Special EDITION

Believe in love. Overcome obstacles. Find happiness.

The Rancher Hits The Road
Melissa Senate

Her Second-Chance Family
Elizabeth Bevarly

MILLS & BOON

THE RANCHER HITS THE ROAD
© 2024 by Melissa Senate
Philippine Copyright 2024
Australian Copyright 2024
New Zealand Copyright 2024

First Published 2024
First Australian Paperback Edition 2024
ISBN 978 1 038 90766 0

HER SECOND-CHANCE FAMILY
© 2024 by Elizabeth Bevarly
Philippine Copyright 2024
Australian Copyright 2024
New Zealand Copyright 2024

First Published 2024
First Australian Paperback Edition 2024
ISBN 978 1 038 90766 0

Published by
Harlequin Mills & Boon
An imprint of Harlequin Enterprises (Australia) Pty Limited
(ABN 47 001 180 918), a subsidiary of HarperCollins
Publishers Australia Pty Limited
(ABN 36 009 913 517)
Level 19, 201 Elizabeth Street
SYDNEY NSW 2000 AUSTRALIA

MIX
Paper | Supporting
responsible forestry
FSC® C001695
www.fsc.org

The Rancher Hits The Road

Melissa Senate

MILLS & BOON

Melissa Senate has written many novels for Harlequin and other publishers, including her debut, *See Jane Date*, which was made into a TV movie. She also wrote seven books for Harlequin Special Heart under the pen name Meg Maxwell. Her novels have been published in over twenty-five countries. Melissa lives on the coast of Maine with her son; their rescue shepherd mix, Flash; and a lap cat named Cleo. For more information, please visit her website, melissasenate.com.

Dear Reader,

Stood up at her big outdoor ranch wedding, Ashley McCray is determined to confront her runaway groom and demand back every penny her family spent on the wedding. That's when the McCray Ranch foreman, widower Shane Dawson, gets an out-there idea: he's headed to the same town she is to drop off his twin five-year-old daughters at their maternal grandparents' house for a visit. The grandparents think he's doing a *terrible* job at parenting. They've even been talking about seeking custody. So Shane offers to drive Ashley to find her ex-groom if she'll give his girls pointers in acting like little ladies to appease their grandparents.

Ashley agrees and off they go on a very unexpected road trip across Wyoming. Along the way there are a few stops and many surprises, including feelings for each other that Shane and Ashley never anticipated...

I hope you enjoy this road trip book and Shane and Ashley's romance. I love to hear from readers, so feel free to email me at MelissaSenate@yahoo.com and check out my website for information on new books coming up.

Happy reading!

Melissa Senate

Chapter One

The groom was forty minutes late to his own wedding.

Shane Dawson, a guest seated on the bride's side at the lavish outdoor event at the McCray Ranch—*too* lavish, given what Shane knew about the ranch's finances—wasn't surprised. The question was: Would the guy show up at all?

From where he sat in the third row, Shane could hear Ashley McCray's parents, grandparents, aunts, uncles and cousins whispering and checking their phones for word from the bridal tent at the far end of the aisle, where the bride and her attendants were waiting. Shane's five-year-old twin daughters, Willow and Violet, junior flower girls, were sharing one chair to his right, glued to a game on his phone to keep them occupied. They'd been in the tent with the rest of the bridal party, but had apparently gotten so bored of standing around that the maid of honor had shooed them out and told them she'd call them when it was time.

At this point, that might be never.

The bride's great-aunt, nervously glancing behind her for any sign of activity in the tents, had unfortunately noticed that Willow's and Violet's fancy updos were coming out of their chignons and had summoned them over twice in the past half hour to fix their hair. She'd tsk-tsked the scuff mark on one of Willow's pink Mary Janes and the wrinkles in both girls' pink beaded flapper-style dresses, complete with fringe. A woman beside the twins had pointed out that Violet's fringe had gotten caught in the mechanics of the white padded folding chair and had spent ten minutes extricating his daughter from it, and now the fringe on the back was frayed.

The good news was that no one was paying any more attention to his "wild" children. They'd drawn plenty of attention earlier, mainly from a group of family friends of the bride's mother.

"Those little girls are pretty but lack decorum," one woman had said, shaking her head. "A little too wild."

"Are they family?" a blonde in a veiled hat had asked, eyeing the twins with haughty disdain.

"They're the foreman's daughters," a lady Shane didn't recognize whispered. "He's a widower," she'd added on a dramatic whisper.

"Ah," the blonde had said, her expression turning from disapproval to that all-too-familiar look that spelled "those poor girls." Then all their gazes had briefly landed on Shane with more pity than compassion.

"Those poor girls" were happy, healthy and loved. So what if they weren't quiet, perfectly behaved, pristine little robots as their own relatives—namely their maternal grandparents—thought they should be?

Don't think about the Shaws right now, he told himself, his tie tightening at his neck. His late wife's parents were full of unjustified criticisms over how he was raising the girls. Shane was doing the best he could. And the way he saw it, his best really *was* good enough. He was doing right by the girls. Yes, Violet liked to run instead of walk and mixed purple leggings with bright orange T-shirt dresses, her favorite color combination. Yes, Willow had a loud voice and a huge laugh—and no, he wouldn't shush her, particularly not in playgrounds, like her grandmother thought he should.

No one would stifle his girls. Not from their natural personalities. Not from who they were. Not from becoming who they were meant to be.

The problem was that after a weeklong visit with the girls last Christmas, the Shaws had emailed Shane a list of the girls' wrongdoings—everything from how Violet went flying down the stairs despite being told to walk nicely to the way Willow used inappropriate language for a little girl. Like "stupid dumbhead."

At the end of the email was an ultimatum about custody.

If you don't...if they don't...we'll be forced to consider whether they would be better served in our home and care...

A chill had run up Shane's spine even as he dismissed the "threat" as unwarranted. Racing down the stairs and referring to a classmate as a stupid dumbhead were hardly reasons for a judge to give custody of his daughters to their grandparents.

But the list was much longer than that. Violet had three fading black-and-blue bruises on her knees because of her need for speed. *If you won't teach the girls to walk properly and safely... Willow refuses to eat vegetables of any kind. You must know this isn't healthy...*

Again his tie tightened around his neck, and he slid in a finger to loosen it. He needed air—and he was *outside*.

If this wedding didn't get started soon, it couldn't *end* soon. And Shane could barely wait for that.

"Daaaaaaddyyyyyyy," Willow whined in her highest-pitched voice, her big green eyes moving from his phone to his face. "When's it gonna start?"

"Yeah, when?" Violet seconded, her matching green eyes never leaving the phone screen. "I want everyone to see Ashley in her gown already. She looks like a princess." She pumped a fist in the air at her game progress. "Yeah! Got you! That's twelve more points!"

"She does," Willow said with a nod. "A real princess."

Shane didn't want to imagine Ashley in her wedding gown. The moment he'd heard about the engagement six months ago, he knew it wasn't something to celebrate. Ashley was making a mistake. She was also a grown woman of twenty-eight, very intelligent, independent and thoughtful. So she *had* to know she was making a mistake—and was choosing to make it anyway. Shane had witnessed or overheard the boyfriend-then-fiancé disappoint Ashley several times. The few occasions that Shane couldn't bite his tongue, when he'd said something to Ashley, like *You deserve better*, she'd glared at him and snapped that he should mind his own business.

So that was what he'd done, all through the wedding preparations. And now here they were—waiting for the wedding to start, with Shane torn between wanting desperately to get it over with and also secretly hoping that something would happen to cancel it at the last minute.

Shane's daughters were now standing on their chairs, craning their necks to see if there was any action coming from the tents. Bridal to the left, groomsmen's to the right.

"Girls, down!" Shane whisper-yelled. Each girl sighed

and hopped down, more strands of honey-brown hair falling from their fancy updos.

Violet fell to her knees on the grass, a new stain appearing on the hem of her dress—and probably a fresh bruise just waiting to make an appearance in time to see their grandparents tomorrow. This was a school vacation week, and he'd promised to drop off the girls at the Shaws' home in Jackson Hole for a five-day visit. Where they'd no doubt assess the twins for any signs of better behavior—and then maybe follow through on their threats.

Don't think about that. Get through now.

Violet popped up with a giggle. Willow dropped to her own knees and also giggled. Then the twins high-fived each other.

He looked at his kind, interesting, smart, curious, bighearted, beautiful daughters, his heart overcome with love for them. "I'm sure it'll start soon, girls."

Maybe the groom's eighty-thousand-dollar Range Rover had gotten a flat tire en route to the ranch. Maybe he really was just running late. Maybe the fact that he was now fifty minutes late to his wedding had nothing to do with cold feet.

Or maybe it was the result of a complete change of heart.

He pictured Ashley in the bridal tent, pacing, worrying, frantically calling and texting her fiancé of six months with Where are you?

"Yes, I'm sure it'll start soon," he repeated more for Ashley's sake than anything. It didn't feel appropriate to say the truth—that she might be better off if the wedding never started.

Suddenly, Anthony McCray, the bride's father, was kneeling beside him in the aisle. "How do you know, Shane?" he asked, panic in his deep voice. "Did you hear something? Do you know something? Did you see Harrington come in?"

Harrington Harris IV was the groom.

"I'm sure he'll be here any minute," Shane told his boss, whom he liked and respected. It was Anthony McCray who'd invited him since his daughter, not Shane's biggest fan, hadn't, even though she'd asked his twins to be her flower girls.

Anthony bit his lip and glanced over at the tents. No action. No movement. No sounds. "That's it," he said, his brown eyes worried. "I'm going to the groomsmen's tent to see if any of them know what's going on." He marched off, guests eyeing him.

A few minutes later, as Shane's daughters both lay on their chairs, heads where their knees should be, legs and feet up against the backrest as they counted clouds, Anthony hurried back past Shane's row. He whispered to his wife, but his voice was so naturally booming and deep that Shane could hear.

"None of Harrington's party has heard from him," Anthony said. "They've been texting and calling and get no response."

Shane could see Harrington's parents, over in the first row on the right side, standing and pacing, their phones out, their heads shaking. Every now and then, someone or a group of someones would come up to them, and Shane would see the parents shrug nervously. *Resignedly* might be the better word. Clearly they were used to their son's behavior and attitude.

Ashley should have been too.

But the woman was an optimist. Shane had gotten to know her pretty well over the past five years that he'd worked for the McCrays. She lived in a cabin near the big barn, where he naturally spent a good amount of time and where she worked as a groomer, horse trainer and all-around cowgirl to help out on the ranch, which hadn't been doing well the past six months.

Harrington Harris IV, whose wealthy family owned a very prosperous ranch and had made a fortune in oil too, hadn't worked a day in his privileged life. The running of the businesses was left to a management company.

Murmuring among the guests got his attention, and he turned around to see two of Ashley's bridesmaids walking down the aisle, their expressions stricken, tears in their eyes.

Uh-oh.

They got to the stage and cleared their throats, but all attention was already on them.

"I'm very sorry to report that the wedding is off," the redheaded bridesmaid called out.

Gasps could be heard all around. Including from Willow and Violet, who had leaped to their feet, eyes wide as they stared at the two women on stage.

"Unfortunately," the angrier-looking of the two bridesmaids added, "Harrington texted Ashley just a moment ago that he's very sorry, but he can't marry her. He thought he loved her but realized at the eleventh hour that he does *not*."

More gasps.

Oh, Ashley, Shane thought. He couldn't even imagine how she must feel right now.

His daughters' mouths were hanging open, their eyes darting to his, waiting for some kind of explanation.

"Apparently," the redhead said, "Harrington is already on the road to his family's summer mansion in Jackson

Hole, where he'll be 'working on himself,'" she added with air quotes and absolute disdain, "and determining what he wants to do with his life."

The two women sent a glare over toward the groom's side of the aisle, where there was lots more head shaking and whispering.

"Thank you all for coming," the other bridesmaid said, emotion clogging her voice, "but there will be no wedding today."

His daughters were now standing in front of him, their knees knocking into his in the narrow space between the chair in front of them and his own. "Daddy? Why didn't Harrington come?"

Before he could respond, Ingrid, Ashley's mother, ran toward the bridal tent. In moments she was back, flinging herself at her husband, who wrapped his arms around her. "She's not there! Her maid of honor said she ran out the back way after getting the text from Harrington. A few of the gals tried to find her, but she's not in her cabin or in the main house. Where could she be?"

Shane would wager a million dollars, not that he had a million dollars, that he knew exactly where Ashley was.

"Daddy?" Violet said. "What happened? Why isn't the wedding happening?"

"You heard what Cathy said," Willow told her sister. "Harrington sent her a text that he couldn't marry her."

"But why?" Violet asked.

"Yeah, why?" Willow said.

Being a dad—and a single dad, at that—was never easy. Moments like this, questions like this, were downright hard as he struggled to say the right thing, in the right way, on a level the five-year-olds could understand. He always strove to protect them while being honest. That balance was always near impossible.

He took a hand each and held on to them. "Sometimes people change their minds, even about important things. They realize something doesn't feel right, so they decide to do something else."

"Is Ashley sad?" Violet asked, her tone worried.

"She has to be, right?" Willow said. "Everyone kept calling this the biggest day of her life."

He squeezed both their hands and then pulled them in for hugs. "I'm sure she's sad. And when you're sad, you just have to let yourself feel what you feel, right?"

They both nodded. "When I see Ashley, I'm gonna give her a flower from the garden," Violet said.

"Me too," Willow said.

"That's a nice idea," he assured them.

As the guests continued to pile out, murmuring and whispering, and stopping to hug this person or that, Shane nudged the girls toward the aisle.

"Daddy, will you change your mind about being our dad?" Willow asked, looking up at him.

"Like Mommy had to," Violet said.

Both girls looked at each other, their expressions reaching into his heart and twisting. Their mother had died in a car accident when they were just three months old.

"Going to heaven isn't the same thing as deciding something," Violet said. "Right, Daddy?"

"Yeah, because she didn't *decide* to go to heaven," Willow responded.

"That's right," he said.

He wrapped them both in another hug. "I love you two more than anything in the world. I'd never change my mind about that. Never. That's a promise. And I always keep my promises, right?"

"Right, Daddy," they both said in unison, eyes brightening as they focused on his face.

"Can we go see Ashley to make sure she's okay?" Violet asked.

"Yeah, can we?" Willow seconded. "We can give her a flower and a hug."

Aww. *Take that, Beatrice Shaw.* His girls were thoughtful and sweet. He valued that over *walking nicely down the stairs.* "I have a feeling she needs some time alone right now. But it's really nice that you both care about Ashley."

Thing was, he cared about Ashley too, despite their squabbles and the tension between them the past few months. The real problem between them was that he knew too much, saw too much, heard too much. After an argument with Harrington on the phone or in person, usually in the barn or stables where he could hear loud and clear, she'd see Shane walking in her direction and hurry the other way, spots of red appearing on her cheeks. Sometimes she'd just shoot him a glare, lift her chin and march past him.

He'd go check on her. He was probably the last person she'd want to see right now, but he figured he was the only person who knew where to find her. And he felt compelled to make sure she was all right. Or as all right as she could be.

"Can we go to Katie's birthday party since there isn't a wedding?" Violet asked. "Or is the party over already?"

He pulled out his phone and checked the time. Their kindergarten classmate's sixth birthday party was from 1:30 p.m. to 3:30 p.m., with pizza and cake. "Actually, it's not starting for fifteen minutes," he said. "Let's go home, you two change fast, and I'll take you over to the party."

Their little faces brightened some more, and he was grateful that the complicated lives of adults were wiped from their minds, if only just for right now in anticipation of the party. They walked the ten minutes to their cabin, which had been the foreman's cabin for the entire fifty-plus years the McCray Ranch had been in operation. He glanced at the stables across the path from the big barn. Ashley was in there, no doubt, up in the loft, way in the back.

Another ten minutes later, the girls were in their brightly colored leggings and long-sleeved T-shirts and sneakers. He dropped them off in town at the party house, which was only a fifteen-minute drive, then hurried back to the ranch. While some people were still milling around, lots of cars were already gone. He didn't see the McCrays. Likely they were in the main house, getting a lot of support from family and friends.

He pulled back into his drive at the cabin, then walked the short path up to the ornate stables, Ashley's favorite place. She was in here, he was sure of it.

Now he'd just have to find the right words for her—a lot harder than with five-year-olds.

Ashley heard the stables door open and held her breath as she had every time someone had come in during the past forty minutes. They'd call out, *Ash? Ashley, you in here?* and she'd go stock-still, afraid they'd climb up the loft and peer way in the back where she was hiding in her secret spot. So far, no one had.

She still wasn't ready to talk to anyone. Not her parents or her cousins or even her favorite aunt, Daphie.

Years ago—when she was in high school and going through breakups or mean girl drama or her parents "didn't understand anything!"—she'd brought up a sleeping bag, down pillow and a go bag with provisions to get her through a few hours. After high school, the place had remained a refuge—and the supplies had stayed—but she'd never used it so much as in the past year, since she'd been dating Harrington. She'd found herself climbing up here quite a few times. She'd mull over what had pissed her off or made her feel uneasy or sad, and she'd come back down when it was either time to get back to work or she'd just plain rationalized away whatever had been bothering her, telling herself she was being "too sensitive" or could blame it on the "different worlds" factor between her and Harrison.

He was so cavalier about money, for example, pointlessly buying another vintage car for his collection or a champion racehorse and wanting her to be as excited when he knew she was worried about the McCray Ranch barely breaking even over the past couple of years. Anytime she'd bring it up, he'd say, "Ashley, just say the word and my father could fix everything. His accountant could transfer over a money market account as easily as he'd buy a few new suits at Brooks Brothers. You have nothing to worry about."

But the McCrays, Ashley included, had never been about *taking*. They worked hard, starting with Ashley's paternal grandparents, who'd started a small cattle ranch, grew it and passed it down to the next generation. Yes, there'd been ups and downs, but for the past ten years, things had been solid. Now, not so much.

And when she'd needed Harrington's understanding or support, he'd offer money. She'd try to explain what she *did* need from him, but he'd get impatient or antsy and make excuses to leave.

She should have counted how many times *that* had sent her up here.

Maybe she would have been the one to send a text changing her mind at the last possible second.

But instead she'd overlooked red flags, focusing on what she'd loved about Harrington, what was great between them—and much was, or had been. He had a big heart, and even though he could be clueless sometimes, he seemed to like when she'd point it out. He'd say, with wonder coming over his handsome face, that he'd never dated a woman who wasn't wealthy. That he was used to tossing his money and name around to get what he wanted. He talked a lot about how he never had to do that with Ashley—and in fact, how he knew that if he tried, it would turn her off. That had seemed to turn *him* on.

He'd sobbed for days when his paternal grandfather had died at the start of their romance, and she'd been there for him, bringing them much closer than they probably would have gotten otherwise. At the core, they were friends. Real friends. And she'd thought he did love her.

She'd clearly been wrong.

And now *everyone* knew it too.

She could envision her parents sitting at the kitchen table of their ranch house, worried sick over her, comforting each other, getting hugs from friends and family who were hanging around. Ashley's father had been talking about her wedding since she was a little girl, how she'd have her big day right here on the McCray Ranch and could invite her horse. She could hear him saying that in her head even now, and it managed to bring a small smile.

Despite how independent she was, Ashley was a daddy's girl, and the fantasy he'd stoked about her wedding, about finding her "one true love," had wound its way deep inside her. He'd been dazzled by Harrington as she'd been and had thought of her fiancé as her Prince Charming. Her father had said more than a few times that the only dreams he still had left were to walk her down the aisle, then hold his grandchildren someday. A few times she'd mentioned what Harrington had said about helping out in terms of money, and he'd gotten a bit angry—embarrassed, really—and waved his hand dismissively. *We McCrays built this place from nothing,* he'd say, *and we'll keep it going just like my grandparents did. Life is full of ups and downs, and now is a down. That's all. We don't take handouts.*

Her parents had raised her right, in her opinion. But because her father could be proud and had always been a man of tradition, he'd insisted on paying for most of the wedding, finally agreeing that the Harrises could take care of the videographer since it was a relative of theirs who still charged a small fortune.

Now it was her parents who were out a *real* fortune, piles of money wasted on a wedding that hadn't happened. Money they didn't have to spare. Her father had already sold parcels of land to pay for the wedding and keep the ranch afloat. She hadn't known about that until an aunt—not her favorite one—had slipped and mentioned it.

Ashley felt an ache both deep in her chest and close to the surface. She wrapped her arms around her knees, blinking back a fresh round of tears, waiting for whoever had come in to call her name, but there was only silence. Except for the sudden footsteps—which weren't retreating. Someone was coming—toward the loft.

She could feel her eyes widen as she heard a shoe hit a rung of the loft ladder. The sound got closer and closer. And then there was a familiar face and broad shoulders as Shane Dawson, the foreman at the McCray Ranch, climbed up and over, crouching over to where she was. He sat down along the wall about six inches away, arms around his knees like hers.

Shane Dawson was the last person she wanted to talk to.

"You'll ruin your nice suit," she said, wanting to beat him to the punch of saying whatever he'd come here to say. She knew what he'd come here to say, actually. And she didn't want to hear it.

"Eh, that's okay. It's rare that I ever need it." She could feel him eyeing the hem of her gown. "Straw adds a Western touch to the dress."

She gazed at her ruined gown, poked with straw, dirty in spots and snagged from climbing the ladder. Ashley and her mother and aunts had gone to at least five bridal boutiques in search of The Dress, but the prices had had Ashley shaking her head at them all. She'd ended up finding a beautiful gown online at half the price of the salons. She and her mother sometimes butted heads, but not over Ashley's pick. That day the dress had arrived, folded up and wrinkled, Ashley had tried it on and her mother had burst into tears at how perfect it was. Now tears stung Ashley's eyes and she blinked hard.

"I'm surprised you haven't said 'I told you so' yet, Dawson. I assume that's why you're here. Or did my father ask you to find me?" Figured Shane would think to climb up the loft ladder.

"Nope," he said, turning his head from against the wall to look at her for a moment. "The twins were asking after you, wanting to make sure you were okay."

Aww. "I love those sweetie pies." Violet, with a heart

bigger than Wyoming, and Willow, who knew every kind of horse there was. Ashley had taught the twins all about horses, and Willow in particular had always listened hard just the way Ashley had when her dad used to talk all things equine with her.

"I'm sorry about what happened, Ashley."

She glanced at him, appreciating that. That was really all she needed to hear. *Sorry. That sucks.* "Yeah, me too. I feel like I got stomped on—and it's no fun to get humiliated in front of two hundred of your family and friends."

She felt a warm, strong hand cover hers, and the simple gesture of comfort, of kindness when she needed it most, broke the dam. The tears came fast and furious. She reached for her go bag and pulled out a third box of tissues. Guess she wasn't cried out yet after all.

"I will say one thing, Ashley. He didn't deserve you."

Damned right he didn't. She'd thought they had something real and loving, but his text made it clear everything she thought about their entire relationship was a lie. Some kind of social experiment for Harrington, maybe. Slumming with the middle-class rancher's daughter. Getting a kick out of how she preferred picnics on the Harris Ranch's beautiful land over expensive restaurants. But then when it came right down to it, to their *wedding day*, she wasn't what he wanted. Wasn't enough.

He didn't love her.

Well, it was a little late to come to that conclusion, Harrington Harris IV!

She looked down at her exquisite engagement ring. Two carats, a perfect solitaire in a gold setting. She stared at it, anger building and building and— She grabbed the ring off her finger and flung it hard behind her.

"Um, Ashley," Shane said, looking behind them in the direction she'd thrown the ring. "That cost what? Ten thousand dollars?"

A feeling akin to horror turned her stomach upside down, and her eyes filled with tears. She could sell the ring to pay back some of the costs. She scrambled on her knees, pawing through the straw in search of the ring.

"I'll help," he said, kneeling down and feeling all over for the ring.

Ten minutes later, neither of them had found it.

Shane scooted over by the wall. "Calculating the bounce and probable direction…" he said, turning and digging his hands in the straw. "Got it!" he said without triumph, and she had to appreciate that. He held it out to her.

"I don't want to touch it," she said.

"I'll hang on to it for you." He put it in his pocket.

What had this day turned into?

She swiped at her eyes with the tissue and lifted her chin.

"You know what?" she said, anger radiating. "He's not getting away with this. He's gotten away with way too much the past year. He's going to pay me back—well, my parents—every penny that they spent on the wedding he didn't show up for. I'm going to hand him an itemized bill and demand payment. That ten-thousand-dollar ring won't cover a *fourth* of what my parents spent."

Shane raised an eyebrow. "You think that'll make you feel better? Personally, I doubt it."

"Yes, it will." It wasn't like Shane Dawson *knew* her.

Though sometimes she thought he did. More than once, he'd been annoyingly insightful after he'd caught the tail end of one of her and Harrington's arguments. He would always confirm that she'd been right, and for a moment, she'd revel in the feeling that she wasn't being "sensitive" after all. But then the rush would fade, and she wouldn't know what to do with her victory. The moment would end with her feeling more awkward around him rather than less.

And yet he *had* known exactly where to find her.

She glanced over at Shane, who eyed her back. He'd worked for her parents for just over five years. He'd caught quite a few of her most embarrassing moments. He knew too much about her as it was, and now he was a witness to her biggest humiliation.

Not being loved after all. Chosen and then put back.

Suddenly she felt…exposed. Even more vulnerable than she'd been before Shane's face had appeared over the platform of the loft.

She had to get out of here. She had to get away.

She bolted up, a piece of straw stuck to her wedding dress poking at her leg. She brushed it away.

She knew exactly where to go.

Chapter Two

Uh-oh. Shane knew that look on Ashley's face. Determination—but mixed with fear, worry and can-I-really-do-this?

She was going after Harrington. To present him with an itemized bill for the wedding.

Jackson Hole, where Harrington was on his way to, was seven hours across Wyoming. In her distracted state, Ashley was in no condition to drive.

Then again, her entire family would probably pile in the car with her.

"I suppose you'll be okay as long as someone else drives," he said. "Your mom? The aunt you often go riding with?"

"Daphie," she said, brushing more straw off her dress. "But no. I need to be alone. I need to think. To process. Digest. I really don't love driving on the highway, especially at night. Or in the rain. But I'll blast my playlists and podcasts, pick up some snacks." Her face brightened. "Yeah, I'll be fine. The road trip will help me…get over this—and result in my getting back my parents' money." She nodded to herself. "See you later," she said and started for the ladder.

He envisioned her on the side of the road in a rainstorm, car broken down, all alone…

And then he envisioned her finally getting to the Harrises' summer mansion, marching up to the door and knocking, and

Harrington not exactly being alone himself. Or amenable to seeing her. Or receptive to her demands for the money back. She wasn't thinking about any of this clearly.

"Ashley, I really don't think going after Harrington will make you feel better or—"

She held up a hand, then bent down and continued dusting herself off, straw falling to the loft floor. "Look, Shane," she said, glancing up at him in between wipes of her hands on her gown, "I appreciate that you didn't say 'I told you so' about him, but you're wrong about *me*. I *will* feel better when Harrington hands me a big fat check that will save the McCray Ranch. My parents spent stupid sums of money on this wedding that they didn't have. You very likely know that."

Shane *did* know that. For a few weeks, Anthony had kept his interesting math a secret from his foreman until Shane had found too many deficits. Money was going out faster than it was coming in, not helped by the fact that expected sales of cattle and land hadn't gone through.

"And a long road trip is exactly what I need," she said. "It'll be like the solo honeymoon I didn't expect to take."

She bit her lip, which was slightly trembling. Her face began to crumble. Tears slipped down her cheeks.

He grabbed the box of tissues and held it out for her.

"Whatever," she said, dabbing at her eyes, trying to put some steely resolve in her voice, her expression. It wasn't working. "I'm going and that's that."

"I hope you're planning to change first," he said.

"Of course I am. I *hate* this dress," she added, new tears forming in her hazel eyes. "I'm going to change, pack, let my parents know I'm fine and going on a mission, and then I'm leaving. Jackson Hole, here I come." She turned around and stepped backward onto the ladder and started climbing down.

Jackson Hole. Where he had to be tomorrow to drop off the girls at their grandparents' house. For just a little while, Ashley's situation had wiped that from his mind, but he was going to have to face the Shaws in just a couple of days. And their threat.

Wait a minute.

Huh.

An idea slammed into his head. An idea that could help out both him and Ashley. Maybe save his entire future. Save his *family*.

And hers—if Harris paid her back.

He thought of Ashley McCray in her straw-festooned, snagged, dirty wedding gown—and how she still managed to look elegant. She simply had a regal look about her. Even when she was grooming horses, Ashley looked great. She was what he supposed was called a "girlie-girl." She liked dressing up. Heels. Perfume.

And she was what the Shaws would call a lady. Polite, refined.

Oh, yes. She could help him. And in turn, he could help her. They could help each other.

"I have a bad idea," he called out. "A better bad idea than yours."

She climbed back up until just her head was visible over the floor of the loft. "And what could that possibly be?"

"I have to drop the twins at their grandparents' mansion tomorrow for spring break. Five days. What if *I* drive us to Jackson Hole—I'll drop you at Harrington's summer place, then take the girls to their grandparents."

She tilted her head. Bit her lip.

She looked at him. He looked at her.

Silence.

"I guess we're headed in the same direction, so it's not that bad an idea," she said. "The twins would be great, fun company."

Was that a diss? That *he* wouldn't be great, fun company? He supposed she *was* used to him pointing out her problems.

"There's a catch," he said.

Now it was her turn to raise an eyebrow. "Of course there is. What?"

"In return for me driving you seven hours so you can sit back and process, especially in the dark and in the rain, you'll teach my twins manners. I need them to be little ladies by tomorrow. By the time we arrive at their grandparents' house."

She stared at him in total confusion. "Why on earth would you want them to be little ladies?"

He looked away for a moment, a hard sigh escaping. "Because the Shaws don't think they're being raised right. 'Feral tomboys' is a favorite descriptor. They've dangled a threat to petition for custody."

She gaped at him. "*What?* Willow and Violet are two of the happiest, funniest, most curious, interesting little kids I've ever met. What's wrong with being tomboys?"

"I could hug you right now," he said, then could feel his cheeks slightly burning.

She smiled for the first time since he'd climbed up to the loft. "Huh. I guess we could *both* use a hug."

He tried to imagine hugging Ashley McCray—and couldn't. They just didn't have that kind of friendship. Not that they were friends, really. They just knew each other from the ranch. He just happened to know a lot about her personal life. She'd know about his too—if he had one outside of his role as a father. He'd moved to the ranch to take the job as foreman just a few months before he was widowed. He'd spent the past five years working hard and raising his daughters with absolutely no social life beyond relatives. He was friendly with the McCrays, but they'd always kept their relationship strictly professional.

"That's why I think we'd be good travel companions," he said. "We've both got a lot going on right now—so much that we'll probably be in our own heads most of the time instead of getting into dopey arguments about this or that. And I really do need your help, Ashley. Seriously."

She nodded and extended her hand, the earlier worry and unease gone from her hazel eyes. "It's a deal."

After making a plan with Shane to meet at his cabin in two hours—at 4:00 p.m.—so they could hit the road, Ashley slipped out the back door of the stables. She darted into the woods just a couple of feet away. There was a path she could take just on the other side of the tree line that would lead to the back door of the ranch house.

She did not want to be spotted by any guests still hanging around—and the wedding gown and updo would make her stand out big-time. She hurried along the path, her *peau de soie* pumps as ruined as her dress by now. Every now and then through a gap in the trees, she'd been able to see a few of her relatives hugging one another goodbye in the parking area, all holding a food container. Her parents must have had the dinners boxed up and handed out so they wouldn't go to waste. She had no doubt the wedding cake was still there, intact. She wished she could smash it.

Sigh.

It was over an hour since the wedding had been called off, and it looked like most of the guests had left.

As she pulled open the back door, she could hear people talking in the living room. Her parents. Her grandparents—both sets. Her three aunts—her mother's sisters—Daphie, who was recently divorced, Lila, who went nowhere without her two mini Chihuahuas, and Kate, who Ashley could hear threatening to sue Harrington for "breach of expectations."

She sucked in a deep breath and moved to the doorway of the living room.

"There she is!" Daphie exclaimed. "Oh, my Ashley," she added, rushing over and pulling her into a hug.

The hug felt so good. Ashley hadn't realized just how much she needed warm, strong arms around her. In seconds she was surrounded by embraces and hand squeezes and compassionate murmurs.

She'd thought having a purpose—going after Harrington for all the money her parents had wasted on the non-wedding—had perked her up, made her feel stronger. But suddenly, in the comfort of her family, all the hurt, all the humiliation, came flooding over her, and her eyes filled with tears.

"I'll kill him!" Daphie shrieked. "When I get my hands on that rat—"

"No, I'll kill him!" Kate said. "What an absolute—"

"Cowardly bastard," Lila added, shaking her head, a Chihuahua in each arm.

Her mother ran over, pulling her into a hug. "Are you okay?" she whispered, stepping back to peer at her daughter, her eyes so full of worry and concern. Ingrid McCray put a hand on either side of Ashley's face. "You'll be okay. You're strong. You're a McCray."

Her father nodded and hugged her next. "I'm so darn sorry, sweetums."

That did it again. The sight of her father's sweet brown eyes so filled with anguish for his daughter broke the dam.

"Someone get more tissues," Kate called. "We actually all went through two boxes already."

Ashley's mom darted off and returned with two boxes. Four hands thrust a tissue at her, and she used them all to dab at her eyes.

"I can't wait to tell that rat fink just what I think of him," Daphie spit, her curly red hair bouncing on her shoulders.

"Well, he ran away like the cowardly baby he is," her mother said. "He's halfway to Jackson Hole by now. Safe from our wrath."

"Not mine," Ashley said, lifting her chin, the tears drying up as her plan came back into sharp focus. "*I'm* going after that rat fink. I'm leaving for Jackson Hole in a couple of hours to demand every cent back that you two spent on the wedding."

"What?" her father said. "Ashley, honey, you don't have to do that."

"If she doesn't, I will!" Ashley's mother snapped. "And not for the money, for the principle! Okay, for the money too. How dare he!"

"I'll go too," Daphie said.

Ashley shook her head. "Actually, Shane is driving me."

"Shane?" her father asked. "Really? He offered?"

"Turns out he has to be in Jackson Hole tomorrow to drop off the twins at their grandparents' for spring break," Ashley explained. "So I'm going along."

Her dad was shaking his head. "Ashley, that rat bastard took enough from you. You don't need to waste even more of your time and energy going there to get the money back from him. I'll just sic the sheriff on him. Surely what he did breaks some old Wild West law."

Ashley almost smiled as she envisioned Harrington Harris IV being led away in handcuffs for leaving her at the altar. Until she imagined hearing him whine, *But I don't love her. How could I marry her?* And the sheriff agreeing and uncuffing him.

She sighed. "I want to. The ranch needs it. He's paying us back every cent. Shane's holding on to the engagement ring, which I'll sell when I get back. I need to do this, okay?"

Her parents peered at her, studying her the way they always did when she announced she was doing something a little "out there."

"I do feel more comfortable knowing Shane and his twins will be with you," her mom added. "They're a breath of fresh air—the girls, I mean."

Ashley laughed. "Not Shane?"

Ingrid McCray smiled. "I adore Shane Dawson. He's a great foreman. And he's a great dad. I just meant that Willow and Violet are a hoot. Shane is always pleasant, but he's not a comical five-year-old times two. Those girls will cheer you up for sure."

A great dad. She thought about why he needed her help with the twins on the road trip and almost blurted it out. But his issues with his in-laws were Shane's business, and she didn't think he'd want that getting around. Her parents could be trusted, but her aunt Lila was a huge gossip. Ashley glanced at her—she adored Lila, but the woman loved to dish. With the failed wedding, she was already hanging on every word to report back to her friends and acquaintances in the off-leash dog park where she took her Chihuahuas twice a day.

"Well, since Shane's driving you, I feel better about that too," her dad said. "I'd trust that man with my life."

Ashley did like knowing she'd be in good hands. Safe hands. "He *does* like to poke his nose into my business, though," she said, thinking of the times he'd told her Harrington didn't deserve her.

"Mine too," Anthony McCray said. "But in my case, that's his job. Do you know he refused to take a salary this past month because of how bad the books were getting?"

Ashley gaped at her father. "Really?"

"That's nice and all," Aunt Kate said. "But Shane's wealthy, right? His late wife's family is superrich."

"Actually," Lila said, one Chihuahua nuzzling her neck. "His wife had a trust fund, but she never touched it. And Shane left it alone for the twins when they come of age. They lived on their own salaries—Shane's as foreman, and his wife was a teacher, right?"

Interesting. "How do you know that?" Ashley asked. "I mean, about his wife's finances?"

"Oh, it was big news when she married him," Lila said. "That she married a ranch foreman and that they were not living beyond their own means. That the wife went from her parents' mansion with an indoor *and* outdoor pool to a cabin next to a barn. Plus, I know one of her cousins and got all the scoop."

"Huh," Ashley said again.

"I heard that Shane lets the grandparents pay for summer camp and trips with them every summer to amazing places, and he's fine with gifts for the girls," Lila added, "but on a day-to-day basis, they live on his salary."

"Which he hasn't taken the past month," her father reminded them.

Ashley's busted-up heart softened toward the foreman a little more. Not that being proud and making his own way made him a saint, but that he turned down a salary to help out her father, to help their ranch survive, when he probably needed it... That was something.

Anthony McCray nodded to himself. "Now, *there* is a good man."

"It's good to know they exist," Daphie said.

Ashley crossed her arms over her chest. "Well, he may be a great guy, but I can't say I'm looking forward to sitting next to him in his SUV for the next couple of days. Shane and I are night and day. He's been tsking me all year over Harrington and our arguments." Ashley's chin wobbled. "And he was right too. I'm such an idiot." She covered her face with her hands, the tears threatening again.

Her mother put an arm around her shoulders. "No, honey. You were just in love. And Harrington won us all over. But now he's shown us who he really is."

Ashley nodded, dropping her hands. She sucked in a breath. "I'm getting back our money. I'm going to keep my mind focused on that. And I'll be fine."

"Sweetheart," her dad said. "You really don't need to go after the money or have anything to do with that lying coward again. We'll get through this—just as we would have had the wedding gone ahead. Let's just move on."

Ashley shook her head. "I need to do *something*. Something to help me deal with how stupid I feel. How angry I am. Family and friends flew in from all over the country. Cousin Ben wasted his army leave on a wedding that didn't happen. Harrington is going to pay us back."

"I get it," Daphie said. "When my ex walked out on me, I presented him with a bill for my suffering—twice-weekly therapy and *retail* therapy."

"I don't think it's the money so much as the last word Ashley is after," her eighty-two-year-old maternal grandmother said.

"Oh, Grammy," Ashley said, gently hugging the dear woman. "You've always known me so well."

But it was both. The money and the last word.

And maybe, if she was very honest, she'd admit that she was holding out a little hope that Harrington would take one look at her and tell her he was sorry. That he made the biggest mistake of his life by not showing up, that he just got scared, that of course he loved her and wanted to marry her.

Her chin wobbled again. How did a man spend a year with someone, share in her life, get close to her family and friends, propose, plan a wedding, whisper in her ear just the week before that he'd never been so happy, that he couldn't wait to spend the rest of his life with her, that she was his everything, and then decide days later that he was wrong about all that?

Maybe he would change his mind when he saw her again. And what if he did? What if he took one look at her on his doorstep, his "Sweet Ashley," as he always called her, and realized he'd made the biggest mistake of his life?

And if he *did* say that, what would she say in return? Did she actually want him back? If she *did* take him back, how could she necessarily believe anything he said at this point? How could she ever trust him again? He didn't show up to their wedding! He'd *texted* her that he didn't love her.

He made a fool of her in front of everyone she cared

about. How could she possibly want him to change his mind and love her again?

She happily accepted the fresh round of hugs she got from her family. The aroma of her grandmother's White Shoulders perfume—which had been her great-grandmother's trademark scent—made her feel instantly comforted.

And right now, she needed all the comfort she could get. Her entire life was up in the air. Of course her head was a jumble of crazy thoughts. She'd just have to see what happened when she arrived in Jackson Hole. How she felt. How he felt. Maybe she'd take one look at Harrington Harris IV and vomit. Tell him he was a low-down dirty rat coward and hold out her hand for the big fat check that would save her family's ranch.

And maybe she'd take one look at him and realize that their love story wasn't over. That all he'd have to do to get a second chance from her was admit he'd made a terrible mistake. That he knew now, with a little time to think, a little time apart, that she *was* the one for him. He'd beg forgiveness for the awful way he'd gone about getting to that point. They'd elope to Vegas, and she'd still make him pay for the wedding that wasn't.

Anything could happen.

Suddenly she was really glad she wouldn't be making the trip alone.

Chapter Three

Shane was due to pick up the girls from the birthday party at 3:30 p.m., but at 3:00 p.m. he received a phone call from Allison Waterly, the birthday girl's mother. There was an "unfortunate incident," and could he please come pick up the twins *immediately*?

Uh-oh.

He was in the middle of packing and quickly threw swim trunks in the suitcase open on his bed, his mental list of what he needed to bring zipping out of his head.

"Willow threw a cupcake at one of the other children," Allison said. "Hard. And she also refused to apologize."

Oh, Willow, he thought. *Why are you throwing cupcakes at anyone?*

"I don't know what led up to it," Allison continued, "but as an example for the other children, I'll need you to pick up the girls. Of course it's wrong to punish Violet for Willow's actions, but when I asked Willow why she threw the cupcake at Dylan, Violet shouted it was because he was a 'dumbhead idiot,' and we don't use words like that."

He sighed long and hard internally.

"I'll be right there," he said. "And sorry."

He headed down the hall, grabbed his keys from the hook by the door and went out to his SUV, glancing over at Ashley's cabin about a quarter mile down the path. She was likely in the middle of packing too.

He'd been second-guessing himself for offering to drive her to Jackson Hole. Maybe he should have encouraged her to stay home. He didn't think confronting the ex was a good idea or a good use of her time and energy when an email would do—and document her request just fine. But now, en route to pick up the girls, he was reminded of how badly he needed Ashley's help with them. When she taught them manners, he could ask her to cover *why they can't go around throwing cupcakes—hard—at children. Even if they're "dumbhead idiots."*

He sighed again and got in his SUV and drove out. When he arrived at the Waterlys' home and headed up the walkway, the front door opened. He could see the twins sitting on the entry bench, bright red parting gift bags in each of their hands. They popped up when they saw him coming.

Allison gave him the same look of pity that the McCray relatives had when they learned he was a widower. "Willow did finally apologize to the boy she threw the cupcake at," she said, giving both girls a satisfied nod.

"And I also apologize," he said to the woman. "I know managing a party full of kindergartners is hard enough without having to call a parent for early pickup."

"No worries, Shane. Thank you for coming, girls."

He gave each twin a sharp look.

"Thank you for having us," they said practically in unison.

Allison smiled, and with an arm around each girl, he ushered them out, the door closing behind them.

"We'll talk in the car," he said.

They weren't exactly hanging their heads on the way to

the SUV, which meant Willow felt justified for what she'd done, and her twin agreed.

Once they'd pulled away from the house and were on the road, Shane eyed Willow in the back seat. "Okay, tell me what happened."

In another glance in the rearview mirror, he caught Willow's face fall, her lower lip slightly tremble. She looked at her sister. Violet eyed her, then frowned and looked down.

Huh. He gave them a few seconds.

Willow kept her head down now. "That dumbhead stupid idiot Dylan said that it's weird that we don't have a mother like everyone else." Her voice was low, practically a whisper, and he could tell that she was trying not to cry.

"And what did you say?" he asked. He realized a second too late that he should probably say something about the stupid and dumbhead and idiot, but what they were talking about seemed more important than shutting them down over word choices.

He wondered if their grandmother would agree, given what the issue was. If Beatrice Shaw were in the car with them right now, would she chastise them for their language? Or would she be more focused on what had upset Willow?

Especially because it involved their mother. Beatrice's daughter.

Willow was still staring at her lap. "I said we *do* have a mother. But that she died."

Violet bit her lip. "And I said that our mom is in heaven. And that means she's always with us."

"You know what that dumbhead stupid idiot said?" Willow asked, scrunching up her face in anger. She met his eyes in the rearview mirror. She was on the verge of crying.

"Hang on a sec," Shane said, pulling over. He set the car

in Park and turned around to face his daughters. "What did he say?"

Tears filled Willow's eyes. "He said that our mom is *not* with us because she's *dead.*"

Violet's eyes filled too, her face crumpling. "And he said that dead people aren't walking around or making pancakes or doing anything."

"And that's when I threw my cupcake at him," Willow said.

Shane got out of the car and opened the rear door. Both girls hopped out. He knelt down and they came in for a hug. "Your mom *is* always with you. She is." He pulled back a bit and touched his hand to the region of his heart. "She's in here. For me and for you two. Always."

"I knew Dylan wasn't right," Willow said, her face brightening.

"He's never right," Violet added.

"You know, you wouldn't have gotten in trouble if you'd just told him that. When you get mad, use your words. Your voices. Next time, if you have something in your hand, like a cupcake with frosting, don't throw it at the person you're mad at. First of all, you won't get to eat it that way. Am I right?"

The girls both laughed.

"And no matter how mad you get at someone, throwing things at them is wrong," he added. "It's like hitting. Not allowed, okay? And neither is using bad words. You can tell someone they're wrong without calling them names. Understand?"

"Yes, Daddy," Willow whispered. "I'm sorry." Her sister echoed her words.

"I love you girls so much," he said. "And I have a surprise for you."

"We're not in trouble?" Violet asked, her sweet face brightening.

"You already got in trouble," he said. "You were booted from the birthday party. It's settled, as far as I'm concerned."

Both their narrow shoulders sagged with relief.

"Let's get back in the car and I'll tell you the surprise," he said.

They raced in and buckled up. He pulled back into traffic. "How would you like to take a road trip—with Ashley? And me, of course."

He knew the answer before he asked, of course.

"Yay!" Willow said.

"Yay!" Violet seconded, pumping her goody bag in the air.

"Where are we going, Daddy?" Willow asked.

"You know how I'm taking you to your grandparents tomorrow?" Shane asked, eyeing them in the rearview mirror. "It turns out that Ashley has to go to Jackson Hole too. So we're all going to drive together. It's a long trip. We'll leave in about a half hour and stay overnight at a hotel. But there are rules for the road trip."

"What rules?" Violet asked.

"I want you two to be kind and respectful to Ashley," he said. "By respectful, I mean that you shouldn't ask her questions that she might not feel comfortable answering."

"About her wedding?" Willow asked.

"Exactly," Shane said.

"What shouldn't we ask her?" Violet asked. "And what *can* we ask?"

"Well, you can ask her if she's okay. You guys were there at the wedding. You know what happened. That the wedding *didn't* happen after all. So it's fine to ask her how she is. But I don't think you should ask her questions about why he didn't show up. Stuff like that. She might not want to talk about it, okay?"

He got two solemn nods.

"Is Ashley very sad?" Willow asked.

"She's definitely sad," he admitted.

"We can draw her pictures to cheer her up," Willow said.

"And give her candy and a toy from our goody bags," Violet added, holding up the bright red gift bag.

"That's really nice," he said. "So when we get home, we'll pack for the trip. You'll be at your grandparents' house for five days, so double-check your suitcases that you have play clothes *and* dress-up clothes."

He'd do a final check before they left.

"And scrunchies," Willow said. "Nana doesn't like when our hair is in our faces."

"Or when we're loud," Violet added.

"Or chew with our mouths full."

"Or run hard in the house."

"Well, since you know all that, it'll be easier to remember not to do those things, right?"

"I never remember," Willow said.

Violet nodded. "Me either."

"It's *important* to remember," Shane said. "It means to think before you act. I know it's not easy—for adults *or* five-year-olds. But try, okay? Sometimes, even when something isn't important to you, it's still important to someone else, like your nana, so you do the thing for *them*."

"Okay, Daddy," they both said.

"You know what my favorite thing is about going to Nana and Pops's house?" Violet asked.

"What?" Shane said.

"They have so many pictures of Mommy. All over. They even have pictures of her when she was little."

"I love looking at those pictures," Willow said.

Shane's heart constricted in his chest.

Almost five years after losing Liza, looking at photos of her still wasn't easy. He figured it never would be. He'd loved her very much. They'd had a good marriage. There had been ups and downs, like everyone had. But they'd been solid. And happy.

And just like that, she was gone.

He wasn't about to lose the girls too. Not when he could do everything in his power to keep them. If that meant guiding Willow and Violet to be little ladies on the way to Jackson Hole so that they'd impress—or simply *not horrify*—their grandparents, so be it.

"You take good care of our girl," Ashley heard her father say to Shane as the last of the bags were stacked in the cargo area of Shane's SUV.

Oh, brother. She wasn't one of the horses or cows. She wasn't ranch equipment. Their foreman was simply giving her a ride because he needed her help. But she knew her father was comforted by the idea of his trusty foreman watching out for "our poor baby," which her aunt Kate had actually referred to her as earlier, so she let it be.

She *was* grateful she wasn't making this trip alone. Shane had his downside—butting into her business, getting know-it-all-y—but he *was* trustworthy, and she felt absolutely safe with him. And he came with two absolutely adorable bonuses. She loved that Violet and Willow were already buckled into their booster seats in the back, their faces full of excitement about the trip—because Ashley was unexpectedly coming along. Their sweet heroine worship of her always made her smile, but right now, it was a real balm to her busted-up heart.

And finally, after another round of hugs with her parents, aunts, uncles, cousins and grandparents, the SUV doors closed, the engine started—and they headed down the long drive.

Shane had mentioned he had to make a few quick calls since he hadn't planned on leaving for Jackson Hole today, but the grandparents had been thrilled to hear the girls would be arriving early and he'd been able to change his hotel reservations for the overnight stay.

The seven-hour road trip would be broken into two days of driving, giving Ashley a lot of time and space to think and process. They'd be on the road for a little over two hours today, arriving at the lodge Shane had booked in Bison Creek for a late dinner and maybe a swim in the heated pool before the twins' 8:30 p.m. bedtime. Then they'd hit the road again bright and early, stopping to see a couple of sights along the way, and arrive at the Shaws' home by late afternoon.

Then he'd drop her off at Harrington's.

Shane had planned everything, from the route to the timing to kid-friendly places to stop for breakfast and lunch tomorrow and a petting zoo just a half hour outside Jackson Hole. How she appreciated having him take the reins. To not have to do any of this brain work and research herself—figure out the route and where to stop, not to mention driving for hours by herself without knowing how things would go when she reached her destination. Having him as the driver didn't change that—she still didn't know how things would go when she arrived—but at least she didn't have to concentrate on driving while she worried about it. He'd also let her know he'd put the engagement ring in the safe in the ranch's office.

While she'd been packing, he'd texted the entire itinerary to her along with: I'll wait, of course, while you and Harrington talk. Shouldn't take long to tell him off and get your money back. Then we'll drive home.

She hadn't mentioned that she might not be returning home with Shane. That she and Harrington might want to *really* talk. See how things felt with the pressure of the wedding off the table… Which was why she now found herself thinking that she probably should have brought the ring with her. In case it was slipped back onto her left hand.

She hadn't mentioned that to anyone.

She could barely admit it to herself that she felt a stirring of hope.

"Are we there yet?" Willow asked in a very exaggerated whine.

Violet giggled.

Ashley turned around and grinned. "Um, we've got today and most of tomorrow to go."

"I was kidding!" Willow said, her big green eyes twinkling. "Daddy said we're not allowed to ask that."

"That's right," Shane said, smiling at his daughters in the rearview mirror. "Every parent's favorite rule of the road."

Now the girls were whispering. Something about candy?

"Ashley, since you might be sad," Violet said, "do you want something from our goody bags from the birthday party we went to?"

"Oooh, whatcha got?" Ashley asked. "And it's very nice of you two to be concerned about me and want to cheer me up with treats. Thank you."

The girls beamed at her.

"Three fun-size Snickers," Willow said.

"And four Dum-Dum lollipops," Violet added.

Ashley smiled. "I will definitely take a Snickers. Any cherry lollipops?"

She heard more whispering—loud whispering, which made her smile. "You give her a Snickers," Violet said. "And I'll give her a lollipop 'cause I have cherry."

Once she had her treats, the girls went from quiet to whispering again. She caught Shane glancing at them in the rearview mirror. With a *look*. Ah—she knew what that look was probably about. He'd instructed the girls not to ask her questions. She thought about telling them that they could ask her whatever they wanted. But then again, she'd probably take their earnest questions to heart and get all upset again.

Father knows best, she thought. *Let it go. Eat your Snickers.*

They played a round of I Spy. And I'm Thinking of a Number between One and Twenty. At Ashley's turn to think of a number, Willow guessed sixty and Violet ninety, since both girls could now count up to one hundred by tens, and they all laughed. Then the twins started singing the chorus from their favorite song, and Ashley joined in, which earned her serious bonus points since she knew the words. Then they asked Shane to put in their favorite kiddie mystery podcast.

Five minutes later, she turned around to ask them where they both thought the runaway dog in the podcast was hiding, and she was surprised to see Willow and Violet conked out, fast asleep.

"Wow, they're out cold," she whispered to Shane.

He smiled. "No need to whisper. They sleep through the blasted rooster every morning—unlike me—so you won't wake them by talking. It takes a lot of energy to be them. They nap easily and sleep hard at night."

"I wonder if *I'll* ever sleep again," she said, letting out a sigh. "My entire life is up in the air."

"In the air? What do you mean?"

"I *mean*... I can't really know what will happen when I get to Harrington's."

He glanced at her and she caught the confused look on his face. "You *know* what will happen. You'll hand him the bill for the wedding, he'll pay without hesitation because it's probably the equivalent of a weekend getaway to the Harrises, and we'll be on our way."

"Well, yes, I'm definitely going to ask for the money. But there's always the possibility that Harrington and I will decide to work things out."

A quick look at Shane revealed his face kind of scrunching up. He pulled over on the service road and put the SUV in Park.

"What are you doing?" she asked. "What's wrong?" She instinctively looked back at the twins, but they were as fast asleep as they'd been two minutes ago.

He dropped his hands off the wheel and slightly turned to face her. "You've got to be kidding me, Ashley. You *are* kidding me, right?"

What was he talking ab—

Oh.

The light bulb went off. He was talking about Harrington. About her saying that things might work out between them.

Clearly he hated Harrington. That much had been clear from the way he'd always pointed out the guy's every... imperfection. But she'd never given much weight to his opinion on that point before, and she wasn't about to start now. It was her relationship, so her feelings were what mattered.

"Shane, you don't go from about to marry someone to magically losing all your feelings for that person because they…" *Left you at the altar. Humiliated you—in front of your family and friends and people you never met, since the Harrises had invited a bunch of their own close friends.*

Said in a text that they realized they didn't love you.

She glanced down at her lap, her heart so heavy she might slump over.

"Right," he said. "But you don't hope to get back together with that person either."

She bit her lip, uncertainty *and* a flare of anger shooting up in her gut. Why was she talking to him about this?

"Oh?" she asked with as much sarcasm as she could get into the tiny word. "What do you do, then?"

"You deal with how bad it hurts. And day by day it'll get easier. Until one day, you'll realize you don't feel like you were drop-kicked into a herd of running cattle. You'll feel more like yourself."

Her gaze shot to his face. *Kind of specific there, Dawson.* It occurred to her that he might be talking about himself. How *he'd* dealt with heartbreak.

She certainly wasn't going to argue with him that he didn't understand that kind of pain. He'd lost his wife to a terrible car accident on a rainy night. The mother of his two baby girls. Violet and Willow had only been three months old. For five years he'd been raising them on his own. Yes, he had family close by—she'd met his kindly parents many times when they came to visit him and the twins. But on a day-to-day basis, he was alone with two little girls, all their lives changed in an instant. And he'd been grieving all that time. It couldn't have been easy.

"Let me ask you something," he said suddenly. "What did you—what do you—love about Harrington Harris?"

She felt herself bristle. "I could list fifty of his good traits. But loving someone is about much more than why they're a good person. It's about chemistry and how the person makes you feel, how you *feel* about them. It's about the inexplicable. And yes, the list of traits, of course."

"Let's hear the top ten traits of Harrington Harris IV," Shane said, starting up the engine and pulling back onto the road.

She shot him a glare. Yes, she was defensive. But rightly so. How dare he? She didn't have to justify herself to him.

To herself, maybe. But not to anyone else.

She cleared her throat. "On our first date, we were on our way to dinner when he saw a stray dog limp into the woods and asked if I'd mind if he went after it to bring it to a vet. It took us two hours to find the dog. Harrington carried him out, wrapped him in a blanket in his car, and we took him to the vet. Over a thousand bucks later, Harrington found a foster family for him until he could heal, and that family ended up adopting him and named him Woody."

Shane scowled. "Did you make that up?"

"The name? Of course not. They named him Woody after being rescued from the woods."

"No, I mean the entire story. Your ex-fiancé doesn't strike me as the type to give up the surf and turf and hundred-dollar bottle of wine to save an injured stray."

Ashley gaped at him. "You think I made it up? That I sat here and lied to your face?" Now she was indignant.

"Just doesn't seem like him."

"That's because *you* don't know him. You saw him around the ranch when he came to see me or pick me up or drop me off. You overheard bits and pieces of our private conversations and came to all kinds of unfair conclusions. Harrington is a good guy. Yeah, he can be impatient and a little self-absorbed sometimes. But no one is perfect."

He kept his eyes on the road. "I suppose not."

Ashley straightened up in her seat and looked out the window. She should steer the conversation to small talk. "Wow, we're only in Weaverton?" she asked, noting the sign for the town limits.

"We've been driving for twenty-five minutes," he said. "Gonna be a long trip."

"Yeah," he agreed, still scowling. "No argument from me on *that*."

Now *she* was scowling.

Chapter Four

Shane had not said a word about Harrington Harris for the past hour and twenty minutes, though he'd been dying to. He'd wanted to *what-about* Ashley every five seconds.

What about when your fiancé didn't attend your father's sixtieth birthday party at the ranchers' association lodge because "something suddenly came up" and then you found out that the "something" was drinks with a friend he saw all the time?

What about when you'd been telling him how you didn't like when he answered for you, kept talking over you and interrupted you three times during dinner with his family, and his response was "Wow, I didn't realize you were so sensitive"?

What about when you mentioned you had a craving for fettuccine Alfredo at the Italian restaurant you were headed to on a date, and while getting into his Porsche, he'd said, "Um, Ashley, isn't that really fattening?" and then looked down at your hips and added, "You seem to take after your mother's side, and she and your aunts are all a little..."

Shane had overheard that gem while walking from the barn to where a truck had pulled up with a delivery. He'd given Harrington a death stare, but the brat hadn't even had the decency to look embarrassed. He'd just shrugged and given a *Well, it's true* look back, while Ashley stood stock-still, taking it in before exploding on Harris. She'd given him a piece of her mind and snapped that he could go to dinner alone, and Harrington had looked pained as if he couldn't fathom what he'd said wrong.

He doesn't deserve you, Shane had said for at least the tenth time since they'd started dating, staring Ashley right in the eyes before she'd told him to mind his own beeswax and then stomped off into the stables.

Now he glanced over at her in the passenger seat. They'd made small talk on and off, whether about the weather or Jackson Hole itself, but she'd mostly stayed quiet, looking out the window or playing Wordle and Spelling Bee games on her phone. She was a good speller. Another plus for helping the girls "be their best selves" for the grandparents.

"Ooh, is that our hotel?" Ashley asked, sitting up straight and pointing up ahead where the Bison Creek Lodge, with its steeply pitched green roof, came into view. As they got closer, he could see that two white cats were asleep on the padded swing hanging on the porch, and two small dogs—pugs or French bulldogs, he wasn't sure—were gnawing on rawhide bones on a little rug under the swing. There'd been nothing much on the freeway for the past thirty minutes, and then the white fencing of the lodge appeared, welcoming visitors up its long drive through gorgeous grounds that were both rustic and manicured at the same time. The lodge looked like a luxe log cabin.

"Are we here yet, Daddy?" Willow piped up from the back. Then both girls broke into giggles in the middle of yawns.

He hadn't realized they'd woken up. "I'll allow that since, yes, we are here!" Shane said as he parked in the gravel lot.

Ashley turned to smile at the girls, then got out of the SUV and glanced around. "What a gorgeous place."

The twins unbuckled and hopped out, rushing to Ashley's side. "Yay!" the girls said in unison.

As Shane loaded up the dolly with their bags, Violet and Willow kept up a nonstop commentary on everything they saw and everything they thought. Ashley seemed charmed by them and answered all their questions.

"Let's head in," Shane said, pulling the dolly. "We'll have dinner and see what's fun to do after for a bit before your bedtime."

"But we just woke up," Willow pointed out. On a yawn.

"I have a feeling you two will be zonked by eight thirty," he said.

Ashley held open the door and they went inside the lodge's inviting lobby. Shane checked in, surprised to learn their rooms were connected by an adjoining door. The girls would definitely like that; Ashley might not. Violet and Willow were entertaining and kept you on your toes—but they weren't great to have around when you wanted some peace and quiet.

A smiling porter took the dolly and led the way through a set of hunter green French doors down a hallway. Rooms 106 and 108 were on the first level. The porter opened both doors and pulled in the dolly, and after Shane tipped him, he left. Ashley went into her room and knocked on the adjoining door, which Shane opened.

The girls popped their heads into Ashley's room, swiveling their heads to note the differences between hers and theirs.

"I love both rooms," Willow said.

Ashley said that she did too. They were painted a pale terra-cotta with framed prints of Wyoming landscapes on the walls. Ashley's room held a double bed, and Shane's had a double and two cots, all with fluffy-looking blankets and pillows. Each room also had a small love seat, a desk and a round table and two chairs by the gated patio.

"Me too!" Violet said. She zipped back and forth.

"I have a fun idea," Ashley said to the twins. "Why don't you two bunk with me tonight? It'll be a girls' night."

The twins actually jumped up and down and clapped. "Can we, Daddy?"

"Sure can," he said. Huh. Guess she hadn't had enough of them yet. Then again, they had been asleep most of the ride here. As the twins ran into Ashley's room to explore every nook and cranny, he whispered, "You sure about your little guests?"

She nodded. "Very. I adore the twins. You know that. And I can start assessing what lessons they might need," she added on a whisper. "So far, I don't see any behavior that warrants actual correcting. Nothing an eagle-eyed grandparent could get upset about."

For a moment there, he'd blissfully forgotten about the Shaws. But they were the reason he'd struck the deal with Ashley, and he sorely needed her help. "The Shaws get upset about everything, though. Even overexcitement bothers them. The way they shrieked when you invited them to share your room? That's a no-go with Nana and Pops."

"Anyone who lets himself be called Pops surely has a warm side," she said. She'd met the Shaws in the harrowing days after Liza's death, but just in passing on the ranch grounds, really.

"True. He's much easier than Nana." He glanced at the alarm clock on the bedside table. "Let's figure out dinner.

Then maybe they can hit the pool for a half hour. You'll be able to do some serious assessing, trust me."

"Sounds like a plan," she said with a smile and went into the adjoining room, then came inside. "So we'll just switch rooms."

He took his bags into the other room. As the doors between the rooms shut, her very simple statement struck him. He was so used to taking care of everything on his own—from managing the McCray Ranch as foreman to the day-to-day of raising his daughters. It was nice to have someone else make a phone call and get something done.

The front desk attendant had mentioned the lodge's restaurant was open till nine and room service was available. He grabbed the menu and looked through it. All he needed to see was that there was a kiddie section. Sold.

He knocked on the adjoining door. Ashley opened it—and he was rendered speechless for a moment.

Maybe because she was *right there*. Just inches away. But he was also suddenly struck by how pretty she was. He was always vaguely aware of her beauty; it would be impossible not to notice. Ashley McCray was tall and strong, with long silky light brown hair shot with gold and hazel eyes with gold flecks like a cat's. She had fine, delicate features and a sexy small mole beside her lip.

Jeez. She offered to do one thing to make his life easier and all of a sudden he was noticing her mole? Her catlike eyes? How long and lean and full-breasted she was?

He glanced down fast at the menu. "Uh, I thought we'd order room service. Decent menu. I'm thinking of the mushroom burger and steak fries."

"Ooh, can I have some of your steak fries, Daddy?" Willow asked, rushing over to see the menu.

"Me too!" Violet said, catching up with her sister. "And can I have chicken tenders?" She turned to Willow. "If you get the mac and cheese, we can share."

"I want the mac and cheese, Daddy," Willow said.

Big surprise. "Done and done. And yes, I'll share my fries."

He handed Ashley the menu.

"What are you getting, Ashley?" Willow asked. "Do you like burgers?"

"Do you like pizza?"

"Do you like ham-and-cheese sandwiches?"

"Do you like chocolate ice cream?"

Shane gave Ashley his best *I told you so* look. Then remembered she was too familiar with that look of his as it pertained to *her*. "Anything look good?"

"The whole menu's great," she said. "And yes to all your questions, girls. I like just about everything."

Willow scrunched up her nose. "Even broccoli?"

"Love it. Roasted with a little drizzled butter and salt—heavenly."

The girls made faces at each other.

"Hey, girls," Ashley said. "Do you know that princesses across the world have a special princess rule?"

They stopped moving and talking and stared at her with wide eyes. "What rule?" they asked in unison.

"Well, princesses must represent their kingdoms. That means when they're around other people, no matter who, they have to act a certain nice and polite way. Otherwise, people might say, 'Oh, the princess is messy or noisy or rude, so I guess everyone from her kingdom is like that.'"

Willow tilted her head. "So how do they have to act?"

"Well, you know how I said I love broccoli? Especially

with drizzled butter and salt? And you two looked at each other as if I were from another planet?"

They both nodded.

"Royal princesses would want to be nice and respect what other people like or dislike. So they would simply smile. Or maybe they'd say, 'Isn't that interesting!'"

Willow and Violet turned to each other. "Let's practice it!" Willow said. "I like string beans, but not when they're mushy."

Violet started to giggle, then cleared her throat and smiled. "Isn't that interesting!"

Shane burst out laughing. "Perfect."

"Yup," Ashley said. "You've got it, girls. And speaking of vegetables, I'm going to order the pasta primavera. It has a delicious cream sauce and spring vegetables."

"Isn't that interesting!" Violet said with a big smile.

Shane shook his head on a grin. "I'll call the front desk to order. Why don't you two wash your hands?"

Ashley nodded and slung an arm around the twins. "Come with me, girls. Oh, and I'll have you loving broccoli before the night is over."

"Do you think Ashley has magic powers?" Willow whispered to Violet as they zipped into their room.

"I think so," Violet whispered back.

Shane smiled, catching Ashley's gaze before she headed into her room behind his daughters. She sure seemed to— when it came to the Dawson twins.

So far, so good. Ashley knew exactly how to impart etiquette lessons to the girls in a fun way they could understand and enjoy. And he and Ashley seemed to be back on good footing again. Friends. Or maybe just temporary partners.

Or something.

* * *

It was the Dawson twins who had the magic powers—to make Ashley forget, to get her mind off herself and everything that had happened today. They were so charming and comical and sweet and, yes, whirlwinds, they didn't leave a lot of room for her to brood or sulk…or even be annoyed at their father.

As if she'd make up the story about Harrington dropping everything to rescue Woody the stray dog. As if she'd fall for someone who didn't have a heart. *Marry* someone without a heart.

How dare Shane Dawson?

She sighed as she remembered that she *hadn't* actually married Harrington Harris. Because he hadn't shown up for the wedding.

Great. Just great. A minute ago, she'd been laughing at something Willow said. Now she was pushing pasta primavera around her plate with her fork, her appetite waning. All she could think about at this moment was sitting at the vanity in the bride's tent earlier today, staring at herself in the mirror, at her beautiful veil that was now crumpled in a ball up in the stables loft. The slow, then very fast realization that her fiancé wasn't coming to the wedding.

"I only like the broccoli a little bit," Willow said, her mouth full of the bite of pasta primavera she'd agreed to try. "Even with the good sauce. Is that okay to say?"

Ashley turned her attention to the little girl sitting beside her at the round table by the sliding glass doors to the balcony of the room. She and the Dawsons were just about finished with their room service meals. Willow's twin was staring at her too, waiting for her verdict. Even Shane had paused with his fork midway to his mouth, awaiting her response.

"Willow, I'm really proud of you for trying it," Ashley said. "Do you want to know something?"

"Yes, I do!" Willow said.

I do. I do. I do...

Violet leaned forward, as did her sister.

Even Shane leaned forward a bit, Ashley noticed.

"Every time you take a bite of food," Ashley said, "there's a special thing you have to do. You have to chew with your mouth closed."

"Daddy tells us that all the time," Violet said—her mouth full of a steak fry. "But how will we talk and eat at the same time?"

Ashley glanced at Shane with a smile. "*That's* the special thing. You can't. You can only open your mouth to talk after you swallow! It's a good rule. Want to know why?"

The girls leaned forward again.

"Let's say I took a big bite of my pasta and then kept talking while I chewed. You'd have to watch my dinner jumble around in my mouth. Yuckeroo, am I right?"

Willow seemed to think about that, and then her face fell. "That dumbhead stupid idiot Dylan talks with his mouth full."

Violet nodded at her sister. "He's the dumbest stupid-head."

"If he is," Ashley said, "you definitely don't want to do something he does, right?"

Both girls brightened.

"I'm only going to talk when my mouth is empty from now on!" Willow said.

"Me too," Violet seconded.

"Good." Ashley forked a big bite of her dinner. Chewed. Didn't say a word. Swallowed. "See, easy!"

"I want to try!" Willow said.

The Dawson twins spent the next few minutes chewing with their mouths firmly closed.

Ashley glanced at Shane, who was watching with something of a mystified look on his face, like he'd just seen a unicorn and couldn't quite believe his eyes. "So, girls, tell me. Why don't you like this Dylan? It must be bad, because you've called him some pretty harsh names."

"Oh, he totally deserves it!" Violet said.

"He does. He made me throw my cupcake at him at the party today. And we got sent home early."

Ashley glanced at Shane. She hadn't heard about this.

"Well, girls, we had a good talk about that," Shane said quickly. "Want to check out the pool?"

Their eyes lit up, whatever led to Dylan getting reamed by a cupcake forgotten.

Interesting that Shane didn't want to rehash it. She wondered what that was about.

"Come on, Dawson girls," Ashley said. "Let's go change into swimsuits."

The girls scrambled out of their chairs and ran for their room.

She probably should call them back and teach them to push in their chairs and walk nicely to their room. But why shouldn't they run? Why shouldn't they express their excitement?

She'd have to talk to Shane about that, about instilling manners and a little grandmother-approved etiquette without squashing their personalities and typical five-year-old behavior. There had to be a balance for teaching good manners without constantly addressing their behavior and correcting, to the point where the girls were afraid to be themselves.

This might be a little harder than she'd thought.

The next hour was a lot of fun. The four of them found the indoor pool and had a great time slipping into the heated water. They all stayed in the shallow end, the twins dunking underwater, Shane tossing each girl up and catching her, Ashley throwing plastic rings for them to find at the bottom of the pool.

And because they were in the shallow end, she couldn't help but notice Shane Dawson's body, the top half mostly. Broad shoulders. Muscled chest and arms. Quite a few times she found herself staring and had to drag her eyes off his physique. She was used to seeing him in his Western-style button-downs and jeans or a heavy jacket all winter.

Now he was practically naked.

It was a good thing she barely liked the man or she might actually consider him…attractive. It wasn't as if she could miss that hard chest with defined abs and fine dark hair traveling along his abs and disappearing under the waistband of his swim trunks.

Or his face. Which was quite handsome.

Luckily, just then, Willow came splashing up triumphantly with her red ring Ashley had thrown for her. Attention diverted.

Once it neared the twins' bedtime, they all got out of the pool, all smiles, grabbed their towels and headed back to the rooms. Aww, she figured they didn't ask to stay in the pool longer because they were excited to bunk with her. Shane said he'd take care of bedtime, but Ashley wanted to try it, not that she knew what it was or involved besides tucking them in. She'd never been a babysitter growing up.

"The girls will fill you in on the routine," he told Ashley as he stood in the adjoining doorway between their rooms. "Right, you two? No skipsies."

Ashley laughed. "Like toothbrushing?"

"Exactly," he said.

A half hour later, after Ashley had had a quick shower, the girls had their baths, got changed into their jammies, which were T-shirts and sweat shorts, and Ashley was combing their pretty honey-brown hair, which fell all one length past their shoulders. Had she ever combed anyone's hair other than the horses?

"It's nice to have you comb our hair," Willow said, glancing shyly at Ashley as she slid the comb through her sister's locks.

Violet nodded. "Daddy always brushes our hair after baths and in the mornings before school, but it's nice to have you do it."

Aww. Her heart melted. Ashley could still recall her mother combing her hair, braiding it, gathering it into endless ponytails—but these girls had been motherless since they were babies.

"I like doing it," she found herself whispering back, so touched by these two. "All righty," she added. "How about you hop under the covers?"

They slid into their side-by-side cots across the room from Ashley's bed. Ashley had given them a choice of being read to or hearing a made-up story, and they picked the made-up story. She barely got two minutes into a tale of a horse named Helena when she realized both girls were asleep, an arm curled around their "lovies," a fabric doll for Violet and a squishy stuffed horse for Willow.

She knocked on the adjoining door.

"Come on in," Shane called out.

She opened the door and almost gasped. Shane was sitting on the love seat in worn jeans and a black T-shirt, his hair damp from his own shower.

What was this reaction to him?

He's a good-looking guy—that's all, she told herself. Anyone would find him physically appealing.

"The twins fell asleep on line three of my story," she said on a bit of a stammer, trying not to stare. "You didn't get to say good-night."

"They're so active, I'm used to them falling asleep sometimes as I turn around to grab a book. I'll go give them good-night kisses," he added, standing. His presence was suddenly so…overwhelming. Shane was tall, six foot two, she'd guess, with those broad shoulders.

She moved over by the door to give him some privacy with his daughters. She watched as he bent down to kiss each twin on the forehead and whisper, "I love you. Sweet dreams, my precious girl."

Aww. He was such a loving, doting dad. She'd known that, of course; she'd been watching him interact with his daughters for five years. But up close and personal like this, the love and reverence in his voice, was something else.

"Let's go into my room," he said, leading the way and leaving the door just slightly ajar. "I can make us coffee or tea." He gestured to the single-brew coffee maker and the offerings beside it.

"Perfect." It had been one hell of a day, and though she should opt for caffeine-free, it wasn't like she'd get to sleep for hours anyway. "I'd love the tea—caffeinated."

He brewed two foam cups, one after another, and brought over the nondairy creamer and sugars. They sat side by side on the small two-person love seat, their drinks in front of them on the little square table.

Ashley wrapped her hands around the hot cup, letting the steam soothe her before taking a sip. She felt her mind wander to the canceled wedding. And where she'd expected to go afterward. "I was supposed to be in a much different hotel room right now. Drinking champagne. With a different man." She felt her cheeks flush. "Not that we're together. I mean…" She sighed. "I should stop talking." She hadn't meant to say any of that.

"Hey, it's okay. Your whole life turned upside down today."

She sipped her tea and peered at him. She liked when he was understanding and supportive. Yes, this Shane could stick around.

"You were going to Italy for the honeymoon?" he asked.

She nodded. "Starting off in Rome, near the Trevi Fountain. Then Florence, then Venice. Then day trips. For a few seconds while I was up in the loft in the stables, I actually thought about going on the trip solo. But I'd be miserable. And lonely."

"How *are* you doing?" he asked, holding her gaze.

She gave a small shrug. She'd been so occupied the past hour that she hadn't been focused on the fact that she'd been left at the altar. She remembered the whole sequence of events, starting with one of her bridesmaids whispering in her ear that she'd heard from the groom's tent that Harrington hadn't arrived yet, to the resultant confusion, the worry that something had happened to him en route. Then the slow, sickening realization that he was a half hour late. And finally, the text message that said he wasn't coming.

"Not great," she said. She hadn't known it was possible

to feel such visceral pain and numbness at the same time. "One minute I feel like crying and the next I feel like maybe I dodged a bullet. I guess you think I did."

He turned slightly to face her. They were so close on the small love seat. "What matters is that you feel like hell, and there's no way around that except to let yourself feel every feeling—even when *what* you feel is confusing and in conflict. You'll go up and down for a while, Ashley."

She sighed. "I just... I don't..." She leaned her head back against the cushion. There was always the possibility that she and Harrington would work things out...

Was that what she wanted? Half of her said *yes*. Half of her said *no way. That jerk can go jump in a crocodile-infested lake.*

She just knew she was confused.

And hurt.

She bit her lip. "It's why I'm glad I've got those two funny little roommates. They cheer me up, take my mind off myself."

He reached over and took her hand, the warmth, the contact, the gentle squeeze so comforting that a burst of sadness welled up from deep inside and she almost burst into tears.

Instead, she leaned her head on his shoulder and closed her eyes. She felt him stiffen for a moment, and she almost sat up straight, but he slung his right arm around her, the heavy weight of it feeling so good. She was in such need and this time she couldn't stop the tears.

"Let it out," he whispered.

And so she sat there with her head on his shoulder and cried.

Chapter Five

Shane sat stock-still on the love seat, Ashley still leaning her head on his shoulder, though her tears seemed to have stopped.

He wasn't used to comforting a woman.

The last time a woman had cried in his presence was his wife. The twins had caught some very ordinary infant virus and she'd been scared, as he'd been. They'd hovered over the bassinets, slept in the nursery to check on the babies every half hour, terribly worried new parents, weighed down with responsibility for two precious lives with big fevers.

That was five years ago. Except for two cowgirls at the McCray Ranch, and Ashley, of course, he hadn't spent much time around women. He certainly hadn't dated, much to his mother's disappointment the past year. *It's probably time you got yourself out there again*, she'd say gently. *Something to think about anyway*, she'd add with a hand on his shoulder.

He still didn't feel ready, though. He'd loved his wife. He'd loved their lives, the excitement of welcoming twins, of being new parents. And then slam. Gone in an instant. No goodbyes. One second Liza was there, the next she wasn't.

He'd been laser focused on his baby daughters. On doing right by them. He wasn't a mother, would never be, but he'd come to realize he didn't have to be. That he was their father and he'd be a damned good one. He had great support in his family, and he wasn't alone and didn't feel alone.

Even if the Shaws' threats sent chills up his spine.

His girls and his job—that was what he focused on. If he thought about sex, it was about missing his wife and their *ahhhs* when the twins finally went to bed. He didn't look at women in the grocery store aisles or around town and have a thought in his head about them.

He didn't know if he'd ever be ready to be with someone else.

Even if, like his mother had said, five years was a long time to be alone.

He wasn't alone.

He certainly wasn't right now. With Ashley sitting so close. Her head a gentle weight on his shoulder. He could smell her shampoo, a clean, coconut scent. And he was extremely aware of her in a way he'd never been before.

That he wasn't comfortable with. Neither of them was in the market for romance, particularly with *each other*.

He could use some air.

"Want anything from the vending machine in the lobby?" he asked. He was itching to stand up, to move, to extricate himself from Ashley's nearness, but of course he wouldn't. He'd sit here, be a support, until she was ready to move herself.

She lifted her head suddenly. "I wouldn't mind a candy bar. Snickers. And Cheez-Its."

Phew. He looked at her and smiled. "Back in a jiff. If you're okay."

"I'm okay," she said in a small voice that went straight to his heart.

Ashley was hurting, and that was all he needed to know, needed to respond to.

They could both use a five-minute interlude so he could remind himself of that, he thought as he stepped in the hallway, the door shutting behind him.

Unexpectedly intense, he thought, trying to emotionally distance himself from whatever was going on with him— where Ashley was concerned. Trying and failing because he couldn't get her face out of his mind.

A few minutes later, just being out of the room, the simple act of pressing in the buttons for the snacks and watching them fall with a tiny thud, had him feeling better. Holding her Snickers and cheese crackers and a bag of white cheddar popcorn for himself, he headed back to the room. His phone vibrated in his back pocket, and he stopped to fish it out, balancing the snacks against his midsection.

His boss. Or in this case, Ashley's dad. He had a feeling Anthony McCray was calling strictly as a father, not a rancher.

"Hi, Anthony," Shane said, stepping out an exit door to the side of the lodge. The cool April air felt good on his face, in his hair—in his lungs.

"How's my girl?" Anthony asked. "Give it to me straight. I just called her and she said she's okay, that the twins are cheering her up, that she went swimming and had excellent pasta, and something about a Snickers?"

He smiled and looked at the bounty of treats he was clutching. "I just hit up the vending machine. Snickers and Cheez-Its. I'll be honest, Anthony. She's hurting and confused. But that makes sense, given what happened."

"I could kill that coward," Anthony said, the pain in his voice, the worry for his daughter, evident. "I'm not so sure she should be going to see him at all. I don't care about the money. I never did."

I'm not so sure either.

"Just rest assured that Ashley's in good hands with us, Anthony. Remember that trips are often about the journey instead of the destination. The drive is letting her get away, to have some time to really think and process. And to have fun company in my daughters, who are keeping her very busy. And then there's me to keep her head on straight." He paused. "Not that I have any right to tell her what to do or think, but, well, you know what I mean."

"I do. And I'm grateful. You have my complete trust, Shane. Ingrid and I take a lot of comfort knowing she's with you and the twins. You'll call me if I need to know anything?" Anthony said hesitantly. "I know she's a very capable grown woman, but if she needs us, we're there, okay?"

"Absolutely," he said.

With that, they disconnected and Shane headed back inside the lodge. He let himself into his room to find Ashley standing in front of the sliding glass doors to the patio, arms wrapped around herself, staring out at the darkness. The moon was almost full, lots of stars visible. He wondered if she was wishing on one. Wishing that when she finally arrived at the Harris family summer mansion, she and her ex would get back together.

He mentally shook his head at himself and told himself to stop judging. She loved Harrington, clearly. To the point that she'd been about to marry him. And like Ashley had said herself, those feelings didn't go away just because the person did.

He knew that from firsthand experience.

But like he'd told her dad, some time away to really think

or just *feel* would do her good. Maybe by the time they arrived in Jackson Hole, she'd want to punch Harrington in the stomach just like he and her parents did.

"I come bearing snacks," he said as he stepped farther into the room. He set everything down on the square table in front of the love seat.

Ashley turned around. "Just what I need. I'll get us water from the mini fridge. Or maybe a mini bottle of wine. There's red and white."

"I'll split the white with you," he said.

She smiled and got the waters and the little bottle of wine, pouring half into two foam cups. "Classy with a *K*," she said, holding up her cup.

He held up his, wondering what she'd toast to.

"You do the honors," she said. "I'm plumb out of anything wise to say."

"To figuring it out," he offered.

She took a breath and slowly nodded. "Yeah. To figuring it out. That's what life is all about."

"Right," he said, taking a sip of the pretty bad wine.

She did too, then sat down and grabbed the Snickers. "So what's this about Willow hurling a cupcake at someone at the party?"

He felt himself stiffen, his thoughts jumbled. He took his time sitting down beside her, spending a bit too much time opening his white cheddar popcorn. Talking about this would mean talking about Liza, and he didn't want to. The subject of the girls not having a mother kept him up at night as it was. Mostly because he couldn't see himself ever dating. And no dating meant no stepmother. He didn't want to talk about any of it. He had enough going on right now to stop him from sleeping.

"Want some?" he asked, holding the little bag toward her.

"Nah, but thanks. I'd offer you some of my Snickers but I ate the entire thing already."

He smiled, then felt it fade as he recalled Allison calling him, relaying the incident. His fierce little girls, trying to protect their own hearts at age five, even if they went about it the wrong way.

He sighed inwardly, suddenly unsure if he himself was going about anything right. How he parented. How he handled the loss of their mom and kept her memory alive for Willow and Violet. "Dylan, who you heard all about," he blurted, "said it was weird that they don't have a mother. And when they told him it wasn't weird and that she was in their hearts, he said she wasn't because she was *dead*."

Now, why had he come out with that? He could have deflected. Could have changed the subject to their route for the morning's drive and the sites he wanted to stop at that he thought the girls would enjoy. Instead, he'd answered her question.

Because you want to know what she thinks, he realized.

Ashley's mouth dropped open. "Stupid dumbhead idiot."

"Right?" he said with as much of a smile as he could muster, which wasn't much of one, though he liked that she was on the twins' side.

"If there's a positive to the comments and questions they'll get about their mother, it's that it's out in the open, that the girls are thinking about how they feel—and dealing with it."

"That's a good point," he said. "I instantly go into protection mode, but they really can't be protected from the truth. Their mom *is* gone."

"And now their grandparents want to take away their dad?" she said, anger in her voice. "What is that all about?"

"When it comes right down to it, that's what they'd be doing, so it's how I know they're not thinking clearly or about what's best for the girls. That's it not really about Violet and Willow at all. We're coming up on the five-year anniversary of Liza's death. The grief that never goes away is at work here."

She turned to face him more fully, curling her legs behind her. "What do you mean?"

"The Shaws are hurting. The loss has settled in their bones, as it has mine, as a terrible fact. So with the anniversary coming up, I think they want to see more of Liza in the girls. More of themselves too. But when they look at them, all they see is me. And ranch life."

Ashley stared at him, seeming to take that all in.

"The Shaws always felt like they lost their daughter to a different world and way of life," he continued. "They liked that she became a teacher, but not that she lived on her salary and within her own means. They wanted her to live in a fancy condo, and instead she paid rent for a one-bedroom above the bakery on Main Street. And when she married me instead of…" He paused, realizing what he'd been about to say.

"Instead of someone like Harrington," she finished for him.

He nodded. "They couldn't understand it. I once overheard them ask her, 'But, sweetheart, what is Shane bringing to the table?'"

He shook his head, remembering the anger mixed with shame he'd felt in that moment over what he couldn't give the woman he loved. Liza's parents were both old-money rich. *His* parents would survive on their paychecks from his mother's job as a hairstylist and his father's as a farm machine mechanic. The Dawsons still lived in the small house they'd raised him in. Besides the retirement plan he'd set up for them, Shane had long started a savings account called Mom and Dad, and whenever he collected enough, with a little help from solid investments, he'd hire a contractor to build them a porch or he'd send them on vacation to Disney World or wherever they wanted to go. Liza's parents had five homes. Two in Wyoming. They spent most of their time at the "summer" home in Jackson Hole because their son, who had toddler twins of his own plus a new baby, lived there, and they felt wanted and needed and helpful in a way they hadn't felt the first year after Liza died and they'd lived primarily in Bear Ridge.

He realized that Ashley was staring at him, her head tilted a bit, waiting for him to finish his story. "Sorry," he said. "Got caught up in memories."

She reached for his hand and gave it a soft squeeze, the small gesture a comfort but that damned awareness of her anything but.

Get Ashley McCray out of your head, he ordered himself. *Stop noticing her. Stop thinking about her. Stop.*

He turned away slightly, slipping back into the memory of overhearing the Shaws ask Liza what he brought to the table. "I remember holding my breath, wondering what she'd say. This was just a day after we'd gotten engaged. We'd driven to Jackson Hole to tell them the news in person, and they were pleasant enough to me, but that night, when I'd left the room, I heard them ask her that question."

"What did she say back?" Ashley asked.

"She said, 'He makes me really happy.' And her mom said, 'Oh, honey, a puppy could make you happy too. A husband needs to bring a future.'"

"Oh, God," Ashley said.

He nodded. "Liza ripped into them." He smiled at that memory. "She said that love was everything. That moving to the McCray foreman's cabin, with the chickens and ducks hanging out in the front yard, and raising the family she was excited to start there had her heart bursting with absolute joy."

"Aww," Ashley said.

"Her dad said, 'Well, at least Finnigan likes the good life. That'll dictate his choices.'" He shook his head again on a laugh. "That's Liza's brother. He's a good guy, and he and his wife FaceTime with the twins every week, but he lives in a different world. Their parents' world. Which is fine."

"So the Shaws want the girls to be the Liza they lost when she married you," Ashley said. "But it sounds like she was always her own girl, own woman, own person."

He nodded. "That's why I think it's about their grief. They want the twins to be a reflection of the daughter they expected, even if she turned out to be a rebel." He smiled again. "They think the twins are all me, but they're a lot like Liza. Clearly."

"I'll do whatever I can to help," Ashley said. "If the twins have to learn to be little ladies to get through visits with their grandparents, we can make that happen."

This time it was he who reached for her hand and gave it a squeeze, but he didn't let it go. He stared at her hand in his. "Thank you. I do need help, Ashley."

And then suddenly they were just looking at each other. That damned awareness of her, how pretty she was, how sexy, how much he did need her help, was at the forefront. There was something different in her hazel eyes. The past year she usually looked at him with wariness, as if she expected him to hurl a truth at her that she didn't want to hear. But now there was something softer in her gaze.

She bolted up. "Well, I'd better turn in. This has been some day."

Relief mixed with disappointment. He could sit here all night and talk to her. But he needed the space, and it was obvious she did too.

"It has," he agreed, standing too. "Good night, Ashley."

"Night," she said, moving toward the adjoining door.

"Oh," he called, "expect to be woken up around six a.m. The girls' eyes pop open and they're raring to go."

She turned and smiled. "Good. Last thing I need is to lie in bed and think."

Same, he thought. *About you too now, apparently.*

She hurried into her room.

Leaving him with that damned awareness that didn't let up even with a door between them.

The girls did wake up at 6:00 a.m., and since Ashley had slept fitfully, she was both raring to go herself that early and zonked. But as she'd told Shane last night, she certainly didn't want to lie around in bed thinking about anything. Including the undeniable fact that she was attracted to Shane. After she'd left his room, she'd slipped into bed, expecting the day to come crashing down on her. The canceled wedding. The crying. The mission to get her money—and maybe her ex-fiancé—back.

But she'd found herself flipping from her back to her stomach to her side, thinking about Shane and all she'd learned about him. She and Shane had never been what anyone would call friends; they were simply acquaintances at the ranch who rarely spoke or interacted since there had been little need. As the horse groomer and de facto stable manager, though that part really fell under Shane's job, she'd leave notes tacked up for him on the stable bulletin board or she'd email him with anything the grooming department needed or she wanted special ordered. He was the busy foreman with two young daughters. She was the engaged daughter of the ranch owners, and they'd all kept their relationship more professional than overly friendly. That hadn't stopped him from butting in, of course.

He doesn't deserve you...

And now that she had a little more context for Shane, a deeper understanding of him, he seemed less like a buttinsky and more like...someone who cared.

She thought about everything his wife had given up to live in Shane's world, choosing to live on a teacher's and foreman's salaries—in a two-bedroom cabin on a medium-sized ranch that was having financial difficulty. But look at what she'd had. Shane as her husband. Two precious baby daughters. A career she'd loved. A lifestyle that suited her soul.

Ashley tried to think of Harrington giving up his Porsche for a pickup. He had a pickup, of course, but a souped-up one that had cost more than Ashley earned in two years.

Very briefly last night, when she'd been tossing and turning, she'd found herself wondering what it would have been like if Shane had moved just a few inches over on the love seat and turned to face her. Putting them in kissing distance.

Oh, snap out of it, she told herself. *You're not really attracted to Shane. He's just...a very big comfort to you right now. He's the one here for you. Offering his shoulder. Literally.*

He got you treats. He listens. He...really does seem to care.

Now Ashley sent a shy glance his way. They were sitting on a bench in the lodge's backyard with their take-out coffees from the restaurant, where they and the twins had gone for breakfast. It was almost 7:00 a.m. and they'd be hitting the road soon, but at the moment they were enjoying the April sunshine and watching the girls run around in the playground. There were two other families out there, both with children around the twins' age, and they were all playing nicely together. No "dumbhead stupid idiots" being thrown about—or cupcakes. Violet was coming down the curving slide, and Willow was climbing up the ladder for her third turn.

"I imparted a couple of lessons in the morning routine," she said, then took a sip of her hazelnut coffee. "Little things like making sure they—and by 'they' I mean Willow—put the cap back on the toothpaste. Taking a moment to brush their hair—they both had serious bedhead."

When the girls had burst into his room, ready for the restaurant, he'd said, "I like your ponytail, Willow. And the way your hair is tucked behind your ears, Violet." The girls had given him big smiles. She'd liked that he hadn't said, "Oh, how pretty you look," or, "How elegant." He kept the focus of his compliment where it should be.

"They hate brushing their hair on the weekends or vacations," Shane said, sipping his own coffee. "They didn't give you a hard time like they do me?"

She smiled. "Nope. But I'm a novelty."

"I loved when Willow told Violet she was talking with her mouth full in the restaurant," Shane said. "They might not remember all the time, but for her to bring it up means they're thinking about it. At least Willow is."

Ashley smiled. "And I loved Violet's 'Oh, right! I forgot.'"

Ashley had asked the girls how they liked the breakfast, which came from the buffet, and when they didn't ask her in return, she reminded them that it was nice to ask others about themselves and show curiosity and interest. Between the hair and the corrections, that had felt like enough instruction for an hour-long period after waking up.

"At least out here, on the playground, they can be as loud and wild as they want," Ashley said, just in time to hear an earsplitting shriek from Violet as two slightly older girls pushed her and Willow on the tire swing, the twins bellyover, arms dangling down. They were laughing and playing very well with others, and they could shriek all they wanted.

Shane let out a sigh. "The Shaws have a play set in their backyard. When I've dropped them off in the past and the girls have played out there, Nana and Pops were constantly shushing them and telling them, 'Not so fast, not so loud.'"

Ashley took that in. She thought it seemed ridiculous to expect little girls to be quiet when they were outside on a play set. There was a reason people used the expression "indoor" and "outdoor" voices. Outdoors was where it was supposed to be okay to be loud. But Shaws' house, Shaws' rules. That was the way of the world. "I'll talk to them about that as we get much closer to Jackson Hole, about being considerate of their hosts, even if it's hard to remember to use their indoor voices outdoors," she added with a grin.

"This is a big relief," he said. "Having a partner on this. And someone the twins want to please. Not that they don't want to please me or their grandparents, but hearing the little corrections and advice from you adds a special quality that hearing it from Nana and Pops and their boring old dad can't compete with."

"You're definitely not boring," she blurted out. She felt her cheeks flush.

"I'm not bored, that's for sure. No time for that. Plus, those two," he said, pointing at the twins on the tire swing, "make that impossible. Every minute they're awake is an adventure."

She turned to smile at him, touched at how reverent a father he was, how devoted. "I'll bet. And a grand adventure." She felt her smile fade as she looked at the woman sitting on a nearby bench holding a baby in fleece pj's. The young mother lifted up the baby and said, "See Daddy pushing your big brother on the swing? Upsie-daisy," she added, bringing the baby down and then back up.

Ashley bit her lip, her eyes on the woman, on the baby, that wistfulness coming over her. "I guess that wasn't going to be me anyway," she said.

"What do you mean?" Shane asked, following her gaze to the mother.

What the heck? Why had she said *that*? One embarrassing statement led to another, apparently.

Or maybe she simply found Shane Dawson a little too easy to talk to. She used to find him judgy. But now he seemed more like the friend she hadn't considered him to be before.

A friend she was way too attracted to.

"Harrington wanted to put off starting a family," she said, their conversations about that echoing in her head. "I wanted to try for a baby right away." Her shoulders sagged and she looked away—from the young mother, from Shane. She took a sip of her coffee to try to get her equilibrium back.

"He wanted to wait a couple of years, till you were settled in your marriage?" Shane asked.

"More like he wanted to wait until we were thirty-five and had jet-setted to every hot spot across the world. When I'd bring up wanting a baby as soon as possible, he'd say, 'Ashley, do we *really* want that kind of responsibility in our *twenties*? Kids are great, but they control your life. Let's have a lot of fun first, and then when we've been everywhere, done everything, seen everything, experienced everything, we'll be ready for a child. Okay?'"

"Did you say okay?" he asked.

"Not at first. I kept trying to explain how a child would enhance our lives. But he just couldn't see it. And the person who isn't ready wins. It's just the way it is."

"You two want different things, Ashley. Jet-setting to Istanbul or Japan or Paris or wherever isn't your dream. Settling down, starting a family, is."

Could her shoulders sag any more? "But if he isn't ready, and I love him, then what's wrong with waiting till he's ready? That's called *compromise*. It's what marriage is about."

Even *she* winced at the defensiveness in her voice.

And the fact that she'd used present tense.

"Compromise is vital," Shane said. "But so is sharing the same goals and values and dreams with your spouse. That makes compromise a bit easier. If you want the same things, the compromising is just in the details."

She felt a lonely chill that had nothing to do with the crisp April breeze. She bolted up and looked around for the twins. "I'm gonna go play with the girls for a bit before we pack up." Tears stung her eyes and she blinked them away.

Then she lifted her chin and hurried over to the swings,

where Violet and Willow were high up in the air, chatting and laughing.

"Ashley, look how high I am!" Willow shouted.

"And me!" Violet seconded.

That chill was melted by their big smiles and exuberance. She did want to be a mother—and now, not later. Not when she was thirty-five.

She didn't want to travel the world.

She wanted a husband and child and a family dog and her job as horse groomer and trainer and cowgirl at her parents' ranch.

You want what Shane had, she thought. *What he still has*, she amended. *A family.*

She glanced back at him on the bench. He was looking right at her, his expression part apologetic for upsetting her, part neutral for being…right.

Ugh, he was making her think too much when she needed to process. She wasn't even sure that made sense. Processing *was* thinking. Hadn't they toasted to *figuring it out*?

But, but, but. Now she was all turned around and upside down and wasn't sure about *anything*.

Maybe she and Shane could make it the rest of the way to Jackson Hole without talking.

Chapter Six

They'd been on the road for just over two hours when they stopped for donuts, the best in Wyoming, according to *everyone*—locals, food critics and online reviews from visitors coming and going from the national parks. Shane agreed. He never passed through the tiny town of Bixby without going into Bess and Daughters Donuts and coming out with a few dozen to hand out and keep for himself.

As they entered the small bakery-café, the delicious scent of warm, sugary confections filled the air. Bess and her adult daughters could be seen through the glass-fronted wall between the kitchen and café in various stages of baking—mixing and sliding big trays of donuts into the ovens. As the foursome waited in line—there were at least ten people ahead of them at this random time of 10:13 a.m.—the twins studied the display containing around twenty different flavors.

"Oooh, I want chocolate with different-colored sprinkles!" Violet said.

"I want strawberry with cream. Do they have that, Daddy?" Willow asked.

Shane peered up at the huge blackboard listing the daily offerings and specials. Reading had just started clicking for the girls, but the big menu was overwhelming even for him. "Strawberry with cream with or without sprinkles?"

"With!" Willow said. Both girls grabbed hands and inched up in line, their anticipation and excitement over something so simple making Shane smile.

Ashley cleared her throat, her gaze on the twins.

Then again.

And one more time.

"Oh!" Violet said. She leaned close to her sister and whispered, "We're supposed to be interested in others."

Willow turned to Ashley. "What kind of donut are you getting, Ashley?"

Ashley gave the girls a smile, then perused the blackboard and peered around the person in front of her toward the display case. "I'm thinking the carrot cake donut."

The girls stared at each other for a moment. "How interesting!" Violet said.

"Yeah, how interesting!" Willow seconded.

Shane burst out laughing. "That *is* interesting."

"I love carrot cake!" Ashley said. "How could I resist a donut version?"

"What kind are you getting, Daddy?" Willow asked. "Your favorite? Cider?"

"You know it," he said. "And a box for your grandparents too. I'll get a dozen different kinds."

"Nana likes cider donuts too," Willow said. "Chocolate ones."

Violet nodded. "And Pops likes chocolate ones with cream inside. But there's always too *much* cream."

"I'll make sure to get those in their box," Shane said, giving both girls' heads a caress.

Twenty worth-it minutes later they were back in the

SUV, the girls' donuts consumed at a picnic table out front, a big blue box of a dozen for the Shaws in the cargo area. But the vehicle wouldn't start. Shane tried again. Nothing.

"Uh-oh," he said. "Starter maybe?"

He tried one more time. Dead as could be.

A half hour later, Bixby Auto came to tow the SUV to their shop. They said they'd be in touch within a couple of hours—sorry, but they were already backed up this morning. Shane almost wished they hadn't had their donuts yet so they could easily pass another hour. But they were full and ready to be on the road.

They were back at the picnic table, the twins counting people coming and going and sitting nearby. There wasn't much around in Bixby other than a beautiful nature preserve with a very cool footbridge that the twins loved walking on. That would pass some time.

Shane suggested it, and Ashley said it sounded great. Then her eyes widened.

"I just realized something. Do you know who moved to Bixby a few years ago? My cousin Miranda. She and her husband, Michael, were at the wedding too. You remember them, right?"

"Sure do," he said. The couple had both been ranch hands, working for room and board at the McCray Ranch while Miranda went to school at night for her teaching degree. "Miranda got a teaching job at the regional high school, and they bought a small cattle ranch."

Ashley nodded. "I'll give them a call and see if they're around today. We might be in luck since it's Sunday. I can apologize for them driving all that way to the wedding and getting a sitter for nothing." She sighed. "They had a baby just six months ago. Roxanna—Roxy. So sweet."

"We don't have to call them," he said gently. "They might put you on the spot, asking questions."

He realized he was being protective of Ashley.

"I don't mind. Miranda and I got close when she worked at the ranch, and they did come to the wedding. The twins won't remember Miranda or her husband, but they're assured a fun time if we go over to their place. Plus, I think they have chickens."

The twins would love nothing more than to watch chickens and maybe collect an egg. "Sounds good to me," he said.

"And you know, maybe spending a little time around a baby will make me realize I'm not ready to be a mom," she added, seeming lost in thought for a second.

He highly doubted that. Babies had a way of sneaking their way into hearts no matter how screechy or stinky they were.

As he watched her head a few feet away beside a tree to make her call, that same blast of protectiveness came over him. Maybe he just felt responsible for her. He'd promised her father he'd watch out for her, hadn't he?

A minute later she was back. "Miranda and Michael are going to come pick us up—they'll be here in fifteen minutes. Girls, Miranda is my cousin, my dad's sister's daughter. Miranda and her husband used to work at the McCray Ranch, and now they live here in Bixby. We're invited to meet their baby and chickens and stay for lunch. Oh, and did I mention they have two puppies?"

She was so good with the twins, so aware of their age and interests. She approached all conversations with them so thoughtfully. He'd known she had a great rapport with

Violet and Willow from her interactions with them at the ranch, but he hadn't known just how bighearted she was.

"Puppies *and* chickens!" the girls shouted in unison.

Shane grinned. "Say no more."

As Ashley went on to tell them about what she knew about the chickens and dogs, Shane held up his phone and went over to the same tree Ashley had just left. He pressed in the speed dial for the Shaws.

Beatrice Shaw, aka Nana, answered. "Shane, everything all right? We're not expecting you till five."

Yeah, five o'clock wasn't happening. "We're in Bixby at the moment. We stopped at that famous donut place, came out and my SUV wouldn't start. It's at a local auto shop. They're not even going to call me to diagnose it for a couple of hours. So depending on what it needs, I'm not sure we'll make it to Jackson Hole until late tonight. Or late morning tomorrow."

Silence and then a long sigh. "I made reservations for four at Donatella's at six. I'll need to cancel, *obviously*."

For *four*. Guess he wasn't invited to the Shaws' favorite restaurant this time. Not that he'd want to go to that stuffy place anyway. At least they had a children's menu with a few basics. The girls would always eat spaghetti and meatballs.

"You know, Shane, if you had a reliable vehicle, this wouldn't have happened. You really can't drive the girls around in an old junker. It's not safe. *Obviously*. And now the start of our time with the twins is completely thrown off."

If she said that word one more time…

"I apologize for that, Beatrice. But the SUV is perfectly reliable and barely five years old. Things *do* happen."

"Yes, I'm well aware," she said. "Well, even if you get your car back this afternoon, there's no sense arriving late at night. And in the morning you'll have a five-hour drive, and I suppose you'll stop a time or two. I'll expect you between two and three."

Fine with him. It would give Ashley a bit more time to prepare Violet and Willow to be on their best behavior. "I'll text you as we get closer to let you know an exact time."

And with that, they disconnected. Shane couldn't get off the phone fast enough.

He headed back over to the picnic table, where Ashley was answering questions about chickens. "Change of plans. Since we don't know when we'll get the SUV back, we're not expected at Nana and Pops's house till tomorrow. So we'll be spending the day and night around here. We'll have lunch with Miranda and Michael and meet their pups and chickens, and then we'll figure out the rest of the day."

Fifteen minutes later, a red minivan arrived. Miranda and Michael were both twenty-six, both redheads, though Miranda's hair was long and Michael's very short, and both had big warm smiles. Michael waved and went around to the passenger side to take their baby from the rear-facing car seat.

Ashley, her arms around the twins, took care of the introductions. The girls said shy hellos.

"And this little darling," Michael said, kneeling down slowly in front of the twins, "is Roxanna. She's six months old. We call her Roxy for short." Shane wasn't surprised the baby had a head full of red hair herself.

"She's so cute!" Willow said.

"And teensy!" Violet added.

"What's your favorite donut?" Willow asked, looking from Miranda to Michael before sneaking a look toward Ashley to see if she approved of Willow's attempt to show interest in others.

Shane held back his laugh.

"Chocolate with sprinkles," Miranda said.

"Did you know that Bess's has carrot cake donuts? That's my favorite," Michael added.

The twins looked at each other, then turned back to Michael. "Isn't that interesting!" they said at the same time.

With that, they piled into the Lorings' minivan and fifteen minutes later were at their ranch, a small cattle operation with a long driveway and beautiful land, surrounded by white fencing. Two pups were in a large pen at the side of the house. They barked their hellos.

As Miranda parked, Shane turned to the girls in the back row. He explained that they'd have to ask to pet the puppies, ask if they could touch the chickens, ask, ask, ask. Got it?

They got it, they insisted, seat belts off and raring to get out.

Michael gave the girls the lowdown, then opened the pen, and the pups came rushing out toward the twins, who'd dropped to their knees and were instantly smothered in puppy love.

Yes, this would be a good detour. For all of them.

Except maybe Ashley, who was now holding baby Roxy in her arms and looking at her with such wonder, such reverence. It was clear she couldn't wait to be a mother, no matter what she'd agreed to in order to suit her former fiancé.

At this point, it was anyone's guess what would happen when he dropped her off in Jackson Hole.

* * *

What a day.

Ashley had to admit she was glad Shane's SUV hadn't started and would actually be in the shop overnight because she had that rare feeling that she needed to be exactly here right now, with precisely these people. With her cousin Miranda, whom she'd immediately reconnected with as if they hadn't spent the past few years apart except for rare family get-togethers. There were some people with whom you could just pick up where you left off, with that same closeness, and it was like that with Miranda.

And with Shane and the twins. Every time her gaze would land on Shane, when the group was having lunch in the ranch house or when they visited the chicken coop or were playing with the pups or taking a tour of the ranch, she'd feel a warm familiarity, a sense of trust that told her she wasn't alone in the world. Of course, she had her family, who always had her back. But this was something different, this unexpected connection to Shane. He'd meet her gaze and give her the slightest nod with such warmth that she'd feel something stirring in her chest.

"Okay, I have to ask," Miranda said when the two of them were alone, taking a walk in the fresh April air on the ranch property. Well, not quite alone—baby Roxy was fast asleep in a carrier strapped to Miranda's chest. They were about a half mile from the house, the sky above bright blue with fluffy clouds, the temperature mild, in the low fifties. "Did Harrington not show up because he could see something was going on with you and Shane?"

Ashley stopped in her tracks, her mouth dropping open. "What?"

"Well, clearly something is. And yesterday was your wedding day, so…"

She'd always loved how Miranda just said whatever was on her mind, put it out there. But this was crazy talk!

"Nothing's going on between us," Ashley said. "And nothing was going on yesterday or last week or months ago or ever in the five years I've known Shane Dawson. Miranda, come on."

"I'm not accusing you of having an affair," Miranda was quick to explain. "I just mean that anyone looking can feel your chemistry. Maybe Harrington noticed."

Ha! If Harrington had noticed there was something brewing between her and Shane, it was their *animosity*. But Harrington wasn't one to notice those kinds of things. She frowned, wondering why someone—namely herself— who noticed everything didn't pay attention *that*.

Ashley linked arms with her cousin and resumed walking. "The only thing going on between me and Shane is *why* we're on this road trip together in the first place. We both kind of need each other right now. I'm an emotional mess and he has my back. He's got an issue with his late wife's parents and needs my help in improving the twins' manners before he drops them off at their house. So we've both got some big stuff going on, and we're helping each other out. That's why it seems…" She trailed off, biting her lip.

Miranda smiled. "Seems what?"

"Like we're closer than we are. That's all!"

"Or you're just getting close, period," Miranda countered.

Ashley wanted to argue, but she had to admit that it had certainly felt that way last night. "I suppose we are. He's so easy to talk to."

"And look at," Miranda added with a grin. She wiggled her eyebrows, and Ashley laughed.

But the undeniable sex appeal of Shane Dawson was no laughing matter. She found him so attractive that it was kind of getting in the way. It was difficult to appreciate him as the good friend he was becoming when she thought about…kissing him. Touching him. Being held by him.

"I don't mean to make light of what happened," Miranda said. "I know you must be hurting bad." She tugged Ashley closer via their linked arms. "I'm so sorry, Ash."

"Yeah," she said, sucking in a breath. "It does hurt. But it helps that I'm doing something. I'm gonna get back every penny my parents spent on the wedding." She'd told Miranda about her plan earlier. "And I guess I was thinking that Harrington would take one look at me and realize he'd made the biggest mistake of his life."

Miranda stopped walking, her expression so compassionate that Ashley almost started crying. "Do you think that's what will happen?"

Ashley looked up at the sky at the cloud slowly moving by. "I don't know. I mean, he didn't show up for his own wedding. He told me—via text—that he realized he didn't love me." She let her head drop back, the stark truth of that making her chest hurt all over again. "Like I said, I'm an emotional mess. I don't know anything."

"Well, I'm glad you're not alone—making this trip by yourself," Miranda said as they resumed walking. "That you're with someone you can lean on."

"Me too," Ashley said. She hadn't realized how much she needed that until she found herself with Shane's support.

A fussy wail came from the carrier, and Miranda glanced down, caressing the baby's pink-capped head. "Aww, what's the matter, my sweet? Need a change of position?" She knelt down for safety, unbuckled the harness and scooped Roxy out.

"Aww, she's so precious," Ashley said. "Can I hold her again? I love that baby shampoo smell." Ashley had gently rocked the baby for a good half hour while Miranda and Michael had fixed lunch.

Miranda transferred Roxy into her arms, and again, Ashley was mesmerized by the sweet face, the curious, alert blue eyes looking up at her. The tiny nose and bow lips. How could she have thought that waiting till she was thirty-five to have a baby was something she could possibly do? Just another thing rationalized in the supposed name of compromise. Where was Harrington's compromise? He hadn't met her halfway. He'd never said, *Since you want to start a family right away and I want to wait seven years, why don't we agree on three and a half years?* What she wanted didn't seem to matter.

Why was that okay with you? she asked silently, her gaze on the baby, her yearning so evident her knees almost wobbled.

"Harrington wanted to wait till we were thirty-five to start a family," Ashley blurted out.

"Ash, can I be really honest with you?"

Her eyes swung up to her cousin's.

"I didn't get a great impression of Harrington when I met him at your engagement party. I know you might get back together—and if that happens, I'll regret having said this. But he just seemed so self-absorbed, talking about himself, his big plans. I don't think I heard the word *we* or *our* come out of his mouth. Even when he was right beside you."

Ashley felt the air whoosh out of her lungs. She held on to the baby a bit more tightly. Miranda was right. One hundred percent right. Ashley had long been aware that Harrington, despite his good side, was focused on himself, but she'd attributed that to his being wealthy beyond belief and living in a different world where he always got what he wanted.

"He does have good points," she rushed to say, tears stinging her eyes. "The way he'd look at me when we were alone, the things he'd say. He'd make me feel so special. And he did have a big heart. I'd seen evidence of that time and again."

Did you make that up? she recalled Shane asking after she'd told him about Harrington working so hard to rescue the stray dog.

"I'm sure he did, Ash. You agreed to marry him, after all. You're smart, independent and incredibly grounded. You'd never let yourself get swept off your feet by anything superficial, so I know you loved him for good reasons. But the way he left you at the altar, what he said in that text… My God."

Ashley bit her lip and handed the baby back to Miranda, too emotional to have that precious life in her arms. Once Miranda had her daughter back in the carrier, Ashley wrapped her arms around herself, feeling so…vulnerable. Exposed.

"I'm sorry, hon," Miranda said. "I don't mean to add to the heavy weight on your shoulders. I know you have a ton on your mind."

Ashley laid a hand on her cousin's forearm. "It's okay. It's more than okay, really. It's necessary. The truth hurts but it's *everything*. Shane tells me the truth too. It's why I like having him around."

"Now, Shane I like," Miranda said. "Always have. From day one. Michael feels the same."

I like him too, she wanted to say, but that made her feel even more vulnerable, so she kept it to herself.

Chapter Seven

"Daddy, can we get doodle puppies too?" Violet asked as he tucked her and Willow in at eight thirty that night.

The twins were in the Lorings' guest room and were sharing the double bed. Shane and Ashley would camp out on the huge sectional sofa in the living room, each on one end. He was looking forward to that—spending some solo time with Ashley. He'd rarely gotten to talk to her one-on-one over the course of the fun, busy day. He'd see her across the room or on the other side of the chicken coop or patting the Lorings' two horses in the barn, and sometimes she'd seemed on the sad side. Or maybe just lost in thought. He'd checked in a couple of times with a private text, just asking how she was holding up. She'd gotten through yesterday—and the disaster of a wedding day—and her mind had to be a jumble today, even with all the distractions.

"I actually want chickens more than puppies," Willow said. "Puppies can't lay eggs. And it was fun to find the eggs in the coop."

"Let's get both!" Violet suggested.

"Hmm. Pets are a lot of work," he said. "And we're a pretty busy family. But maybe in the future."

For the next few minutes, Shane answered their questions about what the future meant, when it started and how long it lasted.

Willow yawned and wrapped her arm around her lovey. "Maybe in the future you'll marry Ashley."

Violet yawned too. "And then she'll be our stepmother. Lianna at school has a stepmother and she makes awesome lunches."

Shane's throat closed up. This was unexpected. They'd never said anything about wanting a stepmother before.

"If you marry Ashley, then she'll have a wedding," Willow said, her eyes fluttering closed.

"And she won't be sad," Violet added, clutching her own lovey.

"You two like the idea of a stepmother?" he asked tentatively, not sure he should put too much stock in the sleepytime conversation. Sometimes the twins talked about things in the abstract that he took much more seriously than they did. He'd spend hours contemplating their comments and questions only to find out in the morning that those deep ruminations during the bedtime routine had been completely forgotten. But sometimes, their questions were forefront the next morning, the center of their hearts. It was hard to know. Especially this. About his getting married again.

"We like Ashley," Violet said.

"We love Ashley," Willow amended.

Violet nodded her agreement on that. "Tell Ashley goodnight, Daddy."

Within seconds, both girls were fast asleep.

He sat there, on the edge of the bed, barely able to breathe, to move. They'd never talked like this about anyone before. Not sitters they'd particularly enjoyed their time with. Not even their beloved kindergarten teacher, Ms. Henry, who was single.

But he was sure the subject wouldn't come up in the morning. There would be too many other things to think about, like the anticipation of Michael's promised chocolate chip pancakes and bacon, getting to pour the puppies' kibble into their bowl for their own breakfasts and collecting the eggs in the chicken coop. If the girls were too distracted to remember what they'd said, then all the better. The idea of remarriage wasn't a thought in *his* head, so he'd prefer it wasn't in the girls' either.

There was a soft tap on the door—Ashley.

He stood up, his legs a bit shaky. He sucked in some air and got himself together. "They're out cold. They said to tell you good-night."

"Aww, I wanted to tell them a story, a continuation of the adventures of Helena the horse."

He smiled. "There's always the long car ride tomorrow."

She smiled too, her pretty face lighting up, and he was struck by the desire to kiss her. To feel her against him.

That would not be happening. She was in way too vulnerable a place. With everything going on right now, worrying about the McCray Ranch as its foreman, watching out for Ashley on this journey—both her personal, emotional journey and the road trip—and the impending arrival at the Shaws' home, where they could make good on their threats to sue for custody of the twins, Shane was in no headspace to start something. Particularly with a woman who'd been left at the altar yesterday. A woman he *was* supposed to watch out for—not take advantage of. If she seemed…drawn to him—and he did get that sense—it was because he was her support system right now. That was all. He represented safety. And there was nothing safe in kissing. It could lead somewhere downright dangerous for two vulnerable people.

"Want some coffee?" she asked. "I'm gonna make herbal tea. Miranda has a thousand kinds."

"Actually, I'd like herbal tea too. Pick something for me."

She smiled again and headed for the kitchen, Shane following her and trying to keep his eyes off her moving body, from the sway of her hips in those jeans to her silky long hair down her back.

"I love this farmhouse," she said as she rummaged through the tea selection. "So cozy. Just right."

He agreed. The house was small and just one story, but it had interesting nooks and crannies and managed to be a bit sprawling with three bedrooms, including Roxy's nursery. Shane had lived in ranch housing his entire adult life and had never had a house of his own, but one like this would do nicely. It really was just the right size. The Lorings had mentioned during dinner that they planned to add a family room in the coming year—and another baby. Shane had never thought about moving, whether building or buying a house of his own, because he'd lived his daughters' entire lives in the foreman's cabin. He couldn't imagine wanting to live anywhere else. It was steeped in good memories—sad ones too—and so many important firsts had happened there.

Yet now that the girls were five and they could all use more room, maybe it was time to think about their own place. It would certainly give the Shaws less to complain about. *They don't even have their own home. The cabin is steps from the barn—they live beside cows...*

Once their tea was ready, they decided to split a carrot cake donut and sat down on the sofa. Miranda and Michael's bedroom was at the far end of the hall, so they didn't have to worry about waking them. Ashley had mentioned she'd volunteered to care for the baby anytime Roxy woke up during the night so the couple could get a good night's sleep.

Shane took a bite of the donut. "Huh, this *is* good. I'll have to tell the girls."

"They crack me up," she said. "They've really taken to the 'Isn't that interesting!' comeback in just the right tone. And they're such great sports about the etiquette lessons. I sneaked in a bunch today. They really enjoyed paying the Lorings compliments. 'What a nice house! What a cute baby! I love your red shoes.' And they now like asking, 'May I do this? May I do that? May I pick up that white chicken? May I check for eggs?'"

He grinned. "The Shaws will like that too."

"I'll admit, I wasn't as strict as their grandmother would probably approve of when it came to how they acted outside. I know the Shaws don't like when the girls run and stomp and shriek, but if they're outdoors, I can't see telling them to walk instead of run or lower their voices. I couldn't bear to squash their exuberance while they were exploring the ranch."

"Same," he said. "When we're closer to Jackson Hole and it'll be easier for them to remember, we can give them some basic rules about the Shaws' house that we'd like them to follow. In their grandparents' backyard, they will have to pipe down. Not run at top speed. Then back home, they can go crazy all they want."

She nodded. "They're such great kids. I just adore them."

That went straight to his heart. "They adore you too. They told me so when I was tucking them in."

"They're so full of life and love," she said, wrapping her hands around her mug of tea. She took a sip and seemed lost in thought for a second. "I'm definitely not waiting till

I'm thirty-five to have a baby. Spending the day with Roxy in all her baby glory cemented that for me."

"And if you and Harrington get back together?" he asked and immediately regretted it.

She didn't exactly bristle but she did seem taken aback. "Well, he and I will certainly have a lot to talk about. I mean, at the most basic level, the trust is gone. That has to be dealt with first."

"Ah, so you'll work up to the fact that you want very different things in life, value different things, want a different lifestyle. You'll work on the trust first, then get into equally important fundamentals."

She stared at him and put her mug down. Then her face kind of crumpled. "I don't know what I'm saying or thinking or doing. I don't know anything."

Oh, heck. His intention was to get through to her—not hurt her or break her spirit. He inched closer and took her hand, holding on to it with a gentle squeeze. "I'm sorry that I keep lobbing this stuff at you. I happen to think a lot of you, Ashley. So I guess I'm feeling extra protective. Plus, I promised your dad I'd look out for you."

Her eyes twinkled for a moment. "Aww. I could see him making you promise just that."

"He did. But I've been doing that long before yesterday."

She only half frowned at that. "Yes, you have, haven't you? I didn't like it then, and I still don't. But I'm glad you are, if that makes any sense. I need it, even if I don't like it."

He smiled and was about to move back over a bit to give them some space when she turned to look at him. He realized that their lips were about an inch apart. And they were just staring into each other's eyes, neither saying a word.

He was barely breathing. Ashley seemed both expectant and nervous.

Remember, you're not allowed to kiss her. That's not looking out for her.

But *she* kissed *him*. She leaned in just enough for their lips to touch, her eyes closing, and her soft mouth on his almost did him in. In that moment, all he could do was feel and not think, and he kissed her back. And then she parted her lips and pressed closer to him, her arms slinking around his neck, her lush, full breasts against his chest.

It took everything in him to pull back. "I want this, Ashley. Trust me. But I *don't* want to add to your confusion. I don't want to be the cause of even more confusion."

She bit her lip and looked at him, then looked away and slid over a bit. She picked up her tea and took a sip. "I did just say I didn't know what the hell I was doing or thinking." She sighed. "But that was one hell of a kiss."

Understatement. "Yeah, it was."

She took another sip of her tea and nodded—as if to herself. "What happens on the road trip *stays* on the road trip."

He stared at her for a second, then picked up his own mug. He felt like a necessary bucket of cold water had been poured on his head. What she'd just said was a stark reminder that their real lives were elsewhere. That she *didn't* know how she felt or what she was thinking or where her heart was. Anything could and probably would happen on this trip. They were out of their usual element, on an adventure, both headed for uncertainty when they reached their destination, both on unsure footing. Ashley would have to find her way to herself. And he had to fully focus on the looming threat the Shaws represented. Nothing that happened on this road trip should be analyzed; nothing could be set in stone. A kiss was just a kiss. Nothing more.

Which meant that when it came to his own heart, he had to watch out for himself. He couldn't mistake this for the start of something.

He wasn't even considering bringing romance into his life.

Shane stood up and grabbed the pillows and blankets that Miranda had set out for them. He put a set next to Ashley and grabbed the other, then set up his bedding on the long section of the sofa. Ashley did the same on the chaise.

But the very short distance between them did nothing to make him stop wishing she was curled up next to him.

Ashley had finally dozed off when she woke to the sound of a baby fussing, a short cry. She sat up, disoriented, and for a moment, she had no idea where she was. Until she noticed the long form of a man stretched out on the sofa, a blanket half covering him.

Shane. Fast asleep.

She felt her eyes widen in remembrance of that unexpected kiss and forced her gaze off him, her heart pounding.

She was about to dash into the nursery, but Miranda had told her that if Roxy woke in the night, Ashley should give her a chance to soothe herself back to sleep before rushing in. Ashley waited a beat, her attention drawn back to the man sleeping just a few feet away.

For a moment, she was mesmerized by the sight of Shane lying there on his side, his dark hair tousled, his head resting on a crooked arm on the pillow. The long eyelashes against his cheeks. The strong, straight nose, the chiseled jawline. And those shoulders and arms that the blanket wasn't covering.

She sucked in a breath, recalling how she'd felt in those arms.

He stirred, moving a bit, and she felt a little panicky for a second, but he remained asleep.

Phew. She was not ready to face him. Not at—she glanced at her phone on the coffee table—1:42 a.m. Not after that kiss that she didn't know what to make of.

Just when she thought baby Roxy had gone back to sleep, another little cry came from the nursery. Ashley peeled off her own blanket and tiptoed into the room. "I've got you," she cooed to the beautiful baby.

She heard footsteps behind her and hoped it was anyone but Shane. Hours after that kiss—that incredible, hot kiss—she'd still been thinking about it, feeling the imprint of his mouth on hers, remembering his passion, the desire in his blue eyes. If he hadn't stopped them from going further...

Complicated—on so many levels. And *complicated* was something neither of them needed.

She settled down in the glider chair with Roxy in her arms, glancing toward the doorway to see who'd also woken up.

Shane.

He stood in the doorway in his sexy Wyoming Cowboys T-shirt and sweats and tousled dark hair. And again, the memory of their kiss came over her.

She felt a flush come over her entire body and gave the baby a gentle sway.

Focus on Roxy, not the man in the doorway.

"Is she hungry? Wet?" he asked, getting right down to business.

"Hmm. Miranda said she didn't need a middle-of-the-night bottle anymore. And she's not wet. She seems to be going back to sleep." Roxy's eyes were fluttering closed. But then they'd open slightly, then close again.

"I can't believe what I don't remember," he said, coming into the room and sitting down in the padded chair by the window directly across from her. "Every stage, every year seems to push the last one farther into the recesses."

This was good. Easy conversation about the baby they were up in the middle of the night to care for. Nothing about the kiss.

Maybe I dreamed it, she thought. It *had* been dreamy.

But no, she'd been wide-awake, every cell in her body on red alert.

Get back to the conversation, she chastised herself. *Stop thinking about it!* "Defense mechanism maybe," she said. "New parents don't remember getting up five times in the night, making bottles while half asleep, changing diapers. That way, they'll want to do it all over again with baby number two and so on." Just like childbirth. She smiled. "I can imagine having four of these tiny marvels. Yeah, four."

"Four?" he repeated with a smile. "I can tell you that *two* is a lot."

She laughed. "Well, at the same time, sure." She chuckled. "Like I'd know. But I *hope* to know."

She'd done it again. Opened herself up for a comment about how getting back together with Harrington wouldn't get her what she wanted since Harrington wasn't interested in *one* baby, let alone four. She waited, bracing herself for it. Truth was, she cared what Shane Dawson thought. She respected him, and his opinion had started to matter.

"You'll be a great mother, Ashley," was what he said.

She was so surprised that tears stung her eyes. The conviction in his tone touched her even more than the words themselves. She looked over at him, so handsome, the kiss pushing its way into her thoughts again, and she forced herself to look down at the baby, to keep her focus on where she at least knew she wanted to go. Shane Dawson wasn't going to be part of her future except as foreman of her family's ranch.

What happens on the road trip stays on the road trip...

It had to. For both their sanity. Like the kiss.

Why *had* she kissed him? And she had—she'd made that first move.

Because of the moment. Their growing closeness. And her attraction to him.

If she was attracted to another man, surely that meant she should let go of Harrington and any thoughts of a second chance with the guy she'd expected to marry.

What happens on the road trip...

On the other hand, maybe kissing Shane had been about their toast when they'd shared that mini bottle of white wine in the lodge suite last night. To figuring it out. She didn't have to know how she felt about every little thing. Every big thing either. She just knew she couldn't bury her head in the sand. Better to put herself out there and find out this or that than burrow under the covers, even if that was what she also wanted to do.

"That means a lot," she said almost on a whisper, the emotion in her voice another surprise. Just what was this man doing to her? She turned her attention to the sweet weight in her arms and gently rocked Roxy, who was now asleep again. "I'll put her back in the crib. I hope she doesn't wake up while I transfer her."

"You've got the magic touch," Shane said. "She fell back asleep in like three seconds."

Oh, Shane. If Harrington had twin five-year-olds, he would have said, *Let me do it. I'm a pro*, and practically grabbed Roxy out of Ashley's arms to show her how it was done. To show her *up*.

Roxy went into the crib without a stir, just a little arm shooting up by her face, her bow lips quirking, her chest rising up and down in her orange pj's. *You are a wonder*, Ashley thought, watching the baby sleep.

She turned around to find Shane *right there*. Standing not three inches behind her, peering into the crib and holding up a palm for a high five.

But when she reached up her hand to tap his palm with hers, he held it. While looking right into her eyes. His other hand went to her chin, tilting it up. Kissing distance once again.

And then they both leaned in at the same time.

How could this kiss be even hotter? she wondered, snaking her arms around his neck. She couldn't get close enough to him. He inched away again, but this time he took her hand and led her out of the nursery.

There was a recessed area between the living room and kitchen, and he led her there, pressing her up against the wall, his mouth, his tongue, his hands exploring her. If anyone came out of a bedroom, whether a grown-up or a five-year-old, they could disengage fast and pretend like they'd been heading for the kitchen. But still, they were being risky.

She could feel his erection against her inner thigh, and a burst of heat spread through her belly. His hands were underneath her T-shirt, slowly moving up to her breasts, where they stopped to cup and rub, and then her shirt was lifted up, his mouth following.

She could melt to the floor. He lifted her up, and she wrapped her legs around his hips as he kissed her so passionately she wished she were naked.

"What I would give to make love to you right now," he whispered.

"Me too," she whispered back. "But we're playing with fire in a lot of ways."

"I keep waiting for a door to open," he said.

"I know. It's kind of killing the moment."

He laughed and took her hand and led her back to the big sofa. "I'd snuggle up with you, but we'd fall asleep and big eyes would find us that way in about three hours."

Ashley grinned. "And we'd wake up to the sound of the twins saying, 'Isn't that interesting!'"

Shane laughed again and pulled her against him, giving her one last passionate kiss. "Good night, Ashley."

"I think I'll be able to sleep now," she said.

"I know what you mean. It's like something has been… released."

"Yeah. This," she said, wagging a finger between them, "is still very confusing and probably a bad idea. But…yes. We're clearly attracted to each other and we're going through a crazy time, so here we are…"

He touched her face and slid back under the covers. She did the same.

But she didn't fall asleep for a long time.

Chapter Eight

Shane awoke the way he often did—to a twin or two jumping on him and asking, "Daddy, are you awake?"

"Oh, I think he is now," Ashley said from the other side of the sofa. He turned his head to see her sitting up with a grin, and the girls both scrambled over to her. She slung an arm around each. "Morning, sunshines."

"Morning, Ashley," they said in unison. She must have taught them that yesterday morning because he'd never heard them say it together like that. Some mornings, they didn't say it back to him at all, particularly on school mornings.

"How did you sleep?" Willow asked very politely.

Shane stared at his daughter. Wow. Ashley had worked wonders.

"Did you have any dreams?" Violet asked her.

Ashley gave each of their chins a little squeeze. "I slept very well, thank you for asking. How about you guys?"

"Very well," they both repeated.

"And yes, I did have a dream. A really good one."

"What was it about?" Violet asked.

"Yeah, what?" Willow seconded.

Ashley glanced at Shane with a sly smile. "You know how sometimes you can't remember the dream, you just know it was good? It was like that."

Ah. He had a feeling she'd had the same dream he'd had, which wasn't fit for anyone's ears but theirs. In his dream, he and Ashley had continued their hot encounter, her legs wrapped around his waist. They were at the Mc-Cray Ranch, though, in the hayloft, and things were hazy and fuzzy and weird the way dreams could be. But it was a very good dream.

"Morning, everyone!" called Michael, walking into the living room with baby Roxy in his arms. Miranda was behind him in a fuzzy pink chenille bathrobe.

"Morning!" the twins called out.

"How did you sleep?" Willow asked Michael.

He tilted his head and smiled. "Very well, thank you. And you?"

"Very well," Violet answered for her.

Miranda grinned at the girls. "You two are so polite! I hope you've rubbed off on Roxy. I'll be hitting you guys up to babysit when you're older, for sure."

The girls both clapped and ran over to Miranda to hug her.

"Who wants my world-famous chocolate chip pancakes?" Michael asked.

That got a round of excited yeses. Shane's phone buzzed with a text—the auto body shop letting him know he could pick his SUV up anytime after 8:00 a.m.

They all made a plan—quick showers, and then Shane would help with breakfast while Miranda and Ashley tended to Roxy and brought the girls into the chicken coop to collect eggs.

The shower cleared his head but did nothing to wash away the memories of the kiss or middle-of-the-night encounter, and he was glad for it.

Fifteen minutes later, dressed and ready to make a lot of

pancake batter, he passed Ashley in the hallway on her way to shower. He wanted to grab her in his arms and kiss her, but of course, he couldn't with everyone around. They settled for giving each other knowing looks, which did something funny to his belly. Neither was pretending last night hadn't happened. Or saying it shouldn't have.

He wasn't ready for this—a romantic relationship. But he was going to see it through, wherever it might lead. Maybe none of this was "real" and they'd go their separate ways when they reached Jackson Hole. Maybe she would get back with the cad. Maybe he'd be busy in court with the Shaws, fighting to keep his girls. But right now, whatever was happening with him and Ashley felt good. He couldn't say whether it was right or wrong. But it was definitely good.

He was adding a handful of chocolate chips to the batter, Michael beside him in his Wyoming's Best Dad apron, when Ashley came into the kitchen. She smiled at him, both shyly and hotly, poured herself a cup of coffee and then left with Miranda and the twins to visit the chicken coop.

"I love life," Michael said, sliding a tray of bacon into the oven. "One minute Ashley is stood up at her own wedding and the next she's found a good guy. I'm happy for you both."

Shane held up a hand. "Whoa, there. We're just traveling to Jackson Hole together. We're not a couple."

Michael laughed. "Uh, sure."

"No, really," Shane said, frowning. "We're not. We're supporting each other through a hard time for us both. We're… friends."

Friends? Did friends kiss so passionately that Shane almost lost control? Did friends wrap their legs around friends' waists while backed up against a wall?

"I repeat—uh, sure." Michael grinned and checked the batter. "That looks great. The griddle's ready, so pour away."

Shane ladled six pancakes onto the griddle, watching the bubbles form, the aroma making his mouth water. He'd rather focus on the pancakes than Michael's line of conversation.

"Hey, I just call it like I see it," Michael continued. "There's something serious going on between you two. It was like that with me and Miranda when we met. She'd just come out of a bad relationship, and I was taking care of my sick mom and barely hanging on. Neither of us was looking to get involved, but we didn't really have a say."

Shane frowned again. "You must have had a say."

"Nope. Every time I'd see Miranda around the McCray Ranch, I'd forget what I was doing or even what day it was. She'd ask me to help her with something, and I'd realize I'd do anything for her. I fell in love before we even started dating."

Hey, no one said anything about love. Or dating.

Shane shook his head. "Ashley and I are on separate missions to the same place. That's all. We'll likely be going our separate ways once we reach Jackson Hole."

"Yeah, I doubt that," he said. "Miranda mentioned that Ashley's going to talk to that jerk about getting paid back for the wedding. And that maybe they'd get back together. That's not happening. The last part, I mean."

"How can you be so sure?" Shane asked. He also wanted to be sure, but he wasn't. Ashley had fallen for Harrington once, and maybe working things out with him was more important to her than he realized.

"Because of you," Michael said.

Shane gaped at the guy. "Me? I'm not anyone here, Michael."

Michael shook his head. "It's amazing when someone can't see what's happening in their own life. But that's what makes it so interesting."

Shane flipped the pancakes, narrowing his eyes. "You and Miranda taking bets?"

Michael laughed. "Never. We love you guys. You were very good to us when we worked for you. And Miranda has always adored Cousin Ashley."

Huh. This was worse. Michael was sincere. Which meant he believed every word he said.

What happens on the road trip stays on the road trip. No matter what, he had to remember that. What Michael was seeing wasn't "real life." His and Ashley's everyday lives. This was just an emotionally heightened time for both of them, and they were leaning on each other. Giving in to their attraction to release some of their anxiety and frustration. Whatever was between them was nothing more than a distraction.

Yes, he thought, stacking delicious-smelling pancakes on a big serving plate.

It's a distraction.

But then the chicken coop crew came back in the house, the twins rushing into the kitchen to show Shane the green and blue eggs they'd found, and he and Ashley locked gazes. A look that held so many different emotions he couldn't begin to count each one.

Okay, this might be more than a distraction. But he had no idea *what* it was.

"Girls, time to go!" Shane called out, glancing around.

Ashley expected to hear four feet come pounding into the living room, where the well-fed group was waiting to hit the road and head for the auto body shop so that Shane could pick up his vehicle. It was 7:50 a.m. and the car would be ready at 8:00 a.m. But the twins were nowhere to be found.

And the longer they stood here waiting to leave, the longer she'd daydream about what had gone on during the night with Shane. *A lot* had gone on.

So far, they hadn't talked about it. But she'd catch Shane looking at her, so much in his blue eyes, and she knew he was thinking about it. Like she was.

But thinking about him was...confusing—and threw a major monkey wrench into what she thought she was doing on this trip. What she was supposed to be doing. She had to stop thinking about last night and focus on getting back on the road. To their destinations. To their missions. To the reasons they were here in the first place.

Where were the twins? she wondered, craning her neck to see outside. She didn't hear them either.

"Violet and Willow, to the living room, pronto!" Shane called out.

Silence.

"Maybe they're saying goodbye to the dogs," Ashley said.

She and Shane walked into the living room, expecting to see the girls on the floor with the doodles, but the dogs were in their beds. No sign of the twins. They'd already said goodbye to the chickens, so Ashley knew they weren't outside.

"Willow! Violet!" he called again. "Let's skedaddle!"

It's too quiet, Ashley thought. *Something isn't right.*

"Let me go look in the room they stayed in," Ashley said and headed down the hall.

Ah. She heard whispering in the hall bathroom. She knocked.

Sudden silence.

Then a flurry of whispering.

"Um, just a second," Violet said through the closed door. Nervously.

"Everything okay in there?" Ashley asked, getting worried.

"No," Willow said. "Violet looks funny."

Funny? "Girls, let me in, okay?" Ashley asked.

The door opened and Willow poked her head out. She was biting her lip.

The door opened wider and there was Violet, standing on a step stool in front of the mirror, a pair of nail scissors in her hand.

And "bangs" cut into her long brown hair, except the bangs were about four inches above her eyebrows. And woefully uneven.

Oh, boy.

"Violet, honey, you cut your hair?" Ashley asked, even though the answer was obvious.

Violet's eyes filled with tears, and she turned around on the stool. "I wanted to look like Miranda."

Miranda had long hair too and a swish of bangs—which ended just above her eyebrows. And were perfectly even and looked great.

Violet's hair looked…as Willow had put it: funny.

Ashley heard footsteps, and suddenly Shane was standing outside the bathroom.

"Everything okay?" he asked.

Now it was Ashley who bit her lip. Nana wasn't going to like this haircut.

Yes, hair grew. But not fast enough to be back to normal before they reached Jackson Hole.

Violet looked sheepishly up at Ashley, who nodded, and Violet opened the door wide and burst into tears.

Shane stared at his daughter with the crazily cut bangs. He didn't say a word.

"I wanted to look like Miranda," Violet said, tears streaming down her cheeks. "But I look like a stupid idiot."

She jumped off the step stool and cried, her head hanging. Willow was looking at her father with big eyes, as if holding her breath while she waited to see what he'd say.

Yeah, I'm right there with you, kid, Ashley thought.

Shane knelt in front of Violet. "Honey, listen to me. I never want you to call yourself names. Okay? No matter what you do. You wanted to look like Miranda, so you cut your hair. It's not the end of the world, right?"

"But I don't look like Miranda," she said, the tears streaming harder.

Shane tipped up Violet's chin, his expression compassionate. "Well, I suppose you learned that if you want a hairstyle like someone else, you could ask them where they get it cut, and I can take you there next time."

"Oh," Violet said. "But what do I do now?"

"I can straighten out the bangs," Ashley said. "But mostly, you'll just have to wait for them to grow. A few weeks is all."

"A few weeks is a really long time," Violet said. She stepped closer to Ashley. "Can you really fix my hair?"

Ashley pulled the girl into a hug. Violet sagged against her, wrapping her arms around Ashley. "Sure I can. I can't make them longer, but I can make them straight."

She stood up and glanced at Shane, who whispered a thank-you.

With Willow watching with big eyes, Shane hoisted Violet onto the counter. Ashley took the scissors and snipped just enough so that the bangs were even without hacking into them any farther.

"There," Ashley said, stepping back. "That looks even now."

Willow nodded. "It does, Violet."

Violet took in a breath. "Thank you, Ashley."

"You're welcome," Ashley said.

As they were about to leave the bathroom, Violet threw herself at Ashley for another hug. The little girl didn't say a word. Ashley hugged her back. Aww, now she was going to cry.

"We've really got to get going," Shane said. "Why don't you two go say your goodbyes to the goldendoodles?"

Violet and Willow hurried away.

"You handled that so well," Ashley whispered. "You could easily have gotten upset, given that they're due at their grandparents' this afternoon."

"The twins don't need my worries heaped on them. Violet made a mistake, and she'll absolutely learn an important lesson from it. Never touch scissors to her hair herself."

Ashley smiled. "Definitely."

He gave her hand a squeeze, and they joined the group in the living room, the twins sitting with the dogs, patting away and telling them they hoped to visit again soon.

"Okay, Dawson girls," Shane said. "Time to head out."

Miranda held open the door. As the twins were about to walk through, she said, "I like your bangs, Violet. They're like mine." She gave her hair a swish.

Violet let out something like a gasp. Her entire face brightened, and she gave her own hair a swish. Then she smiled at her sister and out they went.

"Oh," Violet called back. "Thank you, Miranda!"

Ashley glanced at Shane and grinned. The girl might arrive at her grandparents' with bangs very high up on her forehead, but at least her manners were A plus. She turned to Miranda. "Don't tell anyone, but you're my favorite cousin for a reason."

And then, finally, they all got in the car. The Lorings dropped the McCray-Dawson crew at the auto body shop, where Shane's SUV was all ready to go. Ashley wouldn't have minded if the shop had called about a delay, even another whole day. They'd had a great time in Bixby, even including the hair mishap. *And* even though their detour had included some unexpected romance with Shane Dawson. No matter how she tried to compartmentalize what had gone on between them, to rationalize, to tuck it into something easy, she couldn't.

After goodbye hugs with Miranda and Michael, a promise from both sides to text and swap photos, and a kiss dropped on baby Roxy's capped head, they were back on the road.

Oh, I should mention, Miranda had whispered in her ear as they'd hugged. *The right guy is the one driving you to the wrong guy. Just my fifty cents*, she'd added with a smile.

More confusion. Had her former fiancé done the wrong thing to do the right thing—for himself, and really, if she thought about it, *her* too, since he'd made it clear he didn't love her? Or had he simply gotten cold feet so bad that it had messed with his mind, his emotions? If that was the case, perhaps they could just try to be together without the pressure of an engagement.

Maybe it wasn't that Harrington didn't love her but that he just wasn't ready to get married. The past couple of days, that was what had been knocking around her head and her heart. He'd been about to take a huge step, make a major life commitment, only to realize it wasn't what he wanted.

She wasn't sure if she was letting him off the hook by rationalizing or if she was just really thinking hard about the whole thing.

Luckily, Jackson Hole was a good five hours away and they'd be making at least one stop for everyone to stretch their legs. They'd arrive in town around 2:00 p.m. She'd have plenty of time to think, to feel, to consider all the angles. And given that they'd be driving with the girls, there would be no hanky-panky between her and Shane, no conversation about themselves. She could focus on herself, on what she needed.

She slid a glance at the gorgeous, sexy, kind, warm, funny man in the driver's seat. She had to tear her gaze away from his profile, his shoulder, his forearm, his hand on the wheel. The hand that had touched her so intimately last night.

Yeah, she was already doing a bad job of focusing on herself. Or maybe she had that backward.

Chapter Nine

At 1:00 p.m., they made their second stop since leaving Bixby—the first being Bess and Daughters Donuts for another dozen for the Shaws and a few individual ones for themselves. This time, they pulled into the gravel parking lot of a beautiful park with a few well-reviewed food trucks, a petting zoo, a duck pond and two enchanting footbridges. Ashley got out and glanced around, the grounds managing to seem both rustic and manicured at the same time. The moment the girls' feet hit the gravel in the lot, they raced for the bridge just a few feet away, looking at the ducks swimming below and pointing and chattering excitedly.

"Now, Nana and Pops would have a lot to say about that," Shane said, locking the SUV. "They didn't ask if they could go—they just took off and at full speed. Granted, they didn't have to cross the parking lot and the footbridge is three feet in front of us, but still."

"Well, maybe Violet and Willow factored that in," Ashley said, eyeing the girls leaning over the wide stone railing to better see the ducks. "If they did have to cross the lot, I think they would have asked. And they're *right there*," she added.

He nodded, keeping his eyes on his daughters. "But that jogger coming in their direction had to move out of their way or risk being mowed down by speeding five-year-olds. The Shaws would have called them back, made them sit down on that bench and given them a lecture."

Ashley could see he was conflicted about whether he should too. "Well, what would that lecture be?"

"I know exactly what the Shaws would say because I've been with them when they've scolded the girls for running ahead. They'd say, 'Decorum, girls. Remember we taught you that word. That means you conduct yourselves like the little ladies you are. You ask permission to go to the bridge. You hold hands for safety as each other's partners. And you walk nicely. And once there, you admire the ducks quietly. No shouting and being loud and disturbing other people's enjoyment of the park.'"

Ashley thought about all that for a moment. "I think when they're with their grandparents, that's just the law of the land. The girls are expected to behave a certain way and that's fine. It's a little stuffy and highfalutin, but again, their house, their rules. You don't have to have the same rules."

He nodded. "The past couple of years it's been tough trying to make them remember that different rules go for different places. But now that they're five and have just a couple months left of kindergarten, they're used to rules being enforced. There are school rules and home rules and grandparents' rules and all-the-time rules."

"Like talking with their mouths full. They seem to understand that it's an all-the-time rule."

"Right," he said as they started heading over to the bridge. "Meanwhile, running down the stairs at their grandparents' and leaping off the second step and making a thud is a no-go there. At my cabin, it's fine. I think over lunch, we should have that talk with them." He glanced over at them. "Just explain it again in a way that's not overwhelming." He stopped for a moment, his gaze on his daughters. "I want them to be who they are, not constantly stifled. I love who they are."

Ashley could feel his love for his girls radiating from him. She touched his arm for a moment. "I think they'll be just fine. They've got big personalities. Yeah, they'll get their feelings hurt or they'll get criticized and corrected. But no matter what, those girls' personalities, their curiosity, their exuberance and their big hearts will always shine."

He gave her hand a squeeze, and the sudden touch— his warm, strong hand, the *connection*—brought back a vivid memory of last night. She blinked it away and kept her gaze on the twins.

She could hear Violet saying that she wished she could have a pet duck and Willow saying she'd want a swan. "Think Nana will say something about Violet's bangs?" she asked Shane.

Shane sighed. "Definitely. Beatrice won't find it amusing in the slightest, not that I did. But Violet cutting her hair was perfectly age appropriate. And every time she looks in the mirror, she'll see that cutting her own hair was a mistake."

"Their grandparents don't take that into account?"

He shook his head. "The past couple of years, they've been full of criticism. Like, 'The twins have to learn, period. You're too lenient, too soft, and you're not teaching them how to behave in the world.'"

"They're so hard on you," Ashley said. "Honestly, it's unfair. To you and the twins."

"I appreciate that," he said, holding her gaze for a moment.

Reminding her about last night…

"Daddy, Ashley, do you see the ducks?" the twins called, jumping up and down and pointing and leaning over the stone railing again.

"They're so beautiful," Ashley said as they joined Violet and Willow. "I love the one with the green bill."

"So, guys, what does everyone want for lunch?" Shane asked. "I read that the taco truck here has amazing tacos. And really great strawberry lemonade."

"I want tacos!" Violet said.

"Me too!" Willow seconded.

Shane took orders—chicken for the twins and spicy beef for Ashley and strawberry lemonade for everyone—and then headed for the truck.

"Oooh," Violet said, turning to the left. "It's a wedding!"

Ashley turned too. Sure enough, a bride and groom were being photographed on the far side of the bridge. Ashley looked down and noticed a small group off to the side all dressed up, though there weren't any chairs set up. The couple must have gotten married somewhere else and come here for photos.

She thought of her beautiful white gown—still beautiful, even decorated with straw—crumpled in her closet, her veil still up in the stables loft. Her bridal party, in their matching pale pink satin dresses and *peau de soie* peep-toe pumps. Humph—she'd make Harrington reimburse her maid of honor and bridesmaids for that big expense too.

The groom dramatically dipped the bride, the photographer clicking away.

Harrington used to like doing that, dipping her for a kiss. It used to make her feel so special, the drama he brought to even the quickest of kisses. She inwardly sighed, seeing herself in that bridal tent, staring at herself in the mirror, noticing the worry and tension in her face when she began to realize that Harrington wasn't coming. That he wasn't just late.

"Ashley, when you marry Daddy you can take pictures here!" Willow said.

Ashley was immediately shaken from her thoughts—because she'd almost choked on air. *Marry Daddy?* What?

"I think Daddy and Ashley should definitely take pictures here," Violet said. "I hope they get the ducks in the pictures too."

Ashley realized she was staring—hard—at the twins, trying to make sense of what they'd just said. Should she correct them now? Wait for Shane to handle it? Why on earth would they think she was marrying their father? Where had that come from?

"Violet, Willow," she began hesitantly. "Your daddy and I aren't getting married."

"We know you're not getting married *now*," Violet said.

"Yeah, not right *now*!" Willow added with a big grin, the *now* getting a couple of extra syllables.

Phew. Her heart slowed back down to normal.

"We just meant someday," Violet added.

Someday. Ashley suddenly imagined herself in the foreman's cabin, the Dawson home. She saw herself curled up on the sofa in front of the crackling fireplace, snowflakes coming down, as she flipped through a photo album of her and Shane's wedding, the girls beside her, smiling and full of remembrances of the big day. Oh, and in this little winter fantasy, Ashley was eight months pregnant with Violet and Willow's little sister or brother.

What on earth? she thought again. *Now I'm seeing myself married to Shane Dawson? Pregnant with his child?*

Back to reality, Ashley.

"Well, you know what happened a few days ago," she said. "I was supposed to get married, but it didn't happen."

Willow nodded. "Because Harrington didn't come."

"Right," Ashley said. "So, I'm probably going to take my time getting over that, you know?"

"Do you still feel sad?" Willow asked.

"I feel...confused," Ashley said.

"Why?" Violet asked.

"Because planning a wedding is a big deal. And when the groom doesn't show up...well, that's a bigger deal. It raises all sorts of questions."

The girls both nodded.

They'd met Harrington several times when he'd come to pick her up. She wondered if they'd liked him.

Oh, heck, yes, she was going to ask.

"What did you two think of Harrington the times you met him?"

"He was always nice to us," Willow said.

Violet nodded.

Well, at least she had that. He'd been nice to children. She hadn't picked a complete cad.

She inwardly sighed, watching the bride and groom, who'd moved down below where the pond was.

"Tacos for everyone!" Shane called as he approached a nearby picnic table. "Come and get it!"

Ashley's heart fluttered, as did her stomach with a bunch of butterflies. That was new too. This fluttering. The attraction, she was getting used to. Liking this Shane Dawson, the man she'd come to know on this road trip—*that* she'd accepted. But what was this schoolgirl excitement about him coming over with tacos?

Oh, please, she thought, hopping up as the girls ran over. *You were just picturing yourself living in his cabin, married to him, expecting a baby. You've got...feelings for the guy. Accept* that.

Problem was, admitting to herself that she did have feelings for Shane Dawson was a little too scary right now. Too much too soon. Too fast.

The tacos were as good as the online reviews said they'd be. Shane had dragged out this stop in the park for as long as he could, spending a while at the petting zoo, going back to the ducks for a bit, returning to the table for refreshments, wanting to delay the inevitable: the final leg to Jackson Hole. Where he'd have to hand over the girls till Friday, get a lecture of his own from the Shaws and then wait for the impending assessment. *We're sorry, Shane, but we've warned you. The girls are not being raised right, and so you leave us no choice but to petition for custody...*

His stomach rolled.

Oh—and then there was dropping off Ashley at Harrington Harris's summer palace.

His stomach rolled again.

"Ashley, is that a beaver?" Willow asked, pointing at a woodland creature on their way back toward the parking lot.

Ashley peered at it. "Sure looks like it. I see buck teeth!"

"And it has a big flat tail," Violet said excitedly.

"Last one to that tree is a rotten potato chip!" Willow shouted, racing for a big oak with huge and dramatic horizontal branches. It was the perfect climbing tree.

"Last one to the top is a rotten cheese stick!" Violet said, starting her climb.

"Careful, girls!" Shane called. "Watch your footing."

"Trees are so irresistible to kids," Ashley said, tilting her head back to see the girls climb higher and higher.

Shane got out his phone and snapped a few photos, leaning close to Ashley to show her a particularly good one, where he'd caught both girls climbing, the excitement on their faces a thing of beauty.

"I've seen you sitting on a branch pretty high up in that big maple near the stables," Shane said to Ashley. "Quite a few times, actually. It's like the outdoor version of the stables loft for you."

Ashley smiled. "I didn't think anyone knew about my outdoor hiding place. I climb up pretty far behind dense leaves."

"My Ashley McCray radar is pretty strong."

She tilted her head, looking at him for a moment. "Seems so. I guess I didn't realize this whole past year of my relationship with Harrington that you were looking out for me."

"Always," he said, and the connection between them locked his eyes to hers. He couldn't look away if he tried.

"Look at me, Daddy!" Willow called at that exact moment, and he had to smile to himself. Only his daughters could wrest away his focus from Ashley's hazel-gold eyes, her pink-red lips…

He glanced up to see Willow alarmingly high up. Too high. Violet was several feet below, sitting on a limb and looking intently at a leaf. He saw Willow reach for a branch above her head—and miss. She screamed as she slipped, her arm sliding against a branch as she dropped—hard—to the ground.

Shane's heart stopped, then started pounding. He ran over, Ashley right behind him. Willow lay on the ground, looking half shocked, half in pain, the wind knocked out of her.

"Willow!" Violet yelled and looked panicked as she jumped down from her perch, landing on her knees. She rubbed at them, then ran over.

Willow was crying, her face red, and she wasn't moving. "My foot hurts, Daddy. It hurts really bad."

"Oh, no," Shane said. He peered at her ankle, visible above her little orange socks. It was already swollen. "Let's get you to Urgent Care, honey. It might be broken." He scooped her up, careful not to touch her ankle.

They all hurried to the SUV, Willow sobbing in his arms.

"Ashley, will you reach into my pocket and grab the keys?" he asked.

She did and unlocked the doors and held the back seat door open as Shane settled Willow in her booster seat and got her buckled. Ashley got in beside her and buckled up as Violet scrambled into her own seat on the other side.

Once in the driver's seat, he grabbed his phone and typed in: Urgent Care near me. There was one just seven miles from here. Thank God.

He heard Ashley murmuring softly to Willow. A glance in the rearview mirror showed she was holding Willow's hand. He registered that as very thoughtful before another look in the mirror showed Willow's face contorted in agony.

His heart pounded harder.

All he could think as he drove as fast as he could without risking an accident was that his baby girl was hurting.

Because he'd been too busy flirting with Ashley instead of watching his daughters, who he knew were up in that tree.

He could kick himself. Maybe if he'd been watching, paying attention, he could have been a bit closer with his arms ready to catch her.

Instead his daughter landed with a thud on the ground, her ankle reddened and swollen.

He mentally shook his head. There was nothing the Shaws could ever say that would be worse or more critical than what he was yelling at himself right now.

Ashley and Violet sat side by side in the Urgent Care waiting room, Violet playing a game on Ashley's phone, Ashley's gaze darting to the Exam Rooms door every five seconds. She kept hoping Shane and Willow would come through, but a half hour had passed since they'd disappeared inside with a nurse, and there was no sign of them. Violet had tears in her eyes when they'd first arrived, her sister sobbing and wincing in pain, but the phone game seemed to be working to distract her from the wait.

"Do you think her leg is broken?" Violet asked nervously, putting the phone on her lap. "Eli Overman broke his leg from jumping off the monkey bars, and he wasn't even that high up."

"It could be a sprain or it might be broken. We'll have to wait and find out. But either way, the doctor will know what to do. Willow might come out in a cast or a brace to keep her foot secure."

"I'll sign her cast," Violet said with a nod.

"Me too—if she has one. She might only have a brace or something called a boot that comes on and off."

Violet's eyes got all misty again, and she seemed to shrink into herself.

"Want to sit on my lap?" Ashley asked, holding out her arms.

Violet immediately scrambled over, settling herself and turning inward. Ashley put her arms around the little girl, resting her cheek atop her silky hair with the very short bangs for a moment.

The door to the exam rooms finally opened. Violet, who'd normally rush over to her father and twin, seemed nervous and hesitant and stayed on Ashley's lap. Shane's gaze darted to Violet. Unless Ashley was imagining it, he seemed a little upset at the sight of her there. *Stop it, Ashley. Of course he's upset and tense and stressed—it has nothing to do with you.*

Willow was all smiles now. "Guess what? I have to wear this! It's called a boot. It'll keep my ankle steady as it gets better. I have to wear it for six whole weeks. Daddy said that's the rest of school!"

Violet hopped off Ashley's lap and walked over to her twin. "It doesn't hurt anymore?"

"It does a little. But not like before. The doctor wrapped it up with a superlong bandage. It's under the boot."

"No crutches?" Ashley asked. "That's a relief."

"Sure is. She can walk on it in the boot only." He turned to Willow. "And what did the doctor say about taking care of your ankle? About being nice to it? Gentle? Not running or jumping?"

Willow giggled. "He did tell me to be *extra* nice to my ankle. And I will. Pinkie promise!"

Shane smiled and extended his pinkie, which Willow wrapped her own around. "There, that's a solemn promise made." He turned back to Ashley. "Thanks for staying out there with Violet." He walked over to Violet and gave her hair a gentle ruffle. "You okay, honey?"

"Yup," Violet said. "Now that Willow is okay."

He smiled at his daughter and held up his hand for a high five.

Yup, Ashley had had it 100 percent right about his girls' big hearts. And Shane's.

"Okay, we can get back on the road," he said with a soft clap.

He was definitely stressed. About the grandparents' reaction? About the injury? That it happened at all on his watch?

Something else?

You're a little too invested in what Shane Dawson is thinking and feeling right now, she realized. *Because you care about him. And his daughters.*

A lot.

Instead of sitting between the girls like she had on the way to Urgent Care, she got in the front seat. As they pulled out of the lot and got on the highway, the big entrance sign noting Jackson Hole made her tense. Soon enough, they'd be going their separate ways.

Suddenly Ashley didn't like the thought of that.

After a half hour of driving, the quiet in the car had her turning around to check on the twins. They were both asleep. No surprise there, given the drama. Shane had been either quiet or keeping his line of conversation to Willow's injury.

"I figure we'll make one more stop an hour before we're set to arrive," he said. He'd made a quick call to the Shaws, gratefully getting their voice mail, and had left a message updating their ETA, which wasn't too far off course despite the Urgent Care visit. "A coffee shop or convenience store for some refreshments. We can have that talk with the twins about rules for their grandparents' house."

Ashley could only imagine the extra ire and ammunition the Shaws would have now. Even if the girls behaved like "little ladies," the sight of them, Violet with her scraped knee from jumping out of the tree and her extremely short bangs, and Willow with her big black boot on her left foot, would tell their own story—a story the Shaws would interpret their own way.

"You okay?" she asked.

He glanced at her and nodded, his expression softening a bit, which was a relief. "Just worried. About the ankle and the Shaws' reaction. 'Why weren't you watching them? Why weren't you paying attention? Sure, it's just a sprain, but it could have been much worse.' Followed by head shaking. And decisions." He seemed to shiver a bit.

"I wish I could help in some way," she said.

"You have. You've been an incredible help, Ashley. Every step of the way."

She felt her smile reach deep inside. And then, because he seemed lost in thought, she let him be. If he needed to release some tension or talk anything out, he would. And she'd be there.

But she wouldn't be in a few hours. She'd be at Harrington's, which suddenly felt so…wrong.

She had to see him, though. She had to get her parents' money back. Her bridal party's money back. Not to mention even a little of her dignity.

She had to tell him off.

And then something would happen—either he'd break down and tell her that he *did* make the biggest mistake of his life in leaving her at the altar, that the sight of her, standing before him, made him sure of that, and could they please have a second chance without the pressure of the wedding…

Or he'd look at her without any emotion, assured he'd made the right call, and say, *No problem, Ashley. Here's a check...* Maybe he'd apologize but say he'd done the right thing by ditching her, that they weren't meant to be.

Tough luck, kid. Them's the breaks. And close the door in her face.

One of those things would happen.

Now it was her turn to shiver, despite the perfectly comfortable temperature in Shane's SUV, the beautiful April weather outside.

She had a lot of thinking to do. And barely any time left.

Chapter Ten

Shane had been planning to stop in the heart of Jackson Hole, at the park the girls loved so much with the four arches made out of shed elk antlers and the incredible views of the mountain ranges. But given Willow's sprained ankle, he'd opted for a coffee shop near Town Square, where the girls could have chocolate milk and he and Ashley could get some necessary caffeine boosts. They parked very close to the café, Willow managing to walk fine in her boot.

At a table outside with their drinks and two treats to split, Shane had reiterated the rules for the Shaws' house. Indoor voices even outdoors. Walking instead of running, particularly in the house and down the stairs. Not jumping. Saying *please* and *thank you*. Using Ashley's tips and tricks, such as "Isn't that interesting!" in response to the grandparents saying they enjoyed something the twins thought was *the worst*. No name-calling of anyone, even when referring to someone they didn't like, such as Dylan from school. They were to allow Nana to brush their hair and put it up in ponytails. And they were to show interest in others, asking questions that weren't too personal.

"Can we ask Nana and Pops about Mommy?" Violet said, taking a sip from her box of chocolate milk.

Willow tilted her head, staring at Shane, waiting for his answer.

Shane's heart gave a little ping. "Of course you can."

"I like when people ask us about Mommy, but they never do," Violet said.

Willow nodded. "I guess they think we don't want to talk about her, but we do."

"Yeah," Violet said. "We only don't like when people say something mean. Like that stu—" She paused, Shane's words from exactly one minute ago obviously sticking with her. "Like Dylan."

Sweet success. Instead of "stupid idiot," she'd used his name with a little venomous lilt to her voice. Fine with him.

"The kid from the birthday party?" Ashley asked, her gaze soft on the twins.

Violet nodded. "He said it was weird that we don't have a mother. But it's not weird."

"It's not weird," Willow agreed. "It's just the way it is."

The wisdom of five-year-olds sometimes rocked Shane to the core. He reached over and gave both their hands a squeeze across the table. "I think Nana and Pops feel just like you do about Mommy. Your mother was their beloved daughter. Just like you're my beloved daughters. I think they'd love to talk about her. Especially with you two."

The twins' little faces brightened.

"When we're back home at the McCray Ranch," Ashley said, "I'd love to hear what you know about your mommy. I can tell you what I know too."

Violet smiled. "We don't remember her, but we have a lot of stories about her from Daddy."

"We both have Mommy's green eyes," Willow said.

"And we both love horses just like Mommy did," Violet added.

Ashley's eyes were misty. "Well, you guys know how much I love horses too. I remember that your mother had a favorite horse named Duck. I thought that was very funny."

The twins laughed. "Duck!" Violet said. "Daddy told us about that horse. She was brown and white."

Willow nodded. "And a big fluffy white tail, right?"

"Yup," Ashley said with a grin.

The girls had their special smiles on their faces—which told Shane they were lost in thoughts about their mother. When they had those smiles, he knew they were at peace, that they were enchanted by what they knew about their mother, what they'd learned over the years, what they'd heard.

Ashley, as usual, was a master when it came to the twins' hearts and souls. How she always had the right thing to say at the right time amazed him.

Violet scooted close to her sister on the bench and cupped her hand around Willow's ear, whispering something. Usually Shane could hear their "whispers" loud and clear, but not this time.

Violet looked at Ashley. "Want to know a secret?"

"I already know it," Willow said with a nod.

Ashley glanced at Shane, her eyes still misty. She leaned forward on the bench. "I do want to know a secret."

"We like that you knew Mommy and remember her," Violet said. And then she hurried around the table and threw her arms around Ashley.

Willow got up and very slowly walked around too in her boot, doing the same from the other side of Ashley.

"Oh, my heart," Ashley said, tears spilling down her cheeks now. "I'm glad to know that secret. Thank you."

The girls beamed and went back to their seats, their attention taken by a young teenager zipping by on a skateboard. They sipped their chocolate milks and watched him make sharp turns, eyes wide.

"Parenthood," Shane whispered to Ashley, who dabbed under her eyes with a napkin. "It's something else."

"I really can't wait to find out," she whispered back.

His heart pinged again, this time at the idea of Ashley finding out because she was the mother of some other guy's child. A guy she hadn't met yet. Certainly not that cowardly serial disappointer Harrington Harris IV.

Ashley with someone else. As much as Shane wanted her to be happy, he didn't like the idea of her happy with another man.

Unsettled—and he'd been unsettled enough—he plastered on a neutral expression. "Well, everyone ready?"

When that was the last thing he was.

They headed inside the coffee shop so the girls could wash their treat-sticky hands. As he and Ashley waited, something suddenly occurred to him. Something he didn't like one bit.

"So, I guess I'll be dropping you off at Harrington's now?" he asked. "I suppose I should have asked earlier if you'd arranged to see him."

He could feel his scowl deepening.

She frowned herself. "Actually, I haven't gotten in touch with him at all. I figured I'd do that when I arrived. But now that I'm here..." She bit her lip and let out a breath. "I'm just not ready."

He was relieved but worried for her. She was conflicted, her beautiful eyes reflecting that.

"I have an idea," he said. "Why don't you stay in town while I drop off the twins? Walk in the park, do a little shopping, whatever eases your mind. I'll text you when I'm leaving the Shaws' house. Maybe by then you'll have made some decisions, and I'll come pick you up."

He felt little stabs poking at his chest. He didn't want Ashley anywhere near Harrington.

But this certainly wasn't his decision. He'd said his share on the trip here. She knew how he felt about her getting back together with the guy. What she'd do was up to her, and he had to accept her choice.

"That is definitely the plan," she said, perking up some. "I'll do exactly that. Stroll the park and check out the shops. Maybe have two or ten more iced coffees."

He reached his hand to hers and gave it a squeeze. He had no idea what was going to happen. With anything. But he knew, right here, right now, that he couldn't bear the thought of Ashley McCray with another man. Particularly her ex-fiancé, but any other man.

Except him.

But was he ready for a relationship with her? Right now, he was too focused on the Shaws' threats and the holy hell they were going to rain down on him about Willow's injury and Violet's haircut. The scrapes on Violet's knees. The faded bruise on Willow's arm from falling off her bike last month. And those were just the immediately visible issues. Then the twins would open their mouths. Move. And…

"We're ready to go, Daddy!" Violet said as the girls came out the restroom.

He sure wasn't.

"Nana! Pops! We're here! We're here!"

Surely the Shaws would appreciate the twins' excitement at seeing them, Shane thought as the girls raced out—and

Willow was fast in that boot—of the SUV in their grand-parents' driveway, forgetting everything he'd told them twenty minutes ago in town.

Beatrice and Charles Shaw appeared in the doorway of their stately stone house, the Grand Tetons rising in the distance behind it. Shane was always struck whenever he saw the Shaws because there was so much of Liza in them. Beatrice's hair was a deep auburn, and though Liza's had been long and wavy while her mother's was a precise bob to her chin, the similarity in color and texture always caught him off guard. Liza had had her father's green eyes, her mother's perfect nose and alabaster complexion. And height from both tall Shaws.

Beatrice was in her signature outfit, a twinset (he'd learned what it was called from Liza) with dressy pants, and flat shoes with some sort of crest on the toes. Tasteful jewelry, tasteful makeup. Charles, as usual, was dressed in tan chinos and a crisp button-down shirt, this one plaid. Beatrice always had a snooty look about her, but Charles radiated warmth. Liza had had his ready smile.

Violet dashed up the bluestone walkway and threw her arms around her grandmother, then her grandfather, Willow going quite a bit slower in her boot.

The good news? Violet had been so fast running from the car to her grandmother that Beatrice couldn't possibly have noticed the budding hairstylist's bangs. The Shaws' attention was on Willow—her foot, to be exact. Shane hadn't mentioned the reason for the delay in the voice mail.

"What on earth?" Beatrice said, giving Violet a quick hug and then stepping forward to peer at her twin.

Violet remained on the porch. "Willow sprained her ankle and has to wear that boot for six whole weeks!"

Beatrice's gaze traveled from Violet to Willow. She stared at her granddaughter. Well, she'd definitely noticed the hacked bangs now.

"Girls! Welcome!" Charles said. "We're so happy to see you and have you stay for a few days!" He rubbed his chin for a moment. "Hmm, Willow, let me guess... You were running superfast and tripped and landed funny."

"Guess again!" Willow said, making her way to the porch.

Beatrice scowled, her gaze on the black boot.

"You were climbing high at the playground and took a tumble," Charles said.

Willow grinned. "It was actually a tree!"

"And where was your father while you were falling out of trees?" Beatrice muttered.

"Talking to Ashley," Violet said so guilelessly that Shane couldn't fault her for ratting him out. He *had* been talking to Ashley.

"Ashley?" Beatrice said, her chin rising as she shot a quick glance Shane's way. "Who, pray tell, is Ashley?"

"Ashley McCray!" Willow said from the porch.

"Oh, yes," Beatrice said. "The rancher's daughter."

Shane felt himself bristle. That sounded so dismissive. *The rancher's daughter.*

"Ashley's a horse groomer," Violet said. "And her fonsay didn't come to their wedding."

"Her fonsay?" Beatrice repeated.

"Fiancé," Shane offered, his collar tightening even though the first two buttons of his own button-down shirt were open.

"I see you have a new hairstyle," Charles said quickly to Violet as if sensing they should get off the topic of Ashley pronto.

Thank God for Charles. Or actually, maybe not. Beatrice hadn't even gotten to Violet's hair yet. Now she would.

Violet beamed. "I did it myself. I wanted to look like Miranda."

That got Beatrice's attention. The chin lifted just slightly again, and her eyes slightly narrowed. "Miranda? *Who's* Miranda?"

"She's Ashley's cousin. We stayed with her and Michael when Daddy's car was broken."

"Oh, yes, that," Beatrice said. "I almost forgot about the broken-down vehicle." Another glance of disdain was sent Shane's way.

"Ashley came with us on the trip," Violet said. "When he leaves here, Daddy's going to take her to her fonsay's house to get back her money!"

Oh, boy. That was a loaded sentence. Full of things for Beatrice to home in on. To the point that she didn't even correct Violet's pronunciation.

"For the wedding," Willow explained.

For a moment, Beatrice just stared at the girls with a strange expression. "My goodness. How…vulgar," she added under her breath.

But Shane heard it. A burst of anger grew in his gut. There was nothing vulgar about Ashley McCray or her intentions. He stared daggers at Beatrice, which she didn't seem to notice because her attention was moving from Violet's bangs down to her knees. Her scraped knees.

Beatrice walked over to him. "Is Ashley your girlfriend?" she asked in a whisper, her voice cold—but curious.

"She's a family friend. My boss's daughter," Shane said unnecessarily. "We were headed to the same town on the same day, and it made sense for me to give Ashley a ride. The girls adore her."

Beatrice didn't respond. She walked back over to the porch, where Willow had climbed up. Violet was behind her, doing a cartwheel.

Don't knock out a window, he prayed. Or maybe she should. Kick out the whole pane. It would give them something else to talk about.

Beatrice turned to the twins. "Well, I don't know how I can possibly take you two to Climbing Kingdom now." She shook her head with yet another look of disappointment at Shane. "You girls specifically asked to go there on this vacation, but now we can't."

"What matters is that you two are here!" Charles cut in fast. "We're going to have a great bunch of days."

"Yes, of course we will," Beatrice said with a smile at her granddaughters. Then she turned to Shane, the smile gone. "We'll take it from here. Bye now. Girls, say goodbye to your father."

Dismissed. Fine with him. The less time he had to spend with Beatrice Shaw, the better.

The twins came over and hugged him tight. "I'll pick you up on Friday morning, okay? You listen to your grandparents and remember the rules I told you about."

He caught Beatrice raising an eyebrow. They had another round of hugs, and then he held up a hand in goodbye to the Shaws and walked over to his SUV.

Beatrice followed. "A word, Shane."

He turned, dread rising in his throat, desperate to get out of there.

Charles was leading the twins around the side of the house to the backyard, where they had a play area.

Beatrice waited until Charles and the girls were out of sight—and earshot. "I could not be more disappointed," she said. "Well, I'm sure I could. A sprained ankle? Violet playing with sharp scissors and ruining her hair? The scrapes on those girls? The running and yelling the moment they arrived. Nothing's changed. Nothing at all."

"I'm glad for that," he said, deciding he wasn't going to take her criticisms lying down. As much as he wanted to pacify her to keep her from following through on her threat, he wasn't going to let anyone run down his daughters without him standing up to defend them. "Because Willow and Violet are great girls. They're active five-year-olds. They fall because they're playing and enjoying themselves. They're curious. They're smart and interesting and have huge hearts. I'm proud of who they are. I wish you could like them as they are instead of wanting them to turn into people they're not."

"What's wrong with wanting them to be appropriate citizens?" Beatrice said. "That's all I ask. Well-behaved, well-mannered girls."

"They are well-behaved and well-mannered." He mentally shook his head, keeping a lid on his temper. He was well used to Beatrice, and this was nothing new. Except now there was the threat of her taking him to court to fight for custody of his children.

The anger welled up again. *I'll have to be dead first.*

"I'm glad you'll have these days with them," he said, trying to keep the ice out of his own tone. "Because I think you'll see, if you're really looking and listening, how wonderful they are."

"I know they're wonderful, Shane. They're half Liza. Of course they're wonderful. But they're a danger to themselves, and you clearly don't watch them or discipline them. They're not being raised right."

Like hell they weren't.

He wished she would look at him and see the man who loved her granddaughters with everything he was. The man who'd loved her daughter. The man her daughter had loved. Had started a family with. The girls had brought Liza so much joy. But Beatrice had always found something to criticize, no matter how young the twins were. He'd never forget Violet and Willow's second birthday party, which he'd thrown at an indoor toddler play space. They'd been in the throes of the terrible twos the moment they'd hit that milestone. Beatrice had been complaining up a storm about the pretty low-level tantrum they'd both thrown over not getting to have their birthday cake yet. *Unacceptable!* Beatrice had snapped at him. *Liza would have had them behaving like those sweet little girls over there*, she'd said, pointing to the quiet, docile little Hayberry twins, who were nothing like his active whirlwinds.

I'm not the enemy, Beatrice, he'd said to her. *I'm the man who loved your daughter so much that sometimes when I look at the girls and I see her in their faces, I just break down inside. I'm not the enemy*, he'd repeated. *And I'm doing the best that I can—which, yes, is good enough.*

He'd seen her eyes mist before she'd turned away, and he'd been reminded that there was a heart in that body, despite how determinedly she hid it. He'd known she was reacting out of grief. And he'd stuck to his promise to Liza after he'd lost her to always extend his compassion to her mother. To do his best to meet her at her comfort zone until he was pushed too far out of his.

He was there now.

He bristled, anger rising. "They *are* being raised right. They're loved, happy and wonderful children. If I have to fight you in court, I'm prepared."

Beatrice lifted her chin again. "I'll expect you on Friday at ten a.m. to pick them up. That will give you time to return home at a reasonable hour for their bedtime."

A sudden change of subject while still getting in another dig about propriety. She was impossible.

"Just enjoy them," he said. "Liza would be so proud of her daughters. So proud," he added, tears stinging the backs of his eyes at how very true that was. He blinked them away.

Beatrice gave him the quickest of glances but didn't respond. Instead, she turned and headed back to the house. At least she didn't say something awful like, *I'm not so sure about that.*

Still, this had been every bit the disaster of a drop-off that he'd been expecting.

Chapter Eleven

For the past hour, Ashley had been sitting on a bench in the park, so focused on what was very likely going on at the Shaws' house that she barely gave any thought to the reason she'd come to Jackson Hole. All she could think about was the twins' grandmother pulling Shane aside with her litany of complaints and criticisms.

Her threats to take his girls away from him.

He must be so stressed.

She'd seen—up close—how great a father he was, how devoted and loving and caring, how tuned in to his children he was, and how very happy the girls were with him. She adored those Dawson twins and had seen just how lucky they were to have him as a father. Their sole parent.

She pulled out her phone to check the time. He should be texting any moment now. She kept her phone in her hand and lifted her face to the waning sun. She was sitting on a bench in the park, the majestic mountain ranges in full view, the shops and restaurants of Jackson Hole surrounding the square. The air had turned a bit cooler, but there was no wind and it felt so refreshing on her skin, in her hair. She'd been sitting here since they'd parted, unable to imagine window-shopping, let alone going in any stores.

Not when Shane's entire life felt dependent on the grand-parents' reaction, their assessment of the girls' behavior.

Anger stoked in her belly. How unfair. How dare they? Couldn't Beatrice see how he loved Violet and Willow—how loved they were? Couldn't they see how hard he worked, how he balanced his life as a father? He deserved better than to be threatened.

You care about this man, she acknowledged. *A lot.*

Her phone pinged, and she sat up straight. Shane.

Left the Shaws. Feel like hell. Up for some terrible company?

Aww. Her heart flew out to him.

Absolutely, she texted back. Dinner?

And a drink, was his response. Three emojis of wine bottles following.

She texted back a smiley face and her location. He wrote that he'd be there in ten minutes.

As she put her phone away and waited, she realized that right beside her concern for him was excitement at seeing him. To be with Shane, to sit across a table somewhere and share a meal, share their problems.

Maybe…kiss again.

Yes, she thought, some very good, very sexy memories washing over her.

Maybe tonight, they just needed to forget those prob-lems. Put them aside for just a few hours. Several, even. And…enjoy each other's company, which would *not* be ter-rible because they wouldn't be focusing on why they were here in this beautiful town. They'd focus on each other. On pleasure. On forgetting just for tonight.

She'd propose it. Perhaps she wouldn't even have to.

Perhaps the evening would naturally lead to it. She had a feeling it might.

At the fifteen-minute mark, she began looking around for Shane. And there he was, walking down the path toward her. She stood, and he held up a hand in a wave. She could see how tense he was in the set of his shoulders, in the set of his jaw, the lack of light in his eyes.

As he approached, she held out her arms and he stepped right into them. She hugged him and he hugged her back, hard, resting his head atop hers. He definitely was tense, but she could feel him relaxing a bit, more a resignation of what was than letting go of anything.

"How bad was it?" she asked.

He stepped back a bit. "Bad. I'm not raising them right, she said."

Ashley shook her head. "That's the wrongest thing I've ever heard. Ever."

He did manage something of a smile then. "I appreciate that." He held out his hand and she took it, and they started walking. "I could use a steak house. The works. Maybe even creamed spinach. And a really good beer."

"I definitely remember passing a steak house on the way here."

"Rodeo Joe's Steaks," he said.

"We're there."

He smiled again and squeezed her hand, and they continued walking. "What would I have done if you weren't here? I'd be sitting on that bench you just vacated, stewing and shaking and going out of my mind."

"Yeah, same here. If you weren't here, I'd still be on that bench, unable to move or think or know what the hell to do." Not that she *did* know.

"It's a good thing we're both here, then." He squeezed her hand again, and she felt such a connection to him, such solidarity.

"I was thinking," she said. "Let's just go where the night takes us. Talk about what we need to and want to. Do what we need to and want to."

"I'm all for that."

"Good," she said.

This might not be an easy night for either of them, but they'd get through it together.

Rodeo Joe's was crowded, but they'd scored a table for two after just a twenty-minute wait at the bar, where Shane had his good beer and Ashley had sipped a vodka and cranberry. Every time he looked at her, her beautiful face and long silky brown hair, and every time he heard her voice or laughter, he'd be transported away from everything going wrong in both their worlds. By the sweetness of their friendship, the comfort of how they supported each other, the excitement of their attraction and the pressure-free question mark that seemed to hang in the air between them, all his tension would ease and he'd just focus on Ashley McCray.

But then a waiter would pass by with a tray of entrées or a man at a nearby table would laugh loudly and the spell would be broken, diverting his thoughts from Ashley back to the force of everything Beatrice had said, and his shoulders would seize up again. At one point when they'd still been in the bar awaiting their table, Ashley had looked at him with concern, stood up from her stool and given him a mini massage. He'd closed his eyes and let her warm, strong hands work their magic. But then their table had been called and the magic hands had unfortunately lifted.

Now they sat across from each other in front of a window with a view of the mountains, the soft lighting and music helping to relax him again. The woman too. Their waiter had come and gone, and Shane found himself focusing on the good meal he was about to have, the easy conversation and the excellent company. He wasn't sure how great he'd be as a dinner partner, but he'd try to stop thinking about the Shaws for at least the next hour.

The waiter returned with their entrées, and they dug in, talking and laughing and offering each other bites of their meals. It was great at first, but then he started thinking of something equally unpleasant.

Ashley would probably go see Harrington tomorrow. He had the feeling she wasn't going to do that tonight, and he was grateful for that. But tomorrow morning was a different story. She'd go do what she'd come for.

Just demand back the money. Don't hope that he looks at you and realizes he screwed up big-time.

That was what Shane was afraid of, that she still had that lingering hope in her heart. That she needed Harrington to say he was sorry, that he made a mistake, could they try again.

His shoulders started tensing again.

"Hey, you look more stressed than you were when you arrived in the park," Ashley said, fork paused midway to her mouth. "You okay?"

Just say it. This is Ashley, who you can talk to. About anything. Don't hold back the truth. "Just thinking about why you're here. Not in this restaurant. I mean here in Jackson Hole. I figure tomorrow morning, you're going to go see what's-his-name."

"At the very least I need to confront him about the money," she said. "But let's not talk about that, Shane."

At the very least? What the hell did that mean? Those two should have *nothing* to discuss other than the wedding bill. In his opinion anyway.

"Look," she said. "We both have a lot on our minds. But we're here tonight in this beautiful, bustling town, and let's just try to enjoy it, put everything aside, just for tonight."

He held up his beer glass. She held up her wine. They clinked. "To tonight."

"To tonight," she repeated, her gaze and smile softer now. She sipped her wine and forked a spear of asparagus. "But I guess I should ask—you'll be leaving for home in the morning? Then you'll drive back to pick up the girls? You'll have to leave home at the crack of dawn."

He stopped chewing and stared at her for a second. He hadn't really thought about it. But he supposed that would be the plan. It wasn't like he'd want to stick around Jackson Hole with all the uncertainty plaguing him. Better another seven-hour drive to get back to his own turf than risk running into the Shaws in town, even if he'd get to eyeball his girls and give them a hug. No, he should leave and drive back when it was time for the world to feel right again: when he'd be able to be with his children.

Except there was the ole monkey wrench now. Ashley herself.

"I was planning on driving back home, yes," he said. "But I don't like the idea of leaving you on your own here, so…" A decision formed as he said the words. "I'll just stick around. Just in case."

"In case what?" she asked.

"In case you need me."

Her expression showed how touched she was. She put down her fork and reached for his hand and held it across the table. "Now we have to eat holding hands," she said. "Sorry, but that's just the way it has to be." She smiled, her beautiful face lighting up.

"I'd have a hard time letting go anyway," he said.

"Same." She looked up at him, almost shyly.

Tonight was going to be interesting, that much he knew.

"If you're planning to stick around," she said slowly, "maybe...we should find a place to stay for a few days."

Oh, yeah, interesting to say the least.

"There are so many hotels, Airbnbs, guest ranches," Ashley pointed out. "Oooh, maybe we can stay at a guest ranch like your cousins have in Bear Ridge."

Shane loved the place, as did the twins. The Dawson Family Guest Ranch was owned by six siblings, second cousins to Shane. They had opened the dude ranch, re-built from ashes and the doom and gloom of family history, and over the past few years had expanded it into one of the most popular in Wyoming. He and Ashley should definitely pick a place like that, where they could go horseback riding, watch comical goats, walk the land, sit by the river, stare endlessly at the mountains, eat good food and just be together.

And whatever else came up...

"Now we know what we're doing after dinner," he said. "Finding our dude ranch."

Her warm smile mixed with the relief on her pretty face shot straight to his heart.

If anyone had told him a week ago that making Ashley

McCray happy would be so important to him, he wouldn't have believed it. But life was full of surprises—the good and the bad—and right this second, he was dealing with the good and was going with it.

No matter where it led or didn't.

Ahhh, Ashley thought as she and Shane arrived at their cabin at the Mountain Valley Guest Ranch and looked around. Heavenly. The medium-sized ranch was just fifteen minutes from the center of town. Their cabin, a hunter green two-bedroom with a steeply pitched roof and a porch with a swing, overlooked a river and had evergreens creating privacy from the neighbors on either side. Small and cozy with a big stone fireplace, a plush dark tan sofa and a big muted soft area rug, the cabin also had a kitchenette and a bathroom with a spa shower—complete with two fluffy robes on hooks behind the door. Oh, yes, this would do nicely. A relaxing place to spend a few days, to think and plan.

With her new best friend, Shane Dawson.

He'd insisted on covering the cost, including any spa treatments she wanted, and she definitely wanted those. Even just the most rudimentary of facials with cucumber slices over her eyes and a mud mask would be a treat. Ranch attractions included horseback riding on acres of trails, a cafeteria with supposedly amazing burgers and shoestring fries, a petting zoo and Be A Rancher For A Day! Workshops where you could help lead the small herd of cattle out to different pastures or milk cows and learn to make cheese. Yes to all of it, Ashley thought, dropping down on the sofa with a very satisfied sigh. She'd always worked solely with the horses at the McCray Ranch; it would be fun to focus on the cows here.

Shane was scanning the brochure of activities they'd received at check-in. "The entertainment is from nine to eleven at the lodge's club—there's a comedian and also a jazz singer, dancing and moonlit walks along the lit path along the river."

"A comedy show? I love it here already," she said.

"Same." He dropped down next to her, and she turned to him and took his hand.

"Thank you for staying in town with me. Just thank you."

He leaned his head back against the cushion and turned to face her. "Thank you for staying with *me*."

But in separate bedrooms, she wanted to add but didn't. Earlier she'd been planning to let the night go where it would. But maybe tonight needed to be about rest and relaxation— not adding more confusion to the mix. If she and Shane got all romantic again, what did that mean about what she wanted? What she intended? She didn't seem to know how she felt about anything except that Shane was becoming very dear to her. He was there from the outset at the biggest disappointment of her life, there to comfort her, there to offer her a ride, a way to process. And he was here now.

And she was so damned drawn to him, so attracted.

Because he *was* here? Because he *was* there for her when she needed someone most? Someone to count on, someone to turn to, someone who would tell her the truth?

Stop, she chastised herself again. *Don't complicate things further. If you think you might be getting back together with Harrington, if that's a possibility, then no more kissing Shane. No more anything with Shane other than friendship.*

But calling a mental halt to whatever might happen between her and Shane didn't sit well with her either. What was going on here? What did she want? And what if she really fell for Shane? Then what? He wasn't necessarily in the market for a relationship.

Had she ever seen him with a woman in the five years he'd been widowed? Had she ever seen any female besides a relative enter his cabin? Had he ever gone anywhere overnight other than to drop off his daughters at relatives' for visits?

From everything she'd seen and heard, the man didn't date.

But he was…attracted to her. That was the only thing she knew.

You're getting ahead of yourself, Ashley, she told herself. *Just try to enjoy yourself while you're here at the dude ranch. In the morning, you'll make a decision about whether you're ready to go see Harrington and confront him. If you need another day, fine. The reservation for the dude ranch is for three nights.*

Too many contradictory thoughts. Stop thinking.

"Let's take a walk along the river and then go to the comedy show. I could use a laugh."

"Me too," she said. Perfect. A walk on a beautiful evening and a show. Just what she needed. "I'll just go freshen up."

She missed him the moment she closed the bathroom door behind her.

Chapter Twelve

The theater in the Mountain Valley Guest Ranch lodge was on the small side, but pretty crowded, as though all the guests had turned up for the comedian. Who didn't like to laugh? Beatrice Shaw, maybe. But most people did, so Shane wasn't surprised that the show attracted so many folks.

There was a stage and around thirty tables, a few waiters weaving between with trays of drinks and baskets of popcorn. He and Ashley were sitting in the front row, over to the left. The drinks were expensive—fifteen dollars, even draft beer—but the venue had a two-drink minimum. At least there was free popcorn.

The comedian, a tall, skinny guy in a Stetson, bolo tie, huge silver belt buckle and cowboy boots, whose stage name was Cowboy Roy, wasn't all that funny. He tried, but his timing was off and his jokes were a little stale. He got a couple of laughs here and there, mostly when he got a bit vulgar.

"Okay," Cowboy Roy said, peering into the audience, clearly looking for something to turn his bad set around. "Enough about me. Who are *you* people? Any newlyweds? Who's on their honeymoon? I hear this place has a special honeymoon cabin with the works—heart-shaped bed, annulment papers just in case…" That didn't even get him a chuckle—big surprise.

Shane glanced over at Ashley to check her reaction; she didn't crack a smile, but then again, it wasn't laugh-worthy. For the first time, really, Shane homed in on the fact that Ashley's entire life, her future, all the hopes and dreams she'd had for her wedding and marriage, had been taken from her. Shane might think she'd dodged a bullet, but Ashley's heart had been terribly messed with. She'd probably been very excited about her honeymoon—which the Harrises had paid for as their gift—and now, instead of ordering incredible pasta in Italy, a gold wedding ring on her finger, happiness radiating from within, she was here, with him, munching on popcorn and watching a bad co-median joke about honeymoons.

"Huh, no honeymooners," Cowboy Roy continued. "Who's on their third date, then? Third-date rule still a thing? I don't often get past the first date, so I wouldn't know, unfortu-nately." Shane definitely wasn't surprised to hear that. "Ah, you two," he said, his eyes lighting up as he pointed to Shane and Ashley. "*Definitely* on your third date. I can feel the an-ticipation, the tension *radiating* off the two of you."

Every head in the place swiveled to him and Ashley.

Oh, God. Oh, no. There was nothing worse than getting singled out by a comedian.

"People, am I right?" Cowboy Roy said, wiggling his eyebrows. "Oh, my, the sexual tension! Sweetheart, tell us, is he getting lucky tonight?"

This was what passed for humor these days? The guy was not funny in the slightest. Where'd they get him from?

Ashley's cheeks were red. "We're not even a couple," she called out, her eyes darting around a bit. Shane wondered if she was worried she might know someone in the audience, someone who knew about her relationship with Harrington. "We're, um, just…"

Cowboy Roy made a "yeah, right" face, and that did get a laugh from the audience. From everyone but him and Ashley. "Just *friends*? Suuuure. You two will be engaged within three months. Mark my words."

Shane stiffened. Ashley turned redder.

"We're not… I'm not…" Ashley stammered, then clamped her lips shut.

"Sometimes the couple is the last to know," Cowboy Roy said with a wink, then turned to a table of four a row ahead. "Ah, double date…"

Shane breathed a sigh of relief that he'd moved on, that they weren't being responsive enough to continue with. Though Ashley had made it clear there was nothing between them.

We're not a couple…

Of course they weren't a couple. They weren't even dating. They were only together in the strictest sense of the word. They'd had a moment, a couple of moments, that was all.

He and Ashley awkwardly ate popcorn and sipped their drinks. The comedian called for a twenty-minute intermission, reminding everyone that they'd have to order their second drink during the second half, and if they left early, they'd be billed for it anyway.

"I can't take another minute of this guy," Shane said.

Ashley rolled her eyes. "Me either. He's the pits!"

Shane laughed. "Now, *that's* funny."

They got up and headed out. As they walked toward the

cabin on the well-lit path, Ashley said, "What do you think about what he said—I mean about us?"

"That we're third-date material?"

She glanced at him and nodded. Her cheeks were slightly flushed.

"I think," he said slowly, "I think that unfunny comedian was right."

"You do?" she asked.

He stopped and turned to face her. "I can't deny I'm very attracted to you. On all levels."

She let out something of a gasp. "All levels," she repeated on a whisper.

"You're a truly lovely person, Ashley McCray. You're beautiful and incredibly sexy, yes, but you're kind and smart and interesting and fun and very nice to five-year-olds."

She flung her arms around him and hugged him. "I needed to hear that. Thank you."

"You're the first woman I've kissed in five years," he whispered. "To be honest, I had no plans to bring romance into my life again. Not that we're dating or involved, like you said. But you just sort of…happened."

She pulled back, her arms still around his neck, a shy smile on her beautiful face. "You sort of happened too."

He leaned forward and kissed her on the lips. "I'm not ready for anything. You're not sure what you're doing. But here we are. Making out."

She grinned. "We're a pair, all right."

He took her hand and they resumed walking. "You said we should take tonight to just…be. So let's just be. What happens happens."

"And what happens at the Mountain Valley Guest Ranch stays at the Mountain Valley Guest Ranch."

He stopped and turned to her and nodded. "It's like we're each taking baby steps that won't really lead anywhere. Maybe that's what we need, what we *should* be doing. Taking the steps to see what's what with absolutely no pressure."

"Yeah," she whispered. "I think that's exactly what we're doing."

She hooked her hand around his arm and they resumed walking. If he just focused on the beautiful April night, the surprisingly warm breeze, the fresh air, Ashley so close beside him, everything was okay in the world. For tonight anyway.

They approached the cabin, and he unlocked the door, the lamp casting a romantic glow over the interior.

"How about that second drink?" she asked. "The welcome packet said every cabin comes with a complimentary bottle of wine."

"Love some," he said. "And you relax. I've got it."

"You've always got everything. What can't you do?" she asked with a smile. "Seriously."

"Well, I'm kind of used to taking care of stuff and giving people food and beverages. I mix a lot of chocolate milk, make a lot of ham-and-Swiss sandwiches for the girls' lunches. Thank God they both love the same stuff right now. Can you imagine if they had wildly different likes and tastes and personalities?"

She laughed. "They are very alike. Just when I think one is the alpha, the other takes over. I love how close they are."

"Yup." He moved to the kitchenette against the wall and found two wineglasses in the cabinets. "Me too. They'll always have each other." He wished he could FaceTime them right now, but it was late, and even if they weren't asleep—and they probably were, given the big day they'd had—Beatrice Shaw would lay into him.

He brought the bottle, a corkscrew and two glasses. They sat together on the sofa in front of the beautiful stone fireplace but didn't bother lighting it because it was too nice for a fire. He opened the bottle and poured.

"To…right now," he said, holding up his glass.

"To right now," she repeated and they clinked.

Ashley sipped her wine, then put the glass on the coffee table, curled her legs up underneath her and rested her head on Shane's shoulder.

This was…nice. Very nice. He could stay just like this for maybe five more minutes—and then he was going to be overwhelmed with the desire to kiss her.

It turned out he wasn't going to have to wait that long. Because suddenly she was moving, straddling him, her hands against his chest. "I don't know anything, Shane. I just know that I want this right now."

"Same. Exactly. And if that's okay, then…"

"It's okay with me," she whispered.

"And me."

Her mouth was on his neck, trailing kisses up to his ear. He closed his eyes to keep control. It was hard enough to keep a grip on himself when he could feel everything she was doing to him. Seeing her beautiful face, her sexy body, would make his self-control shatter.

He pulled off her sweater and opened his eyes to her lush, full breasts hidden behind a lacy black bra. He needed that thing off now. She reached behind her and unhooked it, arching her back. He groaned, his hands, his mouth exploring every inch of her glorious chest. She moved against him, letting out a breathy moan, and he had to still himself to again regain control. He picked her up, Ashley still straddling him, and kissed her as he carried her to one of the bedrooms.

Within thirty seconds, both their jeans and his shirt were off, and the thin cotton of their underwear was all that was keeping them separated. It had to go too. He peeled down her white lace panties; she pulled down his black boxer briefs.

"Very sexy," she whispered, and he felt her lips on his stomach, kissing downward, a hand sliding onto his erection.

He moaned, groaned, arched his back—all while being unable to stop kissing her. He had to be inside her now.

"Oh, hell," he said, opening his eyes.

Ashley, underneath him, opened hers too. "What could possibly be wrong?" she asked, cupping his face.

"Lack of condoms." He bopped his forehead with the palm of his hand.

She grinned. "My cousin Miranda said the same thing the comedian did. That we're the last to know. She handed me three condoms before we left and insisted I put them in my wallet. Which is where they are now." She scooted over the bed and reached for her jeans and her wallet and plucked out all three condoms.

"Hey, you never know. And we can always get more tomorrow." She ripped open one of the little foil packets.

He grinned and then again went very still as she straddled him again and rolled on the condom. Moments later, she slid down on top of him, his hands on her waist, and moved against him.

Slowly at first. And then faster. Faster.

He reached upward to feel her lush breasts and sat up enough against the headboard to suckle her nipples.

"Oh, Shane," she whispered on a breathy moan, and he knew he was close.

They exploded in pleasure together, and she collapsed down on top of him, their hearts beating so fast in what felt like unison.

He stroked her silky hair and closed his eyes. He felt her kiss him on the cheek before she settled against his chest, and they caught their breath together, holding hands.

He didn't have a thought in his head other than how good this felt, how he wished he could stay like forever.

Ashley awoke in the dark on her side, a warm, strong arm over her.

Ahhh, Shane.

She turned slightly to peer at him. The moonlight coming in through the filmy bedroom curtains cast a beautiful dim glow over part of his face. He was so handsome. The dark tousled hair that she'd run her hands through just hours ago. Long, dark eyelashes against his cheeks. The chiseled jawline, which she'd kissed every bit of.

Mmm, sex with Shane Dawson had been amazing. They'd been in such harmony, moving together so fluidly, effortlessly. There had been so much passion, yet she'd felt so safe, cocooned, as though there was only the two of them in the world.

That's probably not real life, she thought. *That's most likely "road trip" sex. Road-trip romance.*

Or was it? Was she right where she was supposed to be? Would she still feel this way even when they were back in "real life"?

Last night he'd told her that she was the first woman he'd kissed in five years. Which meant she was the first woman he'd slept with since becoming a widower. What was he going to want from this? Maybe nothing at all. Maybe, like he'd said, this was about baby steps toward nothing in particular. At most, toward figuring stuff out that they needed to get a handle on as individuals that had nothing to do with them as a couple. They were doing what felt right in the moment.

Ashley turned and looked out the window. She could see the almost-full moon, and the tops of tree branches with their budding leaves. She slipped out from under Shane's arm and left the bed, tiptoeing from the room, quietly closing the door behind her. She went into the other bedroom, where she'd put her suitcase, and quickly put on a long sweatshirt and yoga pants, then pulled her hair back in a ponytail.

In the living room, she went over to the sliding glass doors that opened out onto the small patio. It was way too chilly to go outside, even though she could use a blast of cool air on her skin, on her brain.

Miranda. She needed to talk to her cousin. She'd help her make sense of what she was feeling without any judgment. And best of all, she'd be awake at—Ashley glanced up at the round clock with little cows for numbers on the kitchen wall—12:17 a.m. Even if baby Roxy was mostly sleeping through the night now, Miranda was a night owl. She sent her a quick text and asked if she was awake and up for FaceTime.

Her video-call app pinged five seconds later.

Ashley smiled. She owed Miranda a lot more than just good donuts for all this. "Hi," she said to her cousin.

"Oooh, something happened—something good," Miranda said, a twinkle in her eyes. "I can see it in your face."

Ashley moved over to a chair farthest from the bedroom she'd just left and glanced at the door to make sure it was still closed. It was, and she didn't hear a peep from inside. "Something did," she whispered. "And it was amazing." She couldn't stop her goofy smile.

"Oh! Well, I am not surprised. I knew you two were going to be together. Just a matter of time. And comfort."

"I don't know how comfortable I am," Ashley said. "I mean, what am I doing? I'm in Jackson Hole for a reason. And I'm sleeping with another man?"

"First of all, you're in Jackson Hole to demand your family's money back from that jerk who stood you up at the altar. And Shane isn't *another* man. There's no other man, Ashley."

She bit her lip. That was true. She wasn't engaged. She wasn't anything with Harrington at the moment. This was why she knew calling Miranda was a good idea. Her cousin would say it straight, even if it did ping her heart. And she knew Miranda thought Harrington Harris needed to be kicked to the curb the way he'd done to Ashley.

"He broke up with you in the worst way, honey. You're not cheating on Harrington, if that's even a thought in your head."

"I know," Ashley said. "But if I harbor any hopes of giving the relationship another chance without all the pressure of a wedding…"

"Well, then ask yourself why you slept with Shane. Test how you feel. About Harrington. About Shane. About everything. Maybe you keep clinging to the idea of another chance with Harrington because you're scared of how you feel about Shane. And I understand that, Ashley."

Huh. She hadn't considered that. Ashley wasn't a dummy—

she knew that Harrington had done her wrong. *I don't love you after all*... Was she sticking with this idea of him in her life because it felt safer than admitting she now had feelings for someone else? Scary feelings?

She let out a big sigh, because it sounded like the truth.

Miranda gave her a gentle smile, full of compassion. "You don't have to know everything. But if you want my opinion, and I think you do because you texted me at midnight, you need to move on from what's-his-name. He's past. Maybe Shane isn't the future—who knows? But he *is* the present, and he's helping you figure things out. He's a great guy, he's safety personified, and he's there for you. And from the look on your face when you popped on-screen, he's great in bed," she added with a devilish grin.

Oh, yeah, he was.

Ashley tried to keep the moony look off her face that the comment had brought on. "I knew I could count on you to set me straight. You're right—I don't know how I feel about anything and I don't have to know. Thank you for talking me through. I owe you."

"All you owe me is a visit sometime soon again. Love you, hon."

"Love you too," she said, and then the screen went dark.

She sat there for a while, looking out at the dark patio, at the moon. Thinking about Shane. Thinking about all Miranda had said.

He's safety personified...

No, he wasn't. Not at all. Shane wasn't safe. He had his own heart, mind and soul, his own reason for being in Jackson Hole and sticking around. His own worries and stressors. Like Miranda had said, she couldn't know if there was any future for them. Maybe all they had was the present.

And if that was the case, she needed to protect herself, and most especially protect her still-healing heart.

Don't fall in love, she told herself. *Whatever you do, do not fall in love with Shane Dawson.*

Their agreed-upon motto, *what happens on the road trip stays on the road trip*, was feeling more and more like utter nonsense. When she did go home, she'd take every memory with her and not forget a moment of it. Especially not after what went on in that bedroom just hours ago.

And Shane would be right there with her at the McCray Ranch.

Tread carefully from here on in, she told herself.

All she wanted right now was to go back into that bedroom and slip into bed beside Shane. She didn't, though. She got up and went into the other room, closing the door behind her.

She had no idea what this meant. Maybe she just needed a little space right now. To think about sleeping with Shane. How she felt about it. Everything Miranda had said.

Maybe she *was* just scared. Of just how deep her feelings for Shane Dawson went.

Chapter Thirteen

Shane woke up in the morning with an instant smile on his face. He kept his eyes closed, wanting to snuggle with Ashley, but when he reached out his hand, all he felt was...bed.

He opened his eyes. He was alone.

Disappointment socked him in the gut until he realized she just might be in the bathroom or the kitchen, making coffee. Maybe she was sitting out on the patio. He listened for signs of her up and moving around, but there was just silence in the cabin.

Shane got up, then rummaged through his suitcase for jeans and a T-shirt and got dressed. He headed out. Ashley wasn't in the living room, kitchen or on the back patio. He walked over to the second bedroom and quietly pulled open the door.

She was in bed, fast asleep.

The disappointment hit him hard again at the proof that at some point in the night, she'd woken up and left him.

He backed out and closed the door, going into the kitchen to start coffee. This was probably a good thing, he thought, choosing a macadamia nut blend K-Cup. *You don't know what you want from this. She doesn't know either.*

What he did know was that last night had been amazing. That he felt relaxed and sated. That he'd missed sex more than he'd realized.

That being with Ashley had felt right and good. They'd come together naturally, out of friendship, caring, attraction, desire. They weren't dating, there were no expectations, no third-date rule. They'd made love because their relationship, whatever it was, had led them there itself.

He liked that.

He drained his coffee and took a quick, hot shower, wishing he had company. When he came out, he saw Ashley on the patio, drinking her own coffee. She turned just then and he held up a hand, and her smile lit up her whole face.

She might have left him in the middle of the night for whatever reason, but that there was something between them, something special, wasn't in doubt.

Let it be, he told himself. *It'll work itself out.*

She came in then, and just as she said she was going to hop in the shower, his phone rang.

He went back into the bedroom and grabbed it. Huh. Beatrice. Calling to complain about the twins' behavior?

"Hello, Beatrice. Everything okay?" he asked, knowing full well it wasn't. She wouldn't be calling otherwise.

"Well, I'm...not sure. Charles and I can't find Violet. We're sure she's somewhere on the property, but we can't find her and she's not responding to us calling her name."

He frowned. "Do you think she's hiding? Did something happen?"

Silence for a moment. Then she said, "I simply told the twins at breakfast that I would be taking Violet to my hairstylist later this morning for an emergency cut to make her hair look more attractive. She seemed upset and said she liked her hair how it was. I told her that was nonsense, that her hair didn't look nice, and she burst into tears and ran off."

Oh, God. "Beatrice…" *How could you? Why can't you see the damage you do?*

"I didn't realize I'd upset her so much. Her hair looks terrible. Anyone can see that. She kept saying 'It looks like Miranda's!' Well, I can't even remember who this person is, for heaven's sake. What matters is that her hair looks awful and needs to be fixed."

He shook his head. Did she hear herself? Did she truly think she was in the right here? "Well, Violet doesn't think so. Does Willow have any idea where her sister is?"

"If she does, she's not saying. She's called out for her a few times, but Violet isn't responding. I'm hoping she's hiding in the house or in the yard. I didn't know if you were still in town or if you'd driven home last night. Maybe you could come find her if you're still around."

If she was asking for his help, she had to have checked everywhere for Violet and was truly nervous that she couldn't find his daughter.

He couldn't imagine Violet having gone far, no matter how upset she was. She was probably in some nook or cranny, either inside or out. "I'm still in town. I'll be there in twenty minutes. Try not to worry, Beatrice. We'll find her."

His words were kinder than she deserved, he thought.

But he could hear the relief in her silence, strangely enough. "Excellent," she said.

Excellent. She never lost her pretentious formality. Fuming, he jammed his phone in his back pocket and paced the cabin, waiting for Ashley to come out of the bathroom.

She did five seconds later. She took one look at his face and her eyes widened. "Oh, no, what's wrong?"

Shane explained about the phone call.

"Oh, poor Violet," Ashley said. "She must have picked a really good hiding place. If she's not coming out, it's probably somewhere she feels safe for the time being. I'd guess that she's someplace either in the house or outside that she's found before."

He immediately thought of finding Ashley in the stables loft after she'd run from the wedding. "I need to think of what her version of the loft would be."

She nodded. "A place her grandparents may even have looked but didn't spot her. That's why I like the loft so much. You can hide in the recesses and go perfectly still and remain unseen, even if people come looking for you. Think of crawl spaces, even in the house. Or she might be way up in a tree outside or tucked far in a spot that a little five-year-old can't be seen."

"Will you come with me?" he asked, surprising himself. But she clearly knew the hiding instinct, knew good spots, and perhaps most importantly, she knew Violet. Ashley would probably find her faster than he or the Shaws would. He couldn't imagine Violet ignoring Ashley if she called for her.

"Bringing me along might not help your case," she said. "I mean, they're your late wife's parents. I'm your boss's daughter, yes, and you gave me a ride to Jackson Hole, but I'm a woman, and it'll be clear to them that we were together when they called you."

He considered that. "I think you're more helpful in this situation than potentially hurtful."

"If you're sure."

"I am. I think Violet and Willow will like it that you're

there too. You may even draw Violet out just from her hearing your voice."

"Give me ten minutes to get dressed and dry my hair," she said.

He nodded. And before she disappeared behind her bedroom door, he called out, "Thank you, Ashley. Really. Thank you."

She poked her head out, drying it with the towel that had been wrapped around it. "Of course."

It seemed more like two minutes when Ashley was grabbing her jacket and heading out the door with him.

"I'm sure Violet's okay," Ashley said as they got inside his SUV. "She has a case of hurt feelings and doesn't want to get her hair cut. But I have no doubt she's safe and nearby. She could even be two feet from where Beatrice stood to call you."

Buckled up, he reached over with his right hand to squeeze her left one. "See, this is another reason why I need you with me for this. You're making me feel a hell of a lot better."

She squeezed back, and he started driving. "Look, just to clear the air so it's not lingering…"

Ah. Last night. Or more accurately, the middle of last night when she left his room and went into her own.

"That's fine, Ashley. You don't need to explain."

She didn't, really. And he wasn't sure he wanted her to even try. He had a feeling that he wouldn't like anything she'd say.

He'd woken up alone and had been surprised to discover he was disappointed. Surprised because he thought he was well used to being on his own. But suddenly she'd created an absence. And maybe he wasn't really ready to think too deeply about any of this.

"It was kind of a big deal," she said. "I mean, that we…"

He glanced at her and smiled. "Yes. It was."

"I woke up at like midnight and was bursting with it, not sure how to feel, where to fit it. So I FaceTimed with Miranda, actually. And then afterward, I guess I felt funny about getting back into bed with you. So I went into the other bedroom."

"Funny why?" he asked.

She gave a little shrug. "I think because I wasn't sure that I belonged back beside you," she added more tentatively.

"Hey," he said gently. "I understand. I have the same doubts. I missed you when I woke up. I absolutely did. But we're both in a confusing place, and we both have to do what feels right in the moment. So it's okay, Ashley."

"Why are you so understanding?" she asked with a shy smile. "You just seem to…get me."

"And you get me."

"Is it because we've known each other for years? I don't think so because we never really interacted all that much. I mean, before this past year when you started butting into my relationship." She laughed. "'He doesn't deserve you, Ashley,'" she said in her best imitation of him, adding his trademark head-shake.

He laughed too. "Well, he doesn't, dammit."

Now it was her turn to squeeze his hand. And then she turned her attention out the window, he supposed to let everything they'd just said settle.

That was fine. Right now, he was more focused on his little girl, upset and probably trying to cry very quietly, wherever she was hiding. What mattered was finding Violet, soothing her wounded spirit and trying to help make things right between her and her nana. He might not like

Beatrice Shaw—and right now, the woman was a huge threat to him—but she was his daughters' grandmother and a very strong connection to their mother. He'd preserve that relationship for their sake.

Not to the point of losing his daughters, though. For that, he'd fight Beatrice Shaw with everything he had.

From the look on Beatrice Shaw's face at the sight of Ashley on her doorstep, it was crystal clear that the woman did not like that she was there. There were assumptions and judgments in her eyes, and she barely glanced at Ashley after opening the door wider to let her and Shane inside. But even in the brief glance, Ashley knew the woman had taken in her sweater and jeans and short red leather jacket, the lack of makeup and loose long hair. Beatrice was dolled up even for just past 8:00 a.m. in a twinset and slacks, her hair coiffed, lipstick and jewelry on.

Willow hurried over to them as best she could in her boot and hugged them both. Ashley could feel her grandmother's eyes boring into the sight they made, her little granddaughter hugging her "father's girlfriend."

Not that she was. But it seemed obvious that Beatrice thought so.

"Beatrice, Charles, I'm sure you remember meeting Ashley a time or two when you visited the McCray Ranch," Shane said.

Ashley wasn't so sure they did. They'd barely paid her any attention then. Or her parents.

"Yes, of course," Charles said graciously, reaching out two hands to hold Ashley's briefly.

Beatrice narrowed her gaze on Ashley, then slid it to Shane. "I didn't realize you were together. Didn't someone say something about a canceled wedding? It's a bit confusing."

Ashley felt her cheeks pinken. *Actually, lady, we are together, whether you like it or not.* She'd only said it in her head, but despite the woman's grief over losing her daughter, Ashley felt like Beatrice deserved some plain talk. It wasn't Ashley's place and she'd keep her mouth shut. But still.

And really, she and Shane weren't *together-together*. They were something but neither knew what.

Shane cleared his throat. "Let's talk about where Violet might be." He turned to Willow. "Sweetheart, any ideas? Does Violet have a favorite place in the house that's easy to hide in? Or maybe outside in the yard?"

Willow shrugged her narrow shoulders. "I can't think of any place."

Shane gently cupped his daughter's chin. "Okay. Don't you worry, hon. We'll find her, okay?"

"I know you will, Daddy." She threw her arms around him and squeezed, and Ashley's heart pinged at her sweet trust. She glanced at Beatrice just in time to catch the woman actually seeming touched, but then Beatrice's gaze shot to Ashley and turned icy again.

"What was she wearing the last time you saw her?" Shane asked. "Violet hates being cold, so if she wasn't wearing a sweatshirt or fleece hoodie, she's probably not outside—she would have come in by now."

Willow bit her lip. "She was just wearing her favorite T-shirt, the red one that says Cowgirl on it."

"Oh, is that her favorite?" Beatrice asked—a bit nervously.

Shane whirled to her. "Did you say something to her about her shirt too?"

"Well, just that she should change into one of the outfits in her closet before we left for the hair salon," Beatrice said, defensiveness in her tone.

"One of the outfits you bought for her," Shane said flatly.

Her chin lifted slightly. "Yes. Clients at Jackson Hole Hair dress to the nines."

"Beatrice, Violet is five. *Five.*"

"We weren't going to the playground, Shane," Beatrice countered. "We were going into town to my high-end salon. There's nothing wrong with dressing appropriately for an outing to somewhere special. And there's certainly nothing wrong with teaching that to a little lady."

Ashley was mentally shaking her head so fast she got a little dizzy. But again, it wasn't her place to say anything, and contradicting Beatrice at this moment wouldn't help Shane or Violet, particularly with Willow listening in. Shane was doing fine without her help.

"Let me look around," Shane said. "I may notice Violet-sized nooks and crannies where she might be. Did you check all the closets?"

Charles lifted a hand. "I did. I don't think any of them are possibilities unless she's really wedged in behind something and I missed her."

"Do you mind if I check all the closets again while Shane looks in all the other spots?" Ashley asked. "Closets were where I hid as a kid when I was upset about something."

"That's fine," Beatrice said. Exasperation was all over her face. The thought of a "stranger" looking through her closets clearly didn't sit well. "What's important is that we find Violet."

"Can you give me the lay of the land?" Ashley asked. "Bedrooms are upstairs?"

Beatrice nodded. "Yes. There are four. Violet and Willow have a room that they share at the end of the hall. They tell me every time they visit that they want to stay together. That room was their mother's before she married Shane, so I suppose it's special to them. Then there are two guest rooms, and our bedroom is the first one off the landing."

Ashley nodded. "I'll head up now." She gave Shane a nod and started up the grand staircase that curved. She saw Shane head into the family room, and then she glanced down in time to see Beatrice throwing up her hands, looking very upset, and Charles walking over to embrace her.

Ashley knew where Violet was. She'd bet anything on it.

She walked down the hallway, shining hardwood with a muted runner. Family photos lined the walls in all shapes and sizes. Ashley was surprised in a good way to see them. Beatrice had struck her as the type to prefer expensive art over family mementos. There were so many, Beatrice and Charles smiling in front of vacation locales, lakes, petting zoos, amusement parks and cities, many with their daughter, Liza, at various ages, and many with the Shaws and the twins. Ashley stopped toward the end of the hall, where a large photo of Liza and Shane, each holding a newborn, had been taken in front of Shane's foreman's cabin. Her hand flew to her heart. What a beautiful photo. The happiness on the new parents' faces was something else. How lovely that whenever the twins visited, whenever they came and went from their room, this greeted them.

The door was ajar, and Ashley stood outside and listened. Quiet. She was 99 percent sure she'd find Violet in the closet, not because it was her and her twin's room, but because it had once been their mother's. And now that she'd seen the photographs, especially the big one with the Dawson family, her surety was 100 percent.

She went into the room and looked around. Very girlie in white and pale yellow, but nothing in the room said Violet and Willow, had their personality, their stamp. There was some of the twins' artwork in frames on the walls, and between the windows a framed "self-portrait" of Liza Shaw, age eight. Ashley's hand went to her heart again. Liza had given herself a purple face and pink hair and green ears and a striped shirt. There were a few dogs beside her—at least Ashley thought they were dogs. They were also multicolored and missing a leg here and there.

Ashley walked over to the closet. She gently pulled open one of the double doors and peered inside. It was a walk-in with lots of hanging clothes and, toward the back, a second row of long coats. Ashley stepped inside. She peered very closely at the floor toward the back. And there, she noticed a flash of green that moved. Like a socked foot. It had darted behind a long red puffer coat.

Ashley had no doubt that coat had belonged to the twins' mother. And that Violet was hiding behind it. Maybe even sitting inside it since it just about reached the closet floor. She went farther in and sat down in front of the red coat.

"Hey, Violet. It's Ashley. I have a feeling you're inside that zipped puffer coat."

Silence. And then a sad little voice said, "My nana is making me get my hair cut to fix it. But I like it. It looks like Miranda's. And Miranda said she likes my hair. You heard her say it, right?"

For the third time in two minutes, Ashley's hand went to her heart.

"Yup, I did. Is that why you're hiding up here? Because you don't want to get your hair cut?"

Violet didn't respond at first. Ashley heard a sniffle. And finally, "I don't think my nana likes me." She heard crying, then sobbing, then movement of the bottom of the coat, and Violet's head peeked out from under it, her green eyes red rimmed, tears falling down her face. She crawled out from under the coat and flew at Ashley.

Ashley wrapped the little girl in her arms and held her, stroking her hair. "Violet, honey, I know your nana loves you very much."

"She doesn't like my hair or my favorite shirt," Violet said through her tears.

"Well, I think your nana has a different style. But she loves the person you are. Inside and out. She always has. I remember one time when your grandparents came to the ranch to visit your parents. You and Willow were just a month old. And your mother was wearing red jeans, a black leather jacket and white studded cowboy boots. And a white studded cowboy hat. Your nana said, 'Oh, Liza, really! What on earth are you wearing?' And do you know what your mommy said back?"

Violet peered at Ashley. "What?" she asked, her eyes wide, the tears drying up.

"Your mommy said, 'You know you love me anyway.' And do you want to know what your nana said back to that?"

Violet nodded. "What did she say?"

"Your nana said—"

Suddenly, the closet door opened and there stood Beatrice Shaw, tears misting her eyes.

Both Violet and Ashley stared up at her, Ashley's heart suddenly pounding.

Beatrice sucked in a breath. "I'll tell you what I said. I said, 'That's right, Liza Lee Shaw Dawson. I do. I love you more than anything on earth except maybe those two babies. I love you all so much my heart feels like it might burst.'"

Violet's mouth dropped open. "Is that what you said?"

Beatrice nodded and ran a quick hand under her eyes to dab at her tears.

"That's exactly what she said," Ashley confirmed. "I remember thinking it was one of the nicest things I'd ever heard anyone say."

"That *is* nice," Violet said, looking shyly up at her nana.

For a moment, Beatrice seemed lost in a memory. "Oh, how your mother loved those white cowboy boots. She'd had them since she was a teenager and they were so beat-up." She smiled shakily.

"I want to get white cowboy boots," Violet said. "Willow will want them too."

"With studs along the toe area," Beatrice added, dabbing under misty eyes.

Ashley could see Violet picturing the boots, her face brightening.

Beatrice knelt down. "Violet, honey, hair grows and yours will too. I won't make you get it fixed if you don't want to."

"You won't?" Violet asked.

"I won't. That's a promise. Your mother was headstrong like you and your sister. Do you know what *headstrong* means?"

Violet shook her head. "You call me and Willow that a lot, but I don't know."

Beatrice touched Violet's chin with gentle fingers. "It means you have your own strong ideas about who you are and what you like. And I should be more respectful of that."

Oh, my heart, Ashley thought. This was going so much better than she could have hoped.

"Do I have to change my shirt?" Violet asked, looking down at the long-sleeved red T-shirt with the sparkly letters spelling *Cowgirl* in rhinestones.

"No," Beatrice said with a smile. "And I have a fun idea for this morning. Since Willow's ankle needs to rest up, why don't we go to the paint-your-own-pottery shop? You two enjoyed that last time you visited."

Violet brightened. "I love that place! There was a dog with long ears I wanted to paint last time but I picked something else. I wonder if they'll still have it."

"Well, we'll go see, won't we," Beatrice said, holding out her hand.

Violet ran over and wrapped her arms around her grandmother's hips.

"Oh, my," Beatrice said, her gaze darting to Ashley for a moment, then back to her granddaughter. "And after pottery, maybe we can go shopping—for white cowboy boots with studs on the toes."

Violet's eyes widened, and she gasped. "Really?"

"Really," Beatrice said, again her eyes teary but a gentle smile on her face.

"I love you, Nana," Violet said.

"I love you too," Beatrice said. "I do indeed." She gave Violet a strong hug and then pulled back. "Ready to go tell everyone about our new plan for the day?"

Violet ran ahead.

"Little ladies walk nicely!" Beatrice called after her.

Ashley mentally sighed. Just when she thought Beatrice had learned something important, something precious about her grandchild, she was back to her old self. Still, the woman got serious points for offering to take the twins shopping for cowboy boots.

And since Ashley had heard a little thud as Violet leaped off the bottom step and called out, "Hi, I'm right here!" she probably hadn't heard her grandmother's request.

Ashley ducked her way out of the closet.

Beatrice stepped back to give her room to come out. "Thank you. You were an enormous help."

"You're very welcome," Ashley said. Even when being nice, the woman was so damned intimidating. But Ashley could see the questions in Beatrice's eyes—everything from, *So, how well did you know my daughter? Were you friendly? I know she wasn't living at the ranch long before...* To, *What is going on with you and Shane? Are you dating?* To, *Didn't I hear you were left at the altar just days ago?*

Beatrice turned slightly. "Well, let's head downstairs and join the others."

Ashley followed her, the woman not saying another word. That Beatrice had questions wasn't in doubt, but Ashley doubted she really wanted answers—or that she'd be happy with them, no matter what Ashley said.

As they reached the bottom steps, Ashley could hear Violet in the living room. "I don't have to change my shirt either! And Nana and Pops are taking us to paint-your-own pottery. Maybe they have that long-eared dog again, Willow. And guess what else?"

"What?" Willow asked with bated breath.

"Nana's taking us shopping for white cowboy boots with

studs at the toes like Mommy had!" Violet said. "Mommy loved hers and had them since she was a teenager."

Ashley glanced at Shane, who now seemed lost in a memory himself—and very surprised that the subject of the boots had come up. There was a question in his eyes—she'd fill him in when she could.

The girls were chattering excitedly. Shane walked over to Ashley.

"I don't know what you did, but thank you," Shane whispered to Ashley.

Beatrice stopped in the living room archway and glanced at both of them for a moment. "Well, I see Charles went outside to look for Violet, so I'll just go tell him the good news. If you'll excuse me." With that, she moved over to the sliding glass doors to the deck and stepped out.

With the twins deep in excited conversation and not paying attention to anyone but each other, Shane pulled Ashley into a quick hug. "Just when I'm not sure if I can trust my instincts or not, you prove me A-OK," he said. "I knew bringing you was a good idea. So what happened? Where'd you find her? And Beatrice was there too? And how on earth did the boots come up in conversation?"

Ashley smiled and whispered a very condensed version of what had gone on upstairs in the closet. "I'll fill you in on the details once we're back in your SUV."

He gave his head a shake, wonder lighting his eyes. "I'd kiss the daylights out of you, but this is definitely not the time or the place."

"Maybe the time, but not the place."

He laughed and squeezed her hand, and they turned to where the twins were still chattering away, now about the boots. Both their faces glowed with happiness. Ashley's heart gave its usual clang where the Dawson girls were concerned. She glanced at Shane as he watched his daughters talking a mile a minute, the relief, the love in his expression, a thing to behold.

And she'd helped. That had felt so good.

Chapter Fourteen

It had been much easier for Shane to say goodbye the second time now that there was some proof that Beatrice wasn't made of stone, that she was capable of changing her mind for the right reasons, that she was able to compromise. The hair and shirt, fine. The running and leaping, no. Okay— he'd take what he could get. He'd smiled as Ashley had told him about the criticism going unheard, Violet already at the bottom of the staircase and calling out that she was back.

Yes, she was. His little girl's spirit was intact. That was what he cared about.

It was what Beatrice should care about too, and he wasn't entirely sure she understood that. She'd been moved by the memory of poking at her daughter's outfit, by Liza's comeback, by her own, and she'd finally connected Liza's free-spirited ways with her children's, which had meant something to her in that moment. To the point that she'd offered to take the twins shopping for boots just like the ones Beatrice had despised the sight of for years. *That* was something, almost a little miracle.

All Shane knew as he drove into town was that he was less worried, less stressed, less scared deep down that the Shaws would petition for custody.

Thanks to Ashley. Had he been there on his own, would

he have come up with that exact memory, with that story? She was gifted in that way, and he was grateful.

They stopped for coffee at a huge bakery-café with a lot of thrift-shop seating—old velvet sofas and benches, over-stuffed chairs. Many people were on laptops with head-phones in. At least twenty people waited to order at the counter. Shane and Ashley got in line.

Could he kiss those daylights out of her now that they were away from the Shaws' home? He sure wanted to, but he was also sure no one in the café wanted to watch him and Ashley make out.

He felt so close to her right now. He yearned to kiss her, hold her, touch her, be one with her again. Like he'd been in bed with her last night. One. Their bodies joined.

And he knew it was much more than that.

Somehow, Ashley McCray was becoming indispensable. She was like a talisman for him and his children.

He linked his arm around hers since it was the most he could hope for at the moment, the connection going straight to all his nerve endings. The smile she sent him lit up his heart.

He was going to have to admit to himself that he and Ashley were more than just partners on a road trip. That there was something so truly special going on between them—something that made him feel like he'd woken up from a long, dry slumber.

She eyed him, tilting her head. "Penny for your thoughts, as my dad always says? You're clearly a million miles away."

Nope, I'm right here. Thinking about you.

"I was…wondering if you were going to ask if they have carrot cake muffins," he said. "Or carrot cake scones," he added, suddenly feeling a little shy in the region of his heart.

She laughed. "Trust me, if they have either or both, I'm in."

He breathed a sigh of relief that they were talking about confections and not themselves, that he hadn't blurted out that he'd been thinking about how much she meant to him. That he had big feelings. He might have Ashley on the heart and soul, but he wasn't quite ready to talk about it.

"I want an iced coffee and something chocolaty," he said. "Maybe a good old-fashioned brownie. Think I can actually find just a plain, amazing brownie?"

"Probably not," she said on a laugh. "It'll have all sorts of stuff in it, maybe oats or even kale chips. But I can see in that display they have a very good lineup of fun bars. Chocolate chip coconut? Oooh."

He tried to peer around the very tall man in front of him, but he kept shifting on his feet and Shane didn't have a good view of the counter. He glanced left out the front window, his attention taken by a huge Great Dane in a pink leather collar walking beside its owner, a petite woman. He was about to point out the dog to Ashley, but then he did a double take.

Behind the woman and the huge dog.

No, it couldn't be. He squinted to peer more closely.

Oh, hell. It *was*.

Harrington Harris IV. Holding the hand of a woman with long blond hair.

Oh, no. No, no, no.

The two of them looked almost like twins. Both blond, fit and tall, super healthy looking, super rich looking. They were definitely not related, however, because they paused just before the door and kissed like they couldn't wait another second.

Repeat: oh, no. *Please keep walking after your stupid kiss. Please don't come in. Keep going. Follow the big dog.*

He took a sidelong glance at Ashley, who was still focused on the display since she had a better view of it to the right. She definitely hadn't been looking out the window—she hadn't seen Harrington. Or the kiss.

The door opened.

Shane sent up a silent prayer. Surely this morning's fortune would bring more luck and it wouldn't be the blond couple who entered. Right now, he didn't see them. Had they passed by when his attention had been on Ashley for those few seconds? Or were they about to walk in behind the family that had just entered?

Dammit.

In walked Ashley's former fiancé, his arm slung around the woman, chuckling away at something.

Hell.

Shane watched Harrington notice Ashley, his expression turning to shock as he stopped short. A guy walking behind him from the cream-and-sugar credenza with a mug of coffee crashed right into Harrington, his coffee sloshing on the floor.

"Jeez, dude, what gives?" the guy muttered.

Harrington quickly turned. "What? Oh, sorry," he said distractedly, reaching into his pocket and pulling out a ten, which he handed the guy—who gave a confused sort-of smile, took the ten and disappeared into the crowd with his sloshed coffee.

At the sound of Harrington's voice, Ashley's head swiveled in that direction.

She gasped.

They were now both staring at each other.

The blonde woman with Harrington was looking at him as if he were having a medical emergency. "Um, Harrington? Baby, what's wrong?"

Shane glanced at Ashley. The look on her face…

"Ashley?" Harrington said in clear disbelief. "What are you doing here?" He then noticed Shane and confusion crossed his features. He was staring at Shane now, clearly trying to place him. *Yeah, try real hard, jerkface.* "You're the foreman, right?"

Shane sighed. He didn't bother responding.

"Baby?" the blonde woman said, looking from Harrington to Ashley. "Who are these people?"

Harrington quickly patted the woman's hand but didn't answer her. "Um, Ashley, can we talk in private?"

Ashley glanced at Shane—and swallowed. "I'll just be a minute, I'm sure."

Shane nodded and attempted to keep the death glare off his face.

Harrington whispered something to the blonde woman, who got in line. Then Harrington walked to the back of the café. Ashley followed. Slowly.

She turned back and looked at Shane again with trepidation in her eyes.

Shane tried to stop glancing over his shoulder to see them, but it was no use. He didn't want to leave Ashley alone with Harrington, even if "alone" didn't mean much in the crowded shop. Either way, Shane felt better simply keeping them in view. They were now sitting across from each other on overstuffed chairs against the wall.

They both looked equally uncomfortable. Horrified, Shane would say.

But that didn't mean that Harrington wasn't about to be

reminded that this was the woman he'd dated for a year, proposed to, was engaged to...the woman he must have had strong feelings for, maybe even loved, if he were capable of loving anyone but himself.

Anything could happen.

And Shane wasn't having it.

If he could march over to them and pull Ashley away, he would. Bring her to safety—away from that dirtbag.

Bring her to *himself.*

It took everything in him to stay where he was.

Ashley stared at the man she'd loved for a year and thought she would marry. He was familiar, of course, the same old Harrington in his Nantucket red faded chinos and white linen shirt, sleeves rolled up, the very expensive watch on his wrist. The slightly long, wavy blond hair and the warm blue eyes.

But something was dramatically different inside her as she looked at him. She didn't feel what she'd expected to when they finally came to face-to-face.

She certainly didn't feel *love.*

To her surprise, she found she no longer cared at all if he took one look at her and realized he'd made the biggest mistake of his life.

She just felt...numb.

Everything Shane had said to her over the past year regarding Harrington suddenly rang so true. *He doesn't deserve you...*

Why had she put up with it? Why had she allowed the man who supposedly loved her to treat her like that? Sure, she hadn't let *everything* slide. Sometimes she'd get upset and tell Harrington to leave or give him the cold shoulder for a couple of days and demand an apology for this or that. But she'd always accepted the apology—which he'd probably never meant.

She'd always gone back for more, intoxicated by *something*. Was it his glamour? His good looks? His wealth? Not that she was a gold digger—far from it—but his aura of sophistication was so different from anything she'd ever experienced. She'd been surprised and flattered that, out of all the women in the world, he'd chosen her, fallen for her. Particularly because she had seen those big glimpses of his heart. She'd fallen hard for him for good reason, even if part of the attraction had been because she'd been dazzled by the trappings. The superficial. The man who could have anyone had fallen for *her*.

Until he realized he didn't love her, of course. Noted by text.

"Why are you here?" he asked, head tilted slightly.

She could feel the scowl pulling at her mouth. "That's what you have to say to me? Not 'I'm sorry'?"

"I figured we were past that, Ashley."

Jerk! Asshat! Scumbucket!

"You left me at the altar, Harrington. In front of all my family and friends. You made everything about our relationship a lie. We're past 'I'm sorry'?"

He shook his head. "Please don't get dramatic. *God*," he added, stretching the word into a very long syllable. "I *am* sorry for everything. But I'm not sorry I didn't marry you."

Nice. Very nice. What a way to put it.

"Because you're involved with the blonde?" she asked, glancing back where the extremely attractive woman was now sitting at a table, sipping an iced coffee and sending nervous glances their way. Ashley's gaze landed on Shane, also sitting at a table, not sipping anything. The hard set of his jaw, the intensity of his expression, told her he was worried about this conversation and how it would end.

"I met her the week before the wedding," Harrington went on. "Not two hours later, two hours in her company, I realized that I loved Gwenyth. That I understood what everyone was always talking about—love at first sight, a chemistry that just grabs you by the heart and soul. You just *know*."

She gaped at him. A week before their wedding date, he'd fallen in love with someone else. A montage of that week rolled in her head—he'd suddenly had to go away on "business" despite not having a job. Something to do with investments, he'd said. He'd had to cancel their rehearsal dinner the night before the ceremony because he couldn't get back till late that same night, but he'd said, *Ashley, I don't need to rehearse to walk down the aisle to you.*

At the time, she'd thought that was so beautiful, so romantic. The man she was marrying loved her deeply, she'd believed.

What a load of bunk! What a lie.

What a fool she'd been. An utter fool.

She'd thought he was in California, dealing with the "investments," when he'd been right in town, in bed with Gwenyth. His real soulmate, apparently.

"I'd never experienced such a powerful feeling before," he continued. "I didn't lie about being in California. I went away with Gwenyth to figure things out. I came back the night before the wedding because it felt like the right thing to do, to face you in the morning. But I couldn't. So I just took off for Jackson Hole with Gwenyth and sent you that text from a gas station."

A gas station. How fitting. Bile inched up in her gut. She felt sick.

"I didn't mean to meet someone," he added. "But I ended up finding my real one true love."

"How special for you," she said, bitterly. But she did feel bitter. Was she supposed to be happy for him? "You owe my parents forty-seven thousand dollars. I subtracted the value of the engagement ring, which I'll sell. You also owe my maid of honor and bridesmaids one thousand seven hundred and sixteen dollars for the dresses and shoes they wasted good money on." She'd left it to the dresses and shoes only, since her parents had paid for the bridesmaids' hair and makeup and had given each woman a gold bangle as a gift. "I want two checks right now. One to my father and one to me so I can reimburse the bridal party. Or you can wire the money. Right now."

He stared at her for a moment, then pulled out his phone and pressed in some numbers. "Clark, HHJ here."

Oh, brother. She'd always hated when he'd referred to himself that way. Harrington Harris Junior. Clark was his wealth management agent and personal accountant. Harrington had often whipped out his phone to call or text the guy during their relationship.

"Can you arrange for two bank checks—one to Anthony McCray in the amount of forty-seven thousand dollars and one to Ashley McCray for one thousand seven hundred sixteen, for pickup at the Bear Ridge Bank and Trust?" he chirped into the phone as though he was ordering room service. "Yes. Perfect." He pocketed the phone and turned his attention back to Ashley. "Done."

She lifted her chin. There. She'd done it. This was what she'd really come for, the no-matter-what reason. To get her family's money back, to get her bridal party's money back too. "Well. Good. Thank you. My parents will appreciate that."

"For what it's worth," he said, "and I know it's not much, I *am* sorry, Ashley. I do wish you the best."

She couldn't say the same. So she said nothing. Harrington stood up and headed to where Gwenyth was waiting. Then the happy couple both quickly left.

Ashley didn't move. Didn't turn. Didn't stand.

Numb. Every bit of her—numb.

She could feel a shadow behind her. Then next to her. She glanced up. Shane. Looking at her with concern.

But instead of flinging herself in his arms the way she wanted to, she just sat there, her body feeling like lead.

Not sure exactly where she'd go from here.

She felt so stupid, so played, so betrayed. Harrington himself almost didn't even factor in. She didn't mourn the loss of him in her life. She mourned *herself*—the person she'd been in the days before her wedding, when she'd been practicing writing *Ashley Harris* over and over in her journal like a sixteen-year-old, when she'd been making lists of baby names, even though that would be years off, when she'd been searching online for recipes of his favorite meals so that she could practice making them…when she'd been so certain she was loved, and all the while, he'd been sleeping with someone else. Deeply involved emotionally with someone else.

And she'd had no clue. That was what had her so upset.

That she hadn't known—about something involving her and her entire life, her future, her hopes and dreams. How could she not have known?

"Ashley?" Shane asked, a warm hand on her shoulder. "How'd it go? Are you okay?"

She sucked in a breath. And didn't answer. Couldn't answer. Couldn't find her voice.

Shane sat down in the chair Harrington had vacated. "Ash, listen, if you just need to go back to the cabin at the dude ranch and lock yourself in your bedroom, that's okay."

Yes. That was what she needed right now. It dimly occurred to her that, of course, Shane Dawson knew that. He always knew what she needed.

But maybe even a very good man like Shane Dawson wasn't what he seemed. She didn't know his private mind and heart, just as she hadn't known Harrington's. Shane had a lot going on. They'd made love, which had to have complicated things for him emotionally where she was concerned.

She couldn't put any stock in even her friendship with Shane.

Great. Now she was being cynical and distrusting, even of the man who'd been nothing but honest and kind and helpful. A lifeline.

"The cabin, yes," she finally said. "That is exactly where I want to be." She looked over at him, her handsome Shane, and her heart did lift a tiny bit. He was her rock. But right now, nothing could break through the numb, the doom and gloom, everything her former fiancé had said so blithely.

She was an idiot. A big stupid idiot.

That actually *did* break the numbness inside her. Because it reminded her of the Dawson twins and their favorite insult that they were probably trying very hard not to use while at their grandparents'.

And suddenly her eyes got misty and she needed to be in that bedroom at the cabin, behind closed doors, under the covers.

Alone.

Chapter Fifteen

Shane had taken one look at Ashley, slumped and dejected in that overstuffed chair at the café, and had taken her hand and led her out of the place with an "I've got you."

And he did. He'd gotten her settled in his SUV and didn't say a word, didn't ask anything of her, even another *You okay?* He could tell that she wasn't. She needed time and rest and someone to take care of her, and he had two days to offer her just that, to be her personal concierge.

At the cabin, she'd gone straight to her bedroom and closed the door, then had come back out a minute later.

She'd told him everything Harrington had said. About falling for the other woman. About lying about a business trip. About the real reason for canceling the rehearsal dinner.

Ah, he'd thought, wishing he could go to her and pull her into his arms, but the pain and anger on her face were like a force field radiating "keep off" vibes, so he stayed put.

But still, he ached for her. She'd been betrayed and had been feeling every bit of it.

"How could I not know?" she'd asked, her face so pale, her eyes devoid of their usual spark. "How could you not know you're being deceived? Does that mean I can't trust myself? My feelings? Others? What the hell?"

He'd understood then that it wasn't so much Harrington or even a broken heart that had her so despondent. Well, of course she had a broken heart in the sense that she'd been hurt and humiliated. But it was her *spirit* that was broken. Her faith—in people and love and everything she'd believed in. Solid ground had turned to sawdust for her.

All he could do was be there for her, let her take her time.

When the world had fallen apart for him, he'd certainly taken his.

Now he looked toward the bedroom door, leaning an ear to hear any signs of movement. Not a peep in the past three hours. A half hour ago, he'd ordered cabin service from the dude ranch's cafeteria, which should arrive any minute. He got a few different things, figuring if he got a good selection, Ashley would find something to like—a cheeseburger with steak fries, a turkey BLT and the chili, which they were apparently known for far and wide. He'd also gotten a Caesar salad since he knew she loved those. And two kinds of desserts.

He had a feeling she'd have little appetite. That was fine and what reheating in ovens and microwaves was for.

He was making himself a cup of coffee at the kitchenette when his phone buzzed; he'd put it on Silent so as not to disturb Ashley.

Anthony McCray.

"Shane, I just got a call from the bank that there's a cashier's check for an enormous sum waiting for me to deposit. And one for Ashley. Both from Harrington. She saw him? How'd it go? Are they together right now?"

Shane didn't know how much to say to her father but opted for a short form of the truth. "They actually ran into each other by chance today. They spoke briefly, five minutes maybe, and then Harrington left. She's taking some time to herself right now. We're staying at a cabin I booked at a dude ranch in Jackson Hole. I'm not sure if she's up for talking just yet, but I can check."

"Aww, poor gal. I'll let her be for now. Thank you for being there, Shane."

"Of course," he said, and they disconnected.

The doorbell rang with their room service. Shane set the bags on the coffee table, then went to knock on Ashley's door.

"Hey," he called. "I ordered a bunch of stuff for lunch. Hungry?"

Silence.

He waited a beat and was about to walk away when the door opened. Ashley, looking tired but more like herself—absolutely beautiful, that sparkle half-back in her eyes—walked up to him and put her arms around him.

"What's this for?" he asked, surprised as could be.

"Just for being you. And I am hungry. I'm surprised, but then again, I came to good realizations while I was under the covers in there, and I'm feeling more okay. Not completely, of course, but a little better."

"I'd love to hear about those realizations," he said, heading to the kitchenette to grab some plates and silverware, which he brought to the coffee table.

They sat down and opened containers. Ashley took half the BLT and a bunch of steak fries. He chose the cheeseburger.

"Ah, this looks so good," she said, then took a bite. She sipped from the bottle of iced tea he'd also ordered. "What I realized is that I'm done with being a confused dummy. Took a few hours under those covers, but I finally got to *anger*. Since the canceled wedding, I've been hurt and upset and unsure, but I wasn't really angry. The past few hours, I felt the full force of it. He betrayed me. Lied to me. Carried on an affair the week before our wedding day—"

He shook his head. For the past several days, Shane had wondered what had really led the jerkface to cancel the wedding, but he hadn't landed on "met someone else."

She swiped a fry in ketchup and popped it into her mouth. "And you know what? Not that I'm letting him off the hook for how he treated me, but I realized something. Even though half of me wishes all sorts of bad things for him, the other half is like, good for him. It's what everyone wants. To find the person you really belong with, the person who makes your heart sing, all that, you know?"

He knew. *Ashley* made his heart sing.

"I wasn't that for him," she continued, "and as I'm sure you'll say, he wasn't that for me. I compromised, let things go, accepted what I shouldn't have. Maybe my soulmate is out there, waiting for me. Who knows, maybe I've already met him at the worst possible time." She shyly smiled and seemed to be holding her breath.

"That's how I feel," he said softly. And it was true.

She let out the breath. "Oh, Shane," she whispered, scooting over and pressing herself against him.

He wrapped her in a hug and put his head against hers. "We feel what we feel, right? Yes, it's bad timing for a few reasons. I didn't think I'd ever be interested in anyone else, Ashley. But here you are. Slammed right into my heart."

"Same," she said, pushing up with her arms against his chest to look at him. "I'm certainly not ready for a new relationship, but I seem to be in one."

"What happens on the road trip doesn't have to *stay on*

the road trip," he said. "We can bring it all home with us if we want."

Her smile lit up her beautiful face, and it took a real effort to keep from kissing her. She'd need a few days to recover from everything that had happened with the jerkface, even if she didn't realize it. And that was fine. Because he needed a few days too—to let himself accept that he had feelings for another woman. That maybe the twins would have a stepmother after all. A mother in their lives to love them, care about them, share in the triumphs and tribulations of raising them. The twins seemed to have them married off in the future anyway. They hadn't brought up the *M* word since that first and only time, but the idea of it was in their heads, in their hearts.

It wasn't necessarily in his. Marriage was a huge step. And he and Ashley weren't even dating. But the label didn't matter. Only what they felt did. "We can both take it as slow as we need," he said. "We don't have to call this anything."

She nodded, the sparkle well back in her hazel eyes. "We'll just take it day by day and know the most important thing— that we have each other's backs, that we're there for each other."

He squeezed her hand. She kissed him on the cheek.

"How is it possible that I felt so betrayed and awful three hours ago and so lucky right now?" she asked.

"That's life for you. Ups and downs. Downs and ups. Sometimes in the same minute."

She leaned her head on his shoulder, linked her arms through his, and they sat like that for a long while.

The next two days were everything Ashley needed. She and Shane spent a lot of time together and made sure to take some time apart too. Ashley went on long walks by herself around the dude ranch, popping in to the petting zoo to see her favorite goats, who always made her laugh as they hopped on and off logs. She'd stop into the cafeteria for iced coffee and to try to get the recipe for the excellent chili out of the longtime cook, who refused to share his secret ingredients. Alone with her thoughts, she had time and space to think and understand and process.

Including how much she felt for Shane Dawson.

They'd shared meals—and a bed—watched TV and movies, borrowed books from the ranch library and curled up on chairs with views of the mountains to read. They took walks together, holding hands, they rode out on the trails, they hiked and had picnic lunches. They talked and laughed and ate and sometimes were quiet, companionably so.

Two days of just what the doctor ordered.

She'd video-called her parents after Shane had let her know her dad had called. She'd assured them she was okay, that she'd be home tomorrow.

Tomorrow. Already?

She wasn't quite ready to leave the dude ranch, but she missed her parents and her horses.

And she did want to see how things would feel with Shane once they were back home. They lived on the same property, only a stone's throw away. They'd see each other all the time, planned or unplanned. They'd both return to their regular, scheduled lives. And Shane was very busy. Not only with his work as the foreman at the McCray Ranch but with his daughters.

Would a new relationship even fit in for him?

She'd discussed this all with Miranda on the phone during her long walks around the dude ranch. Her cousin

thought she and Shane had something very special and that
Ashley was doing exactly what she should be. No labels,
no rushing, no declaring. Just feeling. Just enjoying each
other's company.

But now, as Ashley packed up her clothes and made a
pile of things she needed to return to the lodge, like the library books and a steamer she'd borrowed to get the wrinkles out of the dress she'd worn to the country-and-western
dance last night, she realized she was more than a little
nervous about being involved with Shane.

Scared, really.

Scared that what she'd felt for him was way more intense than anything she'd ever felt for Harrington. It had
to do with their chemistry and closeness, real friendship,
even her relationship with his daughters. She loved those
girls, and now she'd be much more intertwined in their
lives. Her role in what had gone on in the Shaws' house, in
the closet with Violet and Beatrice, had made her feel even
closer to all of them. Even to Beatrice herself. She was en-
meshed in Shane's life in a way that she'd never been with
her former fiancé. She'd never felt a part of Harrington's
family. But would that feeling last when they were back to
their usual lives?

There would be a lot to adapt to once they got home
and settled back.

She glanced at the clock on the bedside table. Almost
five. Shane was helping the owner figure out a problem he
was having with the books—foremen talk. Ashley figured
she'd take the pile of stuff she had to return to the lodge.
She'd stop for iced coffee on the way back and once again
try to get that secret recipe out of the cook. The chili was

that good. And then she and Shane would take a walk on the ranch and then have a special last dinner in town.

A special last night in the cabin too, she thought with a smile as she headed out with her tote bag of things to return.

Ashley pulled open the door to the lodge and headed to the Welcome desk, staffed by Maya, who was usually all smiles and full of fun information about the ranch and the activities. The two had managed to get chummy the past couple of days since Ashley had stopped in often to ask for tips about where to explore or to just say hi. They hadn't gotten too personal, but they'd both shared that they'd gone through recent breakups. Maya had seemed fine, but right now, she looked really glum. And if Ashley wasn't mistaken, she'd been crying.

As she reached the desk, Maya quickly dabbed under her eyes as if wiping away tears. She put on a smile that was definitely forced.

"Maya? Everything okay?"

Maya glanced around. There were some guests milling around by the brochures and a few sitting in the chairs on the far side of the room, but otherwise, no one was waiting for Maya's attention. "Guy problems." She sighed. "I just lost my best friend. The best friend I've ever had." Now tears filled her eyes.

"Aww, what happened?" Ashley asked.

"So you know how I mentioned that a couple of months ago, my boyfriend of three years, who I thought was going to propose, dumped me the night before Valentine's Day? What I didn't get into was the fact that he'd met someone else and he wanted to 'explore' it. So instead of a ring, I got my heart handed to me. I was a wreck for weeks."

"I'm so sorry," Ashley said. "Sounds really hard." And familiar.

"It was. But my best friend—a guy—helped me through. And one thing led to another, and all of a sudden we were a couple. Jonas was just so good to me, so attentive, when I really needed someone. He's the best."

Ashley knew all about that too—from her own life. She was suddenly listening very hard.

"But then *I* met someone else," Maya said. "A new cowboy on the ranch. Oh, my God, Ashley. I've never been so attracted to a man in my life. We just get each other. Understand each other. The connection between us is just unreal. But Jonas and I had become a couple and…I realized it was more a rebound thing. He offered more than friendship suddenly and I saw him in a new light—or thought I did. But now that I've met Daniel, I realize I'm not in love with Jonas and never was."

"Oh, wow," Ashley said. "And you told Jonas?"

"He was so hurt. And furious. He told me we're not friends anymore. That I was a user. He accused me of taking advantage of him for a rebound romance." Her eyes filled with tears. "I do love him—but as my best friend. And now he won't even talk to me. I don't know if he ever will."

"Maybe he just needs time," Ashley offered. "He's hurting and upset, like you said. Give him some time, Maya."

Maya nodded, biting her lip. "I really miss him. His friendship means so much to me, and I screwed up. I should never have gotten involved with him. I was close to his sister also, but she told me off and told me we're through too." Her eyes welled with tears again.

"I'm really sorry, hon," Ashley said. "I think you need to give them both time. In the meantime, be kind to yourself."

A family came in then and headed for the desk, standing behind Ashley.

Ever the professional, Maya smiled at the group. "Be right with you, folks." She leaned closer to Ashley and whispered, "Thanks for talking me through it. I do feel better. It's just a tough situation."

Ashley nodded and gave her hand a squeeze. "I'll come say goodbye at checkout tomorrow." She put the books in the book chute on the side of the desk and handed back the steamer.

Maya checked off its return. "Definitely don't leave without saying goodbye."

As she headed out of the lodge, Ashley's stomach was turning every which way. She dropped down on the bench outside, the fresh April air doing little to reinvigorate her.

Was her relationship with Shane about rebounding? He'd become her best friend on this road trip. And much, much more. Their relationship had deepened in ways she never could have dreamed. That was all very real, though.

But it likely had felt real between Maya and her best friend too. Jonas. Until she met someone who made her realize that her broken and needy heart had innocently mistaken their relationship for more than it was.

Could that be the case with her and Shane? If she hurt him...after what he'd been through... She was his first kiss after being widowed. His first sexual experience after. His first foray into caring about someone again.

Not to mention, if she hurt him, she'd hurt his daughters.

Ashley shivered and bolted up, suddenly needing to move. But not wanting to think. Surely she'd know if something wasn't really there between her and Shane, wouldn't she?

She certainly hadn't known that about her and Harrington. But then again, she felt so much for Shane Dawson.

She *loved* him.

Oh, God, she did. She loved him. Loved his enormous heart. His warmth. His integrity. Loved everything he was. At the start of the road trip, he'd asked for ten reasons why she loved—past tense—Harrington. She could list *hundreds* of reasons very quickly about why she loved Shane.

So it must be real. It wasn't rebound. She wouldn't hurt him or his twins.

But then again, she *hadn't* known Harrington didn't love her. He might not have either until he met Gwenyth. And what about Maya? She was so sweet. Ashley was sure she hadn't meant to hurt her friend Jonas. She just hadn't known that what they had wasn't love...not until it was too late, and she'd already hurt her friend.

It all seemed so complicated now. But was she supposed to step away from Shane just in case he was her rebound relationship? That was nuts. She *did* love him.

Maybe she should talk about it with him. Just tell him about what Maya was going through and see if it provoked anything in him about the parallels. Maybe it wouldn't. Maybe she was just being cautious. Which she should be.

If only love came with guarantees.

Chapter Sixteen

For their last night in Jackson Hole, Shane made reservations at a popular barbecue restaurant known for being more fun than romantic, but he and Ashley both wanted to try it before leaving, especially because Ashley mentioned she would never return to Jackson Hole as long as she lived.

He'd paused at that, a little surprised, maybe a little stung, that she still associated the place with her former fiancé more than with him. But as he'd told himself a few times the past couple of days, these things would take time. One day, surely, the memories would shift. The feelings they'd shared on the road to Jackson Hole, and during their time here, would take over, and the painful parts of the journey would recede.

They'd both dressed up more than the restaurant called for with its bright lights and colorful decor, and he could barely take his eyes off Ashley in her sexy black dress, her silky hair loose around her shoulders, her mouth a glossy red. He was in head-to-toe black, wearing a button-down shirt with the sleeves rolled up and black pants. The restaurant had a dance floor in the bar area, and perhaps after dinner they'd sway together to a few songs before heading back to the cabin for what would be their last night at the dude ranch.

But as he and Ashley were led to their table, he couldn't help but notice that she seemed subdued.

Once they had their drinks and menus, he reached for her hand.

"I'm just gonna ask," he said. "You've been quiet. What's on your mind?" He could guess, but he'd rather not. Speculating never got anybody anywhere.

"This is one of my favorite things about you," she said. "You say what needs to be said. Ask what needs to be asked."

"Uh-oh, though. That means something's wrong."

She told him about returning some things to the lodge and talking to the desk attendant, Maya, who she'd gotten friendly with the past few days.

He bristled but tried not to let it show. "So you think that'll happen with us? That I'm your rebound guy?"

It was possible, of course. Probable, even. She'd been left at the altar days ago, and things between her and the guy helping her through, her rock, had turned romantic. Anybody would call that a rebound. It was one of the oldest stories in the book.

But what was between them was so strong. Their connection was based on deep friendship and wild attraction and explosive chemistry—all very powerful stuff. That was more than just a rebound...wasn't it?

She bit her lip. "I don't think being with you is about rebounding. How could what you are to me be reduced to that?"

Okay, that he liked. She agreed with his assessment of them.

"But," she added, taking a sip of her drink, "Maya didn't think so either. She thought she and her best friend had blossomed into something she never expected. And now he won't talk to her. *You've* become my best friend, Shane. I can't lose that."

"We're not just one thing, though," he said. "You've become my best friend too, Ashley." She certainly had. Talk about unexpected.

"Maybe I shouldn't even have brought it up. Maya's not me. You're not Jonas." She took another sip of her drink, clearly conflicted.

He sat back, his spirit a bit sunk. "You should always bring up everything. It's important to talk things through. Even when we both don't have any answers."

"I want answers, though."

He took a slug of his beer. "I just know that everything in life is a risk. There's no way around it."

She sighed. "I want a guarantee. There, I said it. I want to know for sure that neither of us will hurt each other."

Yeah, me too.

"I'm a widower, Ashley," he blurted out. "My five-year-old daughters haven't had a mother since they were three months old. There *are* no guarantees."

The look on her face. Maybe it wasn't the uplifting thing to say. But it was the truest thing he knew.

He reached across the table to take both her hands. "What's the alternative to us being together? You think I'd give you up just because I fear losing you—to anything? No way."

"But it's not that simple."

"Yup, it is. I want to be with you. That's what I know most of all. Do I have worries? Of course. But you're more important to me. I'd rather have you in my life than not, Ashley. That's what it comes down to."

She reached out her hand to touch his face for just a second. "I want you in my life too. I *need* you in my life." She paused, clearly thinking hard about something. Finally she said, "What if…when we get home, things aren't the same? What if this was a road-trip romance and it just doesn't carry over to real life? If things become strained between us, it'll affect Violet and Willow. Maybe I'm getting way ahead of myself, but those girls mean a lot to me."

This was one of the reasons why he felt so strongly about Ashley McCray—she cared so much about others. His daughters, in particular. "I never want them to hurt, Ashley. But if there's one thing I *absolutely* know, it's that I can't protect them from life itself."

"I know, but—"

The sound of racing footsteps had him glancing over to his right just as he heard a very familiar voice.

"Daddy!"

Suddenly, as if talking about his daughters conjured them, Violet was running toward him in, yes, white studded cowboy boots, Willow trailing in her black boot on one foot, a white cowboy boot that matched her sister's on the other.

Aww. Beatrice had made good on her offer. And the symbolism was very moving.

But—a big but—the Shaws were coming toward the table, Charles with his usual good-natured expression and Beatrice Shaw with her more typical murderous expression, staring at him.

"No running, girls," she hissed with a very forced smile. "This is a restaurant."

The Shaws stopped a few feet from the table. Beatrice was glancing around as if making sure she didn't know anyone dining around them.

"What a great surprise!" Shane said, giving both girls a

hug. It was. Unexpected, yes. But a very nice surprise. He'd missed the twins so much. And seeing their faces right now lifted up his heart like nothing else could. His girls were here beside him—all was right in the world.

They both hugged Ashley, chatting a mile a minute about their day and how much fun they'd had, both lifting up a foot to show their boots. Apparently, the Shaws had given them a last day for the record books. Pony rides. A picnic lunch and then a visit to the toy store in town, where they each got to pick out three special things.

He was about to say, *Wow, that is some amazing day you two had*, but Beatrice was glaring at him. And avoiding looking at Ashley.

"Girls, our table is ready and the host is waiting," Beatrice said, her tone strained.

"You're picking us up tomorrow, right?" Willow whispered in his ear, hand cupped.

"Right? Right?" Violet also whispered, hand cupped.

"Girls, we don't whisper in front of others," Beatrice said in that same strained tone.

Violet and Willow looked at their grandmother with little nods, then back at him.

"Yup," he assured them. "Ten a.m. sharp."

"And, Ashley, you're driving back too, right?" Willow asked.

"Sure am," Ashley confirmed.

Both girls clapped and hurried over to their grandmother. Who was still staring at Shane and looking…pissed off.

Because he appeared to be on a date?

Charles waved, and the four disappeared around a bend into the large dining area.

"That was awkward," Ashley said. "Beatrice didn't even say hello—to either of us."

"She's upset about something. But she always is. And the running and whispering didn't help, I'm sure." He shook his head on a sigh, wishing things could be different with his former mother-in-law. But he had a sinking feeling this was how it would always be.

"I thought you all turned a corner," Ashley said. "With what happened with Violet and her hair and bringing in that sweet memory of their mother. The girls were wearing their white cowboy boots, for heaven's sake."

Nothing positive lasted long with Beatrice, unfortunately. "One step forward, two steps back with Beatrice Shaw. It's always been that way. Just when I think I finally have her approval, she lets me know just how disappointing a father I am to her grandchildren."

"But you're an amazing father!" Ashley practically shouted. She leaned closer, lowering her voice. "You are. Anyone with eyes and ears and a heart should be able to see that plain as day."

He almost laughed at the idea of Beatrice Shaw being some kind of mythical creature without those attributes. A gargoyle, say. It helped.

"Does it get to you?" she asked. "Her opinions of you?"

He sat back. He both hated talking about this and needed to. "It did at first. Especially in those very harrowing weeks and months right after we lost Liza. But I quickly saw there was no pleasing the woman. And I stopped trying. I just did what I felt was right. I'm their father. Their sole parent. Beatrice Shaw isn't the boss of me."

Ashley squeezed his hand. "Yeah. She's not."

But she did have power—and could wield it in the courts.

She could try to make a case for taking custody from him. He couldn't see her complaints actually getting anywhere with a judge, but it was possible. Violet and Willow did have hot dogs for dinner once a week. They did have candy every single day. They did call people stupid dumb idiots. They didn't always remember to brush their teeth before bed, and sometimes he was so tired he'd forget to make sure they did. Violet did get her hands on sharp scissors. Willow did sprain her ankle. They ran in restaurants. They whispered in front of people. Maybe those kinds of things would add up to a judge thinking he was deficient—especially given the Shaws' input.

"You know what helps, Ashley?" He leaned forward and took both her hands again. "I was alone before. Now I'm not. Or at least, I don't feel alone with you in my life."

Her eyes got misty. "I don't feel alone either."

"So maybe that's all we need to know right now—about us, I mean."

She smiled softly and nodded, and he could see she was a bit more at peace about their earlier topic of conversation.

"So let's order from this great-looking menu and enjoy our dinner," he said, opening his. "My girls are in this restaurant, and it's nice knowing exactly where they are and what they're doing. I haven't had that the past few days."

"Aww," she said. "They're always on your mind, aren't they? As they should be."

He nodded. Of course they were.

The waiter came by then and took their orders.

A chill did run up his spine when he thought of the look Beatrice had given him. He supposed from her point of view, it was just emotionally complicated. She might worry a woman in his life would change the dynamic between him and the Shaws, the visitation schedule. She might worry that if he and Ashley broke up, the twins would be hurt because it was clear they liked her so much. He had avoided dating so as not to bring his love life into their worlds. It had been an easy way to protect the three of them because he hadn't wanted to date.

But now what? If he and Ashley did break up a few weeks from now, the twins would be upset. They adored her. If it really upset them, it might even impact how they did at school—maybe they'd have trouble concentrating on their lessons or they'd get into more fights. Would that give the Shaws more ammunition to go for custody?

But a preemptive move when things were so good between them? There was no way he'd end things with Ashley now because of what *might* happen in the future. Even the near future.

Hadn't he just said ten minutes ago that he wouldn't give her up because he feared losing her—to anything?

He wasn't going to spend his last night with this wonderful woman with all this weighing on his mind. He had to let it go for tonight.

He was just having a damned hard time getting there.

As they were leaving the restaurant, Ashley noticed Shane taking a peek around the bend where the dining room continued on. From the looks of that section, families were seated there, couples on dates in the other. The family section sure was loud. But Ashley liked the happy cacophony. It was full of life and love. The couples section was too, she supposed, but in a different way. She'd had a long go of being a couple and definitely saw herself in the family section.

"Are the twins and their grandparents still here?" she asked him.

"I don't see them," he said, and they continued heading toward the exit. "Violet and Willow are pretty quick eaters, and I can't imagine Beatrice wanted to prolong being here with us in the next area. I keep expecting my phone to ring and to see her name flash on the screen so she could deliver a fresh litany of complaints. And maybe the third degree about my love life."

"That's really none of her beeswax," Ashley said.

"No, it's not. But she'll make it hers. 'Are my precious granddaughters being subjected to your sex life?' She's planning to come at me. If not tonight on the phone, tomorrow morning in person when I pick up the girls. I have no doubt."

They passed the entrance to the bar, where the DJ was playing vintage Bee Gees. Had they not run into the Shaws, Ashley would have pulled Shane onto the dance floor when a slow song came on. That would have been a nice goodbye to Jackson Hole, swaying with him, chest to chest, lips to lips. But running into the Shaws had thrown some cold water on their night, and she could tell Shane wanted to get back to the cabin and decompress in private. She did too.

Shane held the door open, the evening April air cool but holding the promise of the warmth of spring. "I had big plans for us to go dancing and make the most of this last night. But between *our* conversation and what's coming from Beatrice, I wouldn't mind sitting on the patio at the cabin and just staring up at the stars with you."

"I think that sounds perfect," she whispered.

Ten minutes later they were heading up the long drive of the dude ranch, where she'd had both a wonderful and painful time. For tonight, since she had no idea what would happen when they got home, she wanted the next several hours to be special.

They'd start by watching the stars, and then Ashley made a mental list of just how she could distract Shane from the threat of his phone ringing. Given that he'd be at the Shaws' house tomorrow morning, Ashley doubted his phone would ring tonight.

Once in the cabin, they grabbed waters from the fridge and went outside on the patio, each taking a side-by-side chaise. Ashley grabbed the big chenille blanket folded in the basket under their chairs and pulled it across them. She noticed Shane had set his phone on the small table beside his chaise.

"Ahh," he said, stretching out and turning to look at her. "Very nice. We've got the moon and the stars and this cozy blanket to keep us warm."

"It's truly heavenly," she said.

For the next few minutes, they both just stared up at the sky. Minutes turned into a half hour. No call. Shane seemed to relax. Ashley felt him reaching around for her under the blanket and then take her hand and hold it.

"I like this," she said, turning to smile at him.

"Me too. Getting chilly?" he asked. "We can go inside and put on some music, have that slow dance after all."

"Sounds perfect," she said on more of a whisper than she'd planned, but he'd managed to touch her, as usual.

Inside, he left on just one lamp and then tapped at his phone, and suddenly Frank Sinatra filled the room, a sweet, slow, romantic oldie. She walked over to him and slid her arms around his neck, resting her head against his chest. His hands were at her waist. Then he slid them around her neck too. They moved slowly on the living room rug, swaying to the music, the song and Shane's heartbeat in her ears, her heart happy and full.

"Let's forget everything but this," she said, pulling back a bit and looking up at him. "How this feels. Because it feels really, really good."

"Agree on all counts." He leaned in for a kiss. Her nerve endings were on fire, her toes slightly curling, a warmth spreading inside her.

She kissed him back, with all the passion she had, and she heard a low groan escape him. Smiling, she took his hand and led him to his bedroom, his playlist still audible from where he'd left his phone in the living room.

She ran her hands under his shirt, then slowly unbuttoned it and slipped it off him, slightly gasping at his chest, which never ceased to delight her. So muscled and hard with a faint line of dark hair running down the center. She kissed that hair line until she was squatting before him and undid his belt, then the button and zipper. Off his pants went until he was standing in just those super-sexy black boxer briefs.

She stayed where she was and slipped a hand inside, his head dropping back with a moan, his muscles tensing. She wrapped her palm around his erection and slid it up and down, up and down, until he growled that he was dangerously close to losing control. She slowly let go and inched down the boxer briefs, trailing her tongue along his erection as she went. His entire body went rigid, and then he picked her up like she weighed nothing and carried her to bed.

He undressed her quickly, practically tearing off her bra, his hands and mouth exploring her breasts as he worked off her panties with one hooked finger, the hands and mouth following. Ashley let out a low scream and arched her back, barely able to contain her pleasure.

She heard a foil packet being ripped open, and she smiled.

And then she felt him inside her, filling her, thrusting inside her slowly, then faster, faster, his hands in her hair, his mouth fused to hers. Then he was kissing her neck, and she heard him whispering her name before she exploded in pure pleasure. He did too just moments later.

And then she wasn't aware of anything except their rapidly beating hearts, making Ella Fitzgerald barely audible from the living room, and the waves of love coming from deep within.

Chapter Seventeen

Everything came down to today.

Shane would pick up his girls—and find out if their grandmother planned to make good on her threats to petition for custody.

Shane would arrive back at the McCray Ranch tonight, drop off Ashley at her cabin, and things could possibly not be the same the next time he saw her.

At least he was as physically relaxed as he could be, given last night. He and Ashley had made love twice, a second time in the middle of the night, and they'd fallen back asleep with her head on his chest. That had ensured that much of his tension had been worked away. Their relationship—as far as a future was concerned—was a bit up in the air. But he'd learned to take things one day at a time years ago. And he'd do that with Ashley.

But now, as he pulled into the Shaws' driveway, Ashley in the passenger seat, his shoulders bunched back up. Ashley herself and their romance factored into what might happen in that house.

"Here goes everything," he said as they both hopped out of the SUV.

"Fingers crossed."

He crossed his too and rang the doorbell.

Charles opened the door, looking somewhat stressed. "The gals are in the living room. They're packed and ready to go, but Beatrice is just having a word with them."

A word. Criticizing them for this and that, he was sure.

Charles led the way into the living room. "Girls, your dad's here."

The twins were sitting on the love seat, side by side, hands folded in their laps, which was unusual and clearly a Beatrice directive. They were each in a play dress, their hair in pigtails, which they hated. They'd been clearly getting a "talking-to."

"Yay!" Violet shouted, both girls leaping up.

Beatrice gave Violet a sharp look. "Young lady, we just discussed this. We don't shout. We don't jump up when someone else was in the middle of speaking to you. Please sit back down."

"But Daddy's here," Willow said, both girls sitting back down, frowns pulling at their sweet faces.

They looked down at the table, then up at each other, then back down. Were they supposed to be robots? Were they not supposed to be excited to see their father and leap into his arms? He sure wanted that.

Enough was enough.

"Beatrice, honestly, is all this really necessary?" he asked, exasperated. For a few years now he'd tried very hard to hold his tongue and let "their house, their rules" keep him from contradicting her when it came to how she disciplined the twins in her home. His sympathy and compassion for her also played a big part in that.

But what the hell, already? She could dictate her relationship with them but not *his* relationship. He was more than happy to have them hug him whenever they wanted. *Leave them alone.*

"Violet went flying down the stairs again this morning and leaped off, landing on her knees," Beatrice said. "She caused a painting to actually fall off the wall in the hallway."

"And this is the end of the world why?" he asked, at the end of his patience with her. "Why can't you let them be five-year-olds who run and jump?"

Beatrice scowled at him and marched over, pointing a finger in his face. "They will learn to be respectful young ladies. They're too wild and undisciplined!"

"I disagree," he said. "And another thing. Until you can love them for who they are instead of what you want them to be, I think a break from visits is a good idea."

Beatrice gasped.

Charles gasped.

The twins' mouths dropped open.

"You want them to be little ladies?" he continued. "Well, they're not. They're five. They are who they are and they're great. Every day is a learning and growing adventure. They're wonderful girls, loving sisters, with curious minds and happy hearts. I won't have you try to break their spirits. I don't think you could, honestly. But I'm done letting you try to squash them."

"How dare you," she snapped—but there was a slight change in her face. Less stony, more tentative. "You leave me no choice but to call my lawyer."

"I'll be doing the same," he snapped back.

"Isn't that interesting," Violet said suddenly, her face crumpling.

"No," Willow responded. "It's not!" And both twins hurried over to Ashley and buried their faces in her stomach. She knelt down and wrapped them in a hug, soothing them with whispers.

Shane doubted the twins even knew what a lawyer was, and they certainly didn't know the context here, but they sure had heard enough tension and anger in the back-and-forth to feel nervous. To need to be soothed.

Dammit. "I'm not proud that we just did this in front of them, Beatrice. But you've pushed us all too far."

Beatrice turned to her husband. "Charles, say something."

The man looked at his wife. "Honestly, dear, I don't know what to say. Neither of you is wrong. You're not wrong. Shane's not wrong. There, I said it. And it's true."

Beatrice's mouth dropped open. Although she was the one who was more authoritative, Shane had always gotten the sense that Charles's voice and opinions were very important to her.

Good for you, Charles, Shane thought. He too had clearly had it with letting Nana run the show.

Violet pulled away from Ashley and walked over to her grandmother. "Nana, I know why you don't like when I run down the stairs and jump off the third step." She spoke in her usual voice—not shyly, not quietly.

Shane stared at his little girl. She had spunk, that was for sure. Her twin was watching, listening hard.

"You're afraid I'll die like Mommy did," Violet said. "And Willow. She already hurt her ankle."

Shane gasped. So did Ashley. And Charles Shaw.

Shane had expected his daughter might say any number of things, but he hadn't figured on *that*.

Beatrice's lower lip was trembling. She turned away for a moment.

Five sets of eyes were staring at her. Shane had no idea what would happen next, how she'd react, what she'd say. His heart went out to Beatrice in that moment. Because he knew Violet was right. One hundred percent.

His girls had heard enough, though. None of what he and their grandmother had said had been meant for their ears. He'd been trying to shield them from all that, but maybe they did need to hear him defending them, standing up for them, as he had.

Yes, he thought. She'd pushed him too far.

Beatrice knelt down in front of Violet, her expression unreadable. "You come here too, Willow," she said.

As Willow slowly walked over, Beatrice opened up her arms. Both girls hesitantly went to her.

"You know what I think, Violet?" Beatrice said, her eyes misting now. "I think you're right."

"You do?" Violet said, her own eyes wide.

"You yell at us all the time so we won't get hurt like Mommy did?" Willow asked.

Beatrice touched each of the girls' chins. "I think so. I think I'm very scared of that. And if you didn't run or jump or climb trees or touch scissors, you wouldn't risk getting hurt. But that's silly, isn't it? Your mother wasn't doing anything reckless when she got into that accident."

"Nana, what does *reckless* mean?" Violet asked.

"It means risky," Beatrice said. "Like driving too fast. Especially in the rain. But your mother wasn't driving fast—in fact, she was driving extra slowly. She simply got into an accident and hit that guardrail. It wasn't anyone's fault, certainly not her own. That's what an accident is."

Oh, Beatrice.

She took in a deep breath. "I've been hard on you girls because I want to keep you safe. And I want you to be like your mother was before she became a teenager and developed not only a mind of her own, but a voice of her own. Oh, she wouldn't listen to a word I said!" She smiled shakily.

Violet's and Willow's eyes were huge. "Did she get in trouble all the time like we do?"

"Yes. I constantly tried to get her to be well-behaved and quiet, to wear pretty dresses and headbands in sleek hair. Instead, she wore ripped flannel shirts, jeans she drew on, huge black boots, and cut her hair into all kinds of weird cuts."

The twins laughed. "Like mine?" Violet asked, touching her bangs.

"Just like yours," Beatrice said with a smile. "But that's the thing. Your hair's not weird if you like it. It's you. And like your father said, you two are wonderful girls. I'm very proud of who you are."

Shane thought he might fall over, he was so surprised. He glanced at Ashley, whose hand was on her heart. She looked half astonished and half like she might cry.

The girls beamed. "Even though we mess up all the time when we're here?"

"You don't mess up," Beatrice said. "I'm the one who messed up. You two are just right."

Well, I'll be, Shane thought, recalling his grandfather's favorite old-timey phrase.

Charles, standing next to his wife, gave her hand a squeeze. Shane could read pride in the man's face loud and clear.

Beatrice hugged the girls, and they hugged her back. "I love you two."

"We love you, Nana," they said in unison.

"Oh, and one more thing," Beatrice said to them. "The other day, your father told me that your mother would be very proud of who you girls were. And he's right. Your mother would be so proud. And I'm proud too."

Violet and Willow beamed again and threw themselves at their nana for another hug.

Beatrice's eyes were all misty, and she gave them a surreptitious swipe. "Why don't you take your pops out to the backyard and show him how high you can swing while I talk to your daddy?"

The twins raced to the door, Charles laughing as he ran behind them. A nice sight to see.

Beatrice stood up. "I owe you an apology, Shane."

"It's not necessary. Everything you just said to them is all I need to hear and know," he said.

She nodded and was quiet for a moment. Then she looked from him to Ashley and back to Shane. "I suppose you two are dating."

"We're trying," Shane said, reaching for Ashley's hand and holding it.

"That's a good way to put it," Ashley said with a gentle smile.

"Well, it's clear to me the twins adore you," Beatrice said to Ashley. "I have a lot to think about and get used to. But I need to put my granddaughters first—not myself."

Shane extended his hand, and Beatrice shook it with a smile. Hugging her was something neither of them was ready for, which made him chuckle. "You're welcome to come visit us anytime."

"I appreciate that," she said.

Shane eyed the girls' suitcases by the door. "Well, I guess we'd better hit the road."

Beatrice led the way to the yard. She ran—actually ran—over to the girls and knelt down again on the wood chips, also a surprise, and called them in for one last hug.

"Wonders never cease," he whispered. "We both need to remember that when we lose faith about anything."

"I would not have believed any of this if you'd told me secondhand," she whispered back with a smile.

He gave her a quick kiss on the cheek, and then it was time to head home.

Where the road trip would end—and maybe take his romance with Ashley with it.

It was almost 8:00 p.m. when Shane pulled up in front of Ashley's cabin at the McCray Ranch. The girls were fast asleep in the back seat. She didn't like the idea of not saying good-night and goodbye—for now anyway—but she couldn't imagine waking them for that when she'd see them in the morning. She lived a literal stone's throw away from their cabin, and the girls played outside in the mornings, particularly when they didn't have school. Before she started work in the stables for the day, she'd have them give a treat to the horses. The twins loved offering them apple slices and carrot bits. It would be a nice way to ease into things being mostly the same but a little different—back home but with their father in a romantic relationship with her. She thought back to when they'd brought up her marrying their father. Now it was a possibility. Before it had seemed crazy to her—but now she wondered how they'd really feel.

She needed to talk to Shane about how they might react to him having a girlfriend. Sure, they adored her like she did them, but this was a whole nother story. They'd never seen their father with a romantic partner before. Not once in their five years.

And they'd just had a very emotional morning at their grandparents' with talk of their mother.

Suddenly Ashley felt unsure of everything.

"You okay?" he asked, hopping out of the SUV and walking around. He gave the girls a glance. Still fast asleep in their booster seats.

She nodded. It was late, he'd just driven seven hours with only a couple of stops, and this was a conversation that would be better left to tomorrow. How to handle their romance in front of his children would need to be his call.

"I know you were just stuck in a car with me for seven hours, but if you want to come over in a little while…"

She smiled. "I absolutely do want to."

She liked the idea of the continuity instead of each of them going to their separate homes and spending the night apart. She wouldn't stay over, of course.

"I'll get the twins settled in bed and then text you," he said. "I'll miss you for the twentyish minutes we're separated."

"I will too," she said, slinging her arms around him for a quick kiss before dashing up the porch and into her cabin.

As she was about to close the cabin door behind her, she noticed him waiting for her to be safely inside. She loved that about him. Harrington had certainly never done that. Shane held up a hand in goodbye before turning back to the SUV. She slid aside the living room curtains and watched his SUV travel down the gravel road to his own cabin, not wanting to break their connection.

She had it bad for the man, that was for sure.

Ashley took a fast shower and dried her hair, pulling it

back into a ponytail, then changed into leggings and an oversize sweatshirt. Ahh, comfort. She texted her parents that she was back and everything was fine.

Her phone pinged with a text. Her mother, not Shane.

Breakfast out on Sunday with us and then lunch with me and your aunts at the house. So glad you're home, sweetie.

Hi, beautiful, her dad texted a moment later. Sweet dreams and see you on Sunday.

Ashley smiled. She was so grateful for her parents.

And then her phone pinged a third time. Shane. Her heart sped up.

My living room awaits...

A rush of happiness welled up inside her, and she headed back out, walking down the path to his cabin. Couldn't beat the proximity just a quarter of a mile away. It wasn't adjoining rooms at the Bison Creek Lodge or the cabin they'd shared, but she'd take it. She'd been worrying for nothing about how things would be once they got back home. Here they were, back home a mere half hour, and all was well. Okay, fine, a half hour was nothing. But they both wanted to be together again, and that was what mattered.

Shane was on the two-person—or one adult, two little kids—porch swing when she arrived. She sat down beside him, and he put his arm around her shoulders, and in that moment all felt right with the world.

"I think things are going to be just fine," he said.

She smiled up at him and then rested her head on his shoulder. "Me too." She lifted her head and leaned back against the cushioned swing. "I've been thinking. How do you think Willow and Violet will feel about you being in a relationship with a woman?"

"As long as it's you, I think we're A-OK there."

That went straight to her heart.

The cool night air felt so good on her face, in her hair. She closed her eyes and could feel herself drifting off. One giant yawn later, Shane said, "I'd walk you home, but I can't. Plight of the single parent."

She laughed. "I'll be fine."

And as they had one hell of a kiss good-night and she started off down the path, she truly believed it. She would be fine. They would be fine.

The future was theirs for the taking, and against all odds, they were taking it.

Chapter Eighteen

Later that weekend, Ashley carried a big platter of the chicken-and-cheese quesadillas she'd spent the last half hour making to the dining room table in her parents' house. Her mom and her three aunts were hosting a "Welcome back, Ashley" lunch, with just the five of them. Early this morning, she and her parents had gone out to breakfast, and then they'd stopped at the bank to each deposit their checks from the wedding canceler. That had felt good. Mission accomplished.

And then some.

Her dad, her uncle Teddy, who'd filled in as foreman for Shane during his absence, and the two ranch hands were out on the range. Shane had told her that he was going to spend the weekend with his daughters, checking in on them emotionally, particularly after the scene right before they'd left Jackson Hole. He'd mentioned he might even bring up the subject of his love life. Then tonight, Ashley's parents were going to babysit the twins once they were asleep while Shane and Ashley went out on the town—her parents' kind offer. They definitely had an inkling the two were *involved*—and were clearly okay with it even so soon after the debacle of Ashley's wedding.

"So where are you two lovebirds going tonight?" Ashley's

aunt Daphie asked as she set out a bowl of sour cream and salsa.

"Umbertos," Ashley said with a smile she couldn't help. She and Shane had missed out on dancing in Jackson Hole, but Umbertos, everyone's favorite Italian restaurant, was famous for its romantic, low-lit dance floor and slow songs only.

"Oooh, maybe he'll propose," Aunt Lila said, slipping a bit of chicken to each of her little Chihuahuas, who were under her chair in a little fluffy dog bed that went everywhere with Lila.

Aunt Daphie's eyes practically popped. "Are you kidding me? They just started dating like a minute ago! And Ashley could use some time on her own."

"Shane is a great guy," Ingrid said, sitting down and plucking a quesadilla from the platter. "And, my, is he handsome. Hardworking, kind, the best of the best."

Ashley smiled at her mom. "He is definitely all that."

Aunt Kate plopped sour cream on her quesadilla. "Mmm, Ashley, these are fabulous. You'll have to give me the recipe. The chicken is perfectly seasoned."

Daphie gaped at her sister. "That's what you have to say, Kate? You're the one who wanted to haul Harrington into court for breach of expectations and the money. Now you agree with her getting engaged two seconds later? Don't you think she needs time on her own to heal and grow?"

"I was staying neutral," Kate responded. "But I do think Ashley should follow her heart—whatever that means and wherever it leads. A great new romance or time on her own. Only she can decide that, busybody."

Ashley found herself listening hard to the argument that ensued. She had these questions herself. On the one hand, Shane was everything she could ever want in a man. On

the other, she had just been through a big emotional up-
heaval and felt shaky in a lot of areas, trust being a big one.

Though Shane was very trustworthy. Her mother brought
that up immediately and listed all the ways that Shane had
been there for the McCray Ranch the past five years, how
he never let them down.

Daphie, who was recently divorced and pro alone, medi-
tation, yoga and working on yourself and becoming your
own best friend, wagged a finger at her oldest sister. "Yes,
he's trustworthy. As a *foreman*. We have no idea if he's a
good life partner."

"He is a great father," Ashley pointed out, spooning more
salsa on her quesadilla. "Devoted, loving, caring, compassionate, fair, warm. Those girls are very lucky to have him
as their dad."

"Again, a devoted dad doesn't mean a devoted husband.
Did Eli not cheat on me even while he attended every one
of our son's lacrosse games? Spend two hours every Saturday helping him study for the SATs?"

Huh. She did have a point. But in a million years, Ashley could not envision Shane cheating on her. On anyone.

"Can we let Ashley enjoy her new relationship without
getting all cynical on her?" Aunt Kate said. "If he hurts
her, we'll just kill him."

Ashley's eyes widened.

"Jeez, I kid, I kid," Kate said. "I'm just saying, let's give
them a chance. He's not Harrington. And Ashley isn't the
same person she was last week. She's been through a lot.
And she's had some unexpected adventures." She wiggled
her eyebrows.

Wow, her aunt Kate was not usually so on the "go for it"
side. She was about caution.

"Plus, being in a good relationship so soon will help Ashley see what she deserves, what she wants," Lila added. "Shane doesn't have to be *the one*. He can be the tester."

Which reminded Ashley of everything Maya had said at the lodge on their final night there about landing in a rebound relationship—and not realizing it until she'd met someone she fell very hard for.

"Look," Ashley's mom said to her sisters. "They're dating. They're not getting engaged at Umbertos tonight. They're enjoying each other's company. I think they're great together. And from everything Ashley told me, they bring out the best in each other. That's what's important."

Ashley felt a shy smile come upon her face. Her mother had called not long after Ashley had returned to her cabin from the brief interlude on Shane's porch swing, checking in, making sure she was really okay, and they'd had a good talk. Ashley had opened up. Her mother had made her feel so positive about her romance with Shane.

She'd explore her feelings and take it day by day.

Saying so got her four nods from her wise mother and aunts, and she was satisfied.

"I do think Ashley will make one hell of a mother," Aunt Daphie said.

"Whoa, now who's getting ahead of herself!" Ashley's mom countered. "Though I am ready to be a grandmother. What should I call myself? Grandmère? Grandmama? Granny? Grammy?"

Ashley grinned at her mom. "You're gonna be amazing at it, that's all I know."

"Those precious little girls do need a mother," Lila said, then took a sip of her iced tea.

It was scary enough worrying about whether she and Shane

were the real deal or a road-trip romance. Add Violet's and Willow's hearts, minds and souls into the mix and she had to tread carefully. She couldn't let those girls get hurt because of her.

They talked motherhood in general for the next twenty minutes, all of them seeming to realize that Ashley was getting a little overwhelmed by the conversation. They moved on to local gossip, and soon enough, the quesadillas were gone. They'd been a big hit and there were just crumbs left.

She suddenly had an urge to go riding. Not necessarily to have some time alone to think about all the things her relatives had just said, but to just let everything settle. She needed the fresh air on her face, in her hair, as she and her favorite mare, Gingersnap, rode far out on the property. Ashley popped up. "My dear aunts, I'm going to take you up on the offer to clean up since I cooked—I'd love to go riding right now, clear my head."

They all thought that was a good idea.

A half hour later, as Ashley saddled up Gingersnap, she wondered what Shane and the girls were doing, where they were. She missed them so much. She'd see them tonight right before bedtime—apparently they'd asked Shane if she could come over and tell them a story and tuck them into bed. She'd love nothing more.

And then a romantic night out with their handsome father? Oh, yeah. She was looking forward to both with equal measure.

"Daddy, can we go see Ashley now?" Violet asked.

He smiled at his daughters, who were down to their last few french fries at the burger joint they went to for dinner in town. "Bored of me already?"

Willow swiped a fry in the little mound of ketchup on her plate. "Daddy, you're not boring! But we miss Ashley."

"Ashley's so great," Violet said.

He took the last bite of his burger, his stomach and heart both full and happy. "I agree."

He did love that the girls adored Ashley. He'd spent the entire day with the twins—both in their white cowboy boots, or boot, in Willow's case—and the girls had spent at least half of it talking about Ashley. How fun she was. How pretty. How smart. How nice. *How she'd said those nice things about Mommy.*

He'd been well aware that Ashley had known his wife, that they'd been acquaintances who said hello and stopped to exchange small talk if they ran into each other. But they hadn't really had the chance to know each other well. Both were busy, Liza as a new, exhausted mother of twin babies, and Ashley as the horse trainer, groomer and stable manager of her family ranch. Now, though, the fact that she had known the twins' mother had special meaning, particularly for Violet and Willow. It was thanks to Ashley's memory of Liza that Ashley had been able to get through to Beatrice in a closet in the twins' bedroom at their grandparents' house—which had led to the sweet boots on their feet. A symbol of their rebellious mother, who'd had her own mind, heart and soul.

As Willow tore her last french fry in half and gave a piece to her sister, which warmed his heart, he realized he hadn't brought up the subject of him and Ashley dating. Willow was out of ketchup but Violet still had some on her plate, and she set her plate on top of her sister's so they could share the condiment. He watched them pop the split fry into their mouths and decided it would be premature to introduce his love life in a big way. No one said he and Ashley had to make their romance obvious to his daughters right away. The girls didn't even have to know. If he and Ashley got serious, that would be a different story. But until then, there was no need to bring his love life into *their* lives.

They had been the ones to bring up the idea of him and Ashley getting married, but they were five. They knew a wedding was about a couple staying together forever. But they didn't know much else about marriage—and the topic didn't really seem to interest them, given that they hadn't brought it up again.

At some point, the twins would happen upon him and Ashley kissing, and they'd *know*. He had a feeling they'd be happy about the kissing too. Which made him smile.

"I know Ashley is spending today with her family," he said as they all gathered up their wrappers and cups, "just like you're spending today with your family. But she did say she'd come visit and read you two a story before bed."

"Yay!" they said in unison.

"So let's go home and get into bed!" Willow said, but then glanced up at the still-bright-blue sky. She frowned. "It's definitely not bedtime yet."

"But we can go to bed *early*," Violet pointed out.

Shane gaped at his daughters. "You actually want it to be bedtime so you can see Ashley?"

They both nodded.

Yup, he had a very strong suspicion they would not mind the idea of him and Ashley as a couple. He glanced at his phone, shaking his head on a smile that reflected the warmth in his heart. "You've got about two hours before bedtime. But maybe Ashley can come over early. Let's head home."

The twins fist-pumped and skipped their way to the SUV. Once they were buckled in the back seat, Shane drove to the McCray Ranch, his own heart speeding up at the idea of seeing Ashley. He knew just how the twins felt and then some.

Once they were back at the cabin, they went straight to their bedroom. When he went to see what they were up to, they were both in pj's and in their beds, blankets pulled up to their chins. Wow, these two were serious.

"Can you call Ashley and tell her we're ready for our story?" Willow asked, her favorite lovey under the crook of her arm.

Violet nodded. "Since it's early, she can tell us a *million* stories about Helena the horsey."

Shane laughed. "She'll probably really like that, actually. I'll go call her, okay?"

He went to find his phone, which he'd tossed in the basket on the coffee table in the living room. Just as he grabbed it, it rang.

Anthony McCray.

"Oh, God, Shane. There's been an accident. Ashley got thrown off the mare she was riding. The only good news is that she was on her way back to the stables and was pretty close—Jack actually *saw* her get thrown and called 911 right away."

Shane had frozen at the word *accident*, his breath caught in his throat, his heart pounding. No. No, no, no.

His hand on the phone was shaking. "She's okay, though? Nothing broken?"

"She was knocked unconscious. The ambulance just came and took her to General. I'm headed there now. Her

mom went in the ambulance with her and just texted me—
no change. She hasn't woken up."

Unconscious. A terrible chill ran up Shane's spine. He
couldn't find his voice.

"Come when you can, okay?" Anthony said. "I know
you'll need a sitter for the girls."

"I'll be there as soon as I can," he said, his voice shaky,
his legs trembling now.

Unconscious. No change...

He started to put the phone in his pocket, but then pulled
it out again. He called Jack, the ranch hand who'd seen
the accident, and asked if his teenage daughter was free
to babysit for a few hours tonight, starting as soon as Jack
could drop her off. Luckily, the answer was yes.

"Was she thrown clear?" Shane asked, his heart pounding so loud he wasn't sure he'd even hear Jack's response.

"Yes, thank God. And it happened on the open path. If
it had happened thirty seconds earlier, she might have been
knocked into the tree line."

He closed his eyes. At least there was that.

Jack assured him he'd drop off his daughter in five minutes, and they disconnected.

Shane had no idea what he was going to tell the twins
right now. They'd be upset enough to learn that Ashley
wasn't coming to read them a million stories. But if he
told them why...

He walked slowly to their bedroom, trying to think, but
his head was jumbled. He sucked in a breath and walked
in, not sure what exactly would come out of his mouth.
Until he had more information, he didn't want to leave
them hanging in worry.

Both girls were asleep, Violet's mouth slightly open,

Willow on her side with her lovey tucked close against her. They'd had another big day, so falling asleep early wasn't a surprise.

And lucky for him. He wouldn't have to tell them why Ashley wasn't coming over. Or that he had to go and would be home later. If they woke up while he was gone, the sitter—a bubbly, funny sixteen-year-old named Elly who'd babysat for them before—would tell them he had to go out for a while, and they'd have a little milk and then go back to sleep.

Jack was true to his word and arrived within minutes. Once his daughter Elly was settled in the house, Shane rushed out.

Jack was waiting. "I wish I had more info for you, Shane. Even though Ashley was thrown clear, she seemed to land hard."

Dammit. "What happened?" he asked as he fished his keys out of his pocket. "Do you know? I mean, what spooked the horse?"

"Delivery truck backfired. Scared the bejesus out of all of us until we realized where the deafening sound came from. It's why I was looking around and happened to see the accident."

"Just tell me one thing," Shane called as he ran over to his SUV. "Was she breathing?"

"I don't know, Shane. I'm sorry."

He nodded and took off for the hospital, which was twenty minutes away. Bluetooth read him a text from Ingrid. No change.

That had to mean she was breathing but still unconscious.

A cold burst of fear traveled up his spine and settled around his neck, squeezing to the point that he had to pull over for a moment and suck in some air. He got back on the road, driving as fast as he could without endangering anyone.

Finally, he made it. He parked and ran inside the Emergency entrance, quickly finding the McCrays and Ashley's three aunts either sitting or pacing. He rushed up to Ashley's parents.

Anthony's eyes were red rimmed. "All they could tell us is that she has a sprained ankle. And hit her head pretty hard, but there's no skull fracture."

A sprained ankle. Like Willow. No skull fracture. Both good signs. "So she'll be okay, right? She'll be okay."

"They can't say yet," he managed in a shaky tone, then dropped down in a chair, then bolted up and began pacing. "She's still out."

Ingrid was being consoled by her sisters, but the three aunts looked very worried, and all of them had the same red-rimmed eyes as Anthony.

Please, God, he sent heavenward. *Please*. He couldn't even get out any more of a prayer. That ice-cold fear ran up his spine again, spreading into his chest. He wrapped his arms around his body. *Please, please, please. Let her be okay.*

He dropped down in a chair, dimly aware that he felt strangely numb, the cold replaced by a nothingness. He squeezed his eyes shut.

Bile clawed at his gut, and that chill was wrapping around him. He was ice-cold again and shaking suddenly.

He'd been here before. In this waiting room.

Waiting. Waiting. Waiting.

The last time he was here, he'd lost his wife. *We're so sorry, Shane. We did everything we could...*

His children had lost their mother. Just three months old and motherless.

A blackness threatened to engulf him. He opened his eyes. *Don't lose it*, he ordered himself. *Ashley needs you right now. Keep it together.*

I can't do this, a small, terrible voice whispered in his head, then started echoing. *I can't do this again.*

Chapter Nineteen

Ashley's first thought when she'd learned from the nurse that she'd sprained her ankle and would need a boot was that she and Willow Dawson would match. Her second thought—her head hurt a bit. She'd been unconscious for almost an hour, but she'd been very lucky—the CT scan showed no sign of injury other than a small goose egg. Her ankle wouldn't require surgery.

Her parents had been in, her three aunts, but where was Shane? According to everyone, he'd arrived very soon after her father had alerted him to the accident and had been sitting in the waiting room looking pale and worried. While she'd been unconscious, she'd been allowed to have visitors for just a few minutes, and apparently, he'd come in to see her but had quickly returned to the waiting room. He was still there. Her aunts had left to relieve Shane's sitter, since Ashley would be here overnight for observation and everyone assumed he'd want to stay with her as long as he could. Her parents had gone to the cafeteria to get her soup and hot tea. Now was a perfect time for Shane to come in, for them to have a little time together alone.

She'd asked a nurse to let Shane know she was awake and wanted to see him, but fifteen minutes later, no Shane.

She looked at the analog clock on the wall. She'd been

here for over three hours. She'd been awake for the past hour. Why hadn't he come in to see her?

A nurse came in to check her vitals. She asked if Shane was still in the waiting room and he was. Yes, the nurse had let him know he could see Ashley anytime until 9:00 p.m., which was coming right up.

And then a terrible idea occurred to her.

He'd been in that waiting room before. For news about his wife after the accident.

His twin three-month-olds in their double stroller beside him, both babies crying, inconsolable on and off for hours.

She knew that because her father had told her. She and her mother and aunts had been away on a girls' trip that weekend. But her father had rushed to the ER the moment he'd heard about the car accident. Liza's parents and brother and Shane's family had been pacing, her mother alternating between crying and demanding information on her daughter's condition.

And then the doctor had come out, and her father had taken one look at the woman's face and knew.

Shane had stood up and dropped to his knees before the doctor had even reached him. And then they'd all heard what the doctor had said.

We're very sorry. We did everything we could...

According to her father, Beatrice had collapsed in her husband's arms and nurses had rushed to help them into chairs.

He'd learned the worst news of his life in that waiting room. Had been crushed in that waiting room. His daughters had become motherless in that waiting room.

And now he was sitting in one of those gray padded chairs.

Oh, Shane, she thought. He must be besieged by memories.

She felt fine now except for the slight headache and wished she could go into the waiting room herself and see Shane, assure him she was okay, that she'd been very lucky.

Maybe it was silly, but she believed he was her talisman. He was in her heart and had been with her when the accident happened—even if not physically. The thought was a comfort.

"Ashley?" she heard him call from behind the ringed curtain.

Her heart sped up a bit. He'd come. *Finally.* She let out a breath, so relieved.

"Come on in," she said.

He was as pale as her parents had mentioned, his expression grim. "You're okay, I hear. Except for a sprained ankle and a goose egg."

"Willow and I have matching ankle boots," she said with a smile. "Oh, gosh, you don't think Violet will try to injure her leg to match, do you?" She chuckled—though it wasn't really funny because Violet just *might*.

He put a hand on her shoulder. "Thank God you're okay. Your parents are back—they brought you some food. They're in the waiting room."

He didn't sound like himself. He sounded like a stranger.

"Shane, are *you* okay?"

He turned away for a moment and didn't say anything, then shook his head. "I'm not."

"I understand," she whispered. *This is hard, but say it, Ashley. Talk about it.* "It must bring back the worst memories."

He sucked in a breath and gave something of a nod. "Now that your folks are back and there's only ten minutes more of visiting hours, I'll let them come and say good-night, and I'll get home and let your aunts go."

He definitely didn't sound like himself. She hoped he'd lean down and hug her, even if that would be difficult to do in their positions, or at least drop a kiss on her lips, on her forehead. But he didn't.

He reached for her hand and held it for a moment and then left. Taking a big piece of her heart with him.

She bit her lip, feeling slightly sick. Worried. Nervous. Scared.

Don't worry, she told herself. *He'll be back in the morning to pick you up. He just needs to get out of here and try to deal with what being back here awakened for him.*

There was an Urgent Care entrance on the other side of the hospital, so he likely hadn't been back to the ER itself in these five years. He would have taken the twins there for their high fevers and minor injuries.

Walking into the ER tonight, sitting in that waiting room for hours...

But her parents had told her that while she'd been un-conscious, the doctors said they'd have to wait to assess her when she came to. *We didn't know how bad it was gonna be*, her father had said, tears in his eyes. *If you'd wake up at all.* He'd burst into tears then, her parents clinging to each other. She'd assured them she was absolutely fine, she'd gotten lucky, and they kept saying they knew it but it was so damned *scary.*

She thought back to her and Shane's conversation in the barbecue restaurant in Jackson Hole. They'd talked about risk. Possible loss. How Ashley had wanted a guarantee.

How he'd said, *You think I'd give you up because I fear losing you—to anything?*

Remembering that made her feel much better. Everything would be okay. Like Shane often said, things took time. This would take time. They'd get through it. They were that strong.

She wished she could sleep beside Shane tonight, just holding him, just there for him, her head pressed against his shoulder.

It was going to be a very long night for them both.

In the morning, Shane put the twins on the school bus, then realized as it was halfway down the road that he'd forgotten to put their lunch boxes in their backpacks; the orange and blue soft sacks were both still on the counter, next to the mess he'd left—the packages of turkey and cheese, the mustard for Willow, the mayo for Violet. The packs of mini pretzels. It vaguely occurred to him that he needed to buy more of those; he was down to his last two.

This was how it had been since the twins had woken up. He was so scatterbrained. He hadn't slept much. He'd set his alarm for their wake-up time just in case he was either asleep or out of his mind, as he'd been much of the night. He'd sat out on the back patio awhile, barely aware that he was cold.

And he'd cried—hard. For a good half hour.

What he knew when the alarm had gone off at 7:00 a.m. was that he couldn't do this. Not that he had a choice; *something* had changed when he'd woken up. The raw aching vulnerability had been replaced by something hard. He could almost feel the metal shutter surrounding his heart, protecting it. *Try to get past me*, it seemed to say in a dead voice.

Yes, something had changed. He'd gone numb again, as

he had those first weeks after he'd lost his wife, become a widowed father to two babies. He'd had so much help then—his family, Liza's family. Beatrice's face gray. Charles constantly crying. But the twins—caring for them, holding them, feeding them, rocking them, consoling them—had gotten them all through. Liza's babies had needed them all. That sense of purpose, along with the knowledge that Liza lived on in these precious infants, had saved them.

He'd felt that way this morning when he'd made Violet's and Willow's lunches, when he'd sat down to brush both girls' hair, when he'd reminded them to brush their teeth, when he'd taken a look in their backpacks to make sure they had their take-home folders. There was such comfort in the everyday tasks. His girls were what kept him going, always.

He'd drop off the girls' lunches on his way to see Ashley in the hospital. He'd tell her he couldn't do this. She'd understand. She'd be disappointed, hurt even, but hadn't she said this might just be a rebound relationship anyway? That she wasn't sure they'd last once they got home?

He'd just be cutting it off now. A preemptive move. A necessary move.

He could not care this much about someone else other than his children. He could not love someone again other than his children.

He could not lose another person he loved.

He wouldn't. And the way to do that was not to date, not to love.

Somewhere inside him he could feel another sharp ache, that metal shutter not doing its job. But that pain was another sure sign that he was doing the right thing by taking himself out, stepping away.

He'd do *his* job—as foreman on the ranch. He'd raise

his girls. He hadn't intended to get involved with another woman, and the road trip had let him compartmentalize; it had been a road-trip romance, but now the trip was over. The romance was stopping with it.

He got back to the cabin, and the sight of all the lunch stuff on the counter made him envision his daughters on the bus. They were probably telling their classmates their adventures these past several days, Willow showing off her black ankle boot, Violet fluffing her very short bangs with pride. Both showing off their white cowboy boots. He squeezed his eyes shut for a moment, then opened them and took a deep breath.

He alternated feeling too much and feeling numb.

Yesterday, the subject of dating Ashley hadn't come up with the twins, and now he was grateful. They hadn't even known their father had briefly been dating her. All they knew was that he and Ashley were good friends. And hopefully, in time, they'd get back to that.

Right now, he could see them going back to the relationship they'd had before the wedding. Acquaintances. But that might be the numbness talking. They would always be more than acquaintances, even if they never spoke again. What was between them ran deep, it was in their veins, and it always would be.

And if she started dating someone else and he didn't like what he saw, he'd butt in again. That was who he was. But he wouldn't get involved in her life beyond that. He just couldn't.

He sucked in a breath and cleared the counter, then grabbed the two lunch boxes and headed out. He liked the idea of going to the elementary school, being in the girls' universe even if he was just going to the office. He'd feel them surrounding him. They were *inside* that metal shutter in his chest—not outside like Ashley was.

Then he'd go to the hospital and he'd tell her how it had to be.

Ashley's aunt Daphie was adamant over FaceTime that Shane would arrive with a huge bouquet of her favorite flowers, which were red tulips and in bloom. That he'd be fine this morning, his head and heart in a better, stronger place. If Daphie thought so, it was easier to let herself hope. Plus, her aunt had always believed in the power of a good night's sleep. But her aunt hadn't seen Shane last night, his face, his eyes, his demeanor, his posture. Or heard his voice, which had had a rawness to it that had made her heart ache.

She was sitting in the guest chair in the hospital room she'd been moved to last night, ready to leave, her phone held up to her face to see her dear aunt. She had her discharge papers and was waiting for Shane. He'd texted last night that he'd pick her up and bring her home.

"Plus, he owes you dinner and dancing at Umbertos," Daphie said. "So once your ankle is all healed, he'll have to make good on that."

"I appreciate your new optimism, Auntie."

Daphie smiled. "I believe in you two. I know I was down on you two getting involved so soon after the wedding disaster. But I was coming from my own long line of man troubles. Last night, your parents told me a lot more about the kind of man Shane is. He's exactly who I want for you, honey."

She bit her lip. "I might not have a say, unfortunately. I just have a bad feeling. A scared feeling. And it's telling me that I've lost him. That he's gone, retreated deep, and I won't be able to reach him."

Daphie gently shook her head. "You two belong together. Might take him a little bit to get there again, but have faith. That's my new motto. Have faith."

Ashley smiled. That was hard-won coming from cynical, I-hate-everyone-and-everything Aunt Daphie. "I'll try. Love you."

"Love you," she said.

They disconnected and Ashley set down her phone, peering out the window, which had a lovely view of the parking lot. Ah—she saw Shane's SUV pull in. She got up slowly, walking carefully on her new boot, which she wasn't quite used to, and looked out, dying for a glimpse of her handsome man. Hopefully he was still *her* handsome man.

But he didn't get out of his vehicle. In fact, she could just make out him sitting in the front seat. He didn't seem to be on his phone. He was just looking straight ahead, then down, then out the side window.

Oh, crud. Her stomach dropped. This wasn't good. He had something hard to tell her.

Like, *I can't do this*. She felt it coming, and her eyes immediately welled with tears.

Dammit.

When she dabbed under her eyes and looked out the window again, she could see Shane making his way to the hospital entrance.

Brace yourself, she thought. *This is gonna hurt.*

She could be wrong, of course. Last night was hard on him. The memories. Being in that waiting room, not knowing how she was, if she'd make it… It must have brought a lot of pain back up for him.

But she was fine. Didn't that count for anything?

There was a tap at her door, and she sucked in a breath. "Come on in."

One look at his face, at his eyes, the set of his jaw, his bunched shoulders, told her everything. He *was* already gone.

"Shane, before you say anything, let me say this. I love you."

She paused, hoping to see some reaction, some change in his expression. But there was none.

She quickly continued so he couldn't get a word in to tell her they were over and walk out. "Before the road trip, I wanted to bop you on the head at least twice a week. In the beginning of the road trip, I was an emotional mess, as you know, unsure of everything, so hurt and dejected that I was actually hoping Harrington would see me and want me back."

She almost couldn't believe she'd been in that headspace. But that was oftentimes how heartbreak worked. You could want to earn the love you'd been denied, that had been snatched from you. You wanted the approval. You wanted to feel good about yourself again.

She mentally shook her head. She could barely remember that woman, and it hadn't been that long ago. That was how different she felt now, how strong, how *sure*—of herself, of Shane, of *them*.

"You helped me change, Shane. You helped me find my way back to myself. You helped me believe in myself and my right to go after what I want. Now that I know this, that this feeling is possible, I'll never again accept anything less."

The look in his eyes almost broke her heart. Because the very air in the room seemed to vibrate with the *I'm sorry* that was coming. Nothing she was saying was reaching inside him. He was listening. But it wasn't getting *in*.

"And, Shane, what was said that final morning at the Shaws' house. About risk—"

He was shaking his head. Fast. Meaning he didn't want to hear this, wouldn't hear this.

"Ashley, I *do* remember what was said. I fully remember Beatrice saying that her daughter wasn't doing anything risky when she got into that accident. That it wasn't her fault. You weren't doing anything risky either when you got into your accident. You were trotting back to the stables. A delivery truck backfired and bam—your horse spooked."

"Right, and—"

"And just like that, reckless, careful—it doesn't matter. The risk is in loving someone in the first place. I've got enough of that with two little girls. I can't take on any more. I've always known I couldn't—it's why I never started dating. But you came along and—"

"And now I'm asking you to let me back in. We both had to go through big changes to find our way to each other. We're so *rare*, Shane."

He was silent, then turned to look out the window.

"And like you said—like my aunt Daphie said," she added, "I have to have faith. You've made me believe that real love exists."

"At least I did that," he said in a low voice, turning to face her. "That does help."

"Help you feel better about walking out of my life, you mean?" she blurted out. She knew that was what he was about to do.

"I'm here to take you home," he said. "But I'm also here

to tell you that I can't do this, Ashley. I wanted to. I thought maybe I could. But I can't. I don't *want* to."

"I'm not worth it?" she said before she could stop herself. Her eyes filled with tears.

"You're worth it. Of course you are. But this isn't about that. It's about me being unwilling to go through what I did five years ago ever again. I can't. I've got those girls to raise. You've seen up close and personal how hard that is, how fraught, how everything changes every five minutes. I'm going to just be their dad. No one's—"

"Husband," she said.

He nodded. "I'm very sorry, Ashley. Hurting you kills me."

"What about what you said in the barbecue restaurant, Shane? That you'd never let me go just because you were afraid of losing me. *You said that.*"

"That was before…" He trailed off, his expression so pained she wanted to go to him and hold him. But of course she couldn't.

He was lost to her right now. Probably for good.

She felt her heart break, snap in two.

"Is there anything I could say that would change your mind in the fifteen minutes it'll take to get to the ranch?" she asked.

He looked at her and shook his head.

She tried to stifle the sob that rose up in her throat. "Then I can't sit there, in your vehicle, with you so close and yet a million miles away from me. I can't do *that*. I'll call my aunt Daphie to pick me up."

"Ashley—"

"Go before I burst into tears," she said.

He looked at her one last time and then slipped through

the door. She'd thought she knew what heartbreak felt like?
She'd had no idea.

She dropped down in the chair and sobbed.

Chapter Twenty

Five days later, Shane was even more miserable than he'd been the day he'd gotten the call from Ashley's father that she'd been thrown. That she was unconscious. That no one knew her condition.

"Daddy," Violet called as she ran from her room in her pj's, her sister right beside her. Shane had tucked them in and turned off the light fifteen minutes ago and had thought they were asleep.

He mentally shook his head to clear it, to be present for his daughters. "Yup, sweethearts? What can I do for you?"

"We have a question," Willow said, biting her lip and looking at her twin.

He tried not to frown. Something in the way they were acting, the hesitance in their voices, made him think this was about Ashley. He hoped it wasn't.

"It's about Ashley," Violet said.

He inwardly sighed.

"Daddy, we were wondering if you and Ashley are still friends."

His heart ached. *We're not friends, actually. We're not... anything.*

Violet nodded. "Because she hasn't come over in a long

time. And we really want her to tell us a bedtime story about Helena the horse."

He knelt down in front of his girls. "Tell you what. I'll ask her if she can tell you guys a story tomorrow night. Tuck you in. I can't promise she'll be able to, though, okay?"

He would ask—for them. And he and Ashley could try to work out some semblance of friendship again. Acquaintanceship, really, since neither of them would be ready to hang out with each other, go for ice cream with the girls, chat about their lives. He certainly wouldn't want to hear about anyone Ashley was dating. Though he had no doubt that would be far off for her.

Or maybe not, he thought glumly. She wanted love. She wanted to start a family.

"She might not?" Willow asked.

She might not. He didn't want to set up false hopes. Or say anything, really.

"Well, I promise to ask her, okay?"

Violet bit her lip and looked at her sister.

They knew, dammit. They knew that something had changed between him and Ashley.

He followed them, tucked them both back in and said, "I'll call her in the morning and ask. I promise."

They nodded and clutched their lovies and closed their eyes.

He kissed their foreheads, wished them sweet dreams and then left the room.

God, his heart felt so heavy. He stood by the sliding glass doors to the patio, looking out at the darkness. At the moon. The stars. Not too long ago he'd sat outside with Ashley sharing that moon and those stars.

Now they weren't anything. He felt like hell.

It's gonna take time, that's all, he told himself. He'd let himself experience something that had been profound and beautiful—a romance with Ashley—and he'd cut it out of his life. Of course it hurt. He just needed to get back to the status quo, his life before the road trip. When everything *had* been fine.

It hadn't been fine, though, he recalled now as he tried to concentrate on inventory in the big barn. The Shaws had been constantly after him. Now they weren't. He'd had all these days of peace, of Beatrice and Charles FaceTiming the girls and overhearing Beatrice say, *Give my love to your daddy.*

She'd never said *that* before this week.

And Ashley had helped set this new relationship with the Shaws in motion when she'd found Violet in the closet in the girls' room. She'd known exactly what to say when Violet needed help with her grandmother, when someone had to step in.

Ashley had. Because she'd been there five years ago when Shane's life had been ripped apart. He and Ashley hadn't been close then, but she'd been there. She *knew*. His history was part of her own memories just because they lived on the same property.

Speaking of which, it had been with absolute dread that he'd texted Anthony McCray the morning after he'd ended things with Ashley.

I ended up hurting Ashley worse than that jerk did. I understand if you need to let me go.

Three gray dots had appeared and disappeared, then reappeared. Finally, Anthony had texted back. You're the best foreman I've ever had. And besides, I asked Ashley if she was doing okay with you and the girls living on the ranch and she said yes. That at least she'll get to see Willow and Violet and have the same relationship with them as before.

That was true. The girls hadn't known there had been a romance to blow up, and so everything was the same to them. And Ashley, because of who she was, gave nothing away. She was herself with the girls. There was no hidden agenda, no asides, no trying to get information out of them. She cared about Willow and Violet and that was evident. He knew this because he'd come upon Ashley and the girls in the stables twice in the past five days, though Ashley hadn't heard him come in. He'd listened to the way she spoke to them, with such kindness, sweetness. He loved the way she answered their big questions, with such thoughtfulness and care.

At least he hadn't destroyed all that, he thought now.

But the twins had noticed she hadn't come over in the past several days. That he didn't take them over to see her. If they ran into her on the ranch property, that was one thing. But neither side was ringing doorbells.

Little kids noticed far more than adults thought they did.

He *would* ask Ashley to read them a story tomorrow night—for the girls' sake. It was a big ask—that he knew. He'd hurt her badly. But he'd make himself scarce so that Ashley wouldn't have to deal with *him*.

He dropped down on the sofa, staring up at the ceiling, thinking about his video call with his cousin Reed last night. Their conversation had been knocking around in Shane's head in the middle of the night and all day today.

He'd FaceTimed with Reed, a cousin he'd always been close to, after being unable to find any damned comfort in the usual ways. Like sitting outside on the porch or patio in the warming spring air. That was out now since it was something he'd done with Ashley, both on the road trip and back here that first night. Even looking in at his sleeping daughters last night hadn't worked its usual magic. Instead of his heart filling with peace and contentment, he worried that, someday soon, there would be discord between him and Ashley, that the end of their romance would lead to some kind of blowout and the girls would be devastated to lose her in their lives.

He'd paced and then grabbed his phone and texted Reed that he could use some advice. Reed had FaceTimed him right away. His cousin was a detective in Bear Ridge, serving with two of his other cousins, the ones who owned the Dawson Family Guest Ranch. Reed had been through hell and back a couple of years ago but had welcomed love into his life not too long ago and had never been happier. A baby in an infant carrier had been left on his desk at the police station with an anonymous note to care for her for a few days. At the time, Reed could barely look at a baby without shattering because of his past.

Shane figured his cousin would have answers to share about how he'd gotten over his own past to be happily remarried now—and raising that little baby girl.

He'd told Reed everything. How close he'd come to actually thinking he could do this, have a relationship with a woman and love someone again.

Someone he could lose.

Believe me, you know I understand, Reed had said.

A couple of years ago, Reed had married a woman who'd been six months pregnant with her ex's baby. The ex had abandoned her. Reed welcomed that baby as if she was his own. But when his wife had an affair with her ex two years into their marriage, he lost not just his wife but all ties and rights to the child he'd thought of as his own. He'd been so heartsick that he'd packed up and moved hours to Bear Ridge to be near family.

I felt the same way, Reed had added. *Scared out of my mind to let myself care about that little helpless baby that had been left in my care for a few days. Scared out of my mind to let myself feel what I was feeling for the social worker I'd been snowbound with along with that baby. And I almost lost both of them to my own stubbornness, my unwillingness to get out of my way.*

How you'd overcome it, though? Shane had asked. That was what he couldn't figure out. He almost felt like he'd had nothing to do with the decision to break off things with Ashley; that his head and heart had simply ganged up on him and taken over. That metal shutter had gone up and that was that.

Same way you will. I was miserable, like you are now. And I realized that not having Aimee and baby Summer in my life was a lot more painful than worrying about losing them.

That had stuck with Shane all last night.

I wouldn't give you up just because I fear losing you— to anything...

He *had* said that. And yes, it was before he had almost lost Ashley.

He got up and paced. This was so damned painful. His heart felt like it might explode.

Did he hear voices suddenly? His daughters', yes, but another voice. Like Beatrice Shaw's. But that was impossible.

He must be going crazy.

He got up and walked over to the twins' bedroom. He definitely heard them talking.

Then Beatrice Shaw responding.

What the heck?

He pushed open the ajar door with a fingertip. His girls were on their stomachs in Willow's bed—his cell phone, which they must have swiped when they'd come out fifteen minutes ago, on the pillow, their grandmother's face filling the screen.

Had they video-called their nana? Why?

Willow turned and noticed him standing in the doorway. Her eyes widened, and she poked her sister.

"Uh-oh," Violet said. She looked at the phone. "Daddy caught us, Nana."

"Sweeties," Beatrice said. "Let me talk to your father, okay? I'll do what I can, okay?"

"Thank you, Nana!" the girls said in unison.

Do what she can? About what?

"Here, Daddy," Violet said in her most innocent tone. "Nana wants to talk to you."

Willow nodded and took the phone from Violet and handed it to him.

He narrowed his eyes at his daughters. "I'll take this in the living room. You two should be asleep."

"Night night," they said and got back under the covers.

He left the room, closing the door behind him. He went into his bedroom and closed the door, away from possibly big ears that might be trying to eavesdrop.

"Beatrice? What's going on?"

Beatrice's eyes were misty. Uh-oh. What was this?

"The girls told me that something is going on. Or not

going on. That you and Ashley don't seem to be friends anymore. They're worried."

He sucked in a breath and looked away for a moment, then found himself breaking down and telling Beatrice everything. *Just about* everything.

"Well, it was plain as day that you two are deeply in love," Beatrice said. "Why do you think I got so emotional that my five-year-old granddaughters had to talk some sense into me?"

"I can't," Shane said, shaking his head. "I can't go through that again."

"I feel the same way. But I certainly can't cut my son out of my life because he might get into a car accident."

Shane almost gasped.

"I know it's a little different," she added, "but the point is the same. And let me tell you something else."

He was a little scared of what that might be now.

"Liza would have wanted you to find love again. I believe that with all my heart. Charles and I talked about that, actually, the morning you picked up the girls. Liza would have wanted you to give them a mother who'd cherish them as she would have."

Now he did gasp.

"Shane, you know how I've spent the past five years trying desperately to control everything around me—especially my granddaughters. But I know now that I can't. I can only love them. And you."

Was it his imagination or did that metal shutter in his chest creak open a bit? Just a bit.

"You can't control love, Shane. It's wild and wonderful and comes with incredible risk, yes. But it's worth everything. Even the loss. I know that now."

He felt his own eyes getting misty. "Now I do too," he said.

She smiled. "Think on it tonight, Shane. Sleep on it. Or better yet, don't waste another second and call Ashley and ask her to come over. Tell her you have some groveling to do."

I would never give you up because I was scared of losing you—to anything.

Like himself. His own stubbornness.

Stupid dumbhead idiot, he chastised himself.

Ashley was finally going to hear from the man she loved that he had made the biggest mistake of his life and loved her. He had to smile about that.

"I think I will," he said. "Thank you, Beatrice. You just might have changed four lives tonight."

The last time he saw the look that was now on Beatrice's face, in her eyes, was the day the twins were born, when she'd held both in her arms for the first time.

"I'll free up the line so you can call Ashley," she said and disconnected.

He just hoped he wasn't too late, that he hadn't been the final straw, causing her to completely give up on love. Lose her faith in happily-ever-after.

And her ability to believe that he *had* made the biggest mistake of his life in letting her go.

Because he sure had. He knew it now.

His girls knew it.

And he was going to fix it.

Ashley had just come out of the shower when her phone pinged with a text.

Shane.

Could you come over now? I need to tell you something right away but I can't leave. Plight of the single parent, remember? I'm hoping to change that, actually.

Her mouth dropped open. She would not read into that last sentence. She would not read into any of the text.

She typed back: On my way.

What could this be about? She quickly got dressed in jeans and a sweater and towel dried her hair, then pulled it into a low ponytail and hurried out the door. On the path to his cabin, she reread the text.

I'm hoping to change that, actually.

Being a single parent?

Stop speculating, she told herself. *You'll find out soon enough.*

Like right now, because she'd arrived. He opened the door before she could even knock and stepped out onto the porch. He gestured to the swing and she sat. Then he sat beside her. Her heart was so full of hope that she had to hold on to the post to keep herself from falling over.

"I've been miserable since the morning I left your hospital room," he said. "It didn't take long for me to realize that living without you is way more painful than the thought of losing you."

Oh, Shane. She was so touched that she couldn't speak. And she didn't want to interrupt. She wanted to hear everything he had to say before she'd fling herself into his arms.

"I made the biggest mistake of my life that morning," he said.

Her hand flew to her heart. "I've been wanting to hear the right man say that."

He smiled and reached up to touch her face. "I love you so much, Ashley," he said, taking her hand and holding it. He kissed her knuckles, then looked at her. "I'm so sorry for hurting you. I promise to make it up to you every day."

"I love you too," she whispered. "So much. And I love Violet and Willow with all my heart."

"I know it. And so do they. To the point that they kind of engineered this. Do you know they stole my phone and FaceTimed their nana tonight for help in getting us back together?"

She smiled and linked her arm through his. "Those girls. Very smart and resourceful."

He laughed. "We'll be a family. The four of us. And maybe a baby brother or sister for the twins."

She was so moved she couldn't speak.

"We want a baby sister!" a little voice called.

"But a brother would be good too," another one added.

What on earth? Shane popped up and looked in the bedroom window, which faced the yard, just inches from the porch. Big ears, indeed.

"You two might as well come on out," Shane called with a smile.

"Yay!" came two little voices. They came rushing out in their orange striped footie pajamas.

Oh, how she did love these girls. So, so much.

"We're going to be a family?" Willow asked, hope in her eyes.

"And have a baby sister or brother?" Violet seconded.

"Hopefully very soon," Shane said. "If Ashley will marry me."

Three sets of eyes looked at her.

She was so happy, so overwhelmed with absolute joy,

that for a second she couldn't speak. "Oh, I'll marry you. *All* of you," she added, wrapping her arms around the girls.

Shane leaned over his daughters' heads to kiss Ashley. "Okay, now it's like ten o'clock and you two need to be asleep immediately."

"I think we'll sleep really good tonight, Daddy," Willow said.

Violet smiled on a firm nod.

They walked the smiling, chattering, yawning girls to their room, tucked them in and kissed their foreheads. Ashley started to tell them a story about Helena the horse, but three lines in, the twins were asleep.

Tears misted Ashley's eyes. "Just think, now I can do that every night. I'm going to be their mother. It's a dream come true. This is all a dream come true."

He pulled her into his arms and held her tight. "It is. I stopped believing in all that. But now I do. And the girls will too."

She leaned up and kissed him. Her Shane. Her heart.

He turned off the lamp between the twins' beds, and they went into the living room. Again, Shane took her in his arms. Ashley rested her head against his chest, Shane's heartbeat precious against her ear.

What happened on the road trip wasn't going to stay on the road trip. It had been a journey that would last forever.

Epilogue

On the first day of summer, another wedding was being held at the McCray Ranch. This time, the groom was there. Sure, he lived on the ranch, but he'd have walked a thousand miles to get there if he had to. Wild horses couldn't have kept him from waiting down at the end of the aisle for his bride.

Ashley McCray was getting married today. For real. And she had no doubt that the wedding would go off without a hitch, that in just fifteen minutes, she'd be Ashley McCray Dawson.

Yes, she'd practiced writing that name last night in her journal, her heart overflowing.

Ashley McCray Dawson, mama to two precious girls, daughters of her heart. She'd love them with everything she had. As she would their father. Forever.

There was no bridal tent this time. Just a big tree on the McCray Ranch that she was waiting behind with her father. There was no bridal party either. No groomsmen.

Just two people very much in love who would say their vows in front of family and friends. Ashley's parents were there. And her aunts and uncles and cousins, including Miranda and her husband. And of course, the Shaws.

The wedding march started, the traditional one that both Shane and Ashley wanted. Ashley's father walked her slowly down the aisle.

Her eyes were getting teary, and she saw her handsome groom, her Shane, surrounded by his girls, *her* girls too, swiping fast under his eyes. The twins were in their favorite play dresses, colorful leggings underneath. No one's hair was in a chignon, except Beatrice's.

Willow was out of her black boot, as was Ashley, and Violet's bangs had grown so long they had to be cut that morning so she wouldn't have to keep swiping them out of her eyes to see her dad get married.

She joined Shane in front of the minister's podium and then knelt down to hug each girl, who were beaming with happiness.

"Hi, Mama," Violet whispered.

"Hi, Mama," Willow seconded.

Last night, the girls had asked her what they should call her after the wedding. Mommy? Mama? Second Mommy? Ashley had told them they could choose. Shane had nodded.

"We want to call you Mama," they'd said together, holding hands.

She'd had to hold back tears, but she'd caught a tear slipping down Shane's cheek.

"Mama it is."

Now, as the minister began the ceremony, Ashley's heart was so full as they recited their vows.

And then they had their wedding kiss, Shane slightly dipping her, and there was cheering and clapping.

The new family of four walked back up the aisle, stopping to hug their relatives and friends.

They had a honeymoon to start, right here on the Mc-Cray Ranch, the four of them together. A family forever.

* * * * *

Her Second-Chance Family
Elizabeth Bevarly

MILLS & BOON

Elizabeth Bevarly is the *New York Times* and *USA TODAY* bestselling author of more than eighty books. She has called home such exotic places as Puerto Rico and New Jersey but now lives outside her hometown of Louisville, Kentucky, with her husband and cat. When she's not writing or reading, she enjoys cooking, tending her kitchen garden and feeding the local wildlife. Visit her at elizabethbevarly.com for news and lots of fun stuff.

Visit the Author Profile page
at millsandboon.com.au for more titles.

Dear Reader,

I've always been a sucker for books about high school sweethearts—possibly because I married mine almost forty years ago—so it was great fun when former adolescent lovebirds Alice and Finn, separated for more than a decade, showed up in my brain. And what a coincidence! They're doing home renovation just like my husband and I are! What are the odds?

Ahem.

Anyway, Alice and Finn have had a few more challenges to their romance than I and my high school sweetheart ever did. Small-town life can be rough when everyone knows everyone else—and everyone else's business. Maybe that's why old hurts and injuries linger longer and are harder to overcome, even in adulthood. And when a ghost from Finn's past that didn't include Alice walks into the picture…

Well. It won't be easy for the pair, that's all. But love never is, is it? One thing that's always a given, though (at least in the books I like), is that it does indeed conquer all. Even better, there's always enough love for one more. Especially a love that creates a family for people who never thought they'd have one again.

I hope you enjoy getting to know Alice and Finn—and Finn's daughter, Riley—as much as I enjoyed writing about them. And, as always…

Happy reading!

Elizabeth

DEDICATION

For David yet *again*.

I mean, it's a book about high school sweethearts after all.

Here's to becoming geriatric sweethearts, as well.

Chapter One

What was he doing here?

Alice Whitlock looked past the minister delivering her mother's graveside eulogy, at the big, blond, bearded man standing between a pair of skeletal maples. Not just any big, blond, bearded man, but literally the last one she thought she would see here: Finn Huxley. The trees were just beginning to bud, despite the spring solstice happening a week ago, and the sky behind Finn was gloomy with gray clouds. Between him and Alice stood a dozen mourners in black and gray, so the picture he painted wasn't exactly a welcoming one. Of course, the bleakness of the day and the jolt of her mother's death weren't the only things that made Finn less than welcome here. The fact that he'd been the cause of the most painful period in Alice's life might also have had something to do with it.

His gaze was as locked on her as hers was on him, but neither of them acknowledged the other in any other way. A shot of cold wind whipped a strand of auburn hair into her eyes, and she reached up automatically to tuck it back behind her ear. Reverend Cunningham asked everyone to pray, and Alice, thankful for a reason to look away, lowered her head. Though not before she noticed that Finn, even though he was staunchly irreligious, lowered his, too.

"Dear Lord," the minister began, "we pray you welcome our dearly departed Noreen into your loving arms."

Alice sighed inwardly. Nora. Her mother's name was Nora. Maybe the Reverend Mr. Cunningham had been hired for the occasion today, since her mother had been unaffiliated with any churches in the tiny Finger Lakes village of Sudbury, New York, but the least he could do was remember the name of the person they were laying to rest.

"Nora," Alice corrected him quietly, her head still bowed, since she'd had to interrupt a petition to the Almighty to do it.

The minister threw her a quick, apologetic look. "Nora," he continued, "was a woman who touched many lives—"

At this, Alice bit back a strangled sound. Her mother had touched exactly two lives during her time on earth—Alice's and Finn's. And neither had been left better off because of it. Alice didn't interrupt the minister to point this out, however. Chances were good that the handful of mourners attending already knew that, since the only way her mother had come close to touching their lives was by paying them for their services. Not a single member of the small party surrounding the open grave had been a friend or family member of Nora Whitlock's. Only Alice had been family. And no one in Sudbury had ever been her mother's friend.

"So let us all remember Nora Whitcomb in our prayers," the minister continued.

"Whitlock," Alice corrected him again, her head still bent.

The minister didn't miss a beat. "Mrs. Whitlock was—"

"Miss," Alice corrected a third time. Her mother had never been married, but she hadn't embraced the "rabid feminism"—her words, not Alice's—of the term *Ms.*, either.

"Ms. Whitlock was a true paragon of virtue," Reverend Cunningham went on…aaaand completely lost Alice after that.

Okay, she knew a funeral was supposed to be a somber affair and a time when the dead were remembered for what they'd contributed to the world they were leaving behind. She also knew that when it came to hiring a clergyperson for an event, you got what you paid for. Reverend Cunningham had been the most, uh, economical shaman in Sudbury that Alice could find. And since the inheritance her mother had left behind for her would only be awarded to Alice in dribs and drabs—even in death, Nora Whitlock would ensure that her daughter was controlled every minute of every day—it didn't allow her to spend frivolously. She'd been forced to embrace economy, even for something like her mother's final send-off—at least the parts her mother hadn't prepaid. So although Alice could correct the minister about the glaring mistakes, such as his erroneous use of her mother's name, it was probably best to just let him get on with his generic discount sermon. The sooner this was over with, the better.

Alice scarcely heard what he said in his prayer after that. Something something her mother's passing, something something her mother's transition to the light, something something her mother's final wishes for her daughter. Alice already knew what Nora Whitlock's final wishes were for her—that Alice would go straight home from the funeral and lock the door behind herself and never, ever, ever see or speak to anyone again and instead spend the rest of her life grieving for her mother and remembering every valuable lesson her mother ever taught her. Isolated and alone, she would marvel at just how fortunate—nay, how blessed—she was to have had such a mother to oversee her and protect her and guide her through life.

After all, Alice had no reason to do anything else, did she? That was something else her mother would have reminded her of, were Nora here right now. Thanks to her mother's foresight and good planning—and, of course, her unlimited concern for her daughter's well-being—Alice had everything she would ever need now that her mother was gone. A house to call her own on which she owed nothing. A car that was equally free of debt. And a trust fund with more than enough in it to cover any other essentials that might arise—food, utilities, taxes, health care and the occasional bit of modest clothing to keep her warm. All paid for directly by said trust fund, lest Alice get any ideas about spending Nora's money on anything that wasn't a necessity.

Honestly, Alice, what more could *you possibly ever need beyond those things?*

It was a question her mother had asked her often enough when she was alive. Even if she'd never once allowed Alice to answer it.

She looked down at the casket that had been lowered into the ground at her feet. The one made of solid mahogany that was trimmed with twenty-four-karat gold, lined in silk and piped with velvet, all preplanned and prepaid by Nora shortly after receiving her lymphoma diagnosis. That casket had probably cost her mother more than she'd spent on Alice over her entire lifetime. And Alice suddenly realized there was nothing to prevent her from answering her mother's question now that she was gone.

What more could I possibly ever need beyond that, Mother? Gee, I don't know. Maybe something in addition to the most meager requirements for the most basic existence? Maybe something that did a little more than allow me to wake up in the morning and slog through the day before turning off the light at night? Maybe something to...oh, I don't know...

grow my experiences? Broaden my education? Enrich my soul? Maybe something to, you know, make me happy?

Reverend Cunningham cleared his throat beside her, and Alice looked up. Everyone else had looked up, too, she noticed, so she knew she had completely missed the part of the prayer where everyone said *Amen*. If her mother had been here now, Alice would have never heard the end of it for letting her mind wander and causing her mother so much embarrassment.

Reverend Cunningham was extending a flower toward her, one he had obviously plucked from the easeled floral arrangement nearest him. A white carnation. It was only the second time in her life a man had given Alice flowers. Or, at least, *a* flower. The first time had been a carnation, too, but it had been a red one. A single red carnation given to her by Finn Huxley on Valentine's Day when they were both sophomores in high school. The junior class had been selling them as a fundraiser for the following year's prom. Alice still had the flower pressed between two pages of a copy of *1984* that had been assigned to her and Finn in English class the same semester.

There was a time when that red carnation had symbolized the beginning of something Alice had thought would be… Well. Something it wound up not being at all. This white carnation symbolized an ending. An ending she still couldn't quite fathom, either.

She took the flower from the minister and, after only a moment's hesitation, tossed it into her mother's grave. It bounced off the coffin and skidded a little, then fell into the dirt beside it. If her mother had been here now, Alice never would have heard the end of it with how much embarrassment that caused, too. The least she could do to honor the woman who had done *so much* for her was chuck a flower to the center of her casket with the precision of an NBA three-point shooter. *Honestly, Alice, how hard could it be?*

No one else present seemed to notice. They followed her example and cast their own flowers and fistfuls of dirt to join hers. Then, one by one, they filed by her to offer awkward condolences.

"Your mother was a good woman," Nora's accountant, Mrs. Delpy, said as she gave Alice's arm a passionless squeeze. "One of my favorite clients."

Alice didn't doubt it for a moment. What accountant didn't love a woman who showed up in her office every April 14 carrying a giant Wegmans shopping bag brimming with unorganized receipts, demanding that her taxes be figured while she waited?

"I'll miss seeing Nora out working in her garden," her mother's neighbor Hiram told Alice as he patted her shoulder.

Alice was sure. Especially the part about how her mother was always planting invasive species, like purple loosestrife and Japanese barberry, which encroached on Hiram's efforts to preserve the local habitat of the Finger Lakes and maintain a balanced ecosystem in his own backyard. *Oh, Alice, who cares if it's killing Hiram's angelica? You can find angelica anywhere in the Finger Lakes.*

"There was no one else in Sudbury like her," Mr. Stampley, the plumber, said as he patted Alice awkwardly on her other shoulder.

That, actually, was probably true. She doubted there were any other plumbers in town who were paid to be on call and commanded to come immediately—often long before or after regular business hours—every time a damp spot appeared on a floor anywhere in the Whitlock home. At least he'd been paid double time for a lot of those calls. Shame about him missing his son's graduation, though.

"I'm sorry I never met your mother," said yet another mourner, this one a newcomer to Sudbury, having lived there only since autumn. Bennett Hadden's family, however, had a long legacy here, having owned Summerlight, the Gilded Age mansion just outside of town, for more than a century. He'd inherited it after his great-aunt's death, along with Haven Moreau, a descendant of the house's original owner, and now they were rehabbing it with the hope of opening it as a hotel within the next year or so.

"I've heard a lot about Nora from Haven, though," Bennett added. "She sounds like she was one of a kind."

Alice hoped that was true. She wasn't sure the world could handle more than one Nora Whitlock.

"She was certainly that," Haven echoed from Bennett's side.

Haven *had* met Alice's mother a few times while working part-time for Finn, performing local repairs to earn some extra cash when she wasn't working to fix something at Summerlight. Not that Nora had been happy to even have one of Finn's employees in her house, mind you. But when there was a jammed chimney flue and single-digit temps and no power from a sudden ice storm, there were some things that could be overlooked.

"Sudbury won't be the same without your mother," Haven added before giving Alice a quick hug and moving on to make way for the next mourner.

No, Sudbury certainly wouldn't be the same without Nora. Alice truly couldn't imagine the tiny town without her. Couldn't imagine her life now without her. So many comments from Nora's fellow Sudburians today had been offered to Alice in an effort to be reassuring. Yet somehow, she felt anything but reassured. Despite that, she somehow managed to thank each of her mother's mourners and was even able to conjure a smile or two as they filed by. Mostly, though, she just looked at the man who was still standing between the two sugar maples, watching her.

What was he doing here?

Why had he come? There had never been any love lost between Finn and her mother. On the contrary, they'd hated each other. Her mother because she'd feared Finn would tempt Alice into doing things Nora would never approve of, and Finn because he'd known her mother would never allow Alice a moment's joy. They'd both had good reasons for feeling the way they had toward each other. And Alice had always been caught in the middle, never being enough for either of them.

The last of the mourners—Sylvia, her mother's hairdresser—gave Alice another perfunctory pat on the arm and told her she would miss her mother's laughter. Which was a nice thing to say, even if it wasn't true, either. Nora Whitlock had never laughed. She may have uttered a sound from time to time that resembled laughter to those who didn't know her well, but she'd never laughed. Alice thanked the woman anyway, patted her arm, too, for some reason, then looked for Finn again.

He was still there. He'd even worn black, something Alice hadn't quite been able to bring herself to do, instead opting for a pearl-gray dress threaded with the tiniest hint of red around the collar and pockets. If her mother had been here now, Alice never would have heard the end of it, wearing something so inappropriate for Nora's final send-off. Finn, though—whether out of respect or simply as a reflection of his mood—was dressed in black trousers and jacket paired with a shirt and tie the color of bittersweet chocolate.

The darkness of his clothing only highlighted the fairness of him otherwise. Even the dismal weather couldn't diminish the light that had always seemed to burn so bright and hot inside him. And although she couldn't note the color of his eyes from this distance, she was certain they were shining as blue and as clear as the waters of the Caribbean.

Not that Alice had ever been to the Caribbean. Not that she'd ever been anywhere outside the state of New York. She'd seen movies at Sudbury's sole movie theater and shows and films on TV. Lots of them. The farther away they took place from Sudbury, the better. And Finn Huxley's eyes had always reminded her of the Caribbean. Or maybe the Maldives. Or Greece. Or Hawaii. Or a million other places they'd always promised themselves back then that they would visit together someday. As soon as she was able to escape from the overbearing, suffocating, unrelenting grasp of her mo—

She halted the thought before it could form and turned her back on Finn to thank Reverend Cunningham. But she didn't even pay attention to the words that came out of her mouth. Instead, she realized she only continued speaking to the minister to give Finn a chance to approach and offer his condolences, too. For long moments, he didn't. Probably because he wasn't sure if he'd be welcome. Truth be told, Alice wasn't sure if he would be, either. Finn had barely spoken a word to her since his return to Sudbury a year and a half ago—not long after her own return to their hometown—when he'd come back to bury his father and ended up staying. Why should he say anything to her now? It wasn't as if she'd tried to talk to him, either. She hadn't even attended his father's funeral—her mother had forbidden it.

And now Nora was gone, too, off to wherever it was Leo

Huxley had ended up. Well, probably. Who knew, really, what lay beyond the grave? Wherever Nora and Leo were, though, it was a sure bet they weren't speaking to each other there, either.

Even though her mother's death hadn't exactly been unexpected—she'd actually outlived her cancer diagnosis by nearly a year—Alice had still been blindsided by her passing. And she still had no idea what she was supposed to do now. Her entire life, save for the few times she had managed to escape Sudbury—once for almost a full year— had been dedicated to her mother in one way or another. First trying to please her, then trying to atone for disappointing her, then taking care of her once her health fell into decline. Now that Nora was gone...

For some reason, that made Alice turn around to look at Finn again. But he wasn't standing between the sugar maples anymore. She glanced around frantically, but there was no sign of him anywhere. Almost as if he'd never been there at all.

And damned if there wasn't a part of her that wished that was the case. That Finn Huxley had never existed. That he'd never given her that red carnation more than a decade ago. That the two of them had never spoken at school. That he'd never lived in Sudbury in the first place. Or, at the very least, that when he left town after their high school graduation, he had stayed gone forever.

Unfortunately, there was a bigger part of her that wished differently. That he had been more patient with her. That he had tried harder to understand. That he had waited a little longer for her to figure things out. Or, at the very least, that he hadn't left Sudbury when they were both so confused and so wounded and so raw.

Yes, he was back now. Yes, things were a lot different than

they had been when they were teenagers. But in so many ways—in too many ways—nothing had changed at all.

As Finn Huxley tugged open his refrigerator to liberate an IPA with one hand, he jerked free the necktie from under his collar and unfastened the top three buttons of his shirt with the other. Then he wrenched off the bottle cap with a vicious hiss and lifted it to his mouth, emptying nearly half of it before lowering it again.

Why the hell had he gone to Nora Whitlock's funeral? The woman had hated him when she was alive, and the feeling had been more than a little mutual. He didn't care how awful that sounded. It was true. Feelings didn't change just because someone died. You didn't suddenly start forgiving and forgetting just because someone couldn't wreak havoc in your life anymore. Especially when what Nora had wreaked had gone way beyond *havoc*. That woman had straight up ruined lives. And she'd ground down her own daughter, day after day after day, until Alice was a near ghost of what she could have been had things gone the way they were supposed to go.

Which was another reason he shouldn't have gone to the woman's funeral. Finn had done everything he could to avoid seeing Alice since he'd come back to Sudbury, and he'd done a damned good job of it, especially in a town whose population had never exceeded four figures. Sure, running into her from time to time had been unavoidable— there was only one grocery store in Sudbury proper, one coffee shop, one bookstore, one liquor store, pretty much one everything—but he'd done his best to visit all of them only when he had to, and only during their slowest hours.

Mostly, that had worked. But not always. Sometimes, when he least expected it, he'd glance up after buying a six-pack of Lagunitas or a tall Americano, or he'd be screwing the cap back onto his gas tank or trying to decide whether he wanted the coconut or the peanut butter Kandy Kakes, and suddenly, right smack in the middle of his vision, there would be Alice. And just like that, the rest of the world would slip away, and all he would see was her, surrounded by that kind of gauzy light that came straight out of a bad melodrama, with a chorus of butt-naked cherubs strumming harps and singing psalms, and *dammit*, it would be all he could do to tear his gaze away and try to remember where he was and what he was supposed to be doing and, hell, what his frickin' name even was.

But today, he'd sought out Alice on purpose. Not the best idea he'd ever had. Even if, deep down, there had been, as always, that singular ribbon of joy that still wound through him whenever he did catch a glimpse of her around town.

It had always been that way with her, since the first day of kindergarten, when she'd walked into the Bluebird class and sat in the chair next to his. Even as a five-year-old, Finn had been smitten. He'd run home that day and told his parents that when he first saw Alice, hearts came out of his eyes like they did for the characters in his favorite cartoons. And he hadn't stopped being smitten throughout grade school, middle school and high school.

He could still remember being sick with nerves after buying her that carnation on Valentine's Day their sophomore year. But he'd been determined to give it to her and make her aware, once and for all, of his complete and utter adoration of her. And when she had confessed her mutual crush on him, he'd soared to heights he never would have thought possible. On that day, fourteen years ago, Finn had been certain his life would be perfect from that day forward. He had the love of Alice Whitlock. Nothing in his life could ever go wrong again. Nothing.

Except that everything had gone wrong. For both of them. And Alice had always blamed Finn for that, even though what happened had been no one's fault. It was hard to make sense of bad things happening to good people when you were a kid. Not that things like that made much sense as an adult, either. And when you had a mother like Nora Whitlock turning the screws, well, that just made an already terrible situation even worse.

But now Nora was gone. Maybe that was why Finn went to the funeral. To make sure it was true. To reassure himself that the woman who had done everything she could to make his and Alice's lives unlivable—not just when they were in high school, but since his return to Sudbury as an adult, too—was really gone. He didn't wish ill of the dead. But with someone like Nora, you kind of wanted to make sure you could finally close the door on them, once and for all.

He muttered a ripe expletive and downed another swallow of his beer. And he thought about how, in spite of the occasion and the bitterness of the day, Alice had looked radiant, her dark red hair a dazzling counterpoint to the cold, monochromatic scene at the cemetery. Spring was generally slow to come to the Finger Lakes, and the mood of the day was fitting. It would probably be a while before warmth and sunlight returned to Sudbury on anything more than a superficial level.

But that was okay. Spring meant there would soon be a lot of work for a guy like him—someone who could do just about anything that needed doing around the house or fix just about anything that needed fixing. He'd gotten that gift from his father, along with the old man's business after Leo passed. Huxley's Habitat, his father's home repair and rehab business—and now Finn's home repair and rehab business—had been the first job he ever had, starting when he was seven years old. After losing his mother to an aneurysm, he'd gone along with his father on all his fix-it jobs whenever he wasn't in school. He'd carried tools bigger than he was and crawled into spaces his father couldn't reach to report back on the condition of whatever project Leo was working on at the time. Fixing things was second nature to Finn at this point. Though some things, he knew from experience, defied repair.

That naturally made him think of Alice again. Did she feel as lost today as Finn had felt the day he buried his father? She was an only child like him, with no visible means of support in town. In his case, that was because he was only a second-generation Sudburian—his dad's family were all on the West Coast, and his mother had been estranged from hers. Alice's family, on the other hand— or, at least, Alice and her mother—had deeper roots in the community, like 99 percent of the town's population. But her mother had managed to alienate pretty much everyone in Sudbury. There couldn't have been more than a dozen people at the funeral today, two of whom Nora had barely known—Haven and Bennett, the new owners of the big mansion on the outskirts of Sudbury that was slowly but surely becoming a hotel. And they were probably only there because they were spearheading a project that would ultimately revamp the whole town, so they were doing their best to become a part of Sudbury, too.

They were also Finn's biggest clients at the moment, since spring was still too inclement for him to be taking on many home improvement projects of his own just yet. He'd spent most of his winter up at Summerlight, the Gilded Age mansion that Haven and Bennett had inherited from Bennett's great-aunt and were turning into a bed-and-breakfast. The place was coming along nicely, though it was still a ways away from being able to open. The new owners were hoping for a Christmas unveiling, which Finn guessed was possible, provided there were no hidden surprises lurking behind walls or under floors. So far, there hadn't been. But you never knew with buildings that were nearly a hundred and fifty years old. Even the ones that had been constructed at a time when things were built to last by people who had more than enough money to ensure their survival. Finn was just glad for the opportunity to work on such a place.

He glanced at his watch. It was coming up on two. He'd promised Haven he would stop by today after the funeral to help her finish drywalling what used to be the ballroom but was fast becoming a trio of luxury suites. It wasn't like he had any other pressing jobs lined up that he needed to do. Or, you know, any jobs at all. And man, did he want to shed the dress shirt and tie he'd driven all the way to Ithaca yesterday to buy when he realized he had nothing suitable to wear to a funeral. Even a funeral for a woman who'd messed up any chance for real happiness he might ever have.

Yeah, it'd be nice to slip into a little denim and flannel to make himself more comfortable. It would be even nicer to have something to do to take his mind off Nora Whitlock's funeral. And off Nora Whitlock herself. But most of all, off Nora Whitlock's daughter.

Hard work. Lots of it. Finn had learned when he was a kid that there were times when that was the only thing that made life bearable. And damned if he didn't feel like one of those times was hovering just this side of the horizon right now.

Chapter Two

If it was Wednesday, Alice thought upon opening her eyes a week after her mother's funeral, it must be baking day. Or was that Thursday this week? Wait, what day was it, anyway? She rubbed her eyes as she folded herself up in her bed and swung her feet to the floor. Tuesday. It was Tuesday, right? Her mother's funeral had been on a Wednesday, and it had been six days since. Hadn't it? She quickly counted in her head. Yes. It was Tuesday. So she didn't work at the bakery today. Today she was scheduled to work at the print shop. Even though Mr. Yao had told her to take some time off and wasn't expecting her in for another few weeks. Even later, if she felt like she needed more time. Mrs. Reyes at the bakery had told Alice the same thing. As had Mr. and Mrs. Kovac at the nursery, and had Cameron, the owner of Jack's Restaurant, where Alice picked up the occasional wait shift.

There had never been a lot of jobs in Sudbury when she was a teenager, so she had always had to pick up odd shifts here and there whenever and wherever she could find them. Back then, she'd needed to get out of the house whenever she could. At first, because she had to escape, even for a few hours, her mother's oppression. Later, it was because she'd genuinely needed the money. She and Finn had had plans back then, big plans. Until those plans were ripped away from both of them. Even after all that—

Well. Even after all that, Alice had kept working wherever she could, whenever she could. Because after that, she'd had even more things she needed to escape. Memories, feelings, a heart so broken, she didn't think it would ever mend. Her mother had thought she was being ridiculous—*Honestly, Alice, why do you want to work so much when you have a mother who gives you everything?*—but Alice hadn't cared. She'd worked until she'd saved enough to run away. Even if, at twenty-one—at least, she'd been twenty-one the first time she left town—she could scarcely be called a runaway. Leaving Sudbury—leaving her mother—even at that age, she had felt like a little girl running away from home. Just because her mother was dead now—

Her thoughts halted there. Her mother was dead. She still couldn't quite wrap her head around that. And she still didn't know what to do.

Coffee, she told herself. *Make a pot of coffee. Then pour a cup. Then add cream and sugar to it. Then drink it.* There. She had plans now. She'd figure out the rest of her life once she struck those things off her to-do list.

She expelled a sigh, tugged on the rag socks she'd tugged off the night before and made her way downstairs to the kitchen. Her mother's house—her house, she corrected herself—wasn't a large one, but it wasn't tiny, either. It would be a good starter home for some newly minted couple. Not that Alice would be starting anything like that herself, here or anywhere else. She was determinedly single and would stay that way forever. She'd tied herself to someone once, had been the half of a whole. Okay, yes, it had been exhilarating and wondrous and joyful. Until it wasn't. Until it was sad and miserable and awful. There was no way she was going to set herself up for something like that again.

Once she had her coffee poured and fixed the way she liked it, she sat at the kitchen table and looked out the window at a day that was just as gray and dreary as the day of her mother's funeral. She took her time sipping in the warmth, since she still had no idea what she was going to do after she'd checked that final *Then drink it* off her to-do list. She really wasn't all that keen to work her shift at the print shop today. But the alternative was hanging around the house, being constantly reminded of her mother and wondering what she was going to do now.

Pour a second cup, she told herself. *Then add cream and sugar to it. Then drink it.* There. She had more plans in place. *Oh, and get dressed.* That was something else she could do. And there was probably at least one load of laundry in the hamper. And she was getting low on a few things. Might have to make a trip to Hop-In-Hop-Out Grocery Store. See? All kinds of plans. Her life was lining up nicely.

Unfortunately, as she stood at her mother's front door an hour later—at her front door, she corrected herself—dressed in faded jeans and a pale lilac turtleneck, with the washing machine gurgling in the laundry room off the kitchen and a *very* short grocery list in her hand, Alice realized the last thing she wanted to do was venture out into public. Even if the possibility of running into Finn was slim—because he seemed to be as assiduous in his efforts to avoid her as she was to avoid him—there had still been the occasional chance encounter since his return to town. Encounters that had left her feeling skittish and breathless and…and…and other things she had no business feeling. Especially not for him. She'd barely gotten over seeing him at the funeral. Why court an incident like that again?

Which was how she found herself standing at the bottom of the front steps of Summerlight, Sudbury's resident historic home on the banks of Cayuga Lake. As surprised as Mr. Yao had been to see her show up for her shift at the print shop, he'd managed to find a few things for her to do. The last of which was dropping off a box of flyers for a job fair at Cornell University that Summerlight's proprietors were planning to attend in Ithaca in a couple of weeks.

It was her first time setting foot on the grounds of the estate, even having grown up within walking distance of it. There had been a time when Summerlight had been a regular field trip for Sudbury's sole elementary, middle and high schools, but that was before Alice was born. The mansion had been occupied when she was a kid, but old Mrs. Hadden, the owner, had been a major recluse who rarely opened her door to anyone. Over the last couple decades— for as long as Alice could remember, anyway—the place had fallen into disrepair and started to look like it was on its last legs. Then, about six months ago, after Mrs. Hadden died, the new owners—her great-nephew, and the great-great-great-whatever-granddaughter of Winston Moreau, the house's original owner, inherited it together.

That had been the talk of Sudbury when it happened, because the century-old feud between the Haddens and the Moreaus over ownership of the house had been legendary in these parts. Everyone in town had been taking bets over which one of the heirs would strangle the other in their sleep first, so deep had been the acrimony between the two families. Instead, much to everyone's surprise—even the two heirs, Alice would guess—Bennett Hadden and Haven Moreau had joined forces. More than joined forces. Word around town was that they'd fallen in love. That they were even talking about getting married once they finished turning Summerlight into a hotel.

Alice hoped the two of them knew what they were doing.

Not just the part about trying to turn a run-down house the size of a small sovereign nation into a hotel, but the part about getting married, too. No way would she undertake the rehab of a place this big and this dilapidated. And no, no, no, *no* way would she ever join herself to another human being permanently. That was just asking for trouble.

The mansion was even bigger close up than it looked from a distance, four towering floors of exhausted splendor in what she'd been told was French revival style. As she climbed the steps to the front door, she saw a note taped to it. On closer viewing, it read, *Doorbell's not working, and we're probably somewhere in the house where we won't hear you knock. But the door is unlocked, so come on in. Just make yourself known when you do.*

Well, alrighty then. Alice balanced the box of flyers in one hand and gave the knob a turn with the other. The door was indeed unlocked, so she pushed it open and entered.

Inside, the house was in better shape than its still-tired-looking exterior. From everything Alice had heard, the new owners still had a lot of work to do on the place before they would be able to open it as a hotel at the end of the year. From where she stood, though, the place was looking pretty good. They must have started in the foyer and been working their way out. The chandelier above her dripped with sparkling crystals, the floor beneath her feet was a creamy marble, and the staircase that wound to the second floor was nothing short of majestic. Antique furniture and accents that looked original to the place gave everything an aura of opulence and conspicuous consumption characteristic of the time the place was built. She couldn't imagine what it must have been like for this to be the private home for a single family. Of course, there probably would have been plenty of servants scurrying around back then, too, but still.

"Hel-looo?" she called out to the cavernous entry. "Anybody home?"

When she didn't receive an answer, she took a few more steps forward, until she had a better view of the upstairs and could look down the corridors spilling away on each side of the lobby. But the house was eerily quiet in every direction she checked.

"Hello?" she called again, a little louder this time.

Still no reply.

Having no idea where anything in the house was—seriously, she hoped they were planning to have one of those "You Are Here" maps for the place when it opened—she tucked the box of flyers under one arm and made her way down the hall to her left. But she didn't see anyone in any of the rooms she passed. Not even the one where there was a ladder unfolded under a wall painted halfway down, along with an open can of paint balancing a brush on its top.

"Hello?" she tried a third time as she made her way farther down the hall. "Is anybody home?" A little less loudly, she added, "Anybody who *isn't* the ghost of a conspicuously consuming Hadden family member who must have called this place home once upon a time?"

"No, just me."

Her stomach clenched at the response that came from behind her. Not because she feared the comment had come from a ghost of Summerlight. But because, even without turning around, she knew it had come from a ghost of her own past.

"Finn," she said quietly.

"Alice," he replied, even more quietly.

She made herself pivot to face him. He'd come out of the room with the ladder and paint she just passed, so he must have been doing something outside her view when she looked in there. He was dressed in faded jeans and a chambray shirt, and battered work boots covered his feet. All of them were spattered with a dozen different colors. Even his pale blond hair was dabbed with the dark blue-green he'd been applying to the walls. It was the first time since his return to Sudbury that she'd seen him alone and this close up. Barely five feet separated them. She'd been right about his eyes. They were still as blue and clear as the waters of a tropical paradise. The rest of him, though...

The dozen years that had passed since he left town showed on him. He was no longer a lanky boy of eighteen, but a man in every way. He was taller now, his shoulders broader. Although his waist was still trim, he had definitely filled out everywhere else. Physical labor did that to a person, and she knew he'd taken over his dad's business after Leo's death. She didn't know what he'd done for a living while he was living in wherever he landed after leaving Sudbury—as gossipy as the small town was, no one gossiped with Alice any more than they would have gossiped with her mother—but it was a safe bet he'd plied the same trade he did now.

The years of hard work showed on him. Not just in the physical fitness of his body, but in the changes to his face, too. It was the beard, mostly, that prevented him from looking like the boy she remembered. It was the same pale blond as his hair, full but well tended, giving him the air of a man much older than he was. Or maybe it was something else that did that. God knew Alice felt much older than she was these days, too. Finn was barely thirty. But he looked as if he'd been through more trials than someone twice his age. There was a hardness about him that hadn't been there before. A sternness. A telling lack of joy.

Finn Huxley hadn't exactly been the most carefree kid in

the world when he was young—losing your mom as a child rather prevented that—but he had been happy. At least he had been while the two of them were together. He'd made Alice happy, too. Evidently, the years since then hadn't been especially kind to either of them. Because the reflection looking back at her from her own mirror these days wasn't exactly that of a blooming young miss. She was only twenty-nine, but no one these days ever stopped to tell her how good she looked.

"You look good," Finn said.

She almost smiled in spite of the grudgingness in his voice when he offered her the compliment. He'd always been able to read her mind when they were young. When they first started dating, that had driven her mad. Toward the end, though, she'd found it kind of comforting. For a little while, anyway.

"You look good, too," she told him.

There was an awkward pause while they each took a quick inventory of the other. No, this Finn didn't look like he had a lot in common with the cute, funny, affectionate boy she remembered from high school. But this Finn, whoever he was, was no less appealing.

"I'm sorry about your mom," he said. "I know the two of you were, um…close."

She bit back the strangled sound that rose to the back of her throat and somehow managed to reply, "Thank you. And thank you for coming to the funeral, too. It was nice of you to honor her memory that way."

The way he was looking at her must have mirrored the way she was looking at him—as if they both knew the other was just trying to be polite and that not a word of what they said was genuine.

"How've you been otherwise?" he asked.

She expelled a long sigh. If she answered that honestly, they'd be here all day. So she only told him, "Fine." *Yeah, right.* "I've been fine. How about you?"

He looked no less eager to answer the question than she had been. But he echoed, "Fine. I've been fine, too." And he sounded no more convincing than she had.

There was another moment of silent consideration with both of them trying to figure out how they were supposed to act around each other now. *Good luck with that,* Alice thought on both their behalves. Especially since she was suddenly starting to feel like she was right back at Sudbury High School.

Finally, Finn told her, "I'm the only one at the house right now. Bennett had to be in Rochester for something today, and Haven's on an errand in the village. I'll try to help with whatever you need, though."

Alice pulled the box out from under her arm. "I just need to drop these off. They're some flyers Haven ordered for a job fair."

He took a step forward to accept them from her and, without thinking, Alice took a step in retreat. He halted immediately, but he didn't seem surprised by her reaction. Only resolved.

"I'm sorry," she immediately said. "I didn't mean—"

"It's fine," he interjected, holding up a hand to stop whatever she might say next. He took a few steps backward, until he was out of the middle of the hall and framed by the doorway of the room where he'd been working, clearing a path for her. "If you want to leave them in the kitchen, I'm sure Haven will find them there."

Alice wanted to apologize again, wanted to explain to him why she had recoiled the way she had. Problem was, she didn't know why she'd reacted that way. It had simply been instinctive to want to keep her distance.

So she only told him, "I don't know where the kitchen is."

"Right." He pointed in the direction from which she'd come. "Just go back down to the lobby and turn left. Go down the hall behind the stairway and keep walking to the end. Turn left, then right, then left again. You can't miss it."

Except that she probably would, because she'd barely heard a word he said. She'd been too caught up in noticing how his voice was different from what it used to be, too. Deeper, somehow, and steadier. And completely lacking the lightness and good humor that had always been there, no matter how dire the situation. Even after everything that happened, there had still been something in Finn's voice that lifted her spirits and made her think everything, eventually, would be okay.

If only it had been that easy.

He hooked his hands on his hips, as if he knew she'd be okay now that he'd told her how to find her way. But Alice was no better at finding her way these days than she'd been in high school. She was worse now, in fact. Because she didn't have her mother there, telling her what to do every minute of every day. And the fact that she was feeling so lost now, when what she should have been feeling was liberated, just made her that much more confused.

She tried to conjure a smile but worried it didn't quite make it. "I lost you at your first 'turn left.'"

He nodded philosophically. "Right."

"Right?" she echoed. "I thought you said left. See? Hopelessly lost, as always."

Surprisingly, she managed another smile after the quip, and this one almost felt genuine. Even more surprisingly, they both managed a chuckle. And for the tiniest, most exhilarating nanosecond, the entire world dissolved, and more than a decade fell away with it, and she and Finn were standing in the hallway at school laughing at something that had just happened in class or at lunch or the night before, and for that tiny, exhilarating nanosecond, Alice remembered what it felt like to be happy and hopeful and completely at peace with the world and oh, my God, how could she have forgotten what it was like to feel so incredibly content, as if nothing could ever—nothing would ever—go wrong again…

And then it was gone—all of it was gone—and she was smacked hard at the back of her brain with the realization that she would never, could never, feel that way again, and it was all she could do not to just hurl the box at Finn and run away. Again. The way she'd always run away—in one way or another—over the past twelve years whenever life became too much for her to bear.

Finn seemed not to notice her turmoil, because he continued to smile, albeit a bit sadly. He moved back out into the hallway and jutted his thumb over his shoulder. But all he said was, "Kitchen's this way."

He started walking before he was even finished speaking, so Alice hurried to catch up. She kept her distance, though, as they traveled, doing her best not to notice how Finn's backside was sturdier and more appealing these days, too. Instead, she focused on the rooms they passed as they made their way to the back of the house. None of them was finished, mostly in the sense that they had yet to be furnished, but all were clearly in better shape than they must have been when the new owners took over. There were still remnants of its neglected past in some of the rooms—bits of faded wallpaper here, a dulled light fixture there—but in other rooms, there were signs of new life in the forms of more cheerful colors and recently refinished wood.

Even though it was twenty times the size of her mother's house—her house, Alice corrected herself...again—Summerlight reminded her of it all the same. Nora's house—*her* house—had also fallen into disrepair, though more recently than the mansion had, and Nora's decorating taste had leaned toward Early Conspicuous Consumption. Her mother had been a meticulous housekeeper when Alice was growing up and had insisted on her daughter being that way, too. But after her health began to decline, she had begun to let things slide. When, two years ago, Alice had been forced for the last time to come home to care for her mother—this time, for good—she had been appalled at the state of both her mother and her home and ashamed of herself for not returning sooner.

She had picked up the slack as much as she could, but between returning to her odd jobs—even in her weakened state, her mother had berated and belittled her to the point where the smallest of escapes became necessary for Alice to maintain her sanity—and ferrying her mother to doctor's appointments and for treatments, it had been hard for her to keep up. And after a couple of particularly harsh winters, wet springs, a sweltering summer and wet fall, the house had deteriorated even more.

Alice had tried to hire help for the repairs, but Huxley's Habitat was the only home maintenance business in Sudbury, and her mother would have rather seen the house fall down around them than allow Finn to come within fifty feet of it. And no one in any neighboring communities wanted to come as far as Sudbury for what they considered small jobs. It was obvious, looking at Summerlight, that Haven hadn't been able to get anyone in any great number to come here to help so far, either. No one except for Finn.

Finn, who, she suddenly realized, had made all the right moves to bring them to the kitchen. Which was also still in a clear state of rehabbed/not rehabbed. The tiled floor was clean but cracked in places, and the plaster walls had noticeable patches. The ceiling was discolored in spots, and the appliances looked as if they belonged in the Smithsonian. She was again reminded of her mother's house—*her* house—whose kitchen was also exhausted and obsolete. The whole house was exhausted and obsolete. Had she been thinking that morning that the place would be a good starter home for someone? Now she was thinking otherwise. It needed far too much work for anyone to be interested in buying it. Especially since there was little reason for anyone to want to move to Sudbury in the first place.

Though now that Haven and Bennett were rehabbing Summerlight, and now that they'd made clear they wanted to rehab all of Sudbury when they were through, new businesses—and new people—would probably come to town. It wouldn't be long before the hotel was up and running, hopefully bringing in some decent tourism. More workers in town meant more people buying places to live there. Maybe there would be an opportunity for Alice to sell her mother's house—*her* house—after all.

That thought brought her up short. Just when had she started thinking about selling her mother's house? *Her* house, she reminded herself *again*. Oh, who was she kidding? The house she currently lived in would always be *her mother's house*. Even if Alice legally owned it now—hell, even if she sold it to someone else—she would always consider it *her mother's house*. The house where she had grown up had simply never felt like hers. Because she'd never felt welcome in it. Even the thought of walking past it if—when—it belonged to someone else filled her with a sense of dread. So really, there was no reason for her to keep it. There was no reason for her to stay in Sudbury at all.

She could leave again, she realized suddenly. And this time, she wouldn't have to come back. Ever. She could go anywhere she wanted now. She wouldn't have to sneak out under cover of darkness while her mother slept and take a bus or train to the end of its line to find work there doing whatever she could for as long as she lasted until her mother wore her down and guilted her enough to come home again. She wouldn't have to be a file clerk at the state archives in Albany until her mother had a fall down the stairs that broke her hip and landed her in home rehab. She wouldn't have to sell cheap souvenirs in Niagara Falls until her mother had to have her gall bladder removed and was in need of a caregiver for a while. And she wouldn't have to serve après-ski martinis and hot cocoa at a resort in the Adirondacks until her mother's cancer diagnosis.

She really had done her best to escape Sudbury the same way Finn had once she'd regained the presence of mind and the financial means to do it after everything that happened. But she'd never been as strong as he was, and she'd always come running back when her mother needed her. *Who else is there to take care of me, Alice? And after all I've done for you, feeding you and clothing you and housing you and keeping you safe from all the terrible things and terrible people out there in the big, bad world? Honestly, Alice, the very least you could do is come home for a few months when I need you.*

Needed her. Right. As if Nora Whitlock had ever actually *needed* anyone but herself. She could have hired in-home care easily enough. She could have checked herself into rehab until she healed. Even with her cancer diagnosis, Nora could have simply hired a professional to manage her care rather than Alice. Somehow, though, she'd always been able to convince her daughter to care for her instead. Alice owed her, after all. It was the least she could do after the many, many, *many* ways and times her mother had helped her throughout her entire life.

Honestly, Alice, you'd be nothing without me.

This time, when Alice left Sudbury, she'd be able to go as far as she wanted and for the rest of her life. This time, she wouldn't have to live in dread, waiting for the moment when her mother found her and cajoled her into coming home. This time, she wouldn't feel like she had to hide herself away, never doing anything to draw attention to herself, like going out or living large or making friends. This time, she could do and be whatever she wanted.

And this time, she would never have to come back.

Wow. Nothing like having an epiphany when one least expected it. Alice did her best to shake her thoughts off for now. Plenty of time for soul-searching later. Plenty of time for planning an entire future she never tried to envision before, since it had genuinely never occurred to her that she might someday have a future to plan. Or, at least, a different future from the one she and Finn had planned, once upon a time.

There was a small table and chairs tucked into one corner of the kitchen that looked as if they were regularly used, so she moved in that direction to set the box of flyers on it, where Haven would be sure to see them. Job now accomplished, Alice turned around to leave and found herself facing Finn again.

Finn, who was suddenly stirring a lot of thoughts in her brain, a brain she had managed to mostly purge of thinking for the last week, and luring her right back into epiphany territory. Because the thoughts he was inciting were ones that wanted very much to invade her plans. Plans she hadn't even had a chance yet to consider. Plans she wasn't even sure she should be making. Plans that, if her mother were here now, Nora would have squashed with the same quickness and repulsion she would have shown squashing an insect.

Plans that might, once they were complete, put Alice in a place where she didn't feel so lost anymore. Or at least, not lost in the way she'd felt lost for so long. Her entire life, really.

"Finn," she said before she could stop herself. "Is there a chance your schedule might be open in the near future? I could really use your help."

Chapter Three

Finn told himself he must have misheard Alice's question, since she hadn't even said hello to him after finding him in the hall, so how could she need his help with anything? Then again, he hadn't said hello to her, either, had he? Hellos were for people who were happy to see each other. People who shared nothing but fond memories of each other. People who wanted to sit and chat for a bit. Of course neither of them would have said hello to the other. Which made it all the weirder that she was asking for his help now. People didn't ask for help from people who made them uncomfortable.

But she was looking at him with such earnestness and expectation that that must have been what she'd asked him for.

She really did look good. Even though the passage of time showed on her face in the form of too much lost weight and a too-forced smile and too-shuttered eyes, she was still... Hell, she was as beautiful as the first day he told her he loved her. Her dark auburn curls were dancing around her shoulders the way they had in high school, and her eyes—the gray-green of sage—were as pale and clear as he remembered. He'd always lost himself in those eyes. They were so different from anyone else's he'd ever meet. Not just their color, but because he was always able to read everything about her just by gazing into them. Alice Whitlock had been an open book when they were kids. Since he'd come back to Sudbury, though, Finn hadn't been able to read her at all. She'd put up more than enough barricades to let him know to keep his distance. How could she be standing here now, asking for his help?

Just to be sure, he asked, "Help?"

"Yes," she assured him without hesitation. "Help."

"Me?"

"Yes. You."

Although he told himself it would be better not to ask, he asked anyway. "With what?"

She expelled a sound that was a mixture of fatigue, contrition and longing. For a moment, she didn't say anything, but her gaze roved around the kitchen before finally settling on him again. She studied him so intently, he could almost feel it. Then she twisted her hands anxiously together in front of her.

"This house is coming along nicely," she said. "Well, not so much the kitchen, but the rest of it where you've been working is starting to look really beautiful. You're doing a good job with it."

Not sure what that had to do with anything, Finn said, "Thanks."

"I mean, it's mostly you doing all the work right now, right? You and Haven? I know she has a lot of experience with rehabbing houses, too. She did a great job on the repairs she made for my mother."

Still not sure where she was going with anything, Finn nodded. "She has a rehab business of her own on Staten Island. I mean, it's on hold right now, while she and Bennett are up here with Summerlight for the year, but yeah. It's just she and I right now. She's actually done more work than I have. But she's got some family coming in to help once spring is further along and the weather's more predictable. And she's making arrangements with a crew in Ithaca to come up for some of the big jobs this summer."

That last bit of info seemed to hearten Alice. "So then you might have some time for other projects in the not-too-distant future?"

Finn hooked his hands on his hips and shifted his weight to one foot. Where the hell was she going with this?

"I might," he said. "Depends on the project."

At this, she seemed to lose steam. "Oh."

"Alice, what is it exactly that you want from me?"

And if there was ever a more loaded question in the history of loaded questions, Finn didn't know what it was.

"I need your help," she told him again.

"So you've said. With what?"

"My mother's house," she finally told him. "I want to fix it up so I can put it up for sale."

Her comment shouldn't have surprised him. Now that her mother was gone, it made sense that Alice would want to put that part of her life behind her. He knew she'd never felt at home in her house and had wanted to be out of it whenever she could be. There had been so many times when she sneaked out without her mother knowing. Days and nights both, going back to long before the two of them started dating. He remembered, more than once, being out somewhere with his friends and seeing Alice with a couple of hers, only to have her mother march into wherever they were all having fun and literally drag her out by her arm. All the while reminding Alice she wasn't allowed to be out until after her chores were done, then listing enough chores to keep an entire staff of housekeepers busy and *Honestly, Alice, how could you keep disappointing me this way when I do* so much *for you?*

By the time she and Finn started dating, though, Alice had learned to elude her mother pretty well. She only left the house during the day after her mother went out, and she never stayed gone for long. And on those nights when they made plans for Finn to meet her in the backyard, she left her window open after climbing out of it, and they never went far enough that she wouldn't be able to hear her mother calling for her, should Nora wake up. There had been so many nights when the two of them disappeared into the corner of her backyard that abutted the alley behind it, lying between the cobblestoned wall and the big rhododendron, gazing at the stars and talking about whatever was on their minds. The book they were reading in English. The latest movie playing at Cayuga Theatre. How to get past the toughest bosses in the hardest games.

All the adventures they would have together once they were old enough to leave Sudbury and backpack all over the world.

So lost was he in his memories that Finn didn't even think about the repercussions when he asked, "How big of a project are we talking about?"

Last fall, after Haven and Bennett had first come to Summerlight, but before they'd made the decision to turn the mansion into a hotel, Haven had come to Finn looking for part-time work for herself to sustain her while she would be in residence there. Something about the conditions of their inheritance required her and Bennett to reside in the mansion for a full year before they could actually own it. Finn had sent her to Alice's house, because he'd known there were some small jobs there that needed doing that Alice hadn't been able to get anyone outside of Sudbury to do but that her mother had forbade him from doing. He hadn't exactly pumped Haven for information about the two women upon her return from those jobs, but he'd naturally wanted to know how Alice, especially, was doing.

Haven had been cagey in her replies, since she wasn't the type to gossip, but he'd gotten the impression that Nora wasn't in good shape, Alice was being run ragged caring for her, and the house, although sturdy, needed a lot more help than Haven was able to give it in the perfunctory visits Nora dictated. So Finn could imagine Alice's "project" could potentially turn into a fairly major undertaking.

"Not a lot," she said. Almost convincingly, too. "Haven has taken care of the worst problems. The house mostly just needs updating and cosmetic work. Make it look prettier and less tired. More appealing to anyone who might be interested in buying it. It would be a great starter home," she hurried on. "Perfect for someone who wanted to start a famil—"

Here, she halted suddenly, looking dashed by the comment she had been about to make. Finn understood completely. The word she'd been about to say was one he avoided using at all costs, too. Because there had been a time when he and Alice had been anticipating the start of a family. A time when there had been a life growing inside her that, although unexpected, and maybe not particularly well timed, had offered a promise of a new life for the two of them—for the three of them—together in a way that would join them together forever. Maybe it hadn't been under ideal conditions, but they'd made plans. A lot of plans. And then, when she lost the baby just after four months—

"A great starter home," she backpedaled, thankfully jerking Finn out of the past and back into the present. "Perfect for a young couple who've just gotten marri—"

Here, she stopped without finishing again. And again, Finn understood. That was a word he tried to avoid these days, too. Because that was another one of the plans they'd made when they were kids.

"Anyway," she hurried to finish, "I don't think it would be anything too invasive or time-consuming. Just a small project."

Spoken like every layperson who'd ever set out to do some kind of home improvement. *Congratulations, Alice. You've just ensured that your "small project" will become a massive undertaking.*

Nah, Finn tried to reassure himself. *It will probably be fine.* He didn't believe in jinxes. Not really. Bad frickin' luck, sure. But not jinxes.

He blew out a restless breath, then did something he knew he shouldn't do. "Maybe I could have a look at the place, and you can tell me what exactly you have in mind."

"Mostly cosmetic," she assured him again. "A little plumbing, maybe. A little electrical. A few replacements and a little updating what's already there. And then painting and maybe redoing the floors. That kind of thing. I just need to sell the place. Get out of Sudbury and go somewhere else. I need a fresh start."

A fresh start, he echoed to himself. Away from Sudbury. Something she'd already tried to do—more than once, from what Finn had heard—and never made work. But that was probably because she'd never been able to get out from under her mother's thumb while Nora was alive. Nora had had a pretty big thumb, after all. So maybe Alice could make it work this time. Maybe she really could start a new life in a new place. Just because Finn had tried that himself after high school, and just because he'd failed miserably at it, didn't mean Alice couldn't make it work. All she needed was a little help from Finn to do it.

If irony were a high school bully, Finn would have his

head in a toilet right now, getting a swirly to end all swirlies. Had things worked out the way they were supposed to back in high school, he and Alice would have gotten a fresh start together. They'd be living a new life now. In a new town. With a new home. And a daughter who would be turning twelve in September. And maybe another one or two that joined the family after her. A red-haired boy who read one book after another like his mother. A blonde girl who could quote hockey stats better than Finn could himself.

He halted the forbidden thoughts in his head before they could turn into feelings in his heart. Suffice it to say, there had been a time when he and Alice had planned for a new everything together. Now she wanted to try it again. Only this time, it would be without him. Why that bothered him so much, Finn couldn't say. It had been more than a decade since their future together became a past. A decade when the two of them hadn't even seen each other, let alone talked. He understood completely why she wanted to put some distance between herself and Sudbury. It was exactly what he'd done after graduation. He told himself he should be happy to help her. Let her find the opportunity to turn things around in her life the way he'd tried to do in his. Just because he'd come full circle back to Sudbury didn't mean she would do the same. In fact, he had a feeling that once Alice left town this time, she would well and truly stay gone. Forever.

Which maybe was another reason he should help her. Put some distance between the two of them again, and this time make it permanent. 'Cause God knew ever since Finn returned—and ever since he'd seen Alice upon her own most recent return—he'd been wondering if maybe he should turn right back around and take himself back to Philadelphia, regardless of the mistakes he'd made there.

He blew out another one of those errant breaths and cupped his hand over his nape, rubbing at a nonexistent ache there. "Look, why don't I come over tomorrow, and we can talk more about it. You do a walk-through beforehand and make a list of everything you'd like to have done. We'll see how doable it is."

He thought she would smile at the offer, or at least look relieved. Instead, for some reason, she looked kind of terrified. Somehow, though, he got the impression it wasn't him she was terrified of. Just what it might be, though...

"Thanks, Finn," she said, in spite of her obvious anxiety. "I appreciate it."

He nodded, but he was starting to feel a little anxious, too. Although the two of them had seen each other nearly every day for almost two years when they were kids, he'd never been inside Alice's house. Nora's house, really, even if it did legally belong to Alice now. Maybe that was why. Nora had done a number on both him and Alice when she was alive. Even in death, the woman was more than a little intimidating.

Which was really the main reason Finn needed to help Alice out. If he still felt this cowed by her mother, he could only imagine how Alice felt. She really did need to start anew, with or without him, if she had any hope of ever being happy. And there would always—always—be a part of Finn that wanted to see Alice happy.

With or without him.

When Finn knocked at the front door the following afternoon, Alice was immediately beset by the same befuddled butterflies that used to buffet her belly every time she saw him when they were kids. For all the good times the two of them shared back then, those times had never been free of her fear, sometimes profound, that her mother would find out what was going on between them and put a brutal end to it. Even though there was no way that would happen now, old habits—and old fears—died hard.

Opening the door to find him on the other side only compounded her misgivings. Once again, she was struck by just how beautiful he was, even with the beard that still seemed so alien. She'd never much been attracted to men with facial hair, but on Finn... Well, Finn wore it well, even with the faint lines bracketing his mouth making him look wearier and more cautious now. His eyes, though...

She bit back an eloquent sigh. Although lines fanned out from his eyes, too, and although they were shadowed, she could still see hints of the playful, funny, gentle guy she fell so irrevocably in love with as a teenager. Maybe it had been a while since Finn had felt or been any of those things, but they were still inside him, somewhere.

She knew that, because the girl she had been before still lived inside her, too, despite her efforts to suppress her. She'd been such a timid, anxious, fearful kid. In a lot of ways, she'd been the antithesis of Finn Huxley. It was kind of amazing, really, that the two of them had ever gotten together in the first place, never mind stayed together as long as they had. At least until tragedy tore them apart.

"Hey," he said, chasing her memories back into the darkest parts of her brain, where they belonged.

"Hi," she replied. Another awkward moment ensued, until she remembered he had come here at her invitation because she needed his help. "Come on in," she added.

She took a step backward and opened the door as wide as it would go. Finn hesitated just long enough to remind her that, in spite of their intimate past, he'd never been inside the house she'd lived in virtually her entire life.

Eventually, though, he crossed the threshold and came inside. Though not without clear reluctance. She closed the door behind him and did her best to quell the terror that her mother might come home and discover him there. Her mother wasn't coming home again, ever. This was Alice's house now. She could make her own rules. And rule number one, she told herself, was that there were no rules. Her mother had made enough of those when the place was hers to last both their lifetimes.

Finn's gaze immediately began to rove about the living room, though whether that was because he'd been thrown back in time, too, or was already assessing what needed to be done to the place, Alice couldn't say. She adjusted her own perception to look at the room from his eyes, since she'd stopped seeing the house decades ago as anything more than the building where she lived. Her mother had settled on the furnishings before Alice was born and hadn't changed a thing in all that time. The colors were pretty dingy by now, the furnishings out of date. And, truth be told, all of it was kind of gaudy. As if the person who chose everything had been striving for cheerful and fun, but had really had no idea what either of those things truly was. Even if Alice hadn't intended to sell the place, she would have changed everything.

Finally, Finn's gaze lit on hers again. "You realize there's *a lot* to do," he said.

She nodded. "I know. But like I told you the other day, it's mostly cosmetic. It won't be that hard or expensive to fix, right? I just want to make sure there's nothing major underneath the, uh, inelegance."

He smiled at that. "Well put."

She smiled back. "Thanks."

"Doesn't look too bad so far."

No, it didn't, other than the color scheme and over-the-top furniture. Just stale and old-fashioned and in need of some actual cheer. The same way Alice's mother had always been. The same way Alice herself felt these days.

"Living rooms usually aren't that worn out, though," Finn added. "Ironically, a lot of times, they're the least lived-in room in the house for some people. And there's no plumbing to worry about. Not much electrical to go wrong. This one probably mostly just needs paint and cleaning."

Alice gritted her teeth. "Yeah, sorry about the clutter." And the dust. And the grime. And the neglect. "The last few months with my mother were pretty demanding. I wasn't able to stay on top of the cleaning like I should have."

"No apology necessary," Finn assured her. "I can only imagine what you've been through since she got sick."

Alice nodded quickly and gestured toward the kitchen. "If you want to check some plumbing, it'll be this way."

Finn followed her though the dining room into the kitchen, making a quick survey of the former as he went. He did a perfunctory check of the sink and appliances and everything else, offering encouragement that she hadn't jinxed herself yesterday, after all, since on first look, everything seemed fine. They surveyed the rest of the first floor—a half bath, two closets and a sunroom—until Alice ended the tour at her mother's bedroom. The door to that room was closed, as it had been since the day she returned to the house after taking her mother to the hospital that final time. She'd come home after her mother's death had been called and had gone straight to this room, to strip all the bedding for washing, then to dust, vacuum and quickly tidy what she could. Then, as she'd left the room, she'd closed the door behind her with a soft *click* that still echoed in her brain. She had no idea why she'd done that. Her mother had never closed her bedroom door when she was alive. Never. She'd always needed it open to keep an eye on the place. And on Alice.

Alice hadn't opened that door since, and for some reason, she really dreaded opening it now. So it was with a moment's hesitation that she finally gripped the knob. It was with a longer moment's hesitation that she turned it. And it was with no small effort that she pushed the door inward.

She was genuinely surprised to find the room exactly as she had left it. Not that she expected her mother's specter to be standing at its center giving her a stern look, but there still seemed to be something of Nora Whitlock lingering in the air. Not the enduring fragrance of Chanel No. 5, the only perfume her mother ever wore, and not the leftover miasma of what cancer and chemotherapy had done to her body. Both of those smells, Alice was certain, were just her imagination. But there was still *some*thing there— something just as unpleasant. An encumbrance of oppression and rigor and demand for protection and—

And now she remembered. That was why she had closed this door and never opened it again.

"Your mom's room," Finn said. Not asked. Said. As if he recognized something in the space that was immediately identifiable as Nora, too.

Alice nodded, but remained mum.

Finn drove his gaze around the room, at the cabbage rose wallpaper, the French provincial furnishings, the reproductions of popular rococo paintings, the sultanate period Turkish rugs. Nora was nothing if not a mixer of decor from luscious time periods—the more ornate, the better. Had Alice remade the bed after washing everything, it would have been covered by velvet Victorian paisley.

Finn returned his gaze to meet Alice's. "Nothing a little nitro and acetylene wouldn't take care of."

She almost smiled at that, because she knew he was speaking less about the over-the-top interior design than he was of the lingering remnants of the woman it represented.

If only it were that easy, she wanted to say. Instead, she muttered, "Mother did enjoy her luxuries."

He looked as if he wanted to reach out to her then, and damned if there wasn't a part of Alice that wished he would. But he only offered her some quiet reassurances about how the downstairs of the house seemed sound enough on first consideration, and she probably wouldn't be faced with any major problems, then asked to see the upstairs, too. So up they went, down the hall, past the second bathroom, two more closets, and a guest bedroom that had never been used—since Nora Whitlock had never had any guests—to the room at the end of the hall, the smallest one in the house.

Alice told herself she didn't deliberately save her bedroom until last, but she did kind of deliberately save her bedroom until last. It was just that, like the rest of the house, her room hadn't changed at all since she was a child. Her mother had kept it as it was after Alice left that first time, even though Alice had assured her then that she was never, ever coming back. Then, when Alice did come back, she hadn't changed it herself, either, because she hadn't wanted to give her mother the impression that she would be staying any longer than she had to.

Not that her mother would have allowed her to change it anyway. Nora had furnished Alice's bedroom before she was born and intended for it to stay that way forever. Every effort Alice had made to change it had been met upon her return home from school the next day with its restoration to Nora's liking, and the reminder from her mother of *My house, my rules*, which had sometimes been punctuated with an additional, *My daughter, my rules*.

The door to her room was closed, too, though Alice had no idea why she closed it, other than the fact that her mother had insisted on having it open when she was a girl. Alice had hated the lack of privacy, but now she had nothing but privacy, regardless of the position of the door. Yet she continued to close it, a small act of defiance of her mother that should bring her some measure of satisfaction but instead somehow only reminded her of how very alone she was now.

As Alice opened the door to that room, she couldn't help thinking how opening it to allow Finn entry was the greatest defiance of all. Her mother must be spinning in her grave already, to have her daughter inviting into her bedroom the man who had been the boy who had almost—almost—been successful in spiriting her daughter away forever.

Where Finn hadn't entered her mother's room at all—neither of them had—he strode into Alice's after only a small hesitation. But he stopped mid-stride only a couple of steps in.

"This is your room?" he asked.

"Yeah," she replied simply.

He gave the space another perfunctory glance around. Perfunctory because there wasn't that much to take in. The cream-colored walls—at least, her mother had always referred to the color as *cream*; Alice had always referred to it as *cadaverous*—were completely bare. Well, save for a single eight-by-ten photograph of Nora smiling benevolently—or perhaps she was grinning smugly—over the room. The twin bed was draped with a faded pale yellow coverlet, its maple headboard the same plain style as the lone dresser and nightstand. There was a small lamp on the latter and a smaller catch-all tray on the former—which had never really caught anything, since Alice had been forbidden to accrue anything that hadn't been Nora-approved, and her mother had approved of very little. The only decoration to be found was a faint—very faint—floral motif in an area rug at the center of the floor, one that wasn't large enough for her to move from one corner of the room to the other without having cold feet.

Since her mother's death, Alice had added a single item to the sparse collection—a paperback mystery. And she would be lying if she said she didn't have to battle some guilt over that. She'd only been allowed to read in the living room when Nora was alive, so that Nora could keep an eye on her daughter's reading material. Alice would never forget her mother's disapproval upon discovering a copy of *Teen Vogue* hidden in the air vent behind the dresser.

Honestly, Alice, don't you know how badly trash like this will rot your brain? Here. Read this instead. I loved The Scarlet Letter *when I was your age.*

She could tell Finn was doing his best to be diplomatic when he continued, "It's, um… Not what I would have expected. I mean, it's not really you, is it?"

She expelled a restless sigh. "I tried to make it mine a couple of times," she told him. "Once I hung up a Zac Efron eight-by-ten I got in return for writing a letter to his fan club, but my mother took it down while I was at school and replaced it with that photo of herself. Another time, I bought a jewelry box and a few pairs of earrings from a thrift store, and that was when the catch-all showed up instead. My mother had a thing about containers. She always wanted things in plain sight."

Which didn't account for why her mother had taken the earrings, too. She'd taken those because she'd told Alice she was much too young to wear jewelry. At fifteen.

Finn nodded. "Yeah, I can see why you'd give up personalizing the place after that."

"For a long time," Alice continued, "I did have some success in at least collecting things that I could use in my apartment someday when I moved out on my eighteenth birthday." Though she wondered what had possessed her to share something like that with Finn, since it added nothing to the information he needed for doing home rehab. "Even so," she continued almost helplessly, "I hid it in a box in the back of my closet under a pile of sweaters and T-shirts. But she eventually found that, too. God knows what she did with it all."

At this, Finn smiled a bit. "What kind of things?"

She crossed her arms over her midsection and told herself it wasn't a defensive gesture. Just a reserved one. She told herself to change the subject and get back to talking about the needs of the house. But it felt so good to be talking to someone besides her mother again—to be talking to Finn again—that she couldn't quite make herself do it.

"For a while, when I was thirteen or fourteen, after I started picking up babysitting gigs—Mother didn't have a problem with me developing a work ethic, as long as she knew who I was sitting for—I went to yard sales and estate sales or I'd find things online on those buy-nothing sites. Anything that caught my fancy. I had a lot of those little metal souvenirs people bring home from their vacations—a Big Ben and a Burj Khalifa and a Taj Mahal. I had an Argentinian *aguayo* and this cool batik coverlet from Java I wanted to use for wall hangings. Some of those Russian nesting dolls and a Japanese tea set. A ton of postcards from all over the place. That kind of thing."

"A collection of other people's travels," he said.

She nodded. "They were placeholders for me until I could gad about the world collecting my own."

Which, of course, she never did. Strangely, she probably could have afforded to at some point. Travel could be done on a shoestring if one knew the ins and outs. And Alice did. She'd spent so much time on the computer at the library when she was a teen, googling how to move around Europe and Asia and South America in exchange for work or services or just by paying near pennies for accommodations and meals. The few times she had managed to escape from Sudbury, she'd been able to save enough to cover airfare someplace, at least. She'd figured once she was on the ground in another country, she could work out the rest. She'd even gotten a passport once she turned eighteen.

But she hadn't done any of those things. Her passport had expired, having gone completely unused. She hadn't even traveled beyond the boundaries of New York State. Every time she'd gotten close to the borders of Vermont or Massachusetts or even Toronto, she'd become physically sick at the thought of crossing one of them. It was as if her mother had had her on an electronic leash that could zap her insides if she tried to go too far without Nora's permission.

"And now you can go gadding about the world all you want," Finn said.

She nodded. That was the plan. Except somehow, the prospect of doing that now didn't feel quite as exciting as it had once upon a time. Not like when she and Finn had planned to do that together.

She pushed the thought away, along with so many others that tried to fight their way into her brain just then. "So you've had the complete tour of the house," she said. "What's your prognosis?"

He cupped a hand around the back of his neck, a gesture she remembered from their time together. It meant he was about to say something he was hesitant to say but that had to be said nonetheless. Like *Alice, your mother is gaslighting you. She's been gaslighting you your entire life.* Or *Alice, you have to stop letting your mother make you feel like you don't deserve to be happy. You deserve to be happy.* Or *Alice, stop saying you're nothing without your mother. The reason she has her hooks in you so deep is because she knows* she's *nothing without* you. Or—

"Alice, there's not a lot to do, but there's *a lot* to do. If you know what I mean."

For one frantic moment, she thought he was talking about the two of them, and something in her heart took flight. It was only then that she realized how very much she wished she *could* work on things with Finn. How much she wished she could try again with him. How much she wished they could be together the way they had been before. Only it would be better this time. Because the fear of being caught by her mother would be gone this time. And because they were both on their own now so they could focus on each other. And because the mistakes they had made were in the past. And so was the tragedy. They could start fresh. Build something different from what they'd had before, but no less loving and happy.

Oh, how she wished they could do that. Could he possibly want that, too? Was there any way that maybe they could?

Then she realized he was talking about repairing the house, not what the two of them had once had together. As much as she might wish for it, deep down, she feared there could be no rebuilding for them.

When she didn't reply, he continued, "The house is in decent shape from what I've been able to see so far. But there are going to be a lot of projects to complete if you want to get it into sellable shape. I'd recommend painting every wall and every inch of trim. Refinishing all the floors, too. You're gonna want new countertops in the kitchen, since the linoleum in there is pretty beat up—butcher block is kind of popular right now and not too expensive—and you should replace the vinyl flooring in there since it's not in great shape, either. Tile or laminate—either one could work. Same goes for the floor in all the bathrooms. And I'd suggest replacing the old vanities in them with new ones or even pedestal sinks."

He continued listing improvements that were as easy and economical as he could make them. Then, after a thoughtful pause, he quoted her a guesstimate for what it might all cost. The number was high, but not impossible. The trust her mother had created allowed for withdrawals for home repairs. All in all, what Finn quoted her, even if it was just an estimate for now, seemed fair to her and was certainly affordable.

"Would you be able to fit all that into your schedule?" she asked.

He lifted one shoulder and let it drop, another gesture she remembered well. "If you don't mind it taking a few more weeks than it might otherwise."

"I'm not in any hurry," she assured him. Then she was surprised to realize that she really wasn't. Which was odd, because she'd kind of been planning her next exit from Sudbury ever since her most recent return.

He blew out an errant breath and drove his gaze around her bedroom again. Then he nodded. "Okay then. I'll double-check with Haven to see what she needs from me up at Summerlight between now and when her workforce shows up. Then I can figure out a schedule and write up a more formal estimate and agreement and email them to you. I have a couple projects at Summerlight I need to wrap up this week, but I can probably at least get started here on Monday. Sound good?"

The part about the cost and scheduling did sound good to Alice. But the other parts, she wasn't sure about. Finn would be back in her life starting next week, even if it wasn't in the way it had been once upon a time. Having him back in her life would inevitably bring back memories she would just as soon keep buried in the darkest corners of her brain. Worse, having him around might bring back old feelings, too, feelings Alice had sworn she would never allow herself to feel again. For anyone.

No, that wouldn't happen, she immediately reassured herself. It had been a decade since she was in love with Finn. And she hadn't come close to feeling that way about anyone else since, even having encountered scores of people since then. She wasn't even sure she knew how to love anyone anymore. Even Finn.

She didn't care how much her head—and her heart— were trying to tell her otherwise.

Chapter Four

Finn knew he'd made a mistake less than twenty minutes after entering Alice's house on Monday morning. Not because of any problems he suddenly noted in the house—it really did seem pretty sound from what he'd seen on his initial pass—but because this third time seeing her up close and conversational was promising to be the proverbial charm. As in, sitting across from her at her dining room table sipping the coffee she'd greeted him with at the front door, he was becoming as bewitched by and attracted to her as he'd been that first day of kindergarten.

Not only had she remembered how he liked his coffee—black with a heaping teaspoon of sugar, just the way he'd been drinking it since he was a teenager—but she'd thrown in two doughnuts from Patsy's Pastries. Not just any doughnuts, but the chocolate-covered and cream-filled ones, since she knew those were his favorites, too. And she was smiling. The same smile that had always been his undoing with her, at once happy and sad, as if being with him brought both joy and anguish. But he'd always understood the reason for that. It hadn't been because of him, but because of her mother. Being with him back then, he knew, had made her happy. But it had also made her feel as if she were betraying her mother, which he supposed she had been, but then Nora had never exactly been the kind of person who invited loyalty. Not for the reasons a person should feel loyal to another, anyway.

So he and Alice were sitting at the dining room table to enjoy breakfast together as if it were the most natural thing in the world for them to do. And God help him, Finn was almost convinced it was.

Hey, why shouldn't this be natural? he asked himself as she refilled his cup with coffee and nudged the sugar bowl toward him. It wasn't unusual for his clients to offer him food or drink at some point during the workday. Though these days, he seldom accepted. Back when he lived in Philadelphia, however, when he was trying to get his business off the ground and struggling to make ends meet? Back when he'd often had to choose between paying the utility bills and eating more than one meal a day? Oh, hell yeah. Back then, he'd jumped at the chance when Mr. Fannelli brought out a plate of his homemade cannoli or Mrs. Szymański was making pierogi for lunch and there was more than enough for two people. Hell, during those years, he was saved more weeks than one by empanadas with Mr. Lopez or banh bao chi with Mrs. Phan. So why should doughnuts with Alice be any different?

He knew the answer to that question immediately. Because all those times, the food and the offer had been superficial and fleeting. Doughnuts with Alice... Well. If things had gone the way they were supposed to once upon a time, doughnuts with Alice might have been a way of life for him by now. A way of life for both of them. It was all he could do not to envision their children—or, at the very least, the child they should have had eleven and a half years ago—sitting at the table with them, face smeared with jelly and powdered sugar, laughing at some dad joke he just made while Alice groaned at its corniness.

He should have realized from the start that what their lives had promised to be once upon a time was just a fairy tale, one too good to come true.

"You still think about her, too, don't you?"

Finn told himself he shouldn't be surprised by Alice's question. It would be impossible for them to be together like this and not be thinking the same thing.

"Yeah," he said. "I do."

"So do I," she told him unnecessarily. "Especially every—"

"September 18," he finished for her.

Because that was the day baby Sarah Madeleine Whitlock Huxley had been due to make her appearance in the world. They were going to name her after Finn's mother and Alice's favorite writer and give her both their last names. They'd found out her sex during the ultrasound Alice had at twelve weeks, one they'd driven all the way to Ithaca for, because neither had wanted to risk one of the handful of doctors in Sudbury telling Nora about Alice's condition— in small towns like theirs, fear of the town bully easily trumped HIPAA, potential lawsuits be damned.

Everything had seemed fine at that point in Alice's pregnancy, just as it had seemed fine the first time they made the drive, for her to have a legitimate test to confirm what the home test had revealed and start regular prenatal visits. And when, a few weeks after the ultrasound, she had felt the flutters of the baby's first movements—flutters that had been too soft for Finn to discern with a hand on her belly, as hard as he'd tried and as much as he'd wanted to share that experience with her—they had started making plans in earnest.

How Alice would hide her condition however she could until the end of the school year. How, the day after they graduated, they would leave Sudbury for good. They both had some money saved, and Finn knew that once they confided in his father, Leo would help them out however he could. He wouldn't be happy that his barely-eighteen-year-old son was about to become a father with his not-quite-eighteen-year-old girlfriend, but once the shock wore off, Finn knew, he would help.

They would move south, they decided—way south—where it was a lot cheaper to live than the northeast. Finn would find work doing whatever odd handyman jobs he could while he found a position as an apprentice somewhere to begin his odyssey toward becoming a master craftsman. Alice would stay home to care for Sarah until she was old enough to start preschool, then she'd find work, too, doing whatever she could. It wouldn't be easy, they both knew. But they could do it. They would do it. For Sarah. And for themselves.

A month after that ultrasound, though, everything changed. Alice woke up to some spotting, so they both skipped school that day to drive to Ithaca again. The ultrasound that time had been devastating. Though it wasn't common for a baby to lose viability in the second trimester, the doctor told them, it did occasionally happen. A few days later, Sarah Madeleine Whitlock Huxley was gone. And with her, every plan and dream Finn and Alice had made for all of them.

"Are we actually going to talk about this?" Finn asked, his heart pounding in his chest at the thought. He looked up from his coffee, where the spoon still holding sugar hovered over his cup. And he met her gaze levelly.

Alice didn't look away, only met his gaze and held it. "We should have talked about it a long time ago."

He was going to point out that he had tried. That he had practically begged Alice to talk about it, but she'd refused. She'd told him she needed space. And time. Reluctantly, he'd given her both, thinking she would eventually need to see him again as badly as he'd needed to see her. He'd still wanted to run away after graduation, even if it would just be the two of them this time, and leave Sudbury behind. Start fresh in a place where they had no obligations to anything or anyone—only to each other. They'd made so many plans for their life together and had been so happy about the prospect of building one somewhere new. He'd been so sure Alice would still want to do that, too. Instead, she'd thwarted every effort he made to see her.

Or, rather, Nora had thwarted every effort he made. She had realized something was terribly wrong with her daughter after Alice miscarried, and Alice, in her shattered state, had ultimately told her mother everything. Although graduation had been less than two months away, Nora had kept her home from school, thinking it better that her daughter be a high-school dropout than to allow her to see Finn. She'd forbidden Alice to go back to work, as well, and had only allowed her very limited contact with the few friends she had—and only then at her home and never theirs.

Reports from her friends was the only way Finn even knew what was going on with Alice. And when he had finally taken it upon himself to boldly knock on the front door and demand to see her, Nora had eyed him venomously in silence before slamming the door in his face.

Finn had done everything he could to talk to Alice back then. And when it became clear that that simply was not going to happen as long as Nora Whitlock had her way, he did the only thing he knew to do: he left Sudbury without her. And he started a new life elsewhere. This time without the people—without the person—he had thought he would spend the rest of his life with. He'd told himself then that he would work hard and save money and go back to Sudbury to reconnect with Alice when they were both more mature and in a better place emotionally, and she was old enough to be free of her mother. But when he finally was able to go back home, Alice was gone, and no one knew where she was. So he'd been forced to return to Philadelphia, feeling raw and more alone than he'd ever felt in his life.

"Yeah. We should have talked about it then," he told her.

"I'm sorry we didn't," she said softly. "I'm sorry I…" She sighed heavily. "I'm just sorry, Finn. For so many things."

"Yeah, me, too," he told her. Understatement of the century. "We were kids," he added lamely.

Not that that really explained anything. In a lot of ways, they'd stopped being kids the minute they realized they were responsible for creating another life that would come into the world. It was hard to be a kid when you knew you were about to have a kid.

"I know you wanted to talk back then," she continued. "I know you tried. And I know my mother made it impossible. Not that that's any excuse," she hurried to add when she saw him open his mouth to comment. "I could have done something. I could have sneaked out to see you, the way I always did before. I could have found a way. I should have found a way. You have to understand that I was such a mess after everything that happened. Emotionally, physically, mentally. I couldn't make sense of anything. And my mother was so—"

Here, she halted abruptly. Which was just as well. Finn really didn't want to know what her mother had said or done after she discovered everything that went down. He'd had years to imagine it. And he was confident his imaginings were nowhere near as bad as Nora had made it for the daughter who had defied her so thoroughly.

"It's okay, Alice," he said. "It was a long time ago."

She sighed again. "I know it was. But sometimes, it feels like it was just yesterday."

Yeah. Sometimes it did.

He said nothing in response to that. He was just grateful she was now acknowledging the effort he'd made to see her after their loss. He'd been terrified back then that she might be thinking badly of him. He'd sent so messages to her via her friends that they'd promised to deliver, but they'd always come back telling him she had nothing to say in reply. After so many years, there were times when he'd almost convinced himself he hadn't tried hard enough. Times when he began to wonder if his memories of everything that went wrong were even accurate. Times when he'd almost wondered if any of it had happened at all.

Then that big black hole would open up in his heart again, and he'd remember that yeah, it happened. And it was horrible. And he'd wondered again if he would ever be able to move past it.

With great care, he asked, "Do you want to talk about it now?"

Her eyes immediately filled with tears, and she nodded. "I do want to talk about it," she said. "Eventually. When the time is right."

He wanted to ask when that time would be, because as far as he was concerned, there was no time like the present. He felt as if he'd been standing on the edge of a building for almost a decade, waiting for a good stiff wind to blow him either into the abyss or back on the roof to safety. But

Alice palmed both eyes quickly and hastily stood to… Do something. Something that had to do with searching the cabinets. For what, he couldn't imagine, since she didn't seem to find anything.

She was making clear that this wasn't the time to talk about, well, anything. Unless it was about home improvement, because she immediately launched into some concerns she had about a spot on a wall in the upstairs bathroom that she was worried might be due to water damage, and whether or not it was possible to discern that without creating a huge mess. Then it was back to the contractor-client relationship of coffee and doughnuts and drywall.

And damned if there wasn't some small part of Finn that welcomed that transition. Maybe Alice was right. Maybe, for now, they should just take it day by day. There would be time for talking later. For the time being, it would probably be best if the two of them just got used to seeing each other again. Talking to each other again. Being close to each other again.

Yeah. Sure. Time. Never mind that so far, time hadn't helped matters at all.

Alice stood in the kitchen doorway watching as Finn rolled a second coat of Beach Oyster over a dining room wall that had been bright poppy for as long as she could remember. It was only day two of home rehab, but already, she was breathing easier. She had feared that their uncomfortable exchange at the kitchen table yesterday morning might set a precedent for how the entire renovation would go. That the two of them would spend the entirety of his time at the house dancing around the tragedy that had set both their lives in a new direction as if it had been no more noteworthy than that time during junior year when

Benny Nolan slipped a bunch of plastic cockroaches into the apple brown Betty at lunch. They'd avoided each other as well as they could after that conversation yesterday, with Finn working in the living room, draping the furniture with drop cloths and washing and priming the walls in there while Alice began packing up things in any room where he wasn't.

And yes, this morning had started off a little tense, too, with more forced smiles and terse greetings. Today, though, Alice was staying close to where Finn was working, since he'd told her before leaving yesterday that he wanted to work on the house in pockets, finishing one or two rooms at a time, so would it be a problem for her to clear out the dining room and kitchen next, since that was the path he wanted to follow. She'd packed up the dining room last night fairly quickly, but the kitchen was promising to be more of a challenge, so crammed was every cabinet and drawer with…stuff. Stuff she couldn't even remember her mother or her ever using. How did kitchens collect so much extraneous…stuff?

She was sorting everything she found into two boxes— one for things to keep, one for things to go—and so far, the *go* box was twice as full as the *keep*. That was, no doubt, a good thing. The more she could get rid of now, the less she would have to pack when the time came for her to move. But letting go of so many things from the past, despite their being of no use anymore, felt wrong somehow. Even if the surrender of each item did kind of feel like the release of one more burden.

In spite of their initial stiff exchange that morning, Alice and Finn had managed to work companionably. They hadn't really talked about much other than her offer of coffee and

Finn's request for her approval of the colors so far, but at least they had managed to talk.

And she did like the color he suggested for both the living and dining rooms, one he said was popular for sellers these days, since it was neutral but still had a bit of warmth in its sandy undertones. For the kitchen, currently a faded version of its original cranberry color, Finn had shown her a chip for a hue that had a mere hint of a bluish-greenish tint she also liked very much. And not just because it was a pale version of his eyes, but because he said it, too, was currently quite trendy.

They'd moved the chunky wooden table and six chairs that had sat in the dining room to the sunroom, where Alice planned to refinish them all before bringing them back. Though she had no idea why there were six chairs in the first place, since she could never remember using more than the two she and her mother always occupied at mealtime, because the Whitlocks never entertained. Oh, wait. Yes, she could remember using another. Finn had sat in one of the other chairs both yesterday and today when they'd shared their coffee. Alice had sat in a different one, too. In fact, she hadn't occupied her usual chair at the table once since her mother's death.

Anyway, in addition to the dining room table and chairs, the boxy sideboard and hutch that matched them would also be getting a new look. Last night, she'd packed up the Wedgwood china that had filled the hutch—one with a pattern spattered with flowers and birds—and had plans to replace it with some plain white ones she'd found online. She'd likewise crated the paintings of English gardens that had hung on the walls and would replace those with simple sketches of…something else. She didn't know what yet. She just knew she wanted something that wasn't paintings of English gardens. Something simple. Something quiet. Something without too much drama.

She hoped that taming the room—a taming she planned to carry out through the whole house as she and Finn worked—would, in a way, exorcise some of the tumult that had always been present there. Not just in the decor but in the house itself. Calmness. That was what Alice hoped to capture for any prospective buyer. And calmness for herself, too.

"Think two coats will be enough?" she asked Finn now.

He stopped mid-roll and turned to look at her. He was wearing the same paint-spattered denim and chambray and work boots he'd had on at Summerlight the other day. Clearly, they were his usual painting attire. She wondered how many years' worth of renovating they represented and whether or not he would be able to identify which projects each of the colors smeared on them belonged to after all this time.

"Maybe?" he said. "I hope so, anyway. Hard to tell with some of these older paints. And I gotta say, the one in here was a doozy."

"I can't believe what a difference it makes just changing a color. It's so much lighter in here already."

She wasn't just talking about the new paint, either. It was so much easier to breathe in there now, too.

"Are you at a stopping point?" she asked. "I could make us some lunch."

The tension returned at her question. She could tell by looking at him that he wished she hadn't asked it.

"You don't have to do that, Alice. I can run out and grab something for lunch. That's what I usually do when I'm working."

"Yeah, but you're usually working for strangers."

This time, she was the one who regretted the remark. Because in a lot of ways, she and Finn were strangers now. Just because they'd managed to make it through a couple of days without either of them falling apart or tearing the other's head off didn't mean everything between them was okay. She'd meant it yesterday when she told him they needed to talk. And she'd meant it when she told him she wasn't ready to do that yet. She still wasn't. The time would come. She knew that. She didn't know when, but it would. It just wouldn't be today.

"I mean…" she began to backpedal. "It's no trouble," she finally said. "I'm going to be fixing something for myself anyway."

She could tell there was a part of him that wanted to decline. But she could also tell there was another part that wanted to accept. After a moment's hesitation, that second part won.

"Thanks," he said softly. "I appreciate it. Just gimme about a half hour to finish this coat."

She nodded. "That's just about how long it will take to whip up some grilled cheese and tomato soup. So perfect timing."

She tried not to wince as those last two words echoed in her ears, since her and Finn's timing had been anything but perfect in the past or the present. Ah, well. At least maybe lunch could be accommodating.

And it was, for the most part. They carried their meal out to the dining table in the sunroom and talked about their plans for the house as they enjoyed it. Beyond the windows, the sky was blue and dotted with puffy white clouds, and the buds on the trees had sprouted with the promise that true spring was just around the corner. Maybe Alice could even change out the storm windows for actual screens by the time they listed the house, to welcome in some fresh air and show prospective buyers how charming the back-yard could be. It was barren right now, so much so that the cobblestoned wall along the back alley was visible, but it wouldn't be long before the tiny yard was filled with color. And where her mother might have been challenged when it came to interior decorating, she'd been a truly gifted gardener. That cobblestoned wall would be obscured by luscious pink rhododendrons by summer, and the wooden fences between her yard and the neighbors' would be lined with lilacs and lilies.

She looked over at Finn and saw him staring out the win-dow, too. Specifically at the far north corner of the yard, where the fence and cobblestone met, a place where, in the summertime, the rhodies grew particularly thick. Her heart hammered hard in her chest. She knew exactly what he was thinking about. The two of them had spent a lot of time behind the rhododendron in that corner of the yard during the summer, lying on the warm, damp earth, star-ing at the stars overhead, murmuring in low tones about anything and everything. That spot had been within ear-shot of the house, should her mother call to her, but hid-den from view in every direction. So many nights, Finn had sneaked into her backyard, and Alice had crawled out her bedroom window, onto a branch of the sycamore tree outside it to clamber down the trunk. So many nights, the two of them had shared quiet conversations and soft kisses in that corner.

And one night, they had made love there. It was the first time for both of them. The first of many. But only once in that spot. The first time. For both of them.

He must have felt her gaze on him, because he turned to look at her, too, his eyes meeting hers unflinchingly. Neither said a word, though. For a moment, they only remembered in silence. Then Alice murmured something about how their soup was going to get cold, and the moment was gone, replaced by meaningless talk about whether American cheese or pepper jack melted best and whether butter or mayonnaise made for a crispier sandwich experience.

Then, in an effort to thwart a pause that threatened to go on too long, Alice said, "So I heard through the Sudbury grapevine that you lived in Philadelphia for a while."

She actually hadn't heard that through the Sudbury grapevine, because no one in Sudbury was close enough to Alice to share even the most idle conversation. She'd heard it from Haven, who had mentioned it in passing last fall, when she'd been at the house to replace a shower head that went kaput. But when Alice had tried to press her for more information about Finn, Haven—who Alice had quickly realized was *not* as gossipy as the rest of Sudbury—had hastily changed the subject to drain stoppers.

Alice might as well have just told Finn she'd heard through the Sudbury grapevine that he was a serial killer, so quickly and coolly did he react. He had been about to lift a spoonful of soup to his mouth, but he dropped the utensil back into the bowl haphazardly enough to splatter tomato onto the table. He immediately apologized and hurried to clean it up with his napkin, replacing the spoon with much more care. Then he inhaled a couple of what she couldn't help thinking were calming breaths and looked at her again.

But all he said was, "Yeah. That's where I moved after graduation."

It was a pretty empty reply for what had been a pretty startling reaction, but Alice didn't push it. For now, anyway. She really didn't know much about what he'd been doing since they were kids. And she really did want to find out.

She told herself it was only natural that she'd be curious. They'd been a big part of each other's lives when they were growing up, especially in high school. Even before the two of them became a couple, they were friends. Of course she'd want to know what her friend had been up to after such a long separation for both of them.

Unable to help herself, she asked, "So what did you do down there?" It was just normal conversation, that was all. Honest. "Handyman stuff?"

He nodded. And although he seemed to relax some at the question, he still looked a little guarded somehow. "Yeah. I actually ended up starting my own business down there. It was called Huxley's Habitat Two. Like t-w-o two, not t-o-o too. My dad lent me some money to get it up and running and he came down from time to time to help me keep it all organized and show me how to manage it, so it was kind of a satellite business of his here in Sudbury."

"That was nice of him," Alice said.

"Good investment for him, too," Finn replied. "I paid back that loan with interest within a few years, and he earned a percentage of my profits every year I was in business."

She smiled at that. "You guys were obviously a good team."

He smiled back. Definitely more relaxed now. Which made Alice feel more relaxed, too. "Damn straight."

She couldn't imagine having the kind of relationship with her mother that Finn had had with his father. Where a tragedy of the Huxleys' past, losing Finn's mother, had brought the two of them a closer, more loving connection, something in her mother's past—Alice had no idea what— had made Nora demand a warped closeness to her daughter that had been in no way genuine and certainly not healthy.

"I've never been to Philadelphia," she told him. "I imagine it was a lot different from Sudbury."

Despite his calmer demeanor, she could tell he wanted to change the subject. But he replied anyway. "Totally. It's such a big city. So many people. Just my neighborhood was probably bigger than Sudbury."

"I bet you made a ton of friends down there," she said.

He'd always been way more sociable than she, always surrounded by people whenever she saw him, at school or around town. Though, strangely, now that she thought about it, he'd never really had a regular crew he ran around with. Never a single best friend. Of course, neither had she, but that was different. She didn't have the kind of personality that lent itself to that. Finn did. It was only natural to assume he'd amassed friends anywhere he went.

Again, he seemed bothered by the comment. "A few," he told her. "Mostly, I just worked."

For the first time, she tried to picture him in the lifestyle of a grown man away from Sudbury. He was eighteen when he left. Still a kid, really, even if neither of them had felt like kids after losing Sarah. He went to a completely new city, one completely different from the one where he grew up, to start a new life by himself. In her mind's eye, she saw him looking as he did then, with the boyish good looks, not the beard, coming home from work at the end of the day, down a busy urban street to a nondescript building on a corner filled with pedestrians waiting for the light to change. Up some uneven cement steps and past a grid of metal mailboxes, then up another flight of stairs and down a dimly lit hall to a tiny apartment to face another night alone. The same way she had faced so many nights alone all the times she left Sudbury.

"Oh, come on," she coaxed him, forcing a brightness

into her voice she didn't feel. "There must have been a lot more to do in a big city like that than there is here. All that history? All the museums? All the sports and recreation? All the food?" Before he could comment on any of that, since, hey, she was on a roll, she asked, "Did you run up the steps of the Museum of Art like Rocky did?"

He smiled at that. "I didn't exactly run, but yeah. I went to the museum a couple times."

"Did you see the Liberty Bell? And Independence Hall?"

He nodded. "Did that, too."

"How about hockey games?" she asked, remembering how he'd always followed the Buffalo Sabres. "Did you go to a lot of those?"

"Only when the Flyers played Buffalo." He sighed melodramatically. "Who invariably lost."

Okay, that covered museums, history and sports. Which left food. So Alice asked the obvious. "Did you eat a lot of cheesesteaks?"

Now he laughed. A laugh she hadn't heard from him since they'd reconnected, a laugh she remembered from when they were young. A laugh that had always made her heart a little lighter. The way it did now. Wow. She'd completely forgotten how good that felt.

"Of course," he told her. "They're delicious. But living above a hoagie shop meant eating those more often. It was always easy to just grab a couple of sandwiches for our dinner on my way up after work."

He looked as surprised by what he'd said as Alice was to hear it. His eyes went wide, two bright spots of pink appeared on his cheeks, and he immediately dropped his gaze back down to his lunch. Heat blossomed in her belly at the reaction. He felt guilty about something. She knew it as well as she knew her own name. There was still enough of a connection between them for her to sense when he was uncomfortable about something. And he was very uncomfortable about what he'd just revealed.

"'A couple of sandwiches?'" she echoed. "'For us?' You had a…a roommate?"

Of course he would have a roommate, she told herself. It must have been crazy expensive living in a city that big, even without trying to get a business off the ground. It had doubtless been essential for him to share expenses with another guy. Right? Lots of people had roommates when they first struck out on their own. So it made sense that Finn would have a roommate when he lived in Philadelphia. Because if it hadn't been a roommate, then that meant it was—

"Um, yeah," he said, still staring down at his food. "For us. I kind of, uh…kind of, um…" He expelled another restless sound. "I kind of…lived with…someone for a while when I was in Philly."

Chapter Five

Alice told herself to just leave it at that. Finn obviously didn't want to elaborate, and she wasn't sure she wanted him to anyway. But something inside her demanded to know.

"So it was a roommate?" she asked.

He expelled a reluctant sound. "I mean, technically, yeah."

The heat in her belly fired hotter. *Technically.* The greatest word in the history of language to aid in skirting reality. She knew then he'd shared his space with someone way more important than a roommate. The person he'd lived with had been—

"Was this roommate a woman?"

He hesitated a telling moment before replying, "Yeah."

"Meaning she was more than a roommate."

This time his hesitation was almost palpable. "Yeah."

Don't push it, she told herself again. She had her answer. Finn had lived with another woman after he left Sudbury. She didn't need any details. Even if some perverted part of her wanted to hear every detail.

She waited a beat longer to see if he would tell her she'd misunderstood, that yes, the person he lived with might not have had a Y chromosome, but that only meant, well, she'd been born without a Y chromosome, and that there hadn't been anything romantic about their arrangement at all, and that the two of them hadn't been—

"Were you and she serious?"

He hesitated again, long enough that she knew if he said something in denial in response, he would be disingenuous. That was only hammered home when he continued to look down at his lunch instead of at her. "No, it was no big deal," he finally said. Disingenuously. "Just a couple of people who met and hit it off and decided to be together for a while, then went their separate ways not long after that." Now, finally, he did look up. And this time, she could tell he was being honest when he added, "I haven't spoken to her in years. I don't even know what she's doing or where she's living now." Before she could reply, he hurried on, "I'm sorry, Alice. It just sorta happened. I was lonely. She was nice. We liked each other enough to move in together for a while. But it was never that serious."

The fact that he would apologize for something he had nothing to be sorry for hit Alice hard. What was wrong with her, feeling so proprietary about him? Especially since she was the one who'd driven him away? Yes, there had been a reason for that, even if it had been a bad one, but she still had no right to expect *anything* from Finn. Not in the past, not now. And he certainly had nothing to apologize for.

"No, *I'm* sorry," she told him. "It's none of my business. I had no right to pry. You have nothing to apologize for. You and I were over, and you were starting a new life. It makes total sense that you would find someone else to—" She closed her eyes and expelled a soft sound. Then she forced herself to finish, "It makes total sense that you would find someone else."

Except that for some reason, it didn't make sense. Although Alice had dated occasionally while she was living away from Sudbury, not once had she been interested in someone enough to share quarters with him. She'd actually been surprised the first time a guy asked her out, wondering how he could think she would be interested. But she was lonely, too, after she left Sudbury. And the guys she dated had also been nice. She hadn't been serious with any of them, either. She certainly couldn't imagine living with any of them. That Finn had done that—

Didn't matter, she reminded herself. It was none of her business what Finn had done after they parted ways.

"She wasn't exactly someone else, Alice," Finn said softly. "She and I met when a barista mixed up our coffee orders. Like I said, she was nice, and I was lonely. We started talking and things between the two of us just kind of happened. But it wasn't serious," he said again. "And it didn't last long."

It had been serious enough for them to live together. And *didn't last long* could mean anything, really. Maybe it lasted a few months. Maybe it lasted a few years. It didn't matter, she told herself again. What Finn had done after leaving Sudbury—what Finn did now that he was back in Sudbury, for that matter—was none of her business. They weren't together anymore. They were friends. Maybe. She still wasn't even sure about that.

"It's fine," she said again.

Even though it wasn't. She opened her mouth to ask him something else, something that would put them back on whatever kind of ground or keel or whatever they had been on before, but he spared her from having to find something.

"How about you?" he asked. "I heard through the grapevine myself that you kind of came and went around Sudbury after graduation."

Not that she had graduated. Not with their class in June, the way she was supposed to, anyway. Her mother had kept her out of school for the rest of the year, then enrolled her in a summer program she could complete from home.

Alice had graduated in August, in the privacy of her living room, by opening a cardboard mailer that held her diploma. Her mother had made tuna noodle casserole for dinner that night. Alice's favorite. And chocolate pudding for dessert. Her other favorite. Both had tasted like ashes in her mouth.

She was no more eager to talk about her experiences since high school than Finn had been, but fair was fair. She nodded. "I went to summer school and finally got my diploma, then worked a few jobs around town to save up some money. I wanted to get out of Sudbury, too."

She didn't add that the reason for that was as much because she wanted to start her life over elsewhere as it was the fact that Sudbury just didn't feel like home to her once Finn left. So she only told him, "I needed to get away from my mother." Which was both true and something he wouldn't press her on, since he understood completely.

"Where did you go?" he asked.

"The first time, it was to Albany."

"And how did you decide to go there?"

She smiled at the memory, even though it was a mix of both happiness and melancholy. Happiness that she was escaping, melancholy that she was doing so alone. And that doing so would mean she really would never see Finn again, if he ever did come back to Sudbury.

"I hitched a ride to Rochester with Mrs. Reyes at the bakery, where I was working at the time. She used to drive up once a week to visit her daughter, so I asked if I could tag along one time to shop for a birthday present for my mom. I had her drop me off not far from the train station, and I made my way there and bought a ticket for whatever train was leaving next. I didn't care where it was going. It happened to be Albany. As it was leaving, I texted Mrs. Reyes to thank her for the ride and tell her how I wouldn't be coming back to Sudbury. She was surprisingly chill about the whole thing. Didn't ask where I was going or why. Just wished me luck."

"I imagine Mrs. Reyes understood completely why you were leaving," Finn said softly. "Even without her knowing what happened. Your mom was never exactly the most popular person in Sudbury."

No, she wasn't. At one time or another, Nora Whitlock had managed to offend or frighten nearly everyone in town. And those she hadn't had only escaped because they'd steered well clear of her.

"So what did you do in Albany?" he asked.

"I got lucky. Found a job in the state archives pretty quickly. Nothing glamorous. Mostly sitting in front of a computer doing transcription all day, but I made enough to be able to keep myself housed and fed. That was all I needed."

"So what made you come back?"

This time, Alice was the one to inhale a few calming breaths. "The first time, it was because my mother fell and broke her hip and needed me to help her with her home rehab."

Finn nodded. "Even though she could have probably afforded to stay at a proper rehab facility."

"She could have," Alice agreed. "But I felt obligated to come back and help her once she found me."

Finn hesitated a moment, then echoed, "Found you. You mean you didn't tell her where you were?"

Alice shook her head. "When I left that first time, I never planned to come back, but I knew she would try to convince me to. I dropped a letter to her in the mail in Rochester before I left, explaining to her why I had to leave and that I wouldn't be returning. I thought that would be the end of it. But she hired a private investigator to find me.

And when I found out she was hurt…" She looked up now and met his gaze. "Like I said. I felt obligated to come back and take care of her."

"You mean she made you feel obligated."

Alice ignored the comment and continued, "I stayed until she was back on her feet, then—"

"And how long did that take?"

Alice sighed. "About a year." Before he could point out that most people recovered from a surgery like that after a matter of months, she hurried on, "Once she was back on her feet, I left again. This time for Niagara Falls, where I worked in a little gift shop for a while."

"Until something happened to Nora that made you have to come back to Sudbury again," he guessed.

"She had to have her gall bladder removed."

"And did she have to hire a PI that time?"

Alice shook her head. "I told her where I landed. In case she needed me again. Good thing, too, since she had to have a caregiver with her at home after her surgery."

Which also should have only been for a couple of months at most, but with Nora, it had been a couple of years. Before Finn could also point that out, Alice continued, "Once she was okay, I left Sudbury again and found work at a resort in the Adirondacks."

Where she truly thought, at the time, she would stay. She'd like it in Saranac Lake. The little village had reminded her a lot of Sudbury. But the good parts of Sudbury. The smallness and coziness. The friendliness of the people. The beautiful panoramas of woodlands and the lake. The gorgeous changes of scenery that came with every new season.

"I really liked it there," she told Finn. "I found a job at an inn a lot like Summerlight is shaping up to be. It was a historic estate, too, once upon a time, and the owners had managed to keep its cozy, homey feel. Only a handful of guests were ever in residence at a time, and they were all the kind of people who coveted their privacy as much as I did mine. I hated having to leave."

"Then why did you?"

She expelled a tired sound. "She had cancer, Finn. Not exactly something she could face alone. She was there for me after I lost—" She halted abruptly. "Maybe she wasn't the most comforting mother in the world then. But she was there for me at a time when no one else was."

At that, he glared at her.

"I didn't mean it like that. I know you were there, too, but—"

"Nora wasn't there for you, she was there for herself," Finn shot back. "She took advantage of our tragedy to dig her hooks into you even deeper. And I will never, ever forgive or forget that. Even if you can."

Well, that certainly escalated quickly. Alice dropped what was left of her sandwich onto her plate, pushed her bowl away, and stood.

"Are you finished?" she asked Finn, hoping he realized she was talking about a lot more than lunch. "Because I am."

"Yeah," he muttered. "I'm done, too."

She gathered up his dishes with hers and turned to head back to the kitchen. She completed three steps before she turned around again, framed in the doorway of the sunroom. Inevitably, her gaze was drawn through the window to that far north corner of the yard, where the brittle branches of the rhododendron almost mocked her in their barrenness. Then she gazed at Finn again. Finn, who was looking everywhere in the room except at her. And that corner of the yard.

Very softly, she said, "You have to understand what it was like to be her daughter, Finn."

Finally, he fixed his gaze on her. "I do understand, Alice."

"No. You don't," she assured him. "I know you think you do, but…" She shook her head and turned away again. "But you don't. You can't."

She managed to complete a few more steps before his quiet voice stopped her. "Alice."

She turned again. Gone was any animosity he might have been feeling toward her mother or toward her. Gone was the uneasiness of their exchange. Gone was the melancholy of sad memories. In their place was only fatigue. The sort of fatigue that went soul deep and never quite disappeared.

"Alice, I really am sorry."

She knew he wasn't talking about anything that happened in Philadelphia this time. Or about the things he had just said about her mother. He was talking about much, much more.

"I'm sorry, too," she told him.

For another moment, they only gazed at each other, then, finally, Alice managed a small smile. Finn returned it, and for a moment, she felt as if everything really would be all right. Someday. Some way. They both just had to figure out how to make that happen.

By Friday afternoon, the tension that had been coiling tight inside Finn during the first week of renovation at Alice's house was gradually beginning to unwind. They managed to make it through three whole days without there being any more moments that were awkward/distressing/bitter/sad/angry/pick one word from each column and move on. Mostly, they accomplished that by avoiding talk about anything other than her plans for the house and how to best go about implementing them. But they also did it by giving each other a wide berth whenever they didn't have to discuss the renovation. Once she cleared a room of its possessions to allow him to begin working on it, she busied herself with packing up knickknacks or taking those knickknacks to be donated or consigned. They learned their lesson about having lunch together. Finn started bringing a lunch with him and ate in his truck, and Alice made herself scarce after preparing something for herself. So by the time Friday afternoon rolled around without further incident, Finn was breathing a sigh of relief that the two of them might actually make it through a *whole week* without suffering any further anguish.

Until Alice came into the kitchen where he was on his knees and had nearly finished ripping up the old vinyl flooring and told him, "We might have a problem."

Damn. Missed it by *that* much.

He retracted his utility knife into its sheath and sat back on his heels to look at her. She was dressed the way she had been all week, in battered jeans and a voluminous button-up shirt, this one short-sleeved, because today was one of those "false spring" days—the kind blessed with warmth and sunshine and blue skies that taunted a person with how beautiful the weather *could* be before returning to the cold and gray and wet of true early spring in the Finger Lakes. Her dark auburn hair was tied atop her head in a pile of loose curls, and there was a streak of dirt smudging one cheek. He tried to remember where she'd told him she'd be working if he needed her. Upstairs bathroom, he recalled. Bathrooms were always ripe for trouble.

"What kind of problem?" he asked.

"I was cleaning out the bathroom closet upstairs—my God, there's some scary stuff in there my mother's mother must have used because they have got to be illegal now—and I found a patch of what could be mold on the back wall."

Crap. "Yeah, that could be a problem all right. Show me."

She spun around, and he followed, doing his best not to notice how she still had that way of walking he'd always loved. Just a completely casual, unselfconscious stride that looked choreographed to some music only she could hear. He followed her down the upstairs hall, past the collection of cleaners and God knows what else she'd found up there—yeah, he was pretty sure nobody much used creosote anymore, never mind the moth killer that proudly proclaimed it contained DDT—past the minuscule bathroom that would have been the one Alice claimed growing up and probably still used now. In spite of the clutter lining the floor on both sides of the hall, the closet was still packed with linens and other odds and ends, but the floor and bottom two shelves had been emptied. It was toward those that Alice gestured before handing him a flashlight she produced from nowhere.

"Back in the far right corner, above the floor baseboard," she said. "Tell me if that's what I suspect it is."

Finn took the flashlight and switched it on, then got down onto his haunches to shine it where she'd directed. It took him a nanosecond to confirm her suspicions.

"Yep, that's mold," he said. "Looks like it's been collecting for a while, too."

"Great," she muttered.

He shone the light higher, across both shelves. "Doesn't look like it's grown up very much, but we'll have to take out the wall to know for sure. It's definitely worst at the bottom. Water's probably been pooling there for a while. Slow leak in one of your pipes."

"Which means?" she asked.

"I'm not sure yet. Like I said, I'll have to take out the wall to assess for sure. With any luck, it's confined to this one area. That won't be too hard to clean up and repair."

"And if it's not confined to this one area?"

He turned to look at her. "Then you're gonna have to hire someone more qualified than me to take care of it. I don't have a lot of experience with mold removal."

"In other words," she said, *"cha-ching."*

"Maybe. Maybe not. Like I said, I'll have to take out the wall to be sure. But it'll be easier to approach it from the bathroom on the other side than from the closet."

She nodded. "Whatever you need to do."

He'd promised Haven he would work at Summerlight next week, and he'd really hoped to take the weekend off. But if there was a chance Alice was going to need to hire an extra hand for this job, it would be best to know as soon as possible.

"I can come back tomorrow to do it," he told her.

"I don't want you to have to work on a Saturday."

He smiled. "What? Don't want to pay me those week-end rates?"

She smiled back. "Don't want to keep you from having a life."

Yeah, well, that ship sailed a long time ago. "It's fine," he told her. "I don't have anything else planned. And it won't take that long to at least have a look and see what we're up against. What *you're* up against," he hastily corrected himself when he realized he was pairing the two of them up in his brain. Again.

He had to stop doing that. All week, whenever he'd thought about the things that needed doing in Alice's house, he'd thought in terms of what *they* had to do, not what *she* had to do or what *he* had to do. This was her house, not his. Not theirs. Their house would have been— -

Well. Their house didn't exist, did it? So he needed to stop thinking about any house, especially this one, as theirs.

"Thanks, Finn," she told him. "I appreciate it."

"If I come at nine, will that be good?"

"Sounds perfect."

He nodded once. "I just have a little more to do downstairs, and then I'll get out of your hair. Let you get on with your evening."

She chuckled. "Yeah, well, I don't have any plans, either, so no rush." She dipped her head toward the bottles, jars and boxes on the floor. "I'm going to box up all this stuff and take it... Gah. I don't know what to do with it. Probably not a good idea to toss it and send it to the landfill."

"Call the recycling center. They can probably steer you in the right direction. Might even take it off your hands themselves."

She shook her head. "I can't believe my mother never got rid of all this stuff."

Yeah, Finn thought, *especially when she wouldn't even let her daughter keep a few perfectly harmless mementos in her own bedroom.*

"Weird what people hold on to sometimes," he said. "She probably didn't even know it was there. Like you said. It may have belonged to her mother."

It was even weirder to think about Nora Whitlock having a mother. That would require thinking about Nora having been a child at some point, and she'd always seemed to him like the kind of person who'd sprung full-grown from Zeus's head or something. Most of what he knew about Nora's origins was what Alice had told him when they were kids. That she had come to Sudbury with her own widowed mother before she started school and had grown up here. That her mother—Alice's grandmother—died before Alice was born. Alice had no idea who her father was or how her mother had even met him. Whenever she'd asked as a child who her father was, her mother told her she didn't have one. When she'd asked as an adolescent who knew it took more than one person to make a baby, Nora had told her her father was dead. Alice had never been able to find out the truth. One day, people in Sudbury had just started noticing that Nora was pregnant. No one had dared ask for details.

Alice seemed in no way concerned about the mention of her grandmother. It was as if earlier Whitlocks were of no more consequence in her life than the kid who bagged her groceries at the Hop-In-Hop-Out.

"No telling what else I'll find over the next couple of weeks," Alice said softly. "I mean, at some point, I'm going to have to go into her room and go through all her things."

Finn was going to make a joke about how there hopefully wouldn't be any dead bodies, but stopped himself. There was still that mystery about Alice's paternity. Maybe Nora had walled up the progenitor of her spawn once the act was over, having consumed his head like a praying mantis or something.

"Yeah, could be interesting," he agreed.

He headed back downstairs to finish in the kitchen and carried out the remnants of the floor to the bulk bag he'd set up in the backyard, near the alley, where it could be picked up by a junk collector next week. He had just tossed in the last fragment when he heard a clamor coming from behind him that sounded like a bird dying a horrible, horrible death. When he spun around, the sound stopped. He scanned the yard from one side to the other but saw nothing that could have made the noise. Shrugging it off as the sound of a bird—a really loud, really annoying bird—he headed toward the back door. He only made it three steps, though, before the sound erupted again.

As he drew closer to the back door, he noted it was coming from that direction, but another quick check of the yard revealed nothing. Not until he looked up at the big sycamore tree, where it finally occurred to him that a bird would be, and found, not a bird, but a kitten staring down at him. It didn't look any bigger than one of his work gloves and was pretty much the same buff color, and it was *waaaaay* up high in the sycamore where he couldn't for the life of him imagine how something that tiny got up that far. Or, worse, how it was going to get down.

"MEOW!" the kitten suddenly screamed down at him, loud enough to make him flinch. *"MEOW MEOW MEOW MEOW MEOW!"*

Damn. The thing must be half lungs for all the racket it was making. How did something that little manage to sound like a soprano chain saw?

"MEOW MEOW MEOW MEOW MEOW!"

"All right, all right," Finn called up to it. "Let me see what I can do."

He was about to go inside and ask Alice if she had a ladder—hopefully one big enough to reach the top of the Chrysler Building—when he saw her stick her head out of her bedroom window above him, having evidently heard the kitten yelling, too.

And just like that, he was a teenager again, having sneaked over the garden wall to toss a pebble at her window. There had been so many nights like that when they were kids, nights when he'd stood at the bottom of this tree, in the very same spot he stood now, while she shinnied down the trunk after climbing through her bedroom window. He'd always been so terrified that she would fall and kill herself, thereby ending any hope the two of them had for a happy future together. But she'd always made it down to earth safely. Then she'd always laughed at the look of concern on his face. After that, she'd always kissed him and told him to stop worrying, that everything would be fine and that nothing—kiss, kiss, *nothing*—could keep the two of them from being together forever.

He could tell by her expression when their gazes connected that she was thinking about those times, too. But all she did was call down, "It'll be easier to get it down from up here."

Then she was sticking one leg, then the other, out the window and lowering herself onto the big branch that had always held her weight just fine, except that it was a little closer to the window now, having had ten years to grow. So, really, she was even safer up there now than she'd been when they were teenagers. That did nothing, however, to quell the very same fear Finn had always felt whenever she did something like this.

But she had all the grace and confidence of a prima ballerina as she maneuvered herself toward the kitten, who turned its attention to her now and started yelling again.

"MEOW MEOW MEOW MEOW MEOW!" it shrieked.

"I know, I know," she murmured barely loud enough for Finn to hear. "It looks scary this high up, but it's fine. We'll get you down."

As she drew nearer to the kitten, it backed toward the juncture where the branch joined the trunk, never once taking its eyes off of Alice and never once interrupting its howling.

"You're gonna be fine, little buddy," she continued as she drew nearer still.

The kitten looked nowhere near convinced. It just kept

screaming and backing up. When it reached the trunk, it turned and dug in its claws and started to climb higher. But Alice scooped it up and pulled it back toward the branch and herself. It still managed to wriggle free, but this time when it grabbed the trunk, it started moving downward instead, inching its way along, its tiny sabers clawing the bark as it went. To make sure it didn't venture upward again, Alice followed, hugging the trunk herself as she followed it down. When the kitten was close enough for Finn to grab, he did, tugging it free of the bark and immediately putting it on the ground to keep himself from getting sliced to ribbons. Once it was on the ground, though, it just kept yelling, only this time, it was glaring at him, too, as if it couldn't believe he'd had the temerity to aid in its rescue.

"MEOW MEOW MEOW MEOW MEOW!"

"What?" he demanded. "We just saved your life."

"MEOW MEOW MEOW MEOW MEOW!"

He looked up to see that Alice was nearly on the ground, too, and automatically—just as he had when they were kids—he reached up to settle both hands on her hips and pull her safely to the ground. And she—just as she had when they were kids—spun around and settled her hands on his shoulders to look up at him with a triumphant smile that she'd once again survived the trip down, just as she always said she would. It was only when he felt himself lowering his head to hers for the traditional *I told you so* kiss that followed her descent, and only when she was tilting her own head back to receive it, did he finally realize what he was doing. What they were doing. But instead of letting go of her—and instead of her pulling away—they only stared at each other in wonder for a moment, as if a decade had dissolved away and they indeed were kids again, sneaking around in her mother's garden. Had it been dark, with the moon and stars overhead, Finn could have completely convinced himself that they had fallen well and truly into that other reality. The one that might have been.

Maybe that was why he didn't stop himself when he covered her mouth with his. And maybe that was why she melted into him when he did, as if it were the most natural thing in the world for them to do.

He brushed his lips lightly over hers, once, twice, three times, four, as she gently looped her arms around his neck and pushed herself up on tiptoe. Then she kissed him the same way, a gentle touch of her mouth on his, tilting her head first one way then the other. A ribbon of pleasure unwound inside him unlike anything he'd felt in years. Twelve years, to be exact. He'd genuinely forgotten just how good he could feel. How good they could feel. How good everything everywhere could feel. The entire planet seemed to shift on its axis as they kissed, setting them back into a spot they'd been gone from for too long. And, just like that, everything—everything—seemed like maybe…possibly… perhaps…would be okay.

And when they finally pulled apart, when Finn finally looked down into Alice's eyes, he knew she was thinking the same thing. Maybe, just maybe, they could—

"MEOW MEOW MEOW MEOW MEOW!"

Maybe they could talk about this later. Because the kitten suddenly lunged onto Finn's jeans and began to climb him as effortlessly as it must have taken on the sycamore. Then it jumped over onto Alice and climbed her, too. The two of them separated just as the kitten latched onto Finn's belt, then used it for a launch pad to his chest—*dammit*, those little scimitars hurt. It didn't stop climbing until it was perching precariously on his shoulder, its claws buried in his collar, its pink triangle nose sniffing his beard, its whiskers tickling his ear.

"MEOW!" yelled the kitten again. *"MEOW MEOW MEOW MEOW MEOW!"*

Finn couldn't help the laughter that escaped him as he tried to free the kitten from his shoulder only to have it dig in harder. Alice laughed, too, and reached out gingerly to help. Between the two of them, they were finally able to free the demonic little ball of fur, who never stopped shouting at them the entire time. Only when Alice gently gathered it by its scruff and cradled it close did it seem to calm down. At least enough to simply mewl at them.

"Are you someone's escaped pet?" he asked the kitten. "You don't have a collar or tag, so I'm thinking you're not supposed to be out and about this way."

"It looks awfully young to be a rescue," Alice said. "Not that I'm an expert or anything, but it's so tiny. I don't think they're supposed to be away from their mother when they're this small. It might not even be weaned."

"Guess there's one way to find out."

Chapter Six

Alice sat cross-legged on the cool cement of the kitchen floor that was only hours ago covered with the ugliest vinyl she had ever seen and watched as the recently rescued kitten lapped at a bowl of water. Finn sat on the floor across from her, leaning against the doorjamb, his legs extended before him as he scrolled through his phone, reading over tips about what to do with it. A quick search of its fur before bringing it inside didn't reveal any evidence of fleas or ticks, and, as he'd pointed out, it was still pretty early in the season for either of those to be a problem. So inside the house with them the little ball of fuzzy energy came, screaming at them some more as Alice looked for something in the pantry to feed it.

Finn had found a veterinary website that said not to give it milk—which she had been about to do until he stopped her, because, hey, why would cartoons lie about something like that? But canned tuna was okay on occasion, he read to her, so she'd flaked a bit of that with some of its oil onto a dinner plate near its rim and set it down. The kitten had then climbed onto the plate from the other side to eat it, snarfing it down as if it were the first solid food it had consumed in days. They estimated its age as somewhere between four and eight weeks, thanks to the site's designation that that was the age when they were old enough to run around but also be difficult to catch. Due to its smallness, though, Alice was going to err on the side of younger rather than older. So maybe no more than sixish weeks. The site had also helped them determine the kitten's sex as female. So that made it no longer an *it* but a *she* instead.

"Looks like she's weaned," Alice said as the kitten slowed her water lapping long enough to take a few breaths.

But when the bundle of buff fur looked up at the sound of her voice, she could see that its face was drenched with the water it hadn't managed to lap into its mouth, and its pink tongue was sweeping around awkwardly at the mess.

"Okay, kind of weaned," she amended. "And she did okay eating the tuna. So mama cat must have at least taught her a few things."

Finn looked up from his phone. "I checked a couple of local missing pet sites, but there's nothing about any missing kittens. So the mom is probably feral."

"Maybe," Alice conceded. "But a lot of people don't post stuff like that online. She could still be somebody's pet."

"Then what was she doing up a giant sycamore in someone else's backyard?"

"She could be somebody's escaped pet."

Finn looked at the kitten again. Now she was awkwardly swiping her paw over her face, doing little more than moving the dampness from one side to the other. "Or she could have been abandoned. People can be pretty awful about stuff like that."

Yeah. They could, Alice thought. The kitten seemed to be satisfied for now, though, because, still awkwardly licking her whiskers, she backed away from the water and into Alice's knee. Then she scrambled into Alice's lap, where she began to lick her paws and swipe them over her face again, and this time, that almost worked. Alice couldn't help chuckling at her near-miss maneuvers. And then, when the kitten began to purr, something inside her buzzed with delight.

"She's purring!" she exclaimed. "She must like us!"

When she glanced up at Finn, he was looking at her in a way that made her want to purr even louder than the kitten. Immediately, her thoughts went back to what had happened under the tree once they had the kitten safely grounded. The same thing that had happened dozens of times when they were kids, greeting each other after being separated only a matter of hours after school as if it had been eons instead. Except that this time, they weren't kids. And this time, they'd been separated a lot longer. And not just by time, either.

"Are we gonna talk about what happened outside?" Finn asked.

She hesitated, then told him, "I don't guess we can avoid it."

In spite of her statement, both sat with their gazes locked as tightly as their lips. Finally, though, Finn said, "Just what exactly did happen out there?"

Alice sighed. "The same thing that happened a million times when we were kids."

Finn uncrossed his ankles and then crossed them again. "Yeah, but when we were kids, it was different."

She grinned and lifted a hand to her cheek, where her skin still felt a little abraded by the facial hair he hadn't had before. "Yeah, when we were kids, you didn't have that scratchy beard."

He lifted a hand to his own face, scrubbing it lightly over his beard, looking mildly offended. "You don't like it?"

It wasn't that she didn't like his beard. She just wasn't used to him having one, even after seeing his bearded self around Sudbury for more than a year.

"No, it's fine," she said noncommittally.

"Fine," he repeated.

"I'm just not used to it."

Especially up close.

"But you're right," she said. "When we were kids, what happened under the tree was different."

"Because when we were kids, we were…" He stumbled over his next words. "We were…in love. Now…"

"Now?" she asked. Mostly because she was no more willing to finish the statement than he clearly was.

He said nothing in response to that. Which was just as well, because probably neither of them knew what was going on between them. She'd told herself over and over since he came back to Sudbury that she wasn't in love with Finn anymore. She couldn't be. Because she was a different person now from the person she had been when she lived here before. Finn was different, too. In a lot of ways, they really were strangers getting to know each other for the first time. But they had shared a life together of sorts a decade ago. Feelings like theirs didn't just go away. Maybe they changed, but… But what did they change into?

Alice sighed again and dropped her gaze to the kitten, who had stopped bathing and curled into a ball in one of her bent knees. Her eyes were closed, and she was still purring. Alice wished she could be half that content.

She looked up again. "Finn, I don't know what's going on between us, either. If there's just something unfinished that needs to be finished or if there's something stirring that wants to reawaken or if it's something that's completely new. But there is something going on between us. Clearly."

He nodded. "Yeah, I don't know, either. But that…" He pointed in the direction of the backyard and smiled. "That was… That was kinda… That was…pretty great."

She smiled back. "Yeah, it was."

She just wished she knew exactly what *it* was. And if it would happen again. And how deep it went. And if it would last.

Another bout of silence ensued. Once again, Finn was the one to break it. "So what do we do about it?"

Alice thought about that for a long time before answering, because there were just too many ways she could reply. They could forget that the kisses under the sycamore today had ever happened and never speak of them again. Or they could acknowledge that yes, they happened, but they were a mistake and should never happen again. Or they could sit here talking about it all night until they figured out what those kisses had meant and why they had happened and how they should probably never happen again. Or...

Here, she inhaled a deep mental breath and steeled herself for the other possibilities tumbling through her brain. Or they could recognize the mistakes of the past, accept that they had been too young to deal with them and see if they could start over again as adults.

Or they could just keep doing what they'd been doing since reconnecting and wait to see what happened next.

Alice knew she could no more forget those kisses today than she could forget the thousands they had shared when they were kids. And they hadn't felt like a mistake at all. They had felt like...like picking up where she and Finn left off twelve years ago. The idea of them trying again, though... That was more than a little scary. There was just so much between them to wade through and make sense of and work out. Too much *woulda-coulda-shoulda* that they might never be able to fully resolve. Too many painful memories and feelings that would inevitably get stirred up again.

Finally, she told him, "I guess what we do is…wait and see what happens next."

She could see he was a little disappointed by her response. But what was she supposed to say? That they *could* just pick up where they left off and move forward? That was impossible. They really were completely different people now. Who was to say they would even like each other now, let alone fall in love again, once they spent more time together toward that goal?

"I'm sorry, Finn, but I don't know what else to say. What happened out there today… It came out of nowhere."

He eyed her levelly. "Did it?"

"Yes," she replied immediately, confidently. "At least it did for me."

And it had, truly. Yes, there had been a lot of tension arcing between them over the past week. But she'd assumed it was just the understandable result of confusion and discomfort and even resentment due to their shared past. It had never occurred to her that it might be the result, however misguided, of some lingering leftover affection for each other that the two of them might still have bubbling inside. Now that she did…

Well, it made her think about the two of them differently. But she still wasn't sure where it put them in the overall scheme of things.

Finn said nothing in response to her assertion, which made her wonder if maybe he *had* been thinking the two of them could still care for each other the way they had when they were kids. And who knew? Maybe they could. Maybe. Or maybe they would just open themselves up to a whole other kind of heartache.

"Let's just take it slow and see what happens," she said softly. "One step at a time."

He hesitated another moment, then nodded slowly. "Okay. So then what's the next step?"

She looked down at the kitten again, whose purrs had turned to borderline snores. "First, we're going to have to get this little girl a few things she needs. At least until we find her owner."

"And if we find out she doesn't have an owner?" he asked. "If, instead, we discover she's all alone in the world and has no idea how to find her way in it?"

Somehow, Alice knew Finn wasn't just talking about the kitten. She looked at him again and smiled. "Then we take it slow and see what happens next. One step at a time."

It was as good as he was going to get from her for now, and he seemed to finally accept that. "Okay," he told her. "We can ask around the neighborhood this weekend to see if anyone is missing her. Could be one of your neighbors is out looking around for her right now."

"In the meantime," Alice said, "I'll make a bed for her in the sunroom. And I'll run up to the Hop-In-Hop-Out for some kitten food."

"I could give you a lift."

She smiled again. "I'd like that."

She would like that. She'd like it a lot. Probably more than she should. But at least there was something happening. At least they were taking a step.

As gently as she could, she roused the sleeping kitten and carried her back to the sunroom. Finn grabbed one of the empty boxes she'd been using to pack up her mother's things along the way and followed. Together, they cut down a part of the box until it was low enough for the kitten to climb into and out of by herself, and together, they located a clean blanket to arrange inside it. Then, together, they identified the sunniest corner of the room and placed the box there. Alice refilled the kitten's water bowl while Finn wadded up a scrap of paper for the tabby to bat around the room and keep herself entertained. Then they closed the door and exchanged hopes that they wouldn't return from the Hop-In-Hop-Out to find that the sunroom had been completely dismantled by a creature not much bigger than their hands.

They made short work of the grocery store, picking up not just wet and dry food for the kitten but a litter box and litter, too. Then they stopped by Furry Friends Pet Supplies to pick up a few other essentials—catnip mousies and one of those fishing-pole things with feathers at the end of a string and some plastic balls with bells inside. And, okay, a new bed since the box they'd put together wasn't exactly ideal, never mind aesthetically pleasing, even if it was no longer usable as a box because they'd cut it up. It could be recycled. And the bed that looked like a little sofa was just supercute. And—all right, all right—they picked up a couple of feeding bowls shaped like a mouse and a fish. Hey, Alice didn't have any small dishes that were kitten-appropriate, as proven by the fact that the kitten had had to climb onto a dinner plate to eat. She reasoned to herself that when she and Finn found the owner—if they found the owner—these purchases could just be like kitty baby shower gifts or something.

Which was when it occurred to Alice that they were shopping for the kitten the same way they might have shopped for their baby once upon a time, had things turned out differently. And it was all she could do in that moment to tamp down the feelings of loss and desolation all over again. It had been twelve years, she reminded herself. Long enough for her to know that time didn't actually heal wounds, but it did blunt them enough to make them manageable. She had been managing for a long time now. Long enough that she knew how to not fall apart anymore. Well, usually.

"Hey, you okay?" Finn asked when he must have noticed her sudden withdrawal.

She nodded. "Yeah, I'm fine. I think we have the essentials," she hurried on before he could press her. "Unless you can think of anything else."

He definitely looked like he was thinking of something else, and she was pretty sure it had nothing to do with the kitten. But he only told her, "No, I think a sofa for a cat pretty much tops anything else we might add to the collection."

They paid for their purchases and loaded everything into the back of Finn's truck. Then they picked up some carry-out from Anabel's Diner and headed home.

No, not home. Back to Alice's house. Her mother's house. The house they were fixing up to sell so that she could get the hell out of Dodge. Except that suddenly, she wasn't sure she wanted to get the hell out of Dodge. Suddenly, Sudbury didn't seem quite as menacing as it used to. Especially while she and Finn enjoyed their dinner sitting in the sunroom with the kitten and watching her explore her new acquisitions before stretching out on her new sofa and plummeting into slumber again.

As they cleaned up their dinner remnants and filled the dishwasher, they talked about anything and everything and nothing, the way two people did when they were getting to know each other all over again. Finn talked about some work he'd just completed for their former biology teacher, Ms. Chandramouli, and how she was still caring for the class pet, a bearded dragon they'd named Kenneth. Alice talked about how she'd taken up knitting while she was living in Niagara Falls—the owner of the store where she'd worked had taught her—and wanted to get back to it because she still had some unfinished mittens that showed a lot of promise.

They ran out of conversation a little after two in the morning but made plans to do something together the following evening. Dinner and a movie on a Saturday night. A totally normal date for two people who were getting to know each other better. The kind of date they'd never been able to have when they were kids. At Alice's front door, they lingered a few moments more, reaffirming the time he would come over in the morning to assess the mold problem in the closet upstairs. Then, after only a small hesitation, Finn leaned forward and kissed her, brushing her mouth lightly with his. Instinctively, she lifted a hand to his face, cupping his jaw the way she had when they were kids. The feel of his beard beneath her fingers, though, was so strange that she impulsively pulled her hand back. Finn noticed the gesture and retreated.

"What's wrong?" he asked softly.

She smiled. "I'm sorry. It's the beard. It just feels weird."

"You really don't like it, do you?"

"It's not that I don't like it. It's just…weird," she repeated.

She couldn't think of any other way to put it. The last time before today that she had kissed Finn—a long time ago, in a galaxy far, far away—he'd been a fresh-faced teenager. She didn't think he'd even shaved back when they dated. Having his face covered in fur now was just…weird.

"I have a weird beard?"

She laughed lightly. "It's a very nice beard. It's just… different. Kissing you with it feels different."

"Bad different or good different?"

She thought about that a moment before replying. Then she said honestly, "I don't know. Just different. It's not what it was like when we were kids. But then nothing is like it was when we were kids," she hurried to add.

He gazed at her thoughtfully for a few seconds, then nodded almost imperceptibly. But all he said was, "Okay."

And he leaned in for another kiss. But just a quick one, as if he didn't want to displease her with his weird beard. Then he smiled and lifted a hand in farewell and made his way down to the street where he'd parked his truck.

One step at a time, Alice reminded herself as she watched him drive off. *Take it slow and see what happens.* Because there was no denying that something was happening between her and Finn. Something that felt good. Something that felt right. Something that made her think that maybe— just maybe—the rift that had separated them for so long might somehow be able to be mended.

Yeah. Maybe for once, things would go right for her and Finn. He was leaving by the front door now, instead of sneaking over the garden wall. This was how it could have been for them when they were kids. How it should have been for them. How it might still be, if they took it slow, one step at a time, and waited to see what happened.

And as she closed her front door and switched off the porch light, Alice realized she truly couldn't wait to see what happened next.

The week following the Great Kitten Rescue Caper felt very much to Finn like a week from the life he and Alice might have had if things had worked out the way they were supposed to back when they were kids. Even before she became pregnant, the two had talked about how they would leave Sudbury together after graduating and start a life together somewhere new. Alice applied, was accepted, and won scholarships to a community college in Poughkeepsie, a city that was far away enough to keep Nora out of their lives but big enough for Finn to find work in. He found a couple of places where he could potentially find a job as an apprentice and start working his way up. It wouldn't be easy, they'd both known, but it would be better than sneaking around in Sudbury for God knew how long.

After discovering Alice was pregnant, though, they'd moved their plans farther away, to a different state, where the cost of living was low enough that Finn would be able to support the three of them until baby Sarah could attend school and Alice could find a job of her own. Again, it wouldn't be easy. But they would have found a way to manage. As long as they were together, building a life for the two—or three—of them, they'd figured then, that was all that mattered.

That second week of working on Alice's house really began to give Finn a glimpse of what might have been. Of what could still be, now that the two of them had opened the lines of communication again and were trying to figure things out.

The mold problem, they discovered, didn't look to be as bad as it could have been, but it was bad enough that its removal would have to be handled by someone other than Finn. Fortunately, he discovered upon talking about it to Haven at Summerlight one day, she had experience and was licensed to do it and could make room in her schedule in a couple of weeks to take care of it. She'd suggested that for now, they treat what they could see with a homemade solution of vinegar, baking soda and borax. Finn couldn't help thinking even that felt like one of those normal moments from any couple's life together—waiting for a repairperson to come fix something in their home.

He and Alice spent nearly every day together that week,

working toward getting her house into shape, then they spent every evening together, taking things slowly, one step at a time. Once, they went out for dinner; other times, they ate at Alice's or at Finn's. If the weather was nice—and spring-time in the Finger Lakes could run the gamut from frosty to fair—they took walks through the neighborhood after-ward or window-shopped in the town proper. The way any normal couple would.

And every evening ended with the same sort of kiss they'd shared that first night after the kiss beneath the syca-more tree. Tentative, inquisitive, slow...and concluding with Alice's hands on her own cheeks because she still couldn't quite acclimate herself to his beard. So Thursday night, when Alice came to his house for dinner, Finn greeted her at the door with a surprise. She noticed it immediately after he opened his front door to her.

"Oh, my God, you shaved!" she cried with a smile.

It was all he needed to hear to realize just how much his beard had bothered her. Not enough for it to be a deterrent, but enough that she clearly preferred him without it. She'd just been too polite to tell him so.

She immediately lifted a hand to his face and curled her fingers under his chin, turning his head first one way, then the other. Then her smile broadened.

"Oh, yeah. There's the guy I used to know and lo—" She halted herself, but she didn't stop smiling. "There's the guy I used to know."

Finn scrubbed a hand over the bare skin he hadn't touched in years. Truth be told, he kind of liked having it gone, too. It could get itchy sometimes.

She dropped her hand but couldn't seem to tear her gaze from his face. "You did this for me, didn't you?"

"Nah," he told her. "I did it for us."

Her response to that was to lean in and brush her lips over first one cheek, then the other. Then she kissed his mouth, a slow, soft, lingering caress that left him—and, he was pretty sure, Alice, too—wanting a little something more. Just as soon as they figured out exactly where the hell all of this was taking them.

He tilted his head back toward the living room. "Come on in."

Tonight Finn had insisted on cooking for Alice, because she'd cooked last night when the repairs he had to make to some of the sunroom windows took longer than planned. But where she'd served up a pasta primavera with a lemon-garlic kale salad and Parmesan basil bread that had been perfect for the spring weather—which had actually *been* spring weather for a change, since the Finger Lakes finally seemed to be shedding its winter coat—Finn had to resort to the sort of manly man cooking his father had taught him: a flank steak marinated in A.1. Sauce, diner-style green beans and a couple of big ol' baked potatoes.

Thanks to daylight saving time, the sky outside the kitchen window was still pale gray, in spite of the clock reading nearly seven thirty. The day had gotten away from them again somehow, but neither had minded. Alice's house was coming along nicely. They'd pretty much finished everything that needed doing on the first floor and had moved upstairs this morning. He figured that in another week, the house would be in good enough shape that she could start contacting Realtors to list it.

They still needed to do some work on the landscaping, but until they could be sure that the last of the freezing weather had come and gone, they didn't want to plant anything. What was there definitely needed some grooming, however, since Nora, as far as he could see, hadn't done any for the past few years. He remembered when Alice's mother had been a consummate gardener and how beautiful the backyard had always been from spring through fall. Of course, a lot of that beauty—at least in the backyard—had been a result of Alice herself, as far as Finn was concerned. But yeah. They had done a lot in the past couple of weeks.

Leaving the steak to marinate for a bit—the potatoes were already in the oven, and the green beans were in the pot, good to go—Finn grabbed another bottle of Genesee beer and exited through the back door to join Alice on the patio. She sat in a chaise with her jeans-clad legs stretched out in front of her, her oversize button-down, the same sage green as her eyes, flowing down to her knees. Her dark red hair was caught at her nape in a loose, curly ponytail, a few tendrils escaping to dance around her chin with the evening breeze. She'd barely touched the glass of wine he'd poured her before starting the dinner prep, and she was staring off at a sky barely stained with the lavenders and ambers of a sun that was dipping beneath the trees.

"What are you thinking about?" he asked.

When she turned to look at him, it seemed almost as if she were moving in slow motion. Her expression was dreamy, her eyes were soft, and her lips were slightly parted. He felt as if he were seeing her through some kind of Hollywood camera lens, one that had been developed to buff all the rough edges off people and soften their imperfections. But Alice didn't have any rough edges to buff, and she was as close to perfect as a human being could be. There was nothing artificial there. Just a woman looking happy and satisfied after a long, productive day.

"I was just thinking," she said, "that if things had gone… differently…when you and I were in high school, we might still be living this exact moment this exact way, but just arrived here taking a different route. I mean, not to get all bleak and grim, but even if I'd never…even if we'd never…" Her brows knit for a moment, and her eyes grew damp, but she hurried on. "Even if we took Sarah out of the equation, and even if you and I hadn't been able to leave Sudbury after graduation together the way we planned, even if we'd gone in totally opposite directions, for that matter, your father still would have had his heart attack, and my mother still would have gotten cancer, and you and I still would have ended up back in Sudbury because of that. You still might have ended up living in the house where you grew up, and I still would have had to get my mother's things in order, including the sale of her house."

He moved to the chair beside the chaise and sat down, then enjoyed a long, thoughtful swallow of his beer. "Yeah. Like, even if you and I had gotten separated some other way," he said, "and even without all the…even without the rough times we went through, we might still have run into each other again and wound up doing all the same things we've been doing for the last couple weeks."

She smiled a little sadly. "Maybe the finger of fate isn't so fickle after all."

"I've been thinking about stuff like that a lot, too," he told her. "There have been times this week when it's just felt like this is the way you and I have been living all along. Just going about our day-to-day business the way we have been since we were kids, without anything to interrupt it."

"Yeah."

"Like this is how our life together could have been— should have been—all along."

"Yeah."

He met her gaze levelly. "Like this is how it could still be." She nodded.

He dropped his gaze to the ground, toeing a crack in the patio cement that had been there since he was a kid. "No reason to think it can't still be."

When Alice didn't reply to that, he braved a look up again. Her eyes were clear and bright and filled with something he didn't dare hope to think was real.

Not until she said, "I still love you, you know. I never stopped."

Something hot and jagged twisted in his chest, hearing the words. There was a time when she hadn't said them to anyone but him, and he couldn't help wondering if she'd ever said them to anyone else. Not that it would make any difference if she had. But he felt a little guilty now about having said them to someone else himself. Even if, at some point, he realized he'd only said them out of a sense of misguided duty, it had still kind of felt like a betrayal to Alice when he had.

He'd lied to her when he told her that what he'd had with the woman he lived with in Philadelphia had been nothing serious. Well, yeah, in the long run, it hadn't been. For a little while, it had been serious enough for the two of them to shack up together. Or, at least, it had seemed serious enough at the time for the two of them to shack up together. After Finn returned to Philadelphia from his first trip back to Sudbury to see Alice, only to discover she'd left town and no one knew where she was, he'd felt lost and more alone than he'd ever been in his life. When he met that other woman, it had been easy to convince himself that he could love someone other than Alice. Then, when he'd realized one day how much she wasn't Alice, he understood that no, he couldn't. That he never really loved that woman at all, even if he had said those words to her, because she wasn't Alice and never would be.

"I still love you, too," he told Alice now. "You're the only person I've ever loved."

And that, at least, was true. He did love Alice. He'd always loved Alice. He always would love Alice. And no one but Alice.

She smiled at that, less sadly this time. "Part of me never thought I'd say or hear those words again. But another part of me kind of feels like I always knew I would. It's weird."

It was weird, Finn had to agree. It really did feel as if the two of them had fallen right back into place this week without ever having skipped a beat. They were entirely different people from the kids they used to be. And yet, somehow, they were exactly the same.

"Like we've been away for way too long," he said softly. "But also like we never left."

"Yeah."

He smiled, too. "Then I have to ask you a very important question about this moment, regardless of how we got here."

"Yes?"

His smile broadened. "How do you like your steak?"

Chapter Seven

As Alice wiped dry the last of the dinner dishes, she couldn't stop staring at Finn. Even after looking at him like this all night, she still couldn't believe he'd shaved off his beard. And he'd done it for her, she was certain, even if he did say he did it for both of them. He looked so different without it. Shaving the beard had shaved years off his appearance, too. He was so much more like his teenage self. So much more like the boy who had been the center of her world when they were kids. He seemed less gruff without it. Less serious. Lighter. Happier. More himself than he'd been since they reconnected.

Or maybe he seemed to be all those things because of all the time the two of them had spent together in the past couple of weeks. God knew she felt lighter and happier these days than she had in years. More like herself. Since, truly, the only time in her life she'd ever really felt like herself was when she had been with Finn. Because Finn had accepted her just the way she was. There had never been any conditions with him, the way there had always been with her mother. He'd liked her. Period. He'd loved her. Period. Simply because she was Alice.

"So…any idea what color you want to paint your bedroom?" he asked her for perhaps the thousandth time this week.

Although there were still enough unfinished projects to last them until the end of April, her room was the only room in the house whose paint they had yet to buy. She sighed and replied to his question the way she always did.

"It doesn't matter. Whatever will make it look best."

It wouldn't be her room for much longer anyway. Not that it had ever felt much like her room to begin with.

Where before Finn always replied with some platitude like *Well, just give it some thought,* he took a different tack this time. "It does matter," he told her emphatically. "You're taking back the house you grew up in, Alice, even if you're planning on selling it. Maybe someone else is going to own it before long, but you want to leave something of yourself behind there, even if it's only something of yourself that's been there for a couple of months."

"Why would I want to leave something of myself behind there?" she asked. "I was never happy in that house."

He grinned. A little lasciviously, she couldn't help thinking. "Maybe not inside it, but out in the garden…"

She felt her face flame at the memories of all their adolescent make-out sessions behind the rhododendron, not to mention the first time they made love there. Okay, maybe she'd experienced the absolute peak of joy at that house in some ways. Even inside sometimes, on those nights when she lay in bed thinking about Finn or waiting to hear the rattle of the pebble he tossed at her window to let her know he was there. But even those moments of happiness in her room had been mixed with fears that her mother would find out what was going on between them. Even so, maybe she should paint it a color to commemorate the good feelings that came with thinking about Finn, if nothing else. She just wondered if there was a hue out there called Hunka Hunka Burnin' Love.

"Okay, I'll pick one out next time we're at the hardware store," she promised. And she'd do her best to make sure it wasn't something in the flaming red family.

They finished tidying up in the kitchen, but with darkness having fallen completely by now, it was too chilly to return to the patio. Alice wasn't ready to go home just yet, though. Finn clearly wasn't ready for the night to end, either, because he refilled her glass with wine and grabbed himself another beer, twisting off the top with a wet hiss.

He looked toward the back door and must have come to the same conclusion she had herself. So he dipped his head toward the living room and, with a silent nod in agreement, she followed him there.

In all their years together as teenagers, Alice had never come to Finn's house. She wasn't sure why. His father had known the two of them were seeing each other, and he'd been fine with it. Happy, even, because Leo Huxley had thought Alice was a nice girl, even if her mother wasn't. She'd just always thought it would be strange to go to Finn's house when he wasn't allowed in hers. Or maybe doing that might have added an element of intimacy to their relationship neither of them was quite ready to introduce to it. It was one thing to have sex together—that was a natural response to perfectly healthy hormones. It was normal to be in love—teenagers were more prone to those emotions than even adults were. Being in Finn's house, though, existing in the same space that belonged to his family, where love took on a whole new meaning, because family love went way deeper and was way more binding than romantic love… For some reason, Alice had always been reluctant to infringe on that. Maybe because her own family dynamics had been so *un*healthy that she'd feared she might taint

Finn's. She only knew she had never felt right, when they were kids, about invading that space.

Finn's parents had made his house as warm and inviting as Alice's mother had made theirs cool and standoffish. Nora had never had anyone over, after all. Why should she make her place welcoming? It was hers and hers alone, and it would let anyone who dared enter it know that. Finn's house, though…

It was clear he hadn't done much to update his home from their childhood, either, though she suspected in his case, it was because he had such fond memories of growing up there. The living room was a time capsule of the "shabby chic" that had been so fashionable when they were kids, its sofa and chairs well used and well loved, the flowered wool hooked rug spanning the hardwood floor almost bare in spots. Feral plants in bright pots filled a corner near the broad bay window. Family photos hung on one wall, with Finn being the primary subject, from babyhood through high school graduation. Another wall sported shelves holding all the typical mom touches that most homes had when they were kids—books at every angle interspersed with mason jars filled with seashells and keys and other knick-knacks, bric-a-brac commemorating family vacations and celebrations, all of it surrounding one of those inescapable Live, Laugh, Love signs.

Of course, a sign like that probably hadn't been blustering or pretentious for Finn's house. There had probably been a lot of living, laughing and loving there when his mother was still alive.

He moved to the fireplace, where logs and kindling had been set. Although the spring days had started to turn warmish and pleasant, nights in the Finger Lakes still had a bit of a bite to them, and tonight was no exception. As

Finn set a match to the tinder, Alice moved to the sofa, setting her wine on the side table. He joined her once he was confident the fire had taken, setting his beer on the other end table. For the past two weeks, they'd never had trouble finding something to talk about, but suddenly, for some reason, neither seemed to know what to say.

"Supposed to get down in the low forties tonight," he finally said. "Figured it would be a good night for a fire."

Alice nodded. "I always hated that our house didn't have a fireplace when I was growing up."

"Yeah, kinda odd, that," he said. "Most houses in Sudbury do. Especially the older ones like ours."

Finn's house had been built around the same time as Alice's had been, in the early twentieth century, when industrialization was starting to bustle in upstate New York. Like hers, it was a bungalow, though larger in scale, with four bedrooms and three full baths as opposed to her two bedrooms and two-and-a-half baths. The rooms were larger, as well, with more windows. She remembered Finn telling her when they were kids that when his parents married, they'd planned to have three or four children. But that had never come about.

Alice couldn't help thinking now that the house would have been perfect for a family that size. Big enough that they would be able to escape one another from time to time, but small enough that such escapes wouldn't isolate any of them. A house like this would compel a family to be a family, whether in good times or bad, simply because they would have to be close both physically and emotionally, provided theirs was a healthy, loving dynamic. And with parents like Finn's, how could a family of theirs not have that?

A part of her wondered why Finn had kept the place

after his father's death, since it was far too big for one person. Or, at the very least, why he hadn't redecorated to update his surroundings and better suit his own needs. But being in the house now, and feeling the warmth of both the fire and the room itself, another part of her didn't wonder about that at all.

"Your house was obviously designed to attract someone with a family," she said. "I think maybe my house was built more for older couples whose kids were grown or for single people who intended to stay single."

"Yeah, I guess that makes sense," he said.

Alice nodded.

And then silence fell between them again. Fortunately, the fire was crackling nicely, so the quiet didn't become disquieting. Well, not *too* disquieting anyway. Not until it began to drag on indefinitely.

"So," Alice said in an effort to liven things up. "Other than paint for my bedroom, is there anything else we still need to buy for the rest of the renovation? I'm putting together my financial plan for the rest of April and the first part of May, and want to make sure I budget for everything I'm going to need."

Finn thought for a minute. "Let's see… We have the tile and grout for the upstairs bathroom, the quarter-round and baseboards for after I refinish the floors…" He listed a few other minor purchases, then reminded her of the big one. "Furniture," he said. "You've gotten rid of almost all of your mom's old stuff."

Yeah, because she couldn't stand to look at any of it anymore. No way was she going to take any of it with her when she moved, and she still wasn't sure how far she would be going once she did. Yes, things with Finn were going nicely. But it was still too new—and their feelings from the past were still lingering in their present—for her to know what was going to happen. There was still a chance, albeit small—and it was growing smaller with every minute she spent with Finn—that she might leave Sudbury. It would be a lot easier if she didn't have to take a moving van with her when—if—she did. And even if she stayed here, she was still selling the house and moving into a smaller, more accommodating place until she did figure everything out. It would be better to wait to buy anything until she knew just what kind of space she would be furnishing.

"Is that really necessary?" she asked. "I thought I'd just wait until I settled somewhere else."

Finn's expression clouded when she said the words *somewhere else*. But she said nothing to clarify them. How could she, when she still wasn't sure what her intentions were herself?

"You really should put something in their place for showing the house," he told her. "Staged homes are a lot easier to sell and sell a lot faster than empty ones. And they bring in more money."

Alice really wasn't all that worried about the *more money* part of his statement. But the ease and speed-to-sell were both fairly major concerns. The sooner she could be out of that house, so steeped in past unhappiness and bad memories, the better. If that meant spending on a few essentials earlier than she'd planned, then she would do it.

"Okay," she told him. "Maybe we can go out next week and look for a few things."

His expression cleared some at that. "Sounds good."

Only then did she realize she had just invited Finn to tag along on plans that involved her future, however vague they were at the moment. But that was what they were doing, wasn't it? she reminded herself. Waiting and seeing what happened and taking it one step at a time. The fact that she had just taken a step forward, even if it was just a baby one, and included him in it, was significant. It meant that a part of her, at least, was thinking about a future with him.

"Thanks again for all your help with this," she told him.

He grinned. "Hey, you paid half up front, and you'll be getting a bill for the other half when it's all done."

She grinned back. "Well, you were the most affordable bid, after all. Not to mention, you know, the only bid."

At this, he chuckled in a way that reminded her of their adolescence, a sound that seemed even more genuine coupled with his newly shaved state. It was a sound completely free of stress or anxiety or anything bad, really. He had always been able to do that—free himself of emotions that never did anybody any good. He always joked that Alice felt enough stress and anxiety for both of them. Which, in a way, had been true. She'd always wished she knew what that was like—to be completely free of uncertainty and apprehension. She still couldn't imagine it. But Finn, on some level, could still feel and be like the kid he used to be.

Because of seeing a hint of his old self, she began to feel a little like her old self, too. Scooting across what little distance separated them, she cupped her hand over his warm jaw and leaned in to kiss him. He was taken aback by the suddenness of the gesture for a moment, but it didn't take long before he kissed her back. And kissed her and kissed her and kissed her.

They'd enjoyed a lot of kisses since reconnecting. Usually, those kisses were soft and fairly chaste, like those first ones under the sycamore tree. A few times, they'd grown a little more passionate. But never for long. One or the other of them—usually Alice—pulled back before things went too far. This time, though, for some reason...

This time Alice didn't want to pull back. And neither, evidently, did Finn.

Because he roped both arms around her waist and pulled her into his lap. This allowed her to reach over and snap off the sole lamp that had been burning, throwing the room into the pale gold of the firelight. Then she curled into him as if she were a missing part of him, tangling the fingers of one hand in his hair as she curled the others around his nape.

For a long time, they only kissed, each one longer and deeper than the one before it, until they were fairly consuming each other. She felt his hand at her waist dip below her shirt and scoot higher, until he was cupping the lower curve of her breast in the vee of his thumb and forefinger. When he cupped his hand completely over the swell of her breast, she gasped, but he caught her mouth with his again and kissed her more deeply still. As they vied for possession of the embrace, Alice dropped her hand to the top button of his blue jeans and unfastened it. Then she unfastened the next one. And the next. And the next and the next, until she could tuck her hand completely beneath the worn denim.

He groaned when she pressed her hand against him, swelling to life against her fingers. As he thumbed the sensitive peak of her breast over the cotton of her bra, she stroked her fingers along his hard length over his boxers. Little by little, they each grew more frantic, until Alice somehow managed to find the presence of mind to pull herself out of their intimate touches and into the soft glow of the room.

She met his gaze levelly and asked softly, "Is this really going to happen?"

Instead of answering, he turned the question on her. "Do you want it to happen?"

"I don't know," she answered honestly. "Are we ready for it?"

He grinned. "We said we'd wait and see what happens. This kinda seems to be happening now."

He had a point. If they'd gotten this far, on some level, they were probably ready.

"There's just one problem," she told him. "I'm not using anything. Birth control, I mean. Since I came back to Sudbury to take care of my mother, there hasn't been any need for me to."

"I could use something," he told her. He hurried to add, "I mean, I haven't had any need since I came back to Sudbury, either."

Meaning he, like Alice, hadn't been with anyone for a while. Somehow, that made her feel a little more confident that what was happening between them now—even if maybe it wasn't exactly happening slowly—was a good thing. Was the right thing.

"But I have some condoms upstairs. If you want to… I mean… If you don't want to…" He expelled a restless sound. "Look, Alice, I know what I want. I've wanted it ever since you came back to Sudbury. I want to be with you. The way we used to be when we were kids. The way we always said back then that we'd be when we were adults. But if you want something else…" He kissed her again, softly this time, tenderly, then pulled back and met her gaze intently. "What do you want, Alice?"

"If you don't use protection, I could get pregnant," she told him plainly. She was curious to see how he would react.

His reaction was to simply meet her gaze and say nothing.

"I mean, the timing probably isn't right for that to happen," she told him. "But it's possible."

He gave her another one of those sweet, gentle kisses.

Then he looked at her again and repeated, "What do you want, Alice?"

She knew she should want him to use protection. She knew he actually should use protection. It was the smart thing to do. Not using it that one time when they were kids had led to nothing but heartbreak. Okay, that wasn't quite true. It hadn't led to *nothing* but heartbreak. There had been some happiness in there, too, for a little while. Once they'd gotten over the shock and the fear, when they started thinking about a future together for them and baby Sarah... They hadn't lied to themselves that it would be easy. But they'd still found reasons to be joyful about the new life growing inside her. That had made losing the baby all the more devastating.

And even if there was a good chance any future pregnancies she might have would be perfectly normal ones, even if there was no reason to think she and Finn would lose another child, were they ready to try for a family again? Even if the past two weeks had felt as if they were simply picking up where they left off, even if they both loved each other, even if they both still wanted a future together... Was it a good idea for them to take that chance now?

He should use something, she told herself, since she wasn't. They were still in the early stages of whatever was happening, even if there was less hindering them now than there had been back then. Even if they were adults now. Even if they'd finished with their schooling and had each built a life of sorts for themselves. Even if they were both financially secure. And still in love. And...

What do you want, Alice?

He'd asked a question that required an answer. So Alice told him the truth.

"I want you," she said softly. "I want us. I want everything to be the way it was supposed to be. I want to try again, Finn, to be all the things we said we would be. I still want that."

He smiled again, and whatever tension had been left between them completely evaporated. As he covered her mouth with his, he lay back on the sofa, pulling her along with him, until she lay atop him from head to toe. He'd pulled the curtains closed after starting the fire, so the room was as intimate as it could be. He kissed her again— or maybe she kissed him this time—and they took their time enjoying it. She tangled her fingers in his hair as he ducked his hands beneath her shirt to caress her bare back with both hands. Instinctively, they wove their legs together until their hips were aligned, his thigh pressed against the most intimate part of her. When he moved his hands lower, taking advantage of her open jeans to cup the tender flesh of her buttocks, she gasped. And when he moved his leg against her, she couldn't stifle the murmur of satisfaction that rose from deep inside her. As one, they turned their bodies until his back was pressed against the back of the sofa, and she tucked her hands between their bodies, moving her fingers into the open fly of his jeans to stroke him once, twice, three times, reveling in the quickness and heat of his erection. Finn growled his pleasure in response, tasting her more deeply as he pushed her body more intimately into his.

He moved their bodies again until he was sitting with her astride him, his mouth never leaving hers. Button by button, he opened her shirt, then reached behind her to unfasten her bra, pushing both it and her shirt from her body. When Alice pulled away from the kiss for a breath, he ducked his head to take her breast into his mouth instead. She sighed at the sensation as he laved her with the flat of his tongue, then teased her with its tip. He moved one hand into her jeans, to the juncture of her legs, and pressed a long finger into the damp folds of flesh that he could reach. Alice's entire body jerked forward in response, and she writhed and gasped with every new stroke until she nearly came apart at the seams.

Without thinking, she stood to shed the jeans and panties that were still in their way. Finn rose, too, discarding his clothes as quickly and carelessly as she did. He tugged the afghan from the back of the sofa and spread it over the cushions, then urged Alice down upon it on her back. Then he moved himself between her legs, pushing one so that her foot was on the floor and pulling the other up over his shoulder. Then he lowered his body between her legs, until his mouth was at the damp, heated core of her and…

Oh. Oh, oh, *oh*. Did things he'd *never* done when they were kids.

Alice wouldn't have thought it would be possible for the two of them to make love better than they had when they were teenagers. But the raging hormones of youth had nothing on the raging hormones of two adults who had gone too long without enjoying each other.

As she tangled her fingers in his hair, Finn drove her to the edge of delirium. Then he moved once more, lifting her hips from the sofa to enter her—deeply, heavily, completely. Again and again, he thrust into her, until she wasn't sure where her body ended and his began. She pressed her hands to his firm buttocks, pulling him forward hard as she bucked her hips against him, as if doing that might somehow propel him farther inside, when they were already as close as two human beings could be. For long moments, their bodies writhed and buffeted together until, in one long, luscious climax, the two of them came together.

Alice went still as Finn spilled himself inside her, shuddering from the aftershocks of delight that quaked through her. Then he moved them both until he was on his back again with her atop him, curling his arms around her waist, his face buried in her neck, telling her again and again how much he loved her.

When Alice was finally coherent enough to process thought, she waited for the regrets, fears and concerns she told herself she should be feeling. But she only felt euphoric. Euphoric and hopeful and satisfied. As if nothing in the world could go wrong again. She and Finn were together, the way they were meant to be. And this time, she was certain, everything was going to happen exactly the way it should have before.

Chapter Eight

Finn awoke Monday morning with a jerk to a sound he almost didn't recognize—the ringing of his phone. No one ever called him. He didn't even get that many spam calls, thanks to him rarely giving out his number. Most of the friends he'd made as a child in Sudbury had scattered to other parts of the state, and he didn't have any family to whom he was close enough to want to be in touch. He snatched the phone from the nightstand and squinted at his clock in the murky morning light. He wasn't due at Alice's until ten. After a weekend spent together that he could only describe as *absolutely perfect*, they'd decided to spend last night in their own beds in order to get some much-needed sleep and start back at her house late in the morning today. It was just past eight. Still a chance for another hour of sleep. If it weren't for whoever was on the other end of the call.

The number staring back at him from the phone screen wasn't one he recognized, and there was no name above it from his contacts list, which was made up mostly of regular clients. So spam. He thumbed the button to silence the ringing and placed it back down. After a few moments, though, an alert pinged to let him know he had a voice mail. He grumbled a ripe oath and jackknifed up in bed. He was awake enough now that he knew he wasn't going to get any more sleep.

When he looked at the number again, he noted that the area code wasn't from around here. But that didn't mean it wasn't a local call. The message was probably just someone trying to get in touch with him about his car's extended warranty—yeah, right—but on the outside chance it was a potential new client, he put the phone on speaker and tapped Play.

And then heard a message that dropped a solid block of ice into his belly.

Certain he must still be asleep and dreaming, he played the message again. The caller told him she was on the other side of the country, about as far south in Florida as a person could go, but her words took him back to a place he scarcely thought about now. And a time he thought about even less. The ten years he lived in Philadelphia after he graduated from high school, a point in his life where he had been so lost, and so confused, and so…dammit, so sad… that, for most of them, he hadn't been thinking straight. Those years in Philly, especially the early ones, felt now like they had been lived by another person. In a way, he supposed they had been. The man he was now bore little in common with the one who'd lived in a tiny apartment above the hoagie shop on South Street. He bore even less in common with the man who'd shared that apartment for a little while with someone else.

His wife. Denise. His lie to Alice when he told her the woman he lived with in Philadelphia wasn't serious had been a real whopper. For a while, she had been serious enough that he'd accepted her proposal when she asked him to marry her. In hindsight, that marriage had been a mistake from the beginning, as evidenced by the fact that it hadn't even lasted two years. Partly because Finn realized too late that he was only attracted to Denise in the first place because she reminded him of Alice. But more because, well, Denise hadn't been Alice. Two things it hadn't taken long for Denise to realize, too.

"Good morning, Mr. Huxley," the woman leaving the message greeted him for the second time. "My name is Mona Ramos, and I'm a social worker for Monroe County in Key West, Florida. I'm handling the case of Denise Sullivan, who passed away a week ago. She has some unsettled affairs concerning you that I need to discuss with you as soon as possible. If you could give me a call back today, I'd appreciate it. Thank you very much." She repeated the number with the area code he hadn't recognized and then hung up. Leaving Finn to stare at the phone in his hand as if it were some kind of alien technology he'd never seen before.

Not sure why, he hit Play again, but even hearing the message a third time didn't make it any clearer. Not just the part about Denise having died—she was only a year older than him—but the part about her having some affairs that involved him, too. In what way could he still be involved in any of her affairs? They'd entered into their marriage with nothing, and they'd left it the same way. They hadn't even spoken in the five years since they signed the divorce papers. Although they'd agreed to an informal separation for six months, during which Denise moved back in with her mother in Allentown, it hadn't taken long for them both to realize the separation would be permanent. Though they'd texted and spoken on the phone occasionally during that time, neither of them had tried to get together in person. Ultimately, they signed the judgment of dissolution of their marriage almost a year to the day from their split.

What the hell could Denise have left behind that included him? And why was it a social worker calling him instead of an attorney?

He started to hit the callback button but stopped himself. He needed to clear his head of its nighttime cobwebs first. Try to conjure some memories from that time, since, in all honesty, he could barely remember what Denise looked like at this point. Every time he tried, her face was superimposed with Alice's.

Coffee, he thought. He needed coffee to help him wake up and spur his thoughts. Surely, whatever Mona Ramos had to tell him could wait for half an hour.

An hour later, though, Finn's thoughts were even more jumbled than they'd been when he first awoke. Because it wasn't a some*thing* concerning Finn that Denise had left behind when she fell asleep at the wheel after working a double shift as an ER nurse. It was a some*one*. A daughter. Named Riley. Who, according to Mona Ramos, was Finn's daughter, too. She was born before the divorce was finalized, meaning that according to Pennsylvania law, whether the child was his by blood or not, he was her father. At least unless he could prove otherwise. But when the social worker told him the exact date of Riley Sullivan's birth, Finn realized she could very well be his not just legally, but biologically, too. He and Denise might have had their problems, but infidelity had never been one of them. She could have been a few weeks pregnant when they split, without either of them knowing it.

Why hadn't she told him once she found out? he wondered as he stared at the dark screen of his phone. Unless maybe she *had* hooked up with someone else before their split and knew Finn wasn't her baby's father. But if that were the case, Mona Ramos would have been calling that guy, not Finn. Even if that guy had just been a casual fling for Denise while the two of them were still together—though he truly could not believe she would have done something like that—Denise wasn't the type, either, to pin paternity on someone who wasn't the father.

Could Riley Sullivan really be Finn's daughter? And if she was, what was he going to do about it? Denise's parents were both dead now, according to the social worker, and Finn already knew she didn't have any siblings. Since she moved to Key West with Riley two years ago, she'd kept a low profile and hadn't made any friends outside of work. Ms. Ramos said they had called everyone in Denise's contact list about Riley, but none had expressed an interest in taking on the girl's care and feeding—not even while they looked for her father. Riley Sullivan was currently in foster care. Not surprisingly, Finn hadn't been included in Denise's contacts himself, and they'd only discovered his name when they located Riley's birth certificate among Denise's effects at her apartment.

Jeez, he might actually have a daughter. A daughter for whom he would be responsible, if she truly was his. How was he supposed to explain any of this to Alice? Especially when he didn't understand any of it himself?

He still didn't know the answer to that when he arrived at her house at just past ten. She opened the door to him with a smile, the kitten, whom they still hadn't named, cradled in her palm. But her smile disappeared immediately when she saw the look on his face. Even the kitten looked concerned.

"What's wrong?" she asked by way of a greeting.

He swallowed hard. "We need to talk."

Now she looked a little panicky. Finn wished he could reassure her, but he was still pretty panicky himself.

She opened the door wider to let him in, and he strode past her. There still wasn't any furniture in the living room, so he headed toward the sunroom, where there was some aged wicker furniture that had enough retro value to be fashionable again. Alice followed, sitting beside him close enough on the couch that their legs touched. He told himself it was a good sign. She could have sat at the other end. Or even in the chair on the other side of the room.

"Finn, what is it?" she asked softly.

The kitten squirmed as anxiously as she spoke, so she set the little fuzzball on the floor, and she trotted off.

He looked up at the ceiling for a moment, trying to remember one of the many ways he'd rehearsed this in his head on the drive over. But none of those explanations came to him now. Probably because none of them had been that good to begin with. Finally, he looked at Alice again.

"You remember when I told you I lived with someone for a little while when I was in Philly?"

She nodded but said nothing. Only looked more distraught than she had before.

"And remember how I told you that it wasn't serious with her?"

She nodded again. Silently again.

"Well, I kind of wasn't honest with you."

Her eyebrows arrowed downward.

"I mean, in hindsight, I realize it really wasn't serious. But at the time... While she and I were together..." He sighed heavily. "At the time, for a little while, it felt like it was serious."

Alice continued to study him in silence.

Just spit it out, he told himself. "Serious enough that she and I..." He sighed again. "Her name was Denise. And for a few years, she was my... She was my wife."

Now Alice's brows shot up to nearly her hairline. "You were *married*?"

At the moment, he felt almost as incredulous as Alice

clearly was. He truly did look back on that time as if it had happened to someone else. Until this morning, he hadn't given Denise a thought for years. She was just that absent from his brain and his life and everything else these days. When he first met her, though...

He had just returned to Philadelphia from a trip to Sudbury—his first time back in four years. By then, his business was running fairly well, and he was earning enough to keep himself afloat. He'd figured it was a good time to try to reconnect with Alice. Even if the two of them hadn't been in contact for years, even if she'd never given any indication when he first left that she would be open to reconnecting at some point in the future, even if things between them might still be raw and painful... He had just thought maybe, somehow, they could try again. So he'd gone back to Sudbury to see Alice.

Only to find that she'd left town months before, and no one knew where she was or how to get in contact with her. She was gone. And he had no way of knowing if he would ever see her again. And if he'd felt devastated and broken before, it was nothing compared to the way he felt after that. What little hope he'd had of reconnecting with Alice in Sudbury was gone. Because Alice was gone. Forever.

He met Denise at a coffee shop the week after he returned to Philly. She really had reminded him a lot of Alice. Not just in looks, but in personality, too. When she'd asked him out, he hadn't been able to resist saying yes. He'd just felt so alone and weary and hopeless. Denise was nice and pretty and easy to talk to. She made him feel less alone.

After getting to know her better, he of course realized she wasn't Alice, but by then, the two of them were pretty tight, and he really had thought they could build a future together. Not the one he would have had with Alice—not even close. But that future was going to be impossible now, and he'd honestly thought he and Denise could be happy together. A different kind of happy than he would have had with Alice, but happy nonetheless. He hadn't realized how much he was deluding himself until it was too late.

"Yeah," he said softly. "I was married."

As he tried to explain all that to Alice, though, he could see she didn't understand. He supposed he didn't blame her. How many nights had the two of them lain in the backyard of this very house talking about how they would never— could never—love another person, and how they would be together forever. Even before Alice got pregnant, they'd been completely devoted to each other and to a long life together. How could he explain that he'd fallen for someone else, enough to make a lifelong commitment to her? How was he supposed to make that make sense to Alice when it didn't even make sense to him now?

"You have to understand, Alice," he said when he finished a quick history of his time with Denise, including how quickly it all went to hell. "I came back from Sudbury after finding out you were gone and no one knew where you were... I was a wreck. And a part of me was still kind of raw with what you and I had been through. I wasn't in a good place. I was..." He expelled a restless sound. "I was lonely, Alice. I was sad. Even before meeting Denise, every day for me was just getting up, getting through and going home. And Denise..." He debated whether or not he should even admit it, but he made himself continue. "Denise, when I first met her, reminded me of you. She looked a little like you. She was kind and smart and funny like you. I think some part of me just sort of switched over to thinking that being with her would be as close to being with you as I would ever be again. But she wasn't you. And once she and

I both realized that, we knew the marriage had been a mistake from the beginning, so we divorced."

Alice had been silent the entire time he spoke, but her expression told him exactly how much his words hurt her. And hell, he hadn't even gotten to the main event. But she hadn't moved from where she sat, either. She was still sitting close to him. That had to be a good sign, right? Even so, he didn't want to continue until he knew just where they stood.

"You're not saying anything," he pointed out unnecessarily.

"That's because I don't know what to say," she told him. "I mean, it was strange enough the other day, hearing that you'd lived with someone else. Now you're telling me you were married to her. You have to give me a little time to absorb that."

He nodded. "Yeah, I know. And I'm sorry, Alice. I just… That time was so long ago. And it was such a weird time, being away from Sudbury, from everything I'd ever known and… And loved. When I think about Philadelphia now, it's like I'm remembering some TV show I used to watch. It doesn't seem real."

"But it was real."

"Yeah. It was."

"You actually loved someone else enough to marry her."

"I thought I did."

"Did you tell her you loved her?"

He hesitated, then said, "Yeah. But not like—"

"So you loved someone else enough to marry her," Alice interjected. "Enough to build a life with her."

This time Finn was the one who remained silent.

"To maybe even someday start a family with her."

And that, when he heard Alice say it, was the worst charge on the line. That he would find with someone else the thing the two of them had been denied together. That, honestly, had never occurred to him when things were happening with Denise. The two of them never talked about having children. Only being together. But he could see why Alice would come to the conclusion that she had. And really, it wasn't exactly an erroneous conclusion. It made sense to assume that if two people made a commitment to spend their lives together, there could very well be kids at some point along the line.

This was the perfect place for him to tell Alice about the existence of a little girl who might possibly be his daughter. She had just provided the perfect verbal cue. But he still had no idea how to tell her what he needed to tell her.

"A life and a family that should have been ours," Alice continued softly. "You tried to find that with someone else. I know it was a long time ago," she hurried on before he could comment. Not that he'd intended to comment. He was actually kind of grateful she kept talking. "And I know, by then, you…by the time you got married, you were probably thinking the two of us would never see each other again. But, Finn…"

Here, she did move away from him. Not a lot. Not quite to the end of the sofa. But she did put some physical distance between them, and that was enough to let him know things were about to go south.

"You did move on without me," she concluded. "And you have to know that hurts to hear."

"I do know that," he assured her. "Now, I do. But eight years ago? Alice, eight years ago, I thought you were gone for good. Or, even if you weren't, you wouldn't want anything to do with me anymore."

She still looked hurt, but she gingerly—very gingerly— moved a hand to cup it over his forearm. "I appreciate you telling me this," she said. "And I'm glad you're doing it now, before things between us... Before they get..." She seemed to be having trouble finding words this morning, too. "I'm glad you're telling me now, so we can move forward without there being any secrets between us. You're just going to have to give me a little time to process it, that's all."

Yeah, well, if she thought she was going to need time to process that, she was really going to have to clear her schedule for the rest of it.

"My marriage to Denise isn't the only thing I have to tell you about," he said. "There's one other thing you need to know."

Her panicked expression returned, but she said nothing.

Finn told himself to just spit it out. "Denise died recently."

Alice's eyes closed tight. "I'm sorry, Finn."

He made himself hurry on, before he could lose his nerve, "And she left behind a daughter. A little girl named Riley."

Now Alice's eyes snapped open again.

"A little girl named Riley," he repeated, "who might be my daughter, too."

Alice would have sworn she couldn't feel any more nauseous than she did when Finn told her he used to be married. The realization that he had moved on in his life with someone else who wasn't her was, she would have been certain, the worst thing she could imagine. But no, there was something that could be worse. That not only had Finn joined his life with another woman who wasn't Alice, but that he might have a child—a daughter—who wasn't Alice's, as well.

Her stomach pitched again at his revelation, and her vision swirled. She honestly thought she might throw up.

Never in a million years would she have thought something like this was possible. That Finn might someday have a family that didn't include her.

She didn't know how she found the wherewithal to do it, but she asked, "You have a daughter?"

"I don't know," he said. "Maybe. A social worker in Florida called me this morning and told me about Denise's death and how she left behind a daughter who is *legally* mine, since she was born in Pennsylvania before my and Denise's divorce was finalized, which, by law, makes me her father."

"So she might not be your daughter," Alice said, her emotions roller-coastering from one place to another. "Biologically, I mean."

"I don't know," he said again. "I mean, after talking to the caseworker for Riley this morning and finding out when she was born, and considering the timing of her birth and when Denise and I separated, and doing the math, it's possible Riley is mine biologically, too. Unless Denise had a boyfriend toward the end there that I didn't know about at the time."

Alice hated it that she felt a moment of relief at the possibility that Finn's wife had cheated on him. "Was she unfaithful?"

"I don't think so," he said. "Things got rocky between us sometimes, but I really don't think infidelity ever played a role in that. I never had any reason to think she was seeing someone else. And she really wasn't the kind of person to do something like that."

But it was possible, Alice told herself, clinging to whatever capricious threads she could, even if they weren't very nice. Maybe Denise's daughter wasn't Finn's after all. Maybe she was another man's daughter. It could happen.

"I'm flying down to Florida tomorrow," he continued,

"to meet with the social worker and take a paternity test to see if I'm Riley's father. It'll take a few days to get the results, and I won't see her before the results come in, but I should know before the end of the week whether or not I'm her father."

"And if you are?" Alice asked.

She already knew the answer to that, even without him saying it. He'd do the right thing. Finn always did the right thing. He was a good guy. If Riley was his daughter, he would accept responsibility for her and bring her back to Sudbury and raise her as his own. And when that happened—if that happened, Alice made herself amend, since, hey, this could all be a mistake—she would…she would…

Her stomach rolled again. *Oh, God.* She didn't know what she would do.

"For now, I just need to know," he said. "One step at a time. See what happens."

She knew he wasn't throwing her words back in her face. Even if it did kind of feel that way. He was just reminding her of the deal the two of them had made after that kiss beneath the sycamore changed everything. But him having a daughter…

This changed things even more. And this she could never have seen coming.

"I'm sorry," he said. "I didn't know. It certainly wasn't planned."

Maybe the daughter part wasn't planned, Alice thought. But his wedding to another woman certainly had been. And she still didn't know what to think—or how to feel—about that. Finn had been able to imagine a life with someone else—without Alice—when she had never been able to imagine one without him. He had lived a life with another woman, however short, when she'd barely even dated. He said he was lonely after leaving Sudbury, that his emotions were raw. She'd been lonely, too, when she was away. And her emotions... Her emotions had been barely restrained beneath the surface. She just didn't understand how he could have moved on with another woman like that. And now, there might be a remnant of his time with that other woman who would be by his side forever. And what happened after that...

Well. Alice didn't even want to think about it.

"It's entirely possible Riley is someone else's daughter," Finn said softly, reading her mind. "I have to believe Denise would have told me about her if she was mine. So I'll go down to Florida and take the test, and then we'll go from there. Because despite what Riley's birth certificate says, and despite what the state of Pennsylvania says, I could very well be coming back to Sudbury alone."

Chapter Nine

She was his daughter.

The moment Finn looked at the kindergarten photo that the social worker scooted across the desk toward him, he knew it. Had he been born a girl, he would have looked just like Riley Sullivan when he was five years old. Although he had stopped at the clinic where the social worker had set up an appointment for his DNA test on the way to her office, he didn't have to wait for the results of that test to know. She was his daughter. He was her father. He was going to be responsible for another human being for the rest of his life. And where there had been a time when he was totally prepared to do that—a time when, ironically, he hadn't been much more than a child himself—now, he had no idea what to do.

He looked back up at Mona Ramos, her black hair liberally threaded with silver and cropped short, her dark gaze pinned to his from behind gray cat-eye glasses. He knew she saw the clear resemblance between him and Riley, too. Beyond that, though, he could no more tell what she was thinking than he could predict the winning numbers for tomorrow's lottery.

"She looks an awful lot like me," he said. He couldn't think of anything else to say, on account of how much his head was spinning.

"Yes, she does."

"So…how do we work this?"

Ms. Ramos released the wallet-size portrait, leaving it where it lay on the desk in front of him. Finn picked it up gingerly, holding one corner between his thumb and fore-finger as if the photo were made of something that would dissolve any second. Riley Sullivan had medium red hair like her mother—the same color that Alice's had been at her age, he couldn't help thinking—and eyes the same blue-green of his own. Her hair was bound in two messy braids, as if she'd been on a windy playground just before the pic-ture was snapped, and she was wearing a T-shirt that said, in rainbow-colored letters, "Smile." She was following that advice in the photo, grinning widely, as if she'd had a very good time on that windy playground before being dragged inside for school photos. Riley Sullivan looked like a happy kid in that pic, he thought. Now she was a kid without a mother. He knew how that felt. It was going to be a while before anyone saw Riley smile like that again.

"We'll need to wait for the results of the test before we can get the paperwork finalized," she told him.

He nodded.

"Provided you want to get the paperwork finalized," Ms. Ramos said.

He looked up at that. Did she honestly think he would leave his daughter behind? "She's my daughter," he pointed out. "Of course I want to get the paperwork finalized."

"You want to accept responsibility for Riley Sullivan if the test comes back indicating you are the father, Mr. Hux-ley?"

"Yes," he said without hesitation.

She nodded once, noncommittally, but somehow Finn got the feeling it was also a nod of approval. As if maybe she had assumed before he came down here that he was going to go home alone, regardless of how everything played out.

"All right then," the social worker said. "I'll get the ball rolling. We should have the results back in a few days, and once your paternity is legally established, I can introduce you to your daughter."

His stomach rolled again. His *daughter*. He had a daughter. The way he was supposed to have had one when he was eighteen. Except that that daughter was supposed to have been with Alice. It was like part of this scenario was playing out exactly the way it was supposed to, putting his life right back on the path he had been jerked off of when he was a kid. But Alice wasn't on that path with him anymore. Because Riley *wasn't* her daughter.

And he just honestly didn't know how she was going to feel about that once he—and his daughter—returned to Sudbury.

From the moment Alice laid eyes on the little girl standing on her porch Saturday afternoon, she understood why Finn had said on the phone earlier in the week that he didn't need to wait for the results of the DNA test to know Riley Sullivan was half him. Her hair was red instead of blond, but her facial features and Aegean-blue eyes were all his. She was about the same age Finn was when Alice first met him in kindergarten. She bet if one of them fished out their class photo from that year and held it up next to the girl, little Finn Huxley in the front row, sitting next to Alice Whitlock, would be Riley Sullivan's mirror image.

Finn had a daughter. Alice didn't. Nor would she be having one anytime soon. If ever. She'd gotten her period yesterday morning. In spite of their not using protection when they made love a week ago, Alice wasn't pregnant. And she had no idea how to feel about that.

Oh, wait. Yes, she did. Because all the feelings suddenly roared up inside her to slap her right across the face. She felt confused. She felt sad. She felt bereft and desolate and betrayed. And alone. Alice felt very much alone in that moment, looking at Finn standing in front of her, holding the hand of the little girl who was his daughter. His family. In fact, Alice felt more alone than she'd ever felt in her life, even during those days after losing Sarah.

Even having had a week to think about Finn having lived a life with another woman who was his wife, she still couldn't wrap her head around how Finn had lived a life with another woman who was his wife. For years. She told herself again, as she had many times in the past several days, how she shouldn't be surprised by any of this. It wasn't as if he'd had himself cryogenically preserved while he waited for her to figure herself out and find her way back to him. He'd had every right to move on with his life without her. She hadn't exactly made it easy for him after they lost their baby. She'd been a mess, emotionally, physically, mentally, hormonally. She'd had no idea what to do next. Her mother sure had, though. And with a mother like Nora, Alice had been as pliable as warm clay. It had been easy for her to convince Alice that there was nothing to bind her to Finn anymore. That the two of them were too young to be together. That they never should have been together in the first place. How Mother knew best and would take care of Alice way better than a boy like Finn ever could.

Looking back now, Alice realized Finn must have been a mess back then, too. He'd been as in love with their future daughter as she had, and he'd been every bit as excited about the plans they made for their family's future. Losing Sarah had to have been as devastating for him as it had been for her. And although her mother's motives had been selfish and manipulative, she had still weirdly been there for Alice during her time of need. Finn hadn't had anyone to share his grief with or lean on. She didn't think he ever told anyone, even his father, about the baby. He'd planned on waiting until just before the two of them ran away together to let Leo know what was going on.

It was no wonder he left Sudbury immediately after graduating, having no one there to help him through his grief. The wonder was that he'd been able to finish school at all.

"Alice," he said softly now, "this is Riley. Riley Sullivan. She's my... She's my daughter."

Riley Sullivan. So she had her mother's last name, not Finn's. She wondered if Finn would correct that. The little girl was dressed in a rainbow tutu-like skirt and a T-shirt with a sparkly unicorn, also rainbow. As was the sweater that hung off one shoulder. Her socks, too, were striped with rainbow colors, and her sneakers—what were left of them, since the canvas was worn nearly down to rags—were just as prismatic. When she shifted her weight from one foot to the other, the soles lit up all over, multicolored lights in every color of the, well, rainbow. She was a colorful kid.

Although the little girl had had her blue gaze as pinned on Alice as Alice had had hers on Riley, when Finn spoke her name, she turned to look up at her— Alice swallowed with some difficulty—at her father. But she said nothing. Finn gazed back at his...at his daughter...and offered her a reassuring smile that was almost convincing. Then he looked back at Alice.

"She doesn't talk much," he said. "Or, you know, at all."

Riley looked at Alice again. But, as before, she remained silent.

"Mona—that's Riley's caseworker in Key West—said she hasn't spoken a word since her mother's dea—" He halted abruptly when he realized what he had been about to say. "Um," he tried again. "She hasn't spoken for nearly two weeks." Now he looked at Riley again. "But we're gonna work on that, aren't we, kid?"

Alice wasn't sure who all Finn was referring to with that *we*. Did he mean he and Riley were going to work on it? Or that he and Riley and a speech therapist were going to work on it? Or all of them and her teacher at her new school were going to work on it? Or was he including Alice in that equation, too? And if he was including Alice, did she really want to be included? With Finn and his daughter who wasn't her daughter, too?

Not for a moment did she hold any animosity toward the little girl. In fact, she felt more compassion than she thought she would. No child should be thrust into the position Riley Sullivan had. Losing the only parent she ever knew and having her care turned over to a total stranger? Moving thousands of miles away from what was probably the only home she remembered, one filled with palm trees and beaches and sunshine, to the bare trees and gray skies of a gasping spring in Sudbury? Having no idea what her future might hold or understanding how everything could have changed so quickly?

Having no one to share her grief with, either. Riley and Finn really were two of a kind.

And that, Alice realized then, was what really lay at the core of her sadness. And her confusion. And her bereavement and desolation and betrayal. Finn and Riley truly were two of a kind. A kind that didn't include her. Father and daughter. The two of them were a family. A family by blood and by what would eventually become, she was certain, love, because Finn was the sort of person who gave love freely and quickly and genuinely. A family that Alice might have been a part of—that she should have been a part of—once upon a time. But Finn had gone and created that family with someone else instead.

"Well, it was nice to meet you, Riley," she told the little girl before that thought could take root any deeper than it already had. Quickly, she lifted her gaze to Finn's. "I'm sure you guys want to go and get settled as soon as you can. I'm sure you both have a lot to—" She stopped herself before finishing *talk about*, since Riley didn't seem to be doing much of that for now. "A lot to get organized," she finished instead.

Finn looked at her as if she'd just betrayed him, too. "But I thought… I mean, I hoped… I mean, I was wondering if—" He halted as abruptly as Alice had, expelled a restless sound, then tried again. "I mean, we came here straight from the airport. We haven't eaten anything since breakfast except for some pretzels and Goldfish crackers. I thought maybe the three of us could have a late lunch together, and then maybe you and I could show Riley around town."

Alice was shaking her head before she even realized she was doing it. "I'm sorry, but I can't," she said. "I have so many things I have to get done this afternoon. So, so many things. So, so, *so* many things."

When she saw Finn's expression and realized he knew she was lying through her teeth, she dropped her gaze to Riley. Finn's daughter was still looking at her intently, much the way her father had done when he was her age. There would never be a time when Alice could look at Riley and not see Finn. The little girl would be a constant reminder that he had started a family without her. Whether he had intended to or not, whether he had even known or not, it didn't matter. Finn had a family that wasn't Alice's. And there was no way to undo that.

"So, so, *so* many things," she repeated, this time to Riley. If she couldn't convince Finn, maybe she could convince his daughter. But Mini Finn didn't look like she believed Alice, either. So she looked at Big Finn again. "Maybe another time," Alice finished as she gripped the door and began to push it closed.

But before she could complete the gesture, the Kitten-Who-Had-Yet-To-Be-Named came galumphing into the living room and skidded to a halt between the door and the jamb.

"MEOW!" she yelled. *"MEOW MEOW MEOW MEOW!"*

Then she leaped onto Alice's jeans and climbed up to her waist, where she perched long enough to yell some more before jumping up to Alice's sweatshirt and climbing onto her shoulder. Where, naturally, she continued to howl.

When Riley laughed softly at the kitten's antics, Finn looked down at her incredulously, then back at Alice. "She laughed," he said. Then he looked at the little girl again. "You laughed."

Naturally, Riley stopped laughing at that and looked at her father somberly. And she went back to being silent. Finn returned his attention to Alice.

"That's the first time I've heard her laugh." He looked down at Riley again, but she dropped her gaze steadfastly to her feet. "That's the first time I've heard her make any sound at all."

Alice looked at the little girl, too. She wondered just how much Riley understood everything that had happened to her. She was probably old enough to realize her mother wasn't coming back, but was she old enough to understand that Finn was her father? The equivalent to being her mother, at least where biology and the law were concerned? Just how did a person explain to a child who might not even know where babies came from yet that half of what made her Riley Sullivan was standing beside her, holding her hand, and that her father would be legally responsible for her for more than a decade and emotionally responsible for her for the rest of her life?

The kitten was still screeching like a heavy metal singer, so Alice delicately freed her from her shoulder and held her down at Riley's height. The little girl looked up when she did, then at the kitten—still howling—then back at Alice.

"Would you like to hold her?" Alice asked.

After a small hesitation, Riley nodded. Then she released her father's hand and extended both of hers to accept the kitten into them. The raucous furball squirmed a bit in her grasp, but immediately stopped yelling once the girl was holding her. And when Riley moved the kitten into the crook of her neck and shoulder to give it a gentle hug, the kitten's purr box spurred to life. Loudly.

Riley laughed again. And again, Finn looked at Alice in amazement.

"Can we hang around for a little while?" he asked. Before she could say no, he hurried on, "Please, Alice? This is the most animated she's been since I met her."

Alice was so desperate to turn down Finn's request that she almost offered to let him take the kitten home for Riley to keep. Almost. But in the weeks since they'd found her in the tree, it had become clear that she didn't have a home, and Alice had formally adopted her. Even if she still had no idea what to name her. The kitten had brought fun and light and joy into a house that had never had any of those things before. Alice had never been allowed to have a pet when she was a child. She'd had no idea how easy it was to fall in love with one. And that's exactly what had happened with the kitten. Alice just loved the little orphan too much to give her up.

That made her look at Riley again. The little girl wasn't exactly an orphan—not technically, anyway—but she probably felt like one. She nuzzled the kitten now in a way that made Alice think her mother hadn't allowed her to have a pet, either. Her grasp on the animal was awkward, but careful, and she touched her nose gingerly against the cat's. Then she laughed again. But she still didn't say anything.

Although it made her feel nauseous to do it, she told Finn, "Okay. You can stay for a little while. I have stuff for sandwiches. We can eat lunch here."

As Alice made them sandwiches, she tried to reassure herself that everything would be fine. But as she listened to Finn and Riley in the living room, playing with the kitten, she couldn't quite convince herself of that. Although the little girl still didn't speak, her soft laughter tumbled in from the other room, followed by Finn's soft words to her about how much she was going to like her new home in Sudbury. He explained to her how they would meet a new social worker, who was coming to visit them from Geneva on Monday, the way Ms. Ramos had visited Riley in Key West. He told her how he would fix up her bedroom at her new house—*her* new house, since it belonged to Finn's family, so of course it would be Riley's now, too—any way she wanted, and she could pick whatever color she wanted for the walls. How she would have her own bathroom that she could decorate however she wanted. He told her how the things she'd left behind in Florida would be arriving in a big moving truck later in the week. How they could go to the grocery store this weekend and pick up some of her favorite stuff to eat. How much he wanted Riley to know that his home was her home now, too.

And it was all Alice could do not to cry. Finn and Riley would be making a home together. Not Alice. Because they were family now.

Not Alice.

She admired how quickly and naturally he was stepping up to take responsibility for his daughter—she did. She was happy that Riley had someone like Finn to be her father— she was. But he should have been Alice's daughter's father, not Denise's. Sarah Madeleine Whitlock Huxley would have been going on twelve now. There would have been a point in *her* young life when Alice and Finn let her choose how her bedroom and bathroom would look, too. The three of them would have shopped for everything their daughter needed. The three of them would have put it all together. The three of them would have made their house a home.

The three of them.

Instead, it would be Finn and Riley doing all those things together. Because Alice had no place in that equation. She wouldn't be living in their house. She wouldn't be making the rules or policies that Finn and his daughter would be living by. She wouldn't be enrolling Riley in school or attending conferences with her teachers. She wouldn't choose a pediatrician or dentist for the little girl. She wouldn't be the one comforting Riley when she woke up from a nightmare or filling her prescription when she got sick. She wouldn't be putting sunscreen on her back at the pool or Band-Aids on her skinned knees. She wouldn't be making Riley's breakfast or meeting her at the bus stop or reading her a story before turning out the light.

Because Riley wasn't Alice's daughter. She was Finn's. All of those things would fall to him, not Alice. And he would do it, she was certain, with his daughter's best interests at heart. Alice would be a part of none of it. Because Alice hadn't donated a second set of chromosomes to Riley. She hadn't nurtured and grown the girl inside her. Alice wasn't part of Riley's family. She never would be. She never could be. Riley's family was Finn.

Somehow, she was able to assemble three sandwiches without making a mess of anything—including herself. Somehow, she was able to place three plates on the kitchen table she and Finn had found at an early yard sale the weekend before he left for Florida to bring home his daughter. Somehow, she kept her voice level and almost convincingly carefree when she told the family in her living room that their lunch was ready. And somehow, she was able to eat part of her own without throwing up.

Riley ate politely, if silently, taking small, careful bites of her sandwich, nibbling at her baby carrots and sipping her milk. Finn did his best to draw her out with questions about her life in Florida and telling her stories about his own childhood. And although he could have included a mention or two of Alice in those stories, since some of them had been experiences he and she shared of school field trips or pool and birthday parties at the homes of mutual friends, he never did. Alice told herself it wasn't a big deal. She had no place in the conversation anyway. Finn was trying to bond with his daughter by showing her how much the two of them had in common. Why would he bring Alice into it?

After lunch, Riley and Finn returned to the living room to play with the kitten while Alice cleaned up the few dishes left behind. The task should have taken about five minutes. But twenty minutes later, she was still wiping down the counters and rearranging the dishwasher and gosh, she hadn't mopped in here all week, and she didn't want her new tile floor to get all grimy, did she? And the fridge was looking a little too smudgy and the oven door could use a good cleaning and, wow, it was amazing how gross one's small appliances could become when one wasn't paying attention, so she might as well clean the toaster oven, too, and—

"Alice?"

She spun around to see Finn framed in the doorway, looking at her as if he were worried about something. Well, of course he was worried about something, she immediately reminded herself. He had a family to think about now.

"What?" she replied.

"Aren't you going to join us out here?"

She almost laughed at that. He sounded like he actually wanted to include her. Instead, she said, "No, I can't. Like I told you earlier, I have so, so, *so* much to do this weekend."

He dipped his head toward the open toaster oven. "Pretty sure that toaster oven hasn't been used in years."

"All the more reason to clean it."

He expelled a tired sound, then leaned against the jamb, crossing his arms over his chest and one ankle over the other. "Look, I know this is all really strange," he said. "But all of this stuff with Riley, it doesn't change anything between you and me."

Now she did laugh. She couldn't help it. Could he possibly be that oblivious? "Finn, Riley changes *every*thing between us."

Wow. He really could be that oblivious. Because now he was looking at her with incredulity. "What? How?" he stammered.

"Your life is going to be completely different now. You're a father. You have a child. She has to be the focus of your life."

He glanced over his shoulder, then took a few steps toward Alice. He kept his voice low enough that Riley wouldn't hear as he drew nearer. "She won't be the focus of my life," he said. "I mean, yeah, maybe for now she is, because everything between her and me is just so…so new. So weird. She and I have to get used to each other. Get to know each other. It's not every day a guy finds out he has a daughter, and I don't know if her mother ever said a word about me to her. So, okay, yeah. For now, things between you and me might…" He sighed heavily. "Might be a little different for a little while. But that won't be the case forever."

Now Alice was the one to cross her arms over her midsection. She knew it was a defensive gesture. That was because she could feel a conflict coming on. "Really," she said, turning the word into a statement, not a question. "So…what? A month from now, you and Riley will have everything sorted out? She'll just open up to you one day and start talking like the two of you have known each other for years? She'll forget all about her mother and make tons of friends in a place that's as alien to her as the moon? You'll stop worrying about every little thing that affects her? This dad thing will all become second nature to you by then?"

"I don't know," he replied, just as defensively. "Probably not a month. I mean, I have to get her enrolled in school and find a therapist for her here to find out why she's not talking and help her cope with her mother's death, and I should probably have her checked out by a pediatrician and dentist in case Denise overlooked stuff like that, and get her involved in some activities so she'll meet other kids, and…" He sighed. "Okay, there's a lot. But she'll adjust to her life in Sudbury. Eventually."

"She'll adjust," Alice echoed blandly. "Okay. And how about you, Finn? Will you adjust, too? Just slip right into the role of being responsible for another human being? Of having her in your home twenty-four-seven and three-six-five after living alone for years? Of answering questions about anything and everything she comes into contact with? Of helping her with her homework and taking care of her when she's sick? You'll just—boom—become a dad overnight?"

"No, not overnight," he said, his words edged with tension. "But yeah, I'll become her dad. Eventually."

"Eventually," she repeated. "There's that word again. And it is so convenient. Eventually. Adverb. Referring to an action at some nebulous point later in time."

His mouth thinned to a tight line. "Look, I realize you're angry about this. And I don't blame you. I've been angry myself with Denise for not telling me five years ago that I had a daughter."

"And what would you have done five years ago if she had told you?" Alice asked. "Would you have gone back to her and tried to make a go of your marriage? Stayed together for the sake of your child? If Denise had told you about Riley five years ago, would you be living in Philadelphia right now with your wife and daughter and any other kids that might have come along? The way you and I were supposed to have lived with Sarah?"

His expression went slack at that, but he said nothing.

But Alice needed to know the answer. "Would you?" she asked.

He hesitated a long time before replying. Long enough that Alice knew he realized she might be right. Finn Huxley was a good guy. One who always did the right thing. They both knew that was exactly what he would have done.

To his credit, he didn't try to sugarcoat it. "I don't know," he finally replied. "Maybe."

At least he was honest. Not that that made hearing the answer any less painful.

"Alice, you and I weren't together when I met Denise," he reminded her gently. "You left Sudbury and didn't tell anyone—even me—where you were. I didn't do anything wrong when I married her. It was clear when I left town that you and I were through. You never tried to contact me, even when you had to know how much I wanted—needed—to talk to you. Then you left town without me, too. For good."

Alice knew that. She did. But his marrying someone else and possibly eventually starting a family with that someone else *felt* wrong. At least it did to Alice.

"No, you didn't do anything wrong," she told him. "But I was in the same position as you for a while. Living in a new place, surrounded by strangers. I was unhappy and lonely, too, Finn. And I met guys who were interesting and interested in me. But I didn't marry any of them. I didn't start a family with them. Because even without kids, that's what happens when you get married. You become a family with someone. My future was always supposed to be with you. My *family* was always supposed to be you. You and *our* daughter. I couldn't imagine having a future—having a family—without you. But you didn't have any problem making one without me."

He sighed again, then nodded slowly. "So that's where all this is coming from," he said. "You're angry because I might have had a life with someone else. Even though the two of us hadn't seen each other for years, and even though you never even tried to contact me during that time, and even though you moved on, too."

"I know you don't think it makes sense," she conceded. "But it does to me. And it's hurtful to me."

"I'm sorry, Alice. But it is what it is. And I have to deal with it."

"Yes, you do," she told him. "You have to deal with it. You, Finn. Not me. Riley is *your* daughter. Not mine."

He opened his mouth to say something else—something angry, by the look of him—but his expression suddenly cleared. "Is that part of it, too? That I have a daughter and you don't? It's not a competition, Alice."

"I know that, Finn. But every time I look at her, I'm going to be reminded of what I lost. What we lost. And what you have now that I never will."

"Alice—"

"You have a family now, Finn. I don't. And there's nothing you can say or do that will change that." She felt tears threatening again and crossed her arms tighter. "You and Riley need to go," she added quickly, finally, before he could say anything else. "You need to go…home."

"Alice—"

"Now. Please. Go."

He studied her with a mix of frustration and anguish. "I'll be back Monday morning. I still have a job to do here."

She expelled an anxious chuckle at that. "No, you won't. You're going to have a million things to do with Riley on Monday. Probably all week long."

Now he looked dismayed. "Then I'll be back later in the week," he insisted. He repeated, "I still have a job to do here."

And why did he make it sound like that job had nothing to do with Alice's house?

"It's not necessary," she said. "I'll manage what's left by myself."

And wow, did that sound like she was talking about a lot more than her house, too.

"What about the mold in the closet upstairs?"

"Haven and I made arrangements while you were gone. She's coming on Tuesday. I'll manage everything else."

"How?"

"I'll manage," she repeated firmly. "Now, please. I need you to go. I need to be alone."

And since she couldn't trust that he would leave, she spun around and left herself. Unfortunately, her nearest escape was out the back door and into the backyard, and the farther she went in that direction, the closer she came to the rhododendron. The rhododendron that was starting to bud, starting to stir back to life, the way she had thought she and Finn were going to do. Everywhere she looked now, she was going to see reminders of him and of what the two of them lost. Not just once, but twice. Because she'd been so sure the two of them were back on track and heading in the direction they should have been on a long time ago. Now, though, they'd jumped right back off it.

She couldn't stay in Sudbury, she realized then. She couldn't stay here and see Finn and his daughter on what was certain to be a regular basis. She couldn't have those constant reminders of what could have been. What should have been. But would never be now.

Looked like she would be getting the hell out of Dodge after all. The sooner, the better.

Chapter Ten

Finn sat on the floor outside his hallway bathroom, now Riley's bathroom—or at least, it would be Riley's bathroom soon—and listened to her splash in the bathtub on the other side of the door. He had been more than a little relieved when she'd closed the door behind herself, pajamas and clean underwear in hand, indicating silently, but pointedly, that she could manage her own bath just fine, thanks. Bathing and dressing were now two fewer care-and-feeding-of-a-child things he had to learn how to do. Which left just under eighty billion things that he did. But he still wanted to sit outside the door, just in case maybe he was wrong about her bath-time independence and would be needed if she got too much water in the tub and started to drown or slipped on the soap and started to drown or didn't wait a full hour after eating and started to drown or was set upon by flying monkeys and started to drown or—

Gah. He'd heard people with kids talk about how they'd had to get used to the constant fear after having their kids, but he'd never been able to understand. Now he was beginning to understand. Even though a week had gone by since he discovered he was a father, he was still dazed and confused about the fact that he was a father. Every morning since Mona Ramos's call, he'd woken up thinking this all must be a dream, only to be reminded that, nope, it was his new reality. Although he'd taken exception to everything Alice had told him earlier today about adjusting to all this, he had to admit that maybe he had, um, misspoken. She was right. He was now responsible for guiding another human being through life. And where most parents had up to nine months to think about and get used to that kind of thing, he'd had no preparation at all. Even back when he and Alice thought they would become parents, they'd lost Sarah before getting a chance to educate themselves about bringing a life into the world.

He closed his eyes and leaned his head back against the wall. What the hell was he supposed to do now? Riley's appearance in his life changed everything. Alice was right about that, too, as much as he hated to admit it. Although he did still think that everything between the two of them would be fine—eventually—he had no idea how long *eventually* would be. Maybe he and Riley would adjust quickly. Kids were resilient, right? Everyone said so. So who knew? Maybe in a month, she *would* be feeling right at home here in Sudbury. Maybe she'd adapt quickly to her new school and make lots of friends right off the bat. She could start trusting Finn enough to talk to him any day now, right? Maybe even start calling him Dad.

His stomach rolled. Dad. Boy, was that a word loaded with implication. All it took to become a father was healthy sperm count. But to be a dad? To be there whenever your kid needed you and give them love and acceptance and respect, no matter what? To be able to take any experience and turn it into a lesson about right and wrong or the way the world worked? To teach by example and always do the right thing? To be a dad like that? The way his father had been a dad to him? Well, hell. That took years of work. No way was Riley going to be looking at Finn as *Dad* for a long, long time. If ever.

And Alice. She was convinced she had no place in his and Riley's life. Okay, yes, Riley was his daughter by another woman, and he guessed he did sort of get why Alice couldn't move past that just yet. To him, it didn't make any sense, but it sort of made total sense. The two of them had always assumed they would have a future together, once they could escape Sudbury and Nora Whitlock. When he was a kid, he had dreamed of building a life with Alice every day and could no more imagine a life without her than he could stop the sun from rising in the morning. But all of that changed when he came back to Sudbury to find her gone and had no way to know where she was. The dreams and imaginings of kids rarely survived to adulthood, for whatever reason. Finn hadn't been any different.

Maybe he shouldn't have married Denise, he thought now. But if he hadn't, the little girl on the other side of that door would never have been born. And of all the other weird things Finn had had to think about this week, that was probably the weirdest of them all.

On the other side of the door, Riley suddenly started to hum. Not loudly, and not any tune that Finn could recognize. But except for her laughter at the kitten—which had erupted a few times that afternoon—this was the first sound he had heard her make. His heartbeat quickened at hearing it. Little by little, the humming grew louder, until he could hear a few breathy words joining it. Something about a thousand hugs from ten thousand lightning bugs teaching her how to dance. And then Finn knew the song that she was singing. It had been all over the radio for a while when he and Alice were in high school, and it had been playing in the coffee shop when he and Denise realized their orders had gotten mixed up and they first began to talk. The fact that she had sung that song to their daughter often enough that Riley knew the words by heart...

Just like that, a million feelings washed over Finn. The joy of falling in love with Alice in high school. The terror of finding out she was pregnant. The cautious delight that followed, when they talked about their future with their child. The devastation of losing Sarah, and then losing Alice, too. The comfort of those first few months with Denise. Now, whenever he heard the song, he would think about Riley, too. And he would feel... *What?* he asked himself as he listened to his daughter—his *daughter*—sing about misty eyes and farewells.

Hope, he finally realized. That was what was bubbling up inside him as he listened to Riley sing. No matter what else she might have brought with her, she brought Finn hope. Hope for both of them. That he would be able to give her a happy life here in Sudbury, where he'd spent most of his own, mostly happy, life. And that she would give him something he might never have had otherwise—a family.

But there was room in that family for more than two, a realization that brought Finn more hope. Whether Alice realized it or not, she belonged in the picture with him and Riley. She could be a part of their family, too, if she wanted. He just didn't know how to make her understand that. And he didn't know if she ever really *would* want to make their twosome a trio. She'd made clear today that the path the two of them had embarked on before he left for Florida was now well and truly obstructed by the barricade that was Riley Sullivan. And she'd offered no indication that there was any way around it. She was convinced Finn and Riley belonged together in a way that didn't include her. And he had no idea how to dissuade her of her certainty.

He heard the dull *thunk* of the bath drain opening, followed by a rush of water swirling through the pipes in the wall behind him. He also heard Riley stop singing. Somehow, he got his emotions under control by the time the door opened to release a damp puff of warm air and Riley. Her pajamas were as rainbow as everything else she seemed to own, spattered as they were with, well, rainbows, and her ruddy ponytail had curled some in the humidity.

"All clean?" he asked.

She nodded but said nothing.

"Been a long day, huh?" he asked.

She nodded again. And still said nothing.

"Guess you're looking forward to getting some sleep."

Another nod. Another bout of silence.

"Okay," Finn said. "So tonight, since I didn't have time to get a room prepared for you before I left…" *On account of I'd been hoping it wouldn't be necessary because you weren't my daughter*, he couldn't keep himself from adding to himself, even though he didn't feel that way at all now. "…I thought you could sleep in my room in the big bed, and I'll sleep in my parents' room up the hall. Sound okay?"

She seemed to give it some thought, then nodded again.

"Tomorrow morning, I'll move all the furniture out of my office down there"—he pointed toward the room next to his own—"and we can go shopping for some stuff to turn that into your room. Sound good?"

Another silent nod.

Finn didn't know why he kept trying, but he asked, "Any idea what color you'd like to paint your new room?"

Here, Riley shrugged. Silently.

"Okay," he said wearily. "I guess we'll figure that out tomorrow at the paint store."

She studied him blankly. And said nothing.

He tilted his head toward his bedroom. "C'mon. I put clean sheets on the bed and everything."

She followed him down the hall and into his bedroom, which suddenly seemed massive with such a small human being in it. Riley scrambled onto the bed he'd turned down earlier and filled with all the plushies she'd brought with her, then immediately started rearranging all the animals in a specific order. Violet fish, indigo cat, blue dragon, and green dog, he noted, followed by yellow…something with only one eye…orange parrot and red horse. A rainbow of stuffies. Why had he not seen that coming and arranged them all that way himself? He would get to a point where he understood his daughter—his *daughter*—and her way of seeing the world. He would. It was just going to take some time.

He pointed at the window. "Open or closed? It's not sup-posed to get too cold tonight."

She lifted a hand, her index finger and thumb indicat-ing a space of about two inches.

"Okay, just a little," he said.

He wasn't sure if her preference was a result of living in a warm climate or something innate, but it made Finn feel strangely satisfied that she slept with her window open just a little, the way he had when he was a kid. Then he re-membered he'd also liked to sleep with a night-light when he was her age, and he was currently fresh out of those.

Now he pointed at the lamp. "Light on or off?"

She gave him a thumbs-up. In the On direction of a light switch. "Okay, I'll leave it on."

She almost smiled. Almost. He'd count it as a win. He made his way to the bedroom door and turned around. Riley had plucked the blue dragon from the collection to hug to herself and snuggled it under the covers. Time to say good-night. This was the part when normal parents would give their kids a little kiss on the cheek or forehead and tell them to have sweet dreams. Finn didn't think he *or* Riley was ready for that. So he crowded his fingers to his mouth, kissed them quickly, then opened them again in her direction.

"Good night, Riley," he said softly. "Sleep tight. Sweet dreams."

She almost smiled again. Then she pulled the covers up closer to her chin and closed her eyes. Finn switched off the overhead light, leaving her in a pale gold slice of lamplight. Then, leaving the door half-open so he could hear her in case she cried out, he made his way down the hall to his parents' old room and put himself to bed, too.

There. They'd made it through day one together, and it hadn't gone horribly, had it? Well, except for the part about Alice thinking she no longer had a place in his life. In their life—his and Riley's. But he could work on that. They could work on that—him and Riley. Alice would come around. She'd learn that she belonged with both of them. He just had to be patient, take it one step at a time and see what happened. It would all work out the way it was supposed to. He was sure of it. Everything would be okay.

Eventually.

When Haven Moreau showed up at the front door on Tuesday morning in what could only be described as a hazmat suit, Alice was more than a little alarmed. If Haven needed to wear that to clean up what Alice had been sleeping within yards of—and breathing nightly—for possibly the last year and a half, or maybe her entire life, perhaps she should start getting her effects in order.

"Don't panic," Haven said with a smile as she adjusted

the giant breathing apparatus atop her disheveled blond hair, clearly reading the alarm in her expression.

Easy for her to say, Alice thought. *Her life isn't coming down in a shambles around her. Oh, wait. She meant the mold. Right.*

"This is all for a 'just in case' scenario," Haven continued. "From what Finn said, this shouldn't take long or make that big a mess."

Also easy for her to say. Even after the mold was gone, Alice still had a big mess to clean up. One that would doubtless take years. If she managed to take care of it at all.

"Even if the problem goes from the second floor down to the first," Haven continued, "it'll mostly be a matter of disposing of the infected drywall and flooring, then using the HEPA air scrubber and vacuum here to take care of any particulates, then, boom, Finn can come back and replace everything with new drywall and flooring."

Alice hesitated. "Actually, is there a chance you might be able to do that last part, too?"

Haven shook her head. "It's not necessary for me to do that last part. Any handyman can do it. It's something Finn can do with his eyes closed."

"But Finn's not working for me anymore," Alice told her.

Haven couldn't have looked more surprised if Alice had just told her her hair was on fire.

"Why not?" She must have realized that was kind of an invasive question to ask, because she immediately amended, "I mean… Is everything okay?"

Still invasive, Alice couldn't help thinking. *But a bit more polite.* Before she could reply, though—since she was still trying to figure out how best to reply—Haven continued.

"I mean, yeah, he told me about Riley, so he has her to think about now. That's gotta be a little weird for both of you, him suddenly having a daughter. Neither of you could have ever anticipated something like that happening."

Oh, if you only knew, Alice thought.

Haven smiled and stated with complete confidence, "But you guys are so great together. You'll work it out."

Spoken like a woman in the throes of new romance who was absolutely certain that love really did conquer all. Alice knew Haven didn't mean to be flip or unfeeling. But she didn't know how much history Alice and Finn had together. And Haven was young—okay, maybe about the same age as Alice chronologically, but much younger emotionally—and, from what Alice had gathered of their limited conversations over the last several months, she was blissfully free of past tragedy. Haven had no idea how Riley's appearance changed things for Alice and Finn.

"And you know Finn," she continued, "He always finishes what he sets out to do."

Not this time, he won't, Alice thought. Because this time, his job was already done with someone else. Oh, wait. She meant with Alice's house, not with his new family. Even so, his work for Alice—with Alice—was done.

Instead of getting into any of that with Haven, though, Alice only stepped aside to allow her entry with all her stuff. "Thank you for making time to do this," she said. "I know you still have a lot to do up at Summerlight."

Haven moved past Alice with all her paraphernalia and started up the stairs behind her. "It'll actually be kinda nice to get away from the place for a day," she said as she ascended. "I mean, I love that house, and it's coming along nicely, but wow, has it consumed my and Bennett's life."

Alice sympathized. Her little house had been the focus of her existence for mere weeks. She couldn't imagine what it would be like to renovate a mansion that was more than a hundred years old and had been neglected far longer than her own place.

Haven discarded her stuff by the hall closet, then proceeded to hang plastic sheeting over the bathroom and closet door.

"You probably should head back downstairs for now," she said as she worked. "I'm going to be stirring up spores, and you don't want to be around for that. I'll let you know more once I have a better look."

Alice nodded and thanked Haven again, then headed back downstairs. She'd closed up the kitten in the sunroom to keep her from getting underfoot, having opened the windows so she could sit and chatter at the birds beyond the screen, as she loved to do. Now Alice opened the rest of the windows on the first floor, too, in spite of the chilly air outside. Although it was nearing May, and even though things were well and truly coming back to life in the Finger Lakes, enough so that she'd taken the plunge and replaced the storm windows with screens, there were still days like this—cloudy, overcast and cold. *Much like my mood*, she couldn't help thinking.

While Haven banged and sawed and whirred upstairs, Alice did her best to keep busy downstairs. Though there really wasn't much left for her to do. The house seemed so empty. In fact, the house *was* empty. She'd gotten rid of so much of her mother's furniture, thanks to its giant proportions and grandiosity making it too unfashionable for a house about to be listed. Okay, okay, and also because Alice just felt better having it gone. All that was left in the living room were two bookcases—both empty, since her mother's knickknacks had been gigantic and flamboyant, too—one side table, and a standing lamp whose frilly Victorian shade was now for sale at Thrifts Ahoy. The master bedroom was just as barren, holding little more than a mid-century armoire and chair. Alice would take none of it when she left, but all the pieces had seemed harmless enough to blend in with anything she might purchase for her own needs that she could move later.

Of course, before, she'd been thinking she wouldn't be going far. Now that she was planning on leaving Sudbury again, there was no reason to buy anything yet. Even if, as Finn had said, doing so would make the house more attractive to potential buyers.

She didn't care. At this point, she just wanted to be rid of the house. If she had to give it away, she would.

She recalled that the armoire in her mother's room still held some of her mother's clothes, things Alice hadn't been up to going through yet. Since her mood was already morose, now was as good a time as any. She was taping up a second box to take to a clothing closet run by a local charity when Haven rapped on the door frame behind her. When Alice spun around, it was to find the other woman still in her work clothes, with the added accessory now of black rubber gloves that went nearly to her elbows. She was also wearing a look of much concern.

"Okay, teeny problem," Haven said.

"What?" Alice asked.

"The mold does indeed go down to the first floor, and it's more invasive than it first seemed."

"Meaning?" Alice asked.

"You're going to have to find a new place to stay for a few days while I work on it. I'm going to have to tear up more wall and floor than I thought, and you don't need to be breathing what I'm going to be stirring up while I do it."

Well, that couldn't be good. "Should I get checked by a doctor?" Alice asked.

Haven shook her head. "No, this stuff has been growing for a while, but it's been confined to a closed space. It's been undisturbed until now, so you're fine. But cleaning it all out is going to disturb it a lot, and it's going to be floating around the house for a while. The air scrubber and vacuum will ultimately take care of all that, and I'll leave a dehumidifier on-site for a while after it's all gone just to be sure, but it'll be a few days before it's all clear enough for you to come back. Good news is I don't have anything going on up at Summerlight for the next few days that I can't postpone, so I can start work here tomorrow and be done before the end of the week."

Alice started to sigh heavily but stopped herself. No point in taking the chance of inhaling something awful. Her chest was heavy enough with lousy feelings as it was.

"Okay," she muttered. "I can get a room at the Masons' B and B in town. I just hope they're pet-friendly, because I'll have the kitten, too."

"Oh, you can't," Haven said. "They're not open for the season yet. Mr. and Mrs. Mason are still in Florida, in fact."

But that was the only hotel in Sudbury, at least until Summerlight opened. Alice didn't want to have to go all the way to Ithaca. She brightened some. "Any chance you have a room available at Summerlight? I mean, I know you guys aren't open yet, either, but I don't mind roughing it. All I need is a bed and a bathroom, and I'm good." She crossed her fingers behind her back as she added, hopefully convincingly, "I promise the kitten is well behaved."

"Sorry, no," Haven told her. "We moved out all the mattresses, since we'll be replacing them with new ones."

"I can sleep on a couch," Alice offered hopefully.

Haven smiled. "You don't want to sleep on Victorian furniture. Trust me. You'll thank me someday, when your geriatrician tells you what surprisingly good shape your back is in, and how you must never have had to sleep on Victorian furniture. Besides, the water's off in all the bathrooms but mine and Bennett's while we work."

"Well, where am I supposed to stay for a few days?" Alice asked the room at large.

Haven gave her a funny look. "Finn's. Duh. That guy's got plenty of room. Even with the kid. I'm sure he'd be happy to have you." At what must have been Alice's troubled look in response, she added, more softly "It'll be fine, Alice. Really. Just give it some time."

The smile Haven gave her then reiterated her certainty that Alice and Finn were such a great couple that they were going to be *juuust fiiine*. Eventually. For all Alice knew, Finn had already told her that, the way he'd tried to convince Alice of the same thing. Haven just didn't understand how impossible the situation truly was.

"Finn and I aren't seeing each other anymore," she told Haven flatly.

Haven laughed lightly at that…until she realized Alice was serious. "You can't be serious," she said.

"I'm going to be leaving Sudbury as soon as this house is sold."

"What? No."

"Things just didn't work out with us."

Boy, was that an understatement.

Haven looked even more devastated than Alice felt. "Jeez, Alice, because of Riley? I know that's got to throw a wrench into things, but you and Finn are so… I mean considering the way you've always talked to me about him… The way he's always talked to me about you…"

She didn't finish the thought, but her expression pretty much indicated her feelings. Haven had done some work around Alice's house last fall, enough that she and Alice had become friendly. Friendly enough that Alice had asked Haven a lot of questions about how Finn was doing. Friendly enough that Haven had told her Finn asked about Alice a lot, too. Alice had never gone into any great detail about their past—presumably Finn hadn't, either—and had just left it at pretty much a "former high-school sweethearts" thing. But Haven wasn't stupid. She'd sussed out that there was a lot more to Alice and Finn's relationship back then than puppy love.

"You guys are great together," Haven said again. "Finn has been so happy for the past few weeks. Like, *really* happy. And you've been happier than I've ever seen you, too."

She shrugged in the way people do when they've never had a wrench like Riley Sullivan thrown into their lives. "So you and Finn wind up with a ready-made family you didn't quite plan on. So what? You ask me, you guys would be great parents."

Haven might as well have just slapped Alice. She realized Haven couldn't possibly know about her and Finn's loss of baby Sarah, so her words weren't delivered with anything other than affection and good will. They still made Alice want to cry.

Instead of replying to those words, Alice only thanked Haven for her work today, then promised she would be out of the house by evening, so that Haven could start working on the problem in the morning.

She finished with, "Is it safe to go upstairs and pack a few things?"

Haven handed her a no-nonsense-looking mask. "Yeah, but put this on first."

Alice took it from her and donned it dutifully, then wordlessly moved past her into the hall.

"You should probably pack for three nights," she heard Haven call from behind. "Shouldn't take any longer than that. Any idea where you're going to go? I mean…in case, you know, anyone asks?"

Alice had no idea. Most of the few friends she'd had from school had taken off for college and never come back, having built new lives for themselves somewhere else. And the ones that were left in town she hadn't spoken to in years. They'd all moved on with their lives, too, marrying and starting families here.

So no. Alice didn't know where she would go. There truly was no place for her in Sudbury anymore.

Chapter Eleven

Ever since the message from Mona Ramos about Denise's death and Riley's existence, Finn had been understandably wary about any notifications that pinged on his phone. So when it went off early in the evening on Tuesday, while he was loading the last of his and Riley's dishes into the dishwasher following a gourmet dinner of Dino Buddies, Tater Tots and apple slices—hey, why should he alter his regular diet just because he had a kid now?—he didn't pull it out of his back pocket right away. Instead, he finished his task, wiped off the countertops and tugged down the window over the sink, because the rain that had started late that afternoon was starting to blow inside. When his phone pinged a second time in those few minutes, though, indicating that the incoming message might be urgent, he flinched. With only a small hesitation, he pulled the phone out and gave it a sideways glance, as if turning his head a little might make whatever the messages said more bearable.

But all both messages said were, Hey, are you home?

Which wouldn't have been anything major, had the sender been anyone but Alice. Heat blossomed in his belly at those four words. It felt like it had been months since he'd spoken to her. He quickly texted back.

Hell, yes, I'm home. What do you need?

He waited, watching for the dots in the bubble below his text to turn into words. Instead of a reply on his phone, however, his doorbell rang. Heart racing, he went to answer it. Seeing Alice on the other side of the door only made his heart pound harder. She looked as miserable as he felt himself, her open trench coat spattered with rain, her hair damp and even curlier than usual, blowing around her face, her expression exhausted.

"I'm sorry to bother you," she said softly.

He stepped aside and opened the door even wider. "You're not bothering me at all. Come on in."

She hesitated, though whether that was because she feared she would be unwelcome—as if—or because she really didn't want to come in, Finn didn't know. And he didn't care. He had no idea why she'd come over, but he was happier to see her than he'd been in, wow, probably fourteen years. Ever since the day he handed her, terrified of her reception, that red carnation, only to have her smile and thank him with a kiss on the cheek.

Finally, she stepped over the threshold, but only far enough that Finn could close the door behind her. It was only then that he noticed she was carrying a duffel bag in one hand and a carrier with the kitten in the other, and his happiness completely evaporated. She was leaving Sudbury? Already? She really had given up on them? She wasn't even going to give them a chance?

Not sure how he managed, he asked, "What's up?"

"I, um, I kind of need a place to stay for a few days. The mold Haven found was worse than you and I realized, so she said I have to vacate the premises until she can get it all cleaned out, and I was wondering if you might have a spare room I could borrow until the end of the week. I'm really, really, really sorry to have to even ask, and I'll completely understand if you say no."

Now relief flooded through him. If this emotional roller coaster went on much longer, he was going to pass out.

"I just don't have anywhere else to go," she hurried on. "The B and B isn't open yet, and Haven said they don't have any beds at Summerlight, and I just…" She looked even more miserable for some reason. "I don't have anywhere to go in Sudbury."

"Of course you can stay here," he told her. *Move in*, he wanted to add. *Stay forever.* "You'll always have a place here, Alice. Stay as long as you need to."

"I'll stay out of your way is what I'll do," she assured him. "Just give me a room, and I won't ever leave it. You and Riley will never know I'm here."

As if to show how wrong that assurance was, however, a creak on the stairs erupted behind them. They both looked over at the sound to see Riley crouching on one step, dressed in rainbow-striped pajamas, gazing at them through the balusters. But she didn't say a word. She still wasn't talking. Though Finn had spent every moment of her bath time the way he had that first night, sitting beside the closed bathroom door because he still worried she might be too young to save herself should an accident happen. Every night, she sang the song about fireflies to herself. Beyond that, she never uttered a sound.

Even her laughter had disappeared because there hadn't been anything for her to laugh about. The kitten that had initially elicited her joy lived with Alice, and Finn hadn't exactly been a barrel of monkeys since they parted ways.

Temporarily, he was quick to add to himself. He and Alice had only parted ways temporarily. But even having told himself that—a million, billion times—it hadn't improved his mood.

The kitten must have been sleeping, and the stair squeak must have roused her, because suddenly her little buff face appeared in the mesh at the front of the carrier, and her little pink pads pushed against it.

"*MEOW!*" she yelled when she saw Riley. "*MEOW MEOW MEOW MEOW!*"

And just like that, Riley smiled and stood, then carefully came down the rest of the stairs. She stopped in front of Alice, tilting her head back to study her with the same intensity she always showed for her, but she said nothing. Alice gazed back at the little girl in a way that was impossible for Finn to read. She didn't say anything, either. Instead, she extended the bag with the still *MEOW*ing kitten toward Riley. After a moment's hesitation, Riley accepted it. Then she carried it to the center of the living room, unzipped the front, and let out the kitten. Who ran immediately into her lap, then down to the floor to run circles around her, then back into her lap. And Riley's soft laughter bloomed with every move the kitten made.

Something inside Finn turned over at hearing it. He was still coming to grips with the myriad new feelings that had arrived with his daughter, trying to find a label for each one. This one, though, was easy. This one was delight.

"Her litter box and food are out in the car," Alice said. "I just wanted to be sure it was okay for us to stay before bringing them in."

"Alice, you know you're welcome here," Finn said softly. "I'm happy you're here. So is Riley."

Alice nodded. "Yeah, I imagine she's missed the kitten."

"And you," he said. "She missed you, too."

She closed her eyes as if he'd just said something hurtful. "Don't," she said very quietly. "Just…don't, Finn. Show me where you want to put me for the next few days, and I'll leave you both alone."

He wouldn't push it. Wouldn't push her. She was still sorting out her feelings about all of this, too. She might even have more to figure out than he did. It was enough, for now, that she was here. They would get it all sorted. They would. They had to.

No way was Finn going to lose his family a second time.

Alice awoke to a room she didn't recognize, and it took her a moment to remember where she was. Finn's house. Specifically, the bedroom that had belonged to his father. Both of his parents, actually, when they were both alive. Even if he hadn't told her that last night while getting her settled, she would have known. Like the rest of his house, it didn't appear to have changed at all since he was a boy. The English cottage theme that permeated the living room had found its way up here, too. Finn's mother had probably been responsible for the decor throughout the house, and doubtless neither of the Huxley men had wanted to change it after she was gone.

The room was full of other family-oriented trappings, as well. More photos of Finn's lifelong accomplishments, school-made projects, some of which Alice remembered completing, too. A heart fashioned from paper that they'd made in art class in fifth grade had been framed and hung above the door. Cut-paper art of a flower vase from sixth grade hung on a wall between the two windows. A clay bowl fired in eighth grade was a catchall on what Alice presumed had been Leo's dresser. She'd made all those things, too, but her mother had kept none of them. At least, Alice hadn't come across any of them as she'd gone through her mother's belongings.

She closed her eyes to shut out all the reminders, then rubbed them. The rain must have made some things blossom during the night that were making her eyes water this morning. She needed to remember not to sleep with the windows cracked.

She rose and dressed in blue jeans, layering a long-sleeved white T-shirt and oversize yellow sweater atop them, since the day would be going from cool this morning to warm this afternoon, so typical for spring in the Finger Lakes. Then she brushed her hair and gathered it in a loose ponytail at her nape and made her way downstairs. Normally, she slept with the kitten, who had taken to curling up on the pillow above her head, but Riley had looked so devastated last night when Alice went to collect her and turn in that she'd told Riley it would be fine if she wanted the tiny tabby to sleep in her room. She was surprised how much she'd missed the company, and the kitten's thrumming purr.

She really did need to return home as soon as possible. The longer she stayed here with Finn and his family, the more of herself she was going to lose.

She heard his voice coming from the kitchen as he prepared Riley's breakfast. He'd told her last night that Sudbury's schools were on spring break this week, so although she was now officially enrolled, she wouldn't be starting until Monday. So in addition to imposing on Finn, Alice was imposing on his family, as well.

"Good morning," Finn said with a smile as she entered the kitchen. His hair was still damp from a shower, and he'd donned a pair of battered brown cargo pants and an oatmeal-colored sweater. Riley was her usual rainbow self, her dark red hair bound in two crooked ponytails Alice somehow knew she had gathered up herself, even though Finn probably wouldn't have done much better of a job himself, had he tried. She looked up the minute Alice walked into the room, her gaze fixed, as it always was, on her face. But although Alice murmured a perfunctory greeting to her, the little girl said nothing in reply.

"You're just in time for waffles," Finn said, his smile going broader.

"You know how to make waffles?" she asked incredulously.

"Sure. Just like my mom made them. Shake 'em out of the box and pop 'em in the toaster." He held up the box in question as if it were a prized trophy. "Want a couple?"

Alice shook her head. "Just coffee for now. Thanks."

She could tell he wanted to press, but thankfully, he didn't. He just told her to take a seat at the table, then went to a cabinet and pulled down a mug, pouring her a cup and fixing it exactly the way she liked it. When he turned back from the counter to head for the table, though, he realized Alice hadn't seated herself there. He opened his mouth to say something, but she interjected a quick thank you and took the mug from him.

Then she told him, "Like I said, I'll stay out of your and Riley's way while I'm here."

She turned to leave, but Finn dropped a gentle hand onto her shoulder to stop her. Warmth spread through her at the simple gesture, moving from her shoulder, to her chest, to her heart. Alice told herself to keep walking. Instead, she stopped. It just felt so good, him touching her again. And she needed to bank as many of these sensations as she could before she left Sudbury. Just like before, when Finn had been missing from her life, her memories of him would be what got her through the day.

"Don't," Finn said, echoing her single word of the night before. "We'd love it if you had breakfast with us."

Oh, *they* would love it, would they? Somehow Alice found it hard to believe that Riley had just started talking and making plans with Finn this morning.

"And come with us to shop for Riley's room today," he continued relentlessly. "I don't have an eye for that kind of thing, and Riley doesn't seem to be too sure about what she wants. We'd love it if you could come with us and give us a hand."

There it was again. *They* would love it.

"Finn, I don't think—"

"But breakfast first," he interjected. "Come on. Have a seat. If you don't want waffles, I have other breakfast stuff."

He kept talking as he bustled about the kitchen, obviously in an effort to keep her from saying anything more. Too tired to argue, Alice did as he asked and sat at the table, in the chair next to Riley instead of across from her, so that their gazes wouldn't be falling on each other every time they looked up. Still, she felt the little girl's scrutiny as she sat down, and it lingered even after Riley went back to eating her waffles.

She was dressed as colorfully as she'd been every time Alice saw her, in a bright blue tunic and rainbow-striped leggings. Call Alice crazy, but if Finn just stuck with a rainbow motif for the girl's bedroom, she was going to go out on a limb and say he'd be fine.

"We thought we'd go into Ithaca to shop," Finn said as he placed a bowl of fruit, a plate of doughnuts, a box of cereal, and some toast in front of her. Wow. He really did have other breakfast stuff. "There will be a lot more choices there than in Sudbury, but the traffic won't be as bad as it is in Rochester."

"Finn, I can't," she said. "Like I told you, I have—"

"I know. So, so, *so* much to do."

"And also that—"

"Also that you need..." Here, he looked at Riley.

But Riley was too busy still studying Alice to realize it. Her expression was almost comically serious, her eyebrows arrowed down over her blue eyes as if someone had glued them on that way, and her mouth curved into a twist of consternation. For the smallest of moments, Alice wondered what the little girl was thinking about. Then she remembered it was none of her business what Riley thought about any more than it was her business what any other five-year-old in Sudbury thought about. Because Riley was no more her responsibility than any of them.

"Also that you need some time to be alone," Finn continued, bringing Alice's attention back to him. "But that's going to be hard to do since you and I have a contract that requires me to come to your house to fix it."

"I told you. I'll manage what's left myself," she reminded him. "I free you from your contract immediately."

"Well, I don't free you. Your project is my weekly paycheck for a while."

And he's going to need that money now that he has an extra mouth to feed, Alice thought.

Alice sighed. "I'll still pay you what we agreed on. But I'll finish the work by my—"

"You look like my mom," Riley said suddenly.

Now Alice and Finn both looked down at the little girl. Her scrutiny was even more severe than before, but not in any way that made Alice feel uneasy. Riley just looked as if she were trying to figure out a puzzle that had no solution. Alice was so surprised by the fact that the little girl had spoken after being silent for days that it took a minute for what she had said to register. Then, when it finally did, she had no idea how to reply.

"Your hair is longer," Riley continued somberly. "And it's curlier than Mom's. But you look like her."

And then, without hesitation, the little girl jumped up from her chair, took a step toward Alice, wrapped her arms around her shoulders, pressed her face into her neck and hugged her. Alice had never been hugged by a child before. It was an odd sensation. But not, she realized, a little awestruck, entirely unpleasant.

Instinctively, she set down her coffee and released it, then realized she had no idea what to do with her hands. This wasn't just some quick hug from a child who had met her only days before. It was a long, silent gesture of affection from a stranger. Even if the stranger was only a child, and a grieving one at that, Alice felt a little…imposed upon. She looked at Finn in silent despair, but he was still looking at Riley. Looking at her in a way that made Alice's heart twist inside her. He already loved his daughter. She could see it in his expression, the way his face went all soft and rosy and luminous. Barely a week after meeting her, he felt genuine love for Riley Sullivan. She knew that shouldn't surprise her, but it did. And it twisted her heart even tighter to realize it.

Although her instincts screamed at her to disengage from Riley's embrace, Alice didn't want to hurt the little girl's feelings. So she swallowed a sound of distress that surged to the back of her throat, packed down her anguish, and… hugged Riley back. Not hard. Not even convincingly, she thought. She just pressed her hands against the little girl's back and left them there. But Riley must have been convinced of Alice's gesture, because she squeezed her even tighter. The whimper Alice had tried to contain escaped her, softly enough that only Finn seemed to hear it. Because he glanced at Alice quickly as Riley continued to embrace her, and to his credit, he seemed to understand.

"Riley," he said softly. "Honey. You need to let go of Alice, okay?"

With one last quick hug, Riley released her. Then she returned to her chair. But she never stopped looking at Alice. This time, though, her expression wasn't so much analytical as it was assured. As if by hugging Alice, she had come to some kind of conclusion that left her feeling better about the world at large than she had before.

Unsure why she did it—and before she could stop herself—Alice said softly, "Riley, I'm not your mother."

Finn looked a little horrified by the statement, but Riley was unfazed. "I know. But you look like her."

Alice nodded. "Okay." She just wanted—needed—what she had said to be made clear. To everyone standing in the room.

"You should come with us today," Finn said again. "You've gotten rid of an awful lot of your mother's stuff, and you're going to need to replace it with something else to stage the house before you list it for sale. It really does bring up the value and interest a lot when prospective buyers tour a house, to show how comfortable and welcoming and happy the place could be."

Oh, right. Like Nora Whitlock's house had ever been any of those things. Still, as much as Alice hated to admit it, Finn did have a point. Even though she'd just been thinking yesterday that she didn't care how quickly the house sold, she did. She looked at Riley and remembered the…odd-ness…of the little girl's hug. The sooner Alice could leave Sudbury, the better.

"All right, fine," she finally, reluctantly, conceded. "I guess it wouldn't hurt to look around."

If someone had told Finn as recently as a couple of weeks ago that he would soon be sitting in a beanbag chair that looked like a basketball, in between a giant stuffed narwhal and a pink princess castle, carrying a granola bar in one pocket and a juice box in another, while a little girl who had been placed in his keeping double-checked the weight capacity of a bunk bed with a sliding board at one end—never mind that he would actually be enjoying himself while doing it—he would have figured that person had one hell of an imagination. But here he was, in exactly that position.

When he and Alice and Riley first entered a shop called Polliwog and Piglet, his daughter's gaze had immediately hit on a bookcase/storage shelf in, naturally, every color of the rainbow. Since then, she'd been choosing furniture and accessories to go with it. At the moment, they'd amassed—in addition to the bookcase and what would clearly be a bunk bed with a sliding board at one end—a multicolored dresser, a multicolored chair shaped like an egg, and a multicolored rug to tie it all together. Not that it was hard to tie together an explosion of color. Since Riley had yet to designate a color for the room, Finn was assuming for now that each wall and the ceiling would be a different color and that the baseboards and doors would be a free-for-all.

She hadn't said a lot since telling Alice she resembled her mother. That alone had been enough to shake Finn to his core—both the speaking itself and what the little girl had said. He would have preferred Riley not make the connection between Denise and Alice. And he *really* would have preferred Alice didn't know how much she had in common with the woman he had married. She had been looking at him funny all afternoon, as if he were an even bigger stranger to her than she'd made him feel like the last time he saw her.

Strangely, what few words Riley had said since this morning had all been directed at Alice. Or maybe that wasn't so strange, after all, if Alice reminded Riley of her mother. What was kind of strange was that Alice was starting to seem a little less uncomfortable around the girl. When he remembered the look on her face when Riley hugged her...

His stomach pitched as badly now as it had when it happened. Alice had looked like she wanted to throw up, too. He could imagine—sort of—what she had been thinking when it happened. That she might have been hugged this way by her own daughter, had things turned out the way they were supposed to when they were expecting Sarah. The fact that she'd initially had no idea what to do with her hands had said pretty clearly that she hadn't been expecting—and didn't like—the hug. That she had no idea how to respond to it. Finn sympathized. It was weird enough holding Riley's hand. Though, truth be told, that felt less weird today than it had the first few times it happened. A full-on hug, on the other hand...

Riley glanced up then, as if he'd spoken the thought aloud. Alice was standing in between the two of them— keeping a safe distance from them both, he couldn't help thinking—and now she looked at Finn, too. Both their expressions were identical, and he knew a moment's panic when he realized that Riley could easily be mistaken for Alice's daughter, too. He really had fallen for Denise because of how much she reminded him of Alice. And he'd ended it with her because he finally realized how little she reminded him of Alice.

"What?" he said to them both when nèither said a word to him.

Riley turned her attention to Alice. "I like this one," she told her. "I think it will be safe."

Safe, Finn echoed to himself. What five-year-old thought about the safety of anything? Then he remembered that Denise was an RN. So she probably thought a lot about things like that. It made sense that she would be on the lookout for her daughter's health and safety.

Finn pushed himself up from the bean-filled basketball and made his way toward his daughter. He stopped when he was next to Alice, but he spoke to Riley when he said, "Alright then. Looks like we've got ourselves a bedroom."

Alice looked a little stricken by his announcement for some reason. When she said, "I guess you both do," he understood. She thought he was excluding her from the *we*, when, in fact, he had been referring to the three of them. She really did think he wanted to exclude her from his family. How was he going to make her understand that that was the furthest thing from the truth? For the first time in his adult life, Finn was actually thinking about having a family. Not just with Riley, but with Alice, too.

He started to tell her that, then realized that inside a crowded furniture store surrounded by people and his five-year-old daughter probably wasn't the best place for it. So he only said, "Let's go find our salesclerk and see when we can get all this stuff delivered. Next stop, the paint store." He looked in mock consternation at Riley, smiling when he said, "I mean it, kid. You need to pick a color for your room today."

She said nothing in reply and nodded. But she did seem to be smiling just the tiniest bit. Finn would take what he could get at this point. He'd moved downstairs to sleep on the couch now that Alice was staying with them, but he'd gone upstairs to check on Riley before he turned in. As had been the case every night since her arrival, he'd heard her sniffling softly on the other side of his bedroom door. He wished he knew what to say to her about her mother's death. But hell, he wasn't even comfortable talking to adults who'd lost a loved one. He had no idea what to say to a kid. Especially a kid he'd only met a week ago. So he'd only stood in the hall and listened, in case she did call out for him or something. She never had, though. And eventually, she'd stopped crying and fallen asleep.

He wished he knew how long it would be before his and Riley's lives went back to normal. Then he gave himself a mental kick. His and Riley's lives would never go back to normal.

He looked at Alice again. Her life had been as upended by this whole thing as theirs had. Her life wasn't going to go back to normal, either. And she'd probably never had a chance to normalize it, anyway, after they lost Sarah. Her mother had made sure of that.

His thoughts were threatening to blacken the mood, which was the last thing any of them needed. So he did what he always did in times of turmoil.

"Hey," he said to the two most important people in his life, "you guys want ice cream before we make our next stop? 'Cause I could really go for some ice cream."

There was a time in Alice's life when ice cream really had solved all of her problems. In fact, she remembered two occasions in particular when a single scoop of the tamest vanilla had shooed away a host of cloudy thoughts. Once, at Damian Kaufman's sixth birthday party, on the afternoon following the morning her mother told her she was far too irresponsible to have a pet and that *Honestly, Alice, only children who* don't *spill their milk at the breakfast table can have those.* And again, on the last day of second grade before winter break, when Mrs. Pulaski handed back their book reports, and Alice saw her grade was a B+, which she knew her mother was going to be *very* disappointed to see. In that last hour of school before going home, though, she was able to forget for a little while how she would have to suffer through her mother's complaints that Alice wasn't applying herself nearly enough and how embarrassing it was for Nora to have a daughter making a B+ when she herself had made it through the entirety of elementary school with all As, and *Honestly, Alice, B+ is a mark only an ignoramus receives.*

Today, however, ice cream was nowhere nearly as effective as it used to be in making things better. Amazing how much difference there was between being told no for what was probably the hundredth time Alice had asked to have a pet and having received an ignoramus grade on a report about Eli Whitney's cotton gin, and knowing the life you'd been starting to think might work out after all would, in fact, be worse than you could ever have imagined. Because as she and Finn and Riley sat in a corner booth in an ice cream shop even more colorful than the little girl's bedroom-to-be, Alice felt more alone than she'd felt in a very long time. Not since losing Sarah and Finn had she felt this way.

Probably because, for much of the day, she'd felt like she was losing them both all over again. Sarah, because being with Riley brought back all the memories of the daughter she never got to know, and Finn, because... Well, because he belonged to Riley now. She was his family.

He had been delighted when his daughter ordered a cake cone with a scoop of caramel butter pecan, because that had always been his go-to when they were kids. Hearing the order come from Riley's lips the way it had—to Alice, no less, not Finn, since she was still restricting her words and only speaking to Alice the few times she did speak—had had the opposite effect on Alice. It seemed like, with every passing hour, Riley was doing something that was reminiscent of Finn in some way. He might not have been present in her life until a week ago, but his genes must be fiercely dominant. Not only did she look identical to him physically and like the same foods he did, but her posture was like his, Alice had noticed. The two of them walked alike, too. When the three of them ate lunch at a diner earlier and the server brought out a menu for Riley to color, Finn had joined her with a crayon of his own, one he held the exact same way she did. Her voice inflections were like his. She even tilted her head the same way when they ate their cones.

Alice was never going to be able to see the two of them together and not be reminded that the two of them were father and daughter. The two of them were family. And she would never stop being reminded of everything she had lost with Finn.

The woman who had scooped their ice cream for them earlier suddenly appeared tableside, holding a small paper bowl with two spoons. She was of an age that could make her Alice's mother, but her gray hair had a single streak of purple that matched her uniform and indicated she would be a lot more fun than Nora ever was. She smiled as she set the bowl on the table between Finn and Riley.

"I had to switch out the carton of caramel butter pecan for a new one, and there wasn't quite enough left in the old one to do anybody much good, but I didn't want to waste it. So I thought you two might enjoy it. On the house."

"Oh, that's really nice of you," Finn said warmly. "Thank you."

Riley, not surprisingly, said nothing, but she offered the woman a brief, small smile as she pulled the bowl toward herself. Finn made a move for the second spoon—Alice told herself there wasn't a third because she'd ordered a different flavor, so the ice cream lady may have thought she didn't like caramel butter pecan, but it somehow didn't do much to reassure her—but Riley batted his hand playfully away. When Finn emitted a sound of mock affront, Riley only smiled and pulled the bowl closer to herself. The two of them bantered back and forth that way—well, as much as a five-year-old who doesn't talk much can actually banter—until, in a melodramatic fit of defeat, Finn gave up and pouted.

The ice cream lady teased them both the whole time, finally giving Finn a reassuring pat on the shoulder when he lost the battle. "That's okay, Daddy," she said with a chuckle. "This is nothing. Just wait until you see the battles you and Mommy here are going to have when your daughter is a teenager."

Here, she smiled at Alice, to include her in the conversation, too. Alice tried to smile back, but it wasn't easy when someone had just slammed a two-by-four into your gut. Finn's expression went slack when he looked first at Alice, then at the ice cream lady, but he said nothing. Like Alice, he probably had no idea what to say.

But that was okay, because the ice cream lady wasn't finished with her unwitting battery. "I just have to say that you three are the cutest family I've ever seen. And I've seen a lot of cute families in this place over the years. I don't know how it's possible, but your daughter is the spitting image of you both."

Finn fumbled a smile and managed to mutter a thank-you before the woman turned and went back to the counter. Riley, thankfully, seemed to be too engrossed in her ice cream to have noticed the exchange. Alice was able to hold herself together for about a nanosecond before tears sprang to her eyes. And when she realized they were only going to be the first of many, it was all she could do to flee the table before falling completely apart.

Chapter Twelve

Finn rose from the booth to follow Alice, but halted when he realized he couldn't leave Riley sitting there alone. Riley, who, he was relieved to see, seemed to have no idea what had just happened because she was too focused on scooping every last bit of ice cream out of the cup.

That such a sweet comment from such a nice lady could be so unbelievably hurtful was telling. Mostly, it told him that things between him and Alice were a lot more complicated than he realized, and that he'd been kidding himself when he thought all he had to do was be patient and wait for her to come around and realize she would always be as much a part of his life as Riley was now. She wasn't going to realize that if she was reminded every day of their past and how much she had lost and Finn had gained. Not unless—not until—he made her realize she was as important to him as his daughter was.

But just how was he supposed to make her realize that?

He looked at Riley, who was wiping her mouth with an ice cream-stained napkin, having missed half of what she was trying to clean off. He sat back down beside her, tugged a clean napkin out of the metal dispenser on the table and, after only a small hesitation, dipped it into Alice's still half-full water glass. He started to wipe Riley's face himself, but still wasn't sure if that was too invasive a gesture at this point in their relationship. So he held it out to her instead.

"You missed a few spots," he told her softly.

She took the napkin from him and tried again. But again, she left a few sticky spots behind. Finn pointed to his own face to show her where the bits of caramel still lingered on her own. But she only arrowed her brows down in frustration and thrust the damp napkin back at him, lifting her face in a silent indication that he should take care of the problem.

He couldn't believe the swell of happiness that went up inside him at her simple indication of trust, however silent. He'd figured out by now that she spoke to Alice instead of him because Alice reminded her of her mother. He wasn't sure how that translated in the little girl's mind, whether she was just bonding with Alice due to that reminder or if she was somehow…superimposing Alice over her mother and seeing her as a potential replacement for Denise. He guessed that was something they could work out in their first meeting with the therapist. But he did wish Riley would talk to him, too. He figured that was something that would come with time and patience, so he wouldn't rush it. *With Alice, though…*

His happiness ebbed at that. With Alice, he had no idea what to do.

Gently, he cleaned up Riley's face, then looked toward the restrooms, where Alice had disappeared. The day had been going surprisingly well. In addition to Riley's things, Alice had found some accessories for her own house for them to take home today and had ordered some furniture to be delivered later in the week. There had been some tension between them—he wasn't going to lie to himself about that—but they'd been getting along pretty well. All three of them had been. At least, that was what he'd thought.

Now, though, he was beginning to wonder if maybe he was just mired in denial. Alice had been almost as quiet as Riley over ice cream. Even in the store earlier, she hadn't said much more than she had to. And when Riley had spoken to her about something, Alice had, half the time, replied to Finn instead. He knew she wasn't trying to hurt the little girl's feelings. She just genuinely didn't seem to know how to react to her.

He looked at Riley again. Riley looked back at him. He looked at his watch. He wasn't sure how long Alice had been gone—maybe ten minutes, maybe ten years—but every passing second made him feel like he'd aged a century. When he looked up, Riley was still watching him. And Alice still hadn't come back.

Finn nodded his head toward the restrooms. "C'mon," he said softly. "Let's see if we can find Alice."

He scooted himself out of the booth, and Riley followed. Where before, he'd always had to be the one to reach for her hand, this time, she readily tucked her fingers into his. That surge of odd happiness wound through him again. She really was beginning to trust him. But he was trusted by dozens of people these days. Every one of his clients put their faith in him and paid him thousands of dollars, trusting he'd do good work on their homes. Why the trust of a five-year-old should affect him so deeply was a mystery. But Riley's trust in him buoyed him more than all those other people combined.

Finn stopped them when they got to the women's room, standing outside the door much as he had with Riley the other night, not wanting to invade Alice's space, but worrying about her nonetheless. There was no way of knowing if she was in there alone or not. As much as he didn't want to send Riley in for reconnaissance, since that might just make Alice feel bad all over again, he didn't know what else to do. So he looked at his daughter, then tilted his head toward the door.

"Think you could go in and check to make sure Alice is okay?"

Riley nodded. Then she suddenly looked very serious, mouth firm, brow knit. She released his hand and pushed open the door. As she entered, Finn could hear sniffling on the other side. Just as he had heard Riley the other night. Man, the two of them really were more alike than Alice realized. Both wounded. Both grieving. Both having lost someone who was more important to them than anyone else in the world.

Both of them more important to Finn than anyone else in the world. Two of a kind, that was what they were. He just wished he knew what to do about them both.

Alice was still locked in the bathroom stall, wiping her nose with the nearly depleted paper towel she'd grabbed on the way in, when a pair of very tiny feet, clad in very tiny sneakers sparkling with multicolored lights, appeared on the floor in front of the door on the other side. Their arrival was followed by the soft rap of very tiny knuckles on the metal door.

Then a very tiny voice asked, "Alice? Are you okay?"

And Alice very nearly burst into tears again. Everything about Riley just made her wonder what Sarah would have been like at that age, had she made it. The little outfits Riley wore. Her little giggle when she played with the kitten. The crooked little ponytails. The little voice. All of it was just so…so little. So…so sweet. So innocent. So vulnerable. Had Sarah been born, she would have been little, too. She would have been sweet. Innocent. Vulnerable. She would have been a lot like Riley Sullivan. And realizing that made Alice respond with feelings she had never felt before. Protective. Watchful. Tender. Caring. As if she would do whatever she could to make sure nothing bad ever happened to her again.

She wondered if this was how Finn felt. Was this what it was like to feel responsible for another human being in the world? But how could Alice feel that way? She wasn't responsible for Riley. Riley wasn't her family. She was Finn's daughter, not Alice's.

The little feet shifted beneath the door, making the lights sparkle again. "Alice?" the little voice came once more. "Are you okay?"

Alice swallowed hard, blew her nose, and said, "Yes. I'm fine. Just give me a minute."

"Okay."

But the feet didn't move away.

"I'll be out in just a second," Alice assured her.

"Okay," came the little voice.

And still the feet didn't move away. Clearly, Riley wasn't quite convinced of Alice's fineness.

"Truly, Riley. I'll be right out."

"Okay."

When the feet still didn't move, Alice did her best to bring herself around. It wasn't like her to weep in public. It wasn't like her to weep at all. Even with everything life had thrown at her, her tears had been few. She had learned early in life that crying over anything was pointless. Her mother had taught her that. Tears fixed nothing. They only made a person look weak and out of control. Lately, though, her tears had been erupting almost daily. Sometimes more than once.

Honestly, Alice, get a hold of yourself. You'll never be happy if you're just going to fall apart over the tiniest things.

She sighed, wiped her eyes, blew her nose, and discarded the tattered paper towel into the metal bin attached to the wall. Then, after only a moment's hesitation, she unlocked and opened the stall door. On the other side, Riley Sullivan was looking at her as if she were trying to read Alice's mind.

Good luck with that, Alice thought. She wasn't even sure what she was thinking herself.

"I'm okay," she told the little girl again.

When Riley's expression didn't change, Alice figured she didn't believe her any more than Alice believed herself.

"Really," she added.

But Riley only continued to look at her in silence. Alice went to the sink, quickly washed her hands and dried them. But when she took a step toward the door, Riley extended her very tiny hand and tucked it into hers. Alice stopped in her tracks. She felt the same way she had when Finn's daughter hugged her—awkward and unsure how to respond, but also weirdly...pleased. Riley's hand was a quarter the size of her own, but she wove her very tiny fingers with Alice's and held firm.

"Why are you sad, Alice?" she asked in her very tiny voice.

Leave it to a five-year-old to just put it out there. Although she had no idea why she did it, Alice replied honestly. "I'm sad because I've been thinking a lot today about someone I loved very much who...who..." She inhaled a shaky breath and released it slowly. "Well, someone who's gone now."

Riley met her gaze intently. "Did they die?"

Wow. Five-year-olds really did ask the tough questions. "Yes," Alice told her. "Yes, she died."

"Like my mom."

Alice nodded. "Like your mom."

"Who was it?"

And that was the toughest question of all. Tears sprang to Alice's eyes again. Instead of wiping them away this time, though, she let them fall. "It was my...my daughter. It happened a long time ago. But I still miss her."

"I miss my mom, too."

"I know you do, sweetie. You'll always miss your mom. The same way I'll always miss my daughter. But it will be okay. Eventually."

Eventually, Alice echoed to herself. She had just spoken the word she had so resented hearing Finn say. But maybe he was right, in a way. Even if it wasn't a concrete destination, *eventually* was a goal that made struggling to reach that destination a little more tolerable. In that way, at least, *eventually* was hopeful. And anything hopeful was good.

"What was your daughter's name?" Riley asked.

"Her name was Sarah."

Riley thought about that for a moment, then said, "Maybe she's with my mom in heaven now."

Alice nodded as more tears spilled. "Maybe she is."

"My mom will take good care of her," Riley assured her. "She was a good mom."

More tears spilled. Alice didn't try to stop those, either. "I know she was."

"How do you know? Did you meet her?"

Alice shook her head. "No. But she raised a good daughter." One who recognized, even at such a young age, that another human being was sad and cared enough to want to help. "So I know your mom must have been good, too."

And also because Finn had loved Riley's mother at one time, in some way. He wouldn't have felt that way for Denise Sullivan if she hadn't been a good person. As conflicted as Alice still was about Finn's marriage, she knew she should never have been surprised by it. He was a person who loved freely and generously. Of course he would find someone to love when he felt lonely and unhappy himself. Had Alice grown up in a family like his—one that loved in abundance and without condition—she might have reacted the same way.

Riley released her hand and went to the paper towel dispenser, then rose up on her tiptoes and stretched her arm as far as she could, until she could pull one free. Then she went back to Alice and handed it to her. Alice accepted it, wiped her eyes, blew her nose, and discarded it into the trash. As soon as she released it, Riley took her hand again.

"I'll hold your hand until you feel better," she said. "That's what my mom always did for me."

Something strange and not altogether unpleasant blossomed in Alice's chest, and it was all she could do not to start crying again. She gave the little girl's hand an impulsive squeeze. "Thank you."

"You're welcome."

When they emerged from the bathroom, Finn was looking at Alice with the same scrutiny Riley had shown, and she realized that was something else the father and daughter had in common. As Riley so often did, he said nothing. Only watched Alice as if he were also trying to read her mind.

"I'm okay," she told him.

"You don't look okay," he said. "You look like you've been crying."

"But I'm not now."

He arrowed his brows down. "Look, maybe today wasn't such a good idea, after all. We can head home if you want."

She started to remind him that she didn't have a home to

return to, because it was being treated for mold. And even if it hadn't been, the house where she grew up had never really been *home*.

Instead, she told him, "No, it's okay. We still need a few more things for Riley's room." Here, she looked down at Riley. "Paint color?" she asked the girl.

"Pink," Riley replied without hesitation.

"Pink isn't in the rainbow," Alice said with much surprise.

"But I like pink," Riley told her.

And that, really, was all the reason anyone needed.

"Okay," Alice told her. "Pink it will be."

Then she realized it wasn't her place to okay the decision, since it was Finn's house being redone, and it was Finn's daughter doing the asking, so it was Finn's approval that was necessary.

"I mean," she quickly amended, "as long as your dad says it's okay."

When she looked at Finn, he was eyeing her with...something. Something she couldn't identify. Something different from the concern and apprehension with which he'd been watching her before. Something that was also strange and not altogether unpleasant.

But all he said was, "Pink is great. Let's go find some pink."

Finn had no idea what happened between Alice and Riley in the ice cream parlor restroom. All he knew was that after they came out, Riley spoke more freely and comfortably, and she talked to both of them equally. There were even a few points when she was downright chatty as she weighed in on familiar sights, like the fast food and store chains they drove past. He also noticed that Riley never once let go of Alice's hand.

Alice, on the other hand, remained quiet, though the aura of melancholy that had enveloped her since she learned of Riley's existence seemed to have eased some. Finn even caught her smiling a couple of times, when the little girl offered observations about their surroundings that only a five-year-old would notice (like how interesting it was that every piece of plywood they passed in aisle twenty-two on their way to paint had a face that reminded her of a character from *Peppa Pig*) or relayed her reason for color preferences (she liked Angel Kiss over Peony Swirl because who wouldn't want to be kissed by an angel?). And Alice never once let go of Riley's hand.

The end of the day found him in his usual spot, sitting in the hall outside the bathroom door, but this time, he was listening to both Riley and Alice on the other side. Riley had refused to get in the tub unless Alice kept her company. The two of them had been chatting like new best friends on the first day of school ever since.

Alice, what's your favorite color?

Green, I think. What's yours?

I like them all. What's your favorite food?

Lasagna. What's yours?

Chocolate chip cookies. What's your favorite number?

Four. Yours?

Seven. If you could be any animal you wanted, what would you be?

Hmm... A golden-crowned kinglet, I guess. We both have the same color hair. How about you?

A tiger. Like Sprinkle.

Who's Sprinkle?

The kitten.

You named the kitten Sprinkle?

Her actual name is Princess Caramel Butter Pecan Sprinkle Cone. But I call her Sprinkle.

And so it had gone, for a good twenty minutes, until Finn learned more about his daughter in that short period of time than he had learned in the ten days since actually meeting her. Hell, he knew more about Alice, too, than he'd learned in a quarter-century of knowing her. He'd had no idea she wanted to be a golden-crowned kinglet. And now, finally, the kitten had a name. One that Alice, judging by her soft laughter after Riley's announcement, approved of.

He told himself that Riley responded so well to Alice because she reminded her of her mother. Something told him, however, that there was more to it than that. Neither had said anything about what happened during those few minutes they were alone together that afternoon, but something clearly had happened. Something that made both of them feel a little better about... Well. About a lot.

The *ka-thunk* of the drain alerted him to the end of bath time, so he rose and made his way back downstairs to wait for Riley to come down and tell him she was ready for bed. Well, tell him by standing in front of him and staring at him until he asked her if she was ready for bed and then nodding silently that she was, but still.

Tonight, though, she wasn't being silent. Tonight, she was, as she had been ever since this afternoon, holding Alice's hand, and she was still pumping her for information about favorite songs, favorite movies and favorite books as they came down the stairs with Sprinkle on their heels. For Alice, they were "Unwritten"—her and Finn's first dance together, at the Spring Fling, not long after the carnation-giving—*Little Miss Sunshine* and *A Wrinkle in Time*. Which, of course, Finn already knew. But it was good to also know now that Riley's were "Play with Sky," *Marcel the Shell with Shoes On*, and *Stellaluna*. He made a mental note to download all three and become familiar with them himself.

Instead of standing silently in front of him to wait for him to ask if she was ready for bed, Riley scrambled up onto the couch beside him and tugged Alice into the spot on her other side. Then she patted the sofa between the two of them for the kitten to claw her way up onto it with her little scimitars. Finn figured he should just forget about having unshredded upholstery for a while. Or, with any luck, forever.

Then Riley said to the room at large, "Tonight is Wednesday. Wednesday night is game night. We should play a game."

Finn looked at Alice. Alice looked at Finn. The only non-electronic games he had were Cards Against Humanity and a poker set.

"Uh…" he said. "I don't really have any games, Riley. And it's kind of late to be starting one. Maybe tomorrow we can do game night."

"But Thursday is dance party night."

Oh, Finn didn't like the sound of that at all. He was a terrible dancer. The only reason he'd danced at the Spring Fling was because he was there with Alice. And he'd trusted her—barely—to not laugh hysterically at his efforts.

Alice seemed to remember this, because she told Riley, "Maybe we can make Thursday a different kind of night. How about…"

She thought for a minute, but before she could come up with anything, Finn had a great idea. "Thursday can be stargazing night," he said.

He'd thought Alice would like the idea, since the two

of them had done so much of that together when they were kids. Instead, she looked a little pained by it. Riley, however, thought the idea was genius.

"That would be good!" she said. "And Friday is movie night. Maybe we can watch *Marcel the Shell*."

"That sounds like fun," Finn told her. Hell, Friday could be medieval torture device night, and he'd be all in. His daughter was actually talking to him. That was all he cared about.

Until he looked at Alice and saw that she still looked hurt. Badly. He wanted to ask her what was wrong, but Riley was making plans for the other days of the week. Evidently, Denise had themed every night for the two of them, and Riley was ready to reinstate all of them. Except dance party night. Finn was going to put the kibosh on that ASAP. That way lay madness. He wasn't too sure about mani-pedi night or cupcake bake night, either, but he could totally get on board with build-a-fort night. Well, suffice to say, they could switch it up a bit when it came to theme nights.

"I'm ready for bed now," Riley finally finished when she had laid out the prospective schedule for the rest of the week. Instead of looking at Finn, though, she hopped off the couch, tugged on Alice's hand, and led her toward the stairs.

But Finn wasn't going to let her go that easily. Saying good-night was the closest thing the two of them had to a routine so far. He didn't mind sharing it with Alice, but he didn't want to be excluded. Riley didn't seem to mind, though, because she smiled at both of them as she and Sprinkle climbed into bed—with Riley still holding Alice's hand. Which Alice seemed not to mind at all. In fact, Alice kind of looked like she didn't want to let go, either.

Riley seemed to realize that, because she lifted their linked hands and asked Alice, "Will you be okay if I let go?"

Alice nodded. "Yes. Thank you, Riley, for holding my hand today."

"I can hold it again tomorrow if you need me to."

"Thank you."

"Good night, Alice."

"Good night, Riley."

Then Finn's daughter did something astonishing. She stood on the bed, leaned forward and brushed her lips over Alice's cheek. Then she selected her plushie-du-jour to cuddle for the night and scurried under the covers. Then she looked at Finn.

"Good night… Should I call you Dad or Finn?"

The question hit him like a ton of bricks. And he had no idea how to answer it. So he only told her, "Call me whatever you want."

His daughter gazed at him for several long, thoughtful moments before finally saying, a little hesitantly, "Good night then."

Guess she didn't know how to answer the question, either. Finn wasn't going to be offended. At least she was weighing the consideration.

"Good night, Riley," he said. And, as he always did, he blew her a fingertips-kiss from the door.

This time, though, Riley reached into the air and caught it, then pressed it to her own cheek. Finn wouldn't have been more delighted if she had just intercepted a pass at the Super Bowl and run the entire length of the field to score a game-winning touchdown.

It was going to be okay, he realized then. He knew he and Riley still had a lot to work out, and that it was going to take some time before they were in a place where things between them were second nature for them both. But it *was* going to be okay with Riley. Now, if he could just figure out what to do to make that the case with Alice, too.

As always, he switched off the overhead light but left on the lamp, its buttery light spilling softly across the room. He waited for Alice to join him at the door, but she took her time, tucking Riley's covers between the mattress and box spring, then making sure her plushies were all within reach. Finally, after a small hesitation, she leaned down and kissed Riley on the forehead. Only then did she turn around and head for the door.

But she kept going when she reached it, pushing past Finn without any hesitation at all. When he followed, he had to hasten his step, so quickly was she moving. She didn't stop until she reached the living room again, but instead of sitting back down on the couch, she paced the length of the room restlessly a few times, then moved to the window, turning her back to him, and looked out at the night. She was clearly still upset about something. He was trying to figure out what to say that would lighten the mood, something light and inconsequential like ask her what her hurry was, but he halted when he saw her swipe both eyes with the palms of her hands. Cautiously, he moved to stand beside her. Instead of looking at him, though, she only continued to stare outside.

"What's wrong?" he asked softly.

Belatedly, he realized it was a stupid thing to ask. It would have been easier for her to tell him what wasn't wrong. Even so, he'd been thinking the day had gone pretty well, in spite of the incident at the ice cream shop. Maybe even because of it. Whatever Alice and Riley talked about in there, it had brought Riley out of her shell, and it had lessened Alice's tension. There was still a lingering sadness about her that was unmistakable, but with everything she'd been through the past few weeks, that wasn't exactly surprising.

He realized she hadn't answered his question—probably because she'd realized how stupid it was, too—so he moved in a different, hopefully happier, direction.

"So what was with the hand-holding thing with Riley all day?" he asked. "She pretty much didn't let go of you once."

Alice continued to look out at the night. "When she saw that I was sad, she told me her mother always held her hand when she was sad, so she would do the same for me."

Finn smiled at that. "Sweet kid."

"Yes. She is."

"I could hold your hand now that she's in bed," he offered. "If you want me to, I mean."

Now she turned to look at him. But he could no more tell what she was thinking than he could turn the darkness to light outside. "Why did you tell Riley tomorrow night could be stargazing night? Why did you suggest that as a theme night for you and her to have every week? Stargazing was always our thing. You and me."

"I didn't suggest it for me and Riley," he told her. "I suggested it for all three of us."

Tears sprang to her eyes again. "But why? Why would you do that? I won't be here for it. I told you. I'm leaving Sudbury once my mother's house is sold."

"Yeah, you did tell me that," he agreed. He wondered if she believed it any more than he did.

She drove a hand into the loose curls hanging over her forehead and spun around, looking at the stairs. "I need to go to bed, too," she said restlessly as she headed in that direction. Over her shoulder, almost as an afterthought, she added, "It's been a day."

It had been that and then some, Finn thought as he watched her go. But it was a day the three of them had spent together. And even if it wasn't exactly ending on a high note, that, truly, was the only thing that mattered.

Chapter Thirteen

The following morning saw the arrival of both yesterday's purchases in Ithaca and Riley's belongings from Florida, something that was a bit of a good news/bad news situation for Alice. The good news was that, after the movers and delivery trucks left, she realized there was enough to unpack and get settled to keep them all busy for most of the day, something she hoped would keep her mind off how much she wanted—no, needed—to get back to her mother's house and finish prepping it for its sale. The bad news was that with every box of Riley's things she opened, she was hit by another reminder of what might have been. Little furniture, little clothes, little toys, little books...

But it was more than just reminders of Sarah Madeleine that made Alice feel so distressed. As she looked around her, she realized that everything in the world that Riley Sullivan owned fit into a little bedroom at Finn's house. And seeing all that, understanding just how alone the little girl was in the world, knowing how much lay ahead for her when it came to her new life in Sudbury, all Alice could feel was...

She watched Finn hooking up Riley's game console while the little girl looked on, voicing her concern that he was going to completely botch it as Sprinkle leaped in and out of the packing paper. And she waited for the wave of sadness that had been her constant companion for weeks. But instead, what washed over her was... Something else. Something she couldn't quite identify. Something she'd never felt before. Something that wasn't sad. Something that was almost... She sighed and let the feeling go. She would figure it out later.

"There," Finn said as he plugged the console into the small TV that had arrived with it. He smiled at Riley. "Fire 'er up."

The little girl didn't have to be told twice. Within seconds, the screen came alive with a familiar game title and music, and Alice couldn't help but smile, too. Her mother had never allowed her to have any gaming systems, but she'd played sometimes at her friends' homes. *Animal Crossing* had been one of her favorites. Something inside her warmed at the realization that it could still be popular with a new generation.

"I loved this game when I was a kid," she said. She was immediately surprised to realize she had spoken her thought aloud.

When Finn and Riley turned to look at her, Alice wondered how she hadn't noticed before now that their smiles, too, were identical.

"It was my mom's favorite," Riley told her. She had a little trouble with the controller, having such little hands and all, but she managed to move through the screens until she was back where she left off. "I'm still learning it. But I like it, too."

Finn patted the floor next to himself. "Come on over," he told her. "There are two controllers."

Alice shook her head. "No, I'll watch you two."

"Nah, c'mon," he cajoled. "You know you want to."

She was surprised to realize that she did want to. A lot.

She couldn't remember the last time she'd played any games. Not that she'd been a huge gamer when she was a kid, thanks to not being able to play whenever she wanted. But she had always enjoyed it when she could. Before she even realized she intended to do it, she was sitting on the floor between Finn and Riley, folding up her legs pretzel-style as she took the controller he extended to her. She thumbed all the buttons to refamiliarize herself with them, asked Riley whom she was playing as, so that Alice could take over the other character, and the two settled in for game time.

A few minutes in, it occurred to Alice that she must be playing the character Riley's mother had played with her, since Riley had said the two played together. She waited for the sadness that should have come with that realization, too. Instead, she found herself feeling grateful that Riley could still enjoy this small aspect of her life before losing her mother, a time when she was happy.

They played through lunch, which Finn prepared and brought up to the room, watching them as they ran around the island catching fish and bugs, digging up fossils, and making friends with the animals. They fixed up their houses in the game as they ignored the bedroom they should be pulling together, and not once did Alice mind. It had been so long since she'd done something like this. Something for which the only point was to enjoy herself.

She wondered when that had stopped being a thing for her. Though, honestly, she wasn't sure that had ever been a thing for her. Her mother had frowned on things like enjoyment, since they did nothing to build a person's character.

After finishing their lunch, Alice reluctantly reminded all of them that they really needed to finish up Riley's room if Riley wanted to sleep in her own bed tonight. And because Riley did very much want to sleep in her own bed tonight, she let herself be convinced to go back to the game later. Little by little, they got everything unpacked and arranged—though not before hearing a story from Riley about pretty much every item that arrived from Florida—until the room was in order with everything where it needed to be.

"At least until she outgrows it," Finn said quietly to Alice as he watched Riley slide the last of her games onto a shelf filled with those and her books. "Which will probably be in, oh…a few weeks."

Alice smiled. "No, it will be years before that happens. It will only seem like a few weeks to us."

He turned his head to look at her. "To us?" he echoed.

Only then did Alice realize how badly she had misspoken. "To you," she quickly corrected herself. "It will only seem like a few weeks to you."

He said nothing in response to that. Only smiled and told her, "I thought I could throw something on the grill for dinner. Should be a nice night. Not too cold after the sun goes down."

"That sounds good," she said a little breathlessly, still stunned by her verbal misstep. "I can put together a salad to go with it."

"That also sounds good." He turned to Riley. "Hey, Riley, will you be okay if Alice and I start making dinner?"

"Yes," she replied without looking up.

And she obviously would be, because she'd found her LEGOs and was currently sorting through those.

Finn turned to Alice. "C'mon. I'll let you open the wine."

The sun had well and truly set by the time Finn covered the dying embers in the grill and touched a match to the tinder in the firepit. The night was that perfect mix of not cold enough to drive them into the house, but cool enough that a fire was welcome. Alice had brewed them some coffee to enjoy post-dinner—along with mixing up a hot chocolate for Riley, who was too busy running around the yard with Sprinkle to have remembered it—and now they sat back in their Adirondack chairs on the patio, beneath a full moon and bright stars that twinkled in the sky like diamonds tossed across black velvet. It wouldn't be long before there were fireflies for Riley to chase, but for now, she made do with trying to catch Sprinkle in the beam of her flashlight, her laughter bubbling up from the darkness at the kitten's antics.

Until a few weeks ago, Finn had become convinced that he would never see a night like this. Sure, he'd imagined it at one time, back when he and Alice were planning for the arrival of their baby and the life they would build together after that. He'd told himself then that there would come a day—eventually—when the two of them owned the kind of house built for a family, one with plenty of room and a big backyard, where their kids could make believe and have lots of adventures and be happy and carefree, with two healthy parents who loved each other and their family to distraction. Maybe the house and the family he'd envisioned then weren't the ones he had now. But the feelings winding through him, feelings of contentment and hope and love… He figured those were pretty close to what he'd planned for all those years ago.

"What are you thinking about?" he heard Alice ask from beside him. "You look very…pensive."

He sighed. But all he told Alice was, "I was just thinking that this was a pretty good day."

She said nothing for a moment, then he heard her sigh, too. The sound was filled with what sounded like…contentment maybe? And hope? And perhaps even...love? Could she be feeling the same thing he was feeling right now? Could she have finally arrived in the same place as he, after all this time and everything that had happened? Could she maybe be feeling those things for both him and Riley? Or was it just wishful thinking on his part?

"It was a pretty good day," she agreed softly. "I think Riley is starting to feel settled. Like she's a part of things here."

He braved a look in Alice's direction. She was gazing out at the chaotic light that was Riley running around, the golden glow of the fire giving her profile an almost dreamy quality.

"And you?" he asked. "Are you starting to feel like you're a part of things here, too?"

He expected her to say no, even though the last two days had made clear that the three of them were already closer to being a family than Alice had ever known—and closer to being a happy family than either of them had known. But when she turned to look at him, it was obvious she wasn't as convinced of the isolation she felt from him and Riley as she was a few days ago.

"I don't know," she told him. "I'm not sure how I feel about anything."

"That's okay," he said. "I'm sure enough for both of us. I love you, Alice," he told her without hesitation. "Riley loves you. And it's not because you remind her of her mother," he hastened to add. "She loves you for the same reason I do. Because you're you."

He waited for her to deny Riley's love for her, too, but she didn't. She didn't agree with him about it, but she wasn't as steadfast in her convictions to the contrary as she had been before.

So Finn pressed on. "Sprinkle loves you, too," he said with a smile, something that made Alice smile back. So he decided to go all in. "And maybe I'm being a little presumptuous here, but I kinda think you love all of us, too. Like maybe, over the last few days, all three of us—all four of us, if you throw in Sprinkle—have laid a pretty solid foundation for, you know…a family."

Her brows arrowed downward, and she swallowed hard. "It's not that easy, Finn."

"Yeah, it is, Alice. What do you think makes a family a family?"

Now she looked very much like she didn't want to have this conversation. Even so, she told him, "Mostly DNA. But it's also sharing the same home. The same traditions. The same customs."

He shook his head. "None of those things make a family. There are people out there who share the same DNA with people they've disowned because they weren't behaving like family. There are people living in the same house who barely speak to each other, because none of them is treating the other like family. And on the flip side, there are plenty of families out there who don't share any DNA, and who don't live together, and who observe totally different traditions and customs, but hey, whaddaya know, they're family. They're family because they respect each other. And they take care of each other. And they have each other's backs. They do all that because they love each other. Unconditionally. And that's all it takes, Alice, to make a family. The people you love who love you back. That's your family. Whether you share the same DNA and address and customs or not."

She was looking into the fire now, not at him. And she was as silent as Riley had been those first few days—until the day she realized she wasn't among strangers, she was among people who loved her. Her *family*. Alice wasn't quite there yet, Finn realized. So he scooted his chair closer to hers. And as Riley had done yesterday—once she realized she and Alice were family—he took her hand in his.

"Do you think your mother was your family?" he asked her.

She turned to look at him, confused. "Of course. She was my mother."

"But was she your family?" he asked again.

Her confusion compounded. But she said nothing. So Finn tried a different tack.

"Did you think you and I were family back when we were kids?"

Her expression softened at the question, but she continued to look a little baffled, and she returned her attention to the flickering fire. "I don't know," she said. "I never really thought about it."

"Think about it now. Because you and I became a family fifteen years ago," he said told her. "The minute we realized we loved each other and made a commitment to be together. Even if we never said it in so many words, you and I were a family back then. And Sarah became a part of our family as soon as she was conceived. That will never change. She will always be a part of our family, Alice. But that's the beautiful thing about family. There's always room for more."

Tears had filled her eyes at his mention of Sarah, and now they spilled free. She swiped at them with her free hand and continued to gaze into the fire. But Finn could see that she had taken what he said to heart.

He was about to say more, about how the two of them were still family, because they still loved each other, and how they had room in their hearts—in their family—to include Riley and any other kids who might come along. But Riley came running up to them, breathless and clinging to a squirming Sprinkle, as oblivious to everything hanging in the air between him and Alice as she was to her muddy sneakers, her grass-stained rainbow hoodie and her tattered ponytails.

"It's Thursday," she announced.

Finn and Alice exchanged glances, then looked back at Riley.

"Stargazing night," she reminded them.

"Right," Finn said. "I'll go get a blanket."

He looked at Alice, to see if she would object, but she didn't. When he released her hand, she took the one Riley extended, then rose and followed the little girl past the edge of the patio and into the darkness beyond it. By the time Finn returned with a beach blanket from the garage that was a remnant of his childhood days spent at Cayuga Lake with his parents, Alice was already pointing at the sky, telling Riley to follow the arc to Arcturus and then speed on to Spica. He grinned when he remembered the lesson from their third-grade science class. Then he spread the blanket on the grass, and all three lay down on their backs, Sprinkle curling up on Riley's chest, and gazed at the black sky above. That was another nice thing about living in a small town. No garish city lights to obscure the stars. And here at Finn's house, at the very edge of Sudbury, they were about as far from the pale streetlights of "downtown" as they could be.

"What's that big shiny star?" he heard Riley ask as she pointed directly above them. "It's not twinkling like the others."

"That's actually not a star," Finn told her. "That's Venus."

"Like, the planet?"

He was kind of surprised she knew that. Just when did they teach that stuff in school?

"Yep," he told her. "And Mars is over there." He pointed toward that planet, too.

"I would like to go to Mars someday," the little girl said. "And Saturn, too. Except you can't stand on Saturn. Did you know that?"

"I did not know that," Finn said. "How do you know that?"

"Saturn is made of gas. I learned it from Ms. Gomez at the library. Mommy took me every week for reading circle, and one week the book was about the planets. Neptune is windy."

"Sudbury Library has something like a weekly reading circle for kids," Alice said. "At least, they used to. I worked part-time there for a little while when I came back to town that first time." She turned to look at Riley. "Would you like to go if they still have it?"

"Yes," Riley told her. "I love the library."

"I love it, too," Alice said.

Finn just loved everything about this evening. He loved most that it was starting to feel like the first of many to follow. He bowed out of the conversation after that, letting Alice and Riley explore the cosmos together. Neither seemed to notice his absence from the conversation, something else he kind of loved. This really had been a good day. And it was being capped off by an even better night.

The two most important women in his life continued to share tidbits about the solar system, until Sprinkle woke up and took off after something only she could see. Riley flicked on her flashlight and followed, leaving only Finn and Alice to look up at the stars. For a long moment, neither said a word, but only lay lost in their thoughts. Which, Finn suspected, were probably pretty similar. Although they'd never stargazed in his backyard, they had stargazed plenty when they were kids. It was what they were doing on the night that became the first time they made love. It was what they were doing when they'd talked about their future together. It was what they were doing when they'd made their plans for Sarah.

Very softly, Alice said, "You can see the sky better from your house than we could from mine."

"We're farther from town here," he replied, just as quietly.

"We're farther from a lot of things here."

"So we are."

More silence followed, but it wasn't the awkward, disjointed silence that had lain between them on so many other occasions since Finn had returned with Riley. And it was punctuated by the sound of the little girl's laughter in the distance, something that made it even sweeter.

"She wasn't, you know," Alice said suddenly. At first, Finn thought she was talking about Sarah. Then she quickly clarified, "My mother, I mean. You were right about her. She wasn't my family. When I was a kid, I thought she was. I thought she was the only family I had. I thought she was the only family I would ever have. I mean, that was what she always told me."

Her voice drifted off on a sigh. Finn reached across the blanket and took her hand.

"She told you that because she wanted you to think you were nothing without her. When the opposite was actually true. She was nothing without you."

"Maybe," Alice murmured. "But even as an adult, until your question a little while ago made me think about it, I just always considered her my family. And that when she died, my family died with her. And then, when you and I got back together, it was like…"

Now she turned onto her side to look at him. So Finn turned, too. But they never let go of each other's hands.

"It was like it was when we were kids again," she continued. "Back then, I felt something for you that I'd never felt before for anyone. Not even my mother. I loved you. I honestly never knew what that was like before I met you. It took a while for me to realize how—" Here, she chuckled a little sadly. "Jeez, it took me almost half my life. But what I felt for you then was so much different than what I felt for my mother. What I felt for her wasn't love. It was never love. It was a feeling of obligation. A sense of duty. The belief that I *had* to be with her because she was my mother. All of those things…that's what I thought family was back then. It's what I thought family was a couple of weeks ago. And when you came back from Florida with Riley, when I realized that she would be your biggest obligation now, that your duty was to her, that you *had* to be with her because you're her father… I just thought you couldn't possibly love *me* anymore. That you would never be *my* family."

"Oh, Alice…"

"But you're right," she hurried on, her eyes shining. "That's not what family is. Family is something else." She gave his hand a squeeze. "Family shouldn't make you feel bad. Or guilty. Or scared. Family should make you feel… happy. And safe. And loved. And that's how you make me feel, Finn. I hope it's how I make you feel, too. You and Riley both. Because I love you. Both of you. And I don't want to lose either of you."

Something warm and wonderful blossomed in the middle of Finn's chest and spread outward with every word she spoke. "I love you, too," he told her. "I have always loved you. I always will love you. You're…" He smiled. "You're my family."

He scooched across the blanket until barely a breath of air separated them. Then he leaned in and covered her mouth with his. She melted into him immediately, the way she had when they were kids, when the two of them became one every time they were together. Not physically so much— well, not always—but just joined in a way neither was joined with anyone else. A way neither could be joined with anyone else. Because they were family. Then and now.

"Ew. Gross."

And so is Riley, Finn thought when he pulled back from Alice to find his daughter standing by the blanket, looking at them as if they were a couple of slices of moldy cheese.

"It's not gross," he told her. "Not when you love someone."

"Do you love Alice?" the little girl asked.

"Yes, I do," he told her with a smile and much conviction.

She looked at Alice. "Alice, do you love my dad?"

Alice smiled, too. "Yes, I do."

Riley looked at them both. "I guess it's okay then."

And then she ran off into the darkness once more, Sprinkle screaming her *MEOW!* on her heels.

"I love you, Finn," Alice said again. She lifted her free hand to thread her fingers through his hair.

"And I love you," he replied.

They sat up after that and let Riley run around until she was too tired to run anymore. Then, together, they went through their nightly ritual of bath and bedtime and goodnights. They closed the door on Riley's new bedroom, and made their way downstairs, back to the patio, where the fire's embers still glowed warmly, and their coffee had gotten cold. Finn didn't care. Neither did Alice. They only sat hand in hand, murmuring about the day's events and making plans for the future.

It really was a good night. The best night. A night Finn was pretty sure neither of them would ever forget. Because it was the night when they both found, once and for all, their family. And family, they both knew, was all that mattered.

Epilogue

Alice lay on the sofa in the house that used to belong to Finn and his family—but which now belonged to Finn and his family—and was *this* close to drifting into slumberland when she heard the sound of her husband and daughter coming through the front door. Finn picked up Riley at school every day after whatever practice she had—if it was springtime, it must be track—after calling it a day himself, and they'd all sit down to dinner in a couple of hours to share their experiences of the day. One of which, Alice could already tell, was going to be a tad contentious.

"Dad. I'm eight now," she heard Riley say. "I'm old enough to play *Silent Hill*."

"Oh, no, you're not," Finn replied in that tone of voice where Alice knew what he was actually thinking was *The hell you are*, but was doing his best to maintain the Dad voice instead of the Finn voice. "But I'll be happy to let you tag along with me on a few jobs if you want to earn some money to save up for the new *Pokémon*."

"But *Pokémon* is for babies!"

"Hey, I love *Pokémon*," Alice protested as she struggled to get into a sitting position…and failed miserably. Her eight-months-pregnant belly foiled her again. "Dangit," she muttered in that tone of voice when what she was actually thinking was… Well. Words that weren't fit for an eight-year-old, never mind a minus-one-month-old, to hear.

When Riley and Finn heard and saw her struggle, they hurried to help her up. But they didn't stop bickering as they maneuvered her into a sitting—kind of—position. They'd been having this argument ever since Riley's birthday last summer, and Alice was fairly confident at this point that it would be going on for the next decade, until their daughter was eighteen and would be able to buy the game on her own. There had been other family battles over the past few years—for instance, Riley's insistence that Sprinkle needed yet another sibling, in addition to her brother Waffles, whom they'd adopted during Humane Society Camp last summer, and her sister Oreo, whom they'd adopted during Humane Society Camp the year before that—and there were sure to be more family battles in the future. But as long as they were family battles—and as long as they were family—they'd handle each and every one with respect, consideration and love.

"Stop arguing," Alice told them both as she finally got her feet on the floor. "You're agitating baby Leo. He's spinning around in there like an out-of-possession basketball."

"Ooo, lemme feel!" Riley cried.

She sat and splayed both hands over Alice's broad belly, laughing at the lively movements as the baby did somersaults, first one way, then another. Then she leaned over and gave her brother a kiss through Alice's shirt.

"Won't be much longer, little brother," she murmured with a final gentle pat. "Then I get to be your babysitter."

Alice opened her mouth to tell her daughter she would not be babysitting her brother when she was still too young to babysit herself, but decided that that could wait a bit. They had a few other things more pressing at the moment.

"Okay, so I put a pork roast into the slow cooker this morning, and I'm reasonably sure I remembered to turn it on." Pregnancy brain, she had learned, was a tad unreliable. "Should be ready in a couple hours. But I'm going to need help with the…the…the…" Okay, pregnancy brain could be extremely unreliable. "The long orange things that come out of the ground," she finished.

"Carrots?" Riley supplied helpfully.

Alice smiled and touched her nose. "Thank you. I'm going to need help cutting those."

"Leave it to me," Finn said. "Sharp stuff falls into the Dad wheelhouse."

"I can make…" Riley began. "Um, what can I make?"

"You can cut open the bag of salad when the time comes."

"Yes!" she said with all the triumph of an NBA champion. Which could happen, because she was also on the school basketball team.

"In the meantime," Alice continued, "if you guys could give me a hand, I'd like to stand up. I have an announcement to make."

With Finn on one side and Riley on the other, they managed to help Alice off the couch and to standing position. Once she knew she had her center of gravity stabilized—seriously, how could she be this big when her ob-gyn assured her the baby didn't weigh more than seven pounds at this point—she held up her hands in an *I can do it myself now, thanks* gesture and cleared her throat.

"My announcement," she said, "is that I have gone an entire day without cupcakes."

Riley and Finn exchanged a cautious glance.

"I think I see a trip to Cupcake Castle in my immediate future," he said.

"Well, I mean, if it's no trouble," Alice replied.

"Get me one of the rainbow ones, Dad," Riley added.

"Or, you know, we could all go into town together. Your mom did say there's still a couple hours till dinner's ready."

Alice nodded. "I like that idea. Maybe we could swing by the Pie Hut, too. 'Cause I haven't had any pie today, either."

"You know," Finn said, "you really don't need to be eating so much sugar. Remember what your doctor said."

"My doctor said there's room in the freezer for anything," Alice told him.

"I don't remember your doctor saying that."

"Well, I do," Alice assured him. Faulty pregnancy memory could work both ways. *Hmpf.*

"Okay then," he said. "I'll just grab my keys. Oh, wait. They're still in my pocket."

"See?" she told him. "It was meant to be. Somebody grab my handbag. I forgot where I put it."

Riley went immediately to the kitchen and returned with Alice's purse. Then she helped her mother into a sweater and shoes that weren't slippers, and the three of them made their way—slowly for the pregnant woman—to the front door.

"I just love these family outings," Finn said as he opened the door for the three of them.

"Me, too," Riley concurred.

Alice did, as well. But even more than the family outings, she loved her family. And she couldn't wait to see what the future held for all of them.

* * * * *

Chapter One

The groom was forty minutes late to his own wedding.

Shane Dawson, a guest seated on the bride's side at the lavish outdoor event at the McCray Ranch—*too* lavish, given what Shane knew about the ranch's finances—wasn't surprised. The question was: would the guy show up at all?

From where he sat in the third row, Shane could hear Ashley McCray's parents, grandparents, aunts, uncles and cousins whispering and checking their phones for word from the bridal tent at the far end of the aisle, where the bride and her attendants were waiting. Shane's five-year-old twin daughters, Willow and Violet, junior flower girls, were sharing one chair to his right, glued to a game on his phone to keep them occupied. They'd been in the tent with the rest of the bridal party, but had apparently gotten so bored of standing around that the maid of honor had shooed them out and told them she'd call them when it was time.

At this point, that might be never.

The bride's great-aunt, nervously glancing behind her for any sign of activity in the tents, had unfortunately noticed that Willow and Violet's fancy updos were coming out of their chignons and had summoned them over twice in the past half hour to fix their hair. She'd tsk-tsked the scuff mark on one of Willow's pink Mary Janes and the wrinkles in both girls' pink beaded flapper-style dresses, complete with fringe. A woman beside the twins had pointed out that Violet's fringe had gotten caught in the mechanics of the white padded folding chair and had spent ten minutes extricating his daughter from it, and now the fringe on the back was frayed.

The good news was that no one was paying any more attention to his "wild" children. They'd drawn plenty of attention earlier, mainly from a group of family friends of the bride's mother.

"Those little girls are pretty but lack decorum," one woman had said, shaking her head. "A little too wild."

"Are they family?" a blonde in a veiled hat had asked, eyeing the twins with haughty disdain.

"They're the foreman's daughters," a lady Shane didn't recognize whispered. "He's a widower," she'd added on a dramatic whisper.

"Ah," the blonde had said, her expression turning from disapproval to that all-too-familiar look that spelled "those poor girls." Then all their gazes had briefly landed on Shane with more pity than compassion.

"Those poor girls" were happy, healthy and loved. So what if they weren't quiet, perfectly behaved, pristine little robots as their own relatives—namely their maternal grandparents—thought they should be.

Don't think about the Shaws right now, he told himself, his tie tightening at his neck. His late wife's parents were full of unjustified criticisms over how he was raising the girls. Shane was doing the best he could. And the way he saw it, his best really *was* good enough. He was doing right by the girls. Yes, Violet liked to run instead of walk and mixed purple leggings with bright orange T-shirt dresses, her favorite color combination. Yes, Willow had a loud voice and a huge laugh—and no, he wouldn't shush her, particularly not in playgrounds, like her grandmother thought he should.

No one would stifle his girls. Not from their natural personalities. Not from who they were. Not from becoming who they were meant to be.

The problem was that after a week-long visit with the girls last Christmas, the Shaws had emailed Shane a list of the girls' wrongdoings—everything from how Violet went flying down the stairs despite being told to walk nicely to the way Willow used inappropriate language for a little girl. Like "stupid dumbhead."

At the end of the email was an ultimatum about custody.

If you don't...if they don't...we'll be forced to consider whether they would be better served in our home and care...

A chill had run up Shane's spine even as he dismissed the "threat" as unwarranted. Racing down the stairs and referring to a classmate as a stupid dumbhead were hardly reasons for a judge to give custody of his daughters to their grandparents.

But the list was much longer than that. Violet had three fading black-and-blue bruises on her knees because of her need for speed. *If you won't teach the girls to walk properly and safely... Willow refuses to eat vegetables of any kind. You must know this isn't healthy...*

Again his tie tightened around his neck, and he slid in a finger to loosen it. He needed air—and he was *outside*.

If this wedding didn't get started soon, it couldn't *end* soon. And Shane could barely wait for that.

"Daaaaaaddyyyyyyy," Willow whined in her highest-pitched voice, her big green eyes moving from his phone to his face. "When's it gonna start?"

"Yeah, when?" Violet seconded, her matching green eyes never leaving the phone screen. "I want everyone to see Ashley in her gown already. She looks like a princess." She pumped a fist in the air at her game progress. "Yeah! Got you! That's twelve more points!"

"She does," Willow said with a nod. "A real princess."

Shane didn't want to imagine Ashley in her wedding gown. The moment he'd heard about the engagement six months ago, he knew it wasn't something to celebrate. Ashley was making a mistake. She was also a grown woman of twenty-eight, very intelligent, independent and thoughtful. So she *had* to know she was making a mistake—and was choosing to make it anyway. Shane had witnessed or overheard the boyfriend-then-fiancé disappoint Ashley several times. The few occasions that Shane couldn't bite his tongue, when he'd said something to Ashley, like, *You deserve better*, she'd glared at him and snapped that he should mind his own business.

So that was what he'd done, all through the wedding preparations. And now, here they were—waiting for the wedding to start, with Shane torn between wanting desperately to get it over with and also secretly hoping that something would happen to cancel it at the last minute.

Shane's daughters were now standing on their chairs, craning their necks to see if there was any action coming from the tents. Bridal to the left, groomsmen's to the right.

"Girls, down!" Shane whisper-yelled. Each girl sighed and hopped down, more strands of honey-brown hair falling from their fancy updos.

Violet fell to her knees on the grass, a new stain appearing on the hem of her dress—and probably a fresh bruise just waiting to make an appearance in time to see their grandparents tomorrow. This was a school vacation week, and he'd promised to drop off the girls at the Shaws' home in Jackson Hole for a five-day visit. Where they'd no doubt assess the twins for any signs of better behavior—and then maybe follow through on their threats.

Don't think about that. Get through now.

Violet popped up with a giggle. Willow dropped to her own knees and also giggled, then the twins high-fived each other.

He looked at his kind, interesting, smart, curious, big-hearted, beautiful daughters, his heart overcome with love for them. "I'm sure it'll start soon, girls."

Maybe the groom's eighty-thousand-dollar Range Rover had gotten a flat tire en route to the ranch. Maybe he really was just running late. Maybe the fact that he was now fifty minutes late to his wedding had nothing to do with cold feet.

Or maybe it was the result of a complete change of heart.

He pictured Ashley in the bridal tent, pacing, worrying, frantically calling and texting her fiancé of six months with Where are you?

"Yes, I'm sure it'll start soon," he repeated more for Ashley's sake than anything. It didn't feel appropriate to say the truth—that she might be better off if the wedding never started.

Suddenly, Anthony McCray, the bride's father, was kneeling beside him in the aisle. "How do you know, Shane?" he asked, panic in his deep voice. "Did you hear something? Do you know something? Did you see Harrington come in?"

Harrington Harris IV was the groom.

"I'm sure he'll be here any minute," Shane told his boss, whom he liked and respected. It was Anthony McCray who'd invited him since his daughter, not Shane's biggest fan, hadn't, even though she'd asked his twins to be her flower girls.

Anthony bit his lip and glanced over at the tents. No action. No movement. No sounds. "That's it," he said, his hazel eyes worried. "I'm going to the groomsmen's tent to see if any of them know what's going on." He marched off, guests eyeing him.

A few minutes later, as Shane's daughters both lay on their chairs, heads where their knees should be, legs and feet up against the backrest as they counted clouds, Anthony hurried back past Shane's row. He whispered to his wife, but his voice was so naturally booming and deep that Shane could hear.

"None of Harrington's party has heard from him," Anthony said. "They've been texting and calling and get no response."

Shane could see Harrington's parents, over in the first row on the right side, standing and pacing, their phones out, their heads shaking. Every now and then, someone or a group of someones would come up to them, and Shane would see the parents shrug nervously. *Resignedly* might be the better word. Clearly they were used to their son's behavior and attitude.

Ashley should have been too.

But the woman was an optimist. Shane had gotten to know her pretty well over the past five years that he'd worked for the McCrays. She lived in a cabin near the big barn, where he naturally spent a good amount of time and where she worked as a groomer, horse trainer and all-around cowgirl to help out on the ranch, which hadn't been doing well the past six months.

Harrington Harris IV, whose wealthy family owned a very prosperous ranch and had made a fortune in oil too, hadn't worked a day in his privileged life. The running of the businesses was left to a management company.

Murmuring among the guests got his attention, and he turned around to see two of Ashley's bridesmaids walking down the aisle, their expressions stricken, tears in their eyes.

Uh-oh.

They got to the stage and cleared their throats, but all attention was already on them.

"I'm very sorry to report that the wedding is off," the redheaded bridesmaid called out.

Gasps could be heard all around. Including from Willow and Violet, who had leaped to their feet, eyes wide as they stared at the two women on stage.

"Unfortunately," the angrier looking of two bridesmaids added, "Harrington texted Ashley just a moment ago that he's very sorry, but he can't marry her. He thought he loved her but realized at the eleventh hour that he does *not*."

More gasps.

Oh, Ashley, Shane thought. He couldn't even imagine how she must feel right now.

His daughters' mouths were hanging open, their eyes darting to his, waiting for some kind of explanation.

"Apparently," the redhead said, "Harrington is already on the road to his family's summer mansion in Jackson Hole, where he'll be 'working on himself,'" she added with air quotes and absolute disdain, "and determining what he wants to do with his life."

The two women sent a glare over toward the groom's side of the aisle, where there was lots more head shaking and whispering.

"Thank you all for coming," the other bridesmaid said, emotion clogging her voice, "but there will be no wedding today."

His daughters were now standing in front of him, their knees knocking into his in the narrow space between the chair in front of them and his own. "Daddy? Why didn't Harrington come?"

Before he could respond, Ingrid, Ashley's mother, ran toward the bridal tent. In moments she was back, flinging herself at her husband, who wrapped his arms around her. "She's not there! Her maid of honor said she ran out the back way after getting the text from Harrington. A few of the gals tried to find her, but she's not in her cabin or in the main house. Where could she be?"

Shane would wager a million dollars, not that he had a million dollars, that he knew exactly where Ashley was.

"Daddy?" Violet said. "What happened? Why isn't the wedding happening?"

"You heard what Cathy said," Willow told her sister. "Harrington sent her a text that he couldn't marry her."

"But why?" Violet asked.

"Yeah, why?" Willow said.

Being a dad—and a single dad, at that—was never easy. Moments like this, questions like this, were downright hard as he struggled to say the right thing, in the right way, on a level the five-year-olds could understand. He always strove to protect them while being honest. That balance was always near impossible.

He took a hand each and held on to them. "Sometimes people change their minds, even about important things. They realize something doesn't feel right so they decide to do something else."

"Is Ashley sad?" Violet asked, her tone worried.

"She has to be, right?" Willow said. "Everyone kept calling this the biggest day of her life."

He squeezed both their hands and then pulled them in

for hugs. "I'm sure she's sad. And when you're sad, you just have to let yourself feel what you feel, right?"

They both nodded. "When I see Ashley, I'm gonna give her a flower from the garden," Violet said.

"Me too," Willow said.

"That's a nice idea," he assured them.

As the guests continued to pile out, murmuring and whispering, and stopping to hug this person or that, Shane nudged the girls toward the aisle.

"Daddy, will you change your mind about being our dad?" Willow asked, looking up at him.

"Like Mommy had to," Violet said.

Both girls looked at each other, their expressions reaching into his heart and twisting. Their mother died in a car accident when they were just three months old.

"Going to heaven isn't the same thing as deciding something," Violet said. "Right, Daddy?"

"Yeah, because she didn't *decide* to go to heaven," Willow responded.

"That's right," he said.

He wrapped them both in another hug. "I love you two more than anything in the world. I'd never change my mind about that. Never. That's a promise. And I always keep my promises, right?"

"Right, Daddy," they both said in unison, eyes brightening as they focused on his face.

"Can we go see Ashley to make sure she's okay?" Violet asked.

"Yeah, can we?" Willow seconded. "We can give her a flower and a hug."

Aww. *Take that, Beatrice Shaw.* His girls were thoughtful and sweet. He valued that over *walking nicely down the stairs.* "I have a feeling she needs some time alone right now. But it's really nice that you both care about Ashley."

Thing was, he cared about Ashley too, despite their squabbles and the tension between them the past few months. The real problem between them was that he knew too much, saw too much, heard too much. After an argument with Harrington on the phone or in person, usually in the barn or stables where he could hear loud and clear, she'd see Shane walking in her direction and hurry the other way, spots of red appearing on her cheeks. Sometimes she'd just shoot him a glare, lift her chin and march past him.

He'd go check on her. He was probably the last person she'd want to see right now, but he figured he was the only person who knew where to find her. And he felt compelled to make sure she was all right. Or as all right as she could be.

"Can we go to Katie's birthday party since there isn't a wedding?" Violet asked. "Or is the party over already?"

He pulled out his phone and checked the time. Their kindergarten classmate's sixth birthday party was from 1:30 p.m. to 3:00 p.m., with pizza and cake. "Actually, it's not starting for fifteen minutes," he said. "Let's go home, you two change fast, and I'll take you over to the party."

Their little faces brightened some more, and he was grateful that the complicated lives of adults were wiped from their minds, if only just for right now in anticipation of the party. They walked the ten minutes to their cabin, which had been the foreman's cabin for the entire fifty-plus years the McCray Ranch had been in operation. He glanced at the stables across the path from the big barn. Ashley was in there, no doubt, up in the loft, way in the back.

Another ten minutes later, the girls were in their brightly colored leggings and long-sleeve T-shirts and sneakers. He dropped them off in town at the party house, which was only a fifteen minute drive, then hurried back to the ranch. While some people were still milling around, lots of cars were already gone. He didn't see the McCrays. Likely they were in the main house, getting a lot of support from family and friends.

He pulled back into his drive at the cabin, then walked the short path up to the ornate stables, Ashley's favorite place. She was in here, he was sure of it.

Now he'd just have to find the right words for her—a lot harder than with five-year-olds.

Ashley heard the stables door open and held her breath as she had every time someone had come in during the past forty minutes. They'd call out, *Ash? Ashley, you in here?* and she'd go stock-still, afraid they'd climb up the loft and peer way in the back where she was hiding in her secret spot. So far, no one had.

She still wasn't ready to talk to anyone. Not her parents or her cousins or even her favorite aunt, Daphie.

Years ago, when she was in high school and going through breakups or mean girl drama or her parents "didn't understand anything!" she'd brought up a sleeping bag, down pillow and a go bag with provisions to get her through a few hours. After high school, the place had remained a refuge—and the supplies had stayed—but she'd never used it so much as in the past year, since she'd been dating Harrington. She'd found herself climbing up here quite a few times. She'd mull over what had pissed her off or made her feel uneasy or sad, and she'd come back down when it was either time to get back to work or she'd just plain rationalized away whatever had been bothering her, telling herself she was being "too sensitive" or could blame it on the "different worlds" factor between her and Harrison.

He was so cavalier about money, for example, pointlessly buying another vintage car for his collection or a champion racehorse and wanting her to be as excited when he knew she was worried about the McCray Ranch barely breaking even over the past couple of years. Any time she'd bring it up, he'd say, "Ashley, just say the word and my father could fix everything. His accountant could transfer over a money market account as easily as he'd buy a few new suits at Brooks Brothers. You have nothing to worry about."

But the McCrays, Ashley included, had never been about *taking*. They worked hard, starting with Ashley's paternal grandparents, who'd started a small cattle ranch, grew it and passed it down to the next generation. Yes, there'd been ups and downs, but for the past ten years, things had been solid. Now, not so much.

And when she'd needed Harrington's understanding or support, he'd offer money. She'd try to explain what she *did* need from him, but he'd get impatient or antsy and make excuses to leave.

She should have counted how many times *that* had sent her up here.

Maybe she would have been the one to send a text changing her mind at the last possible second.

But instead she'd overlooked red flags, focusing on what she'd loved about Harrington, what was great between them—and much was, or had been. He had a big heart, and even though he could be clueless sometimes, he seemed to like when she'd point it out. He'd say, with wonder coming over his handsome face, that he'd never dated a woman who wasn't wealthy. That he was used to tossing his money and name around to get what he wanted. He talked a lot about how he never had to do that with Ashley—and in fact, how he knew that if he tried, it would turn her off. That had seemed to turn *him* on.

He'd sobbed for days when his paternal grandfather had died at the start of their romance, and she'd been there for him, bringing them much closer than they probably would have gotten otherwise. At the core, they were friends. Real friends. And she'd thought he did love her.

She'd clearly been wrong.

And now *everyone* knew it too.

She could envision her parents sitting at the kitchen table of their ranch house, worried sick over her, comforting each other, getting hugs from friends and family who were hanging around. Ashley's father had been talking about her wedding since she was a little girl, how she'd have her big day right here on the McCray Ranch and could invite her horse. She could hear him saying that in her head even now, and it managed to bring a small smile.

Despite how independent she was, Ashley was a daddy's girl, and the fantasy he'd stoked about her wedding, about finding her "one true love" had wound its way deep inside her. He'd been dazzled by Harrington as he'd been and had thought of her fiancé as her Prince Charming. Her father had said more than a few times that the only dreams he still had left were to walk her down the aisle, then hold his grandchildren someday. A few times she'd mentioned what Harrington had said about helping out in terms of money, and he'd gotten a bit angry—embarrassed, really—and waved his hand dismissively. *We McCrays built this place from nothing*, he'd say, *and we'll keep it going just like my grandparents did. Life is full of ups and downs, and now is a down. That's all. We don't take handouts.*

Her parents had raised her right in her opinion. But because her father could be proud and had always been a man of tradition, he'd insisted on paying for most of the wedding, finally agreeing that the Harrises could take care of the videographer since it was a relative of theirs who still charged a small fortune.

Now it was her parents who were out a *real* fortune, piles of money wasted on a wedding that hadn't happened. Money they didn't have to spare. Her father had already sold parcels of land to pay for the wedding and keep the ranch afloat. She hadn't known about that until an aunt— not her favorite one—had slipped and mentioned it.

Ashley felt an ache both deep in her chest and close to the surface. She wrapped her arms around her knees, blinking back a fresh round of tears, waiting for whoever had come in to call her name, but there was only silence. Except for the sudden footsteps—which weren't retreating. Someone was coming—toward the loft.

She could feel her eyes widen as she heard a shoe hit a rung of the loft ladder. The sound got closer and closer. And then there was a familiar face and broad shoulders as Shane Dawson, the foreman at the McCray Ranch, climbed up and over, crouching over to where she was. He sat down along the wall about six inches away, arms around his knees like hers.

Shane Dawson was the last person she wanted to talk to.

"You'll ruin your nice suit," she said, wanting to beat him to the punch of saying whatever he came here to say. She knew what he came here to say, actually. And she didn't want to hear it.

"Eh, that's okay. It's rare that I ever need it." She could feel him eyeing the hem of her gown. "Straw adds a Western touch to the dress."

She gazed at her ruined gown, poked with straw, dirty in spots and snagged from climbing the ladder. Ashley and

her mother and aunts had gone to at least five bridal boutiques in search of The Dress, but the prices had had Ashley shaking her head at them all. She'd ended up finding a
beautiful gown online at half the price of the salons. She
and her mother sometimes butted heads, but not over Ashley's pick. That day the dress had arrived, folded up and
wrinkled, Ashley had tried it on and her mother had burst
into tears at how perfect it was. Now, tears stung Ashley's
eyes and she blinked hard.

"I'm surprised you haven't said 'I told you so' yet, Dawson. I assume that's why you're here. Or did my father ask
you to find me?" Figured Shane would think to climb up
the loft ladder.

"Nope," he said, turning his head from against the wall
to look at her for a moment. "The twins were asking after
you, wanting to make sure you were okay."

Aww. "I love those sweetie pies." Violet with a laugh
bigger than Wyoming, and Willow who knew every kind
of horse there was. Ashley had taught the twins all about
horses, and Willow in particular had always listened hard
just the way Ashley had when her dad used to talk all things
equine with her.

"I'm sorry about what happened, Ashley."

She glanced at him, appreciating that. That was really all
she needed to hear. *Sorry. That sucks.* "Yeah, me too. I feel
like I got stomped on—and it's no fun to get humiliated in
front of two hundred of your family and friends."

She felt a warm strong hand cover hers, and the simple
gesture of comfort, of kindness when she needed it most
broke the dam. The tears came fast and furious. She reached
for her go bag and pulled out a third box of tissues. Guess
she wasn't cried out yet after all.

"I will say one thing, Ashley. He didn't deserve you."

Damned right, he didn't. She'd thought they had something real and loving, but his text made it clear everything she thought about their entire relationship was a lie. Some kind of social experiment for Harrington, maybe. Slumming with the middle-class rancher's daughter. Getting a kick out of how she preferred picnics on the Harris Ranch's beautiful land over expensive restaurants. But then when it came right down to it, to their *wedding day*, she wasn't what he wanted. Wasn't enough.

He didn't love her.

Well, it was a little late to come to that conclusion, Harrington Harris IV!

She looked down at her exquisite engagement ring. Two carats, a perfect solitaire in a gold setting. She stared at it, anger building and building and—she grabbed the ring off her finger and flung it hard behind her.

"Um, Ashley," Shane said, looking behind them in the direction she'd thrown the ring. "That cost what? Ten thousand dollars?"

A feeling akin to horror turned her stomach upside down, and her eyes filled with tears. She could sell the ring to pay back some of the costs. She scrambled on her knees, pawing through the straw in search of the ring.

"I'll help," he said, kneeling down and feeling all over for the ring.

Ten minutes later, neither of them had found it.

Shane scooted over by the wall. "Calculating the bounce and probable direction…" he said, turning and digging his hands in the straw. "Got it!" he said without triumph, and she had to appreciate that. He held it out to her.

"I don't want to touch it," she said.

"I'll hang on to it for you." He put it in his pocket.

What had this day turned into?

She swiped at her eyes with the tissue and lifted her chin.

"You know what?" she said, anger radiating. "He's not getting away with this. He's gotten away with way too much the past year. He's going to pay me back—well, my parents—every penny that they spent on the wedding he didn't show up for. I'm going to hand him an itemized bill and demand payment. That ten thousand dollar ring won't cover a *fourth* of what my parents spent."

Shane raised an eyebrow. "You think that'll make you feel better? Personally, I doubt it."

"Yes, it will." It wasn't like Shane Dawson *knew* her.

Though sometimes she thought he did. More than once, he'd been annoyingly insightful after he'd caught the tail end of one of her and Harrington's arguments. He would always confirm that she'd been right, and for a moment, she'd revel in the feeling that she wasn't being "sensitive" after all. But then the rush would fade, and she wouldn't know what to do with her victory. The moment would end with her feeling more awkward around him rather than less.

And yet, he *had* known exactly where to find her.

She glanced over at Shane, who eyed her back. He'd worked for her parents for just over five years. He'd caught quite a few of her most embarrassing moments. He knew too much about her as it was, and now he was a witness to her biggest humiliation.

Not being loved, after all. Chosen and then put back.

Suddenly she felt…exposed. Even more vulnerable than she'd been before Shane's face had appeared over the platform of the loft.

She had to get out of here. She had to get away.

She bolted up, a piece of straw stuck to her wedding dress poking at her leg. She brushed it away.

She knew exactly where to go.

Chapter Two

Uh-oh. Shane knew that look on Ashley's face. Determination—but mixed with fear, worry and can-I-really-do-this?

She was going after Harrington. To present him with an itemized bill for the wedding.

Jackson Hole, where Harrington was on his way to, was seven hours across Wyoming. In her distracted state, Ashley was in no condition to drive.

Then again, her entire family would probably pile in the car with her.

"I suppose you'll be okay as long as someone else drives," he said. "Your mom? The aunt you often go riding with?"

"Daphie," she said, brushing more straw off her dress. "But no. I need to be alone. I need to think. To process. Digest. I really don't love driving on the highway, especially at night. Or in the rain. But I'll blast my playlists and podcasts, pick up some snacks." Her face brightened. "Yeah, I'll be fine. The road trip will help me…get over this—and result in my getting back my parents' money." She nodded to herself. "See you later," she said and started for the ladder.

He envisioned her on the side of the road in a rainstorm, car broken down, all alone…

And then he envisioned her finally getting to the Harrises' summer mansion, marching up to the door and knocking, and Harrington not exactly being alone himself. Or amenable to seeing her. Or receptive to her demands for the money back. She wasn't thinking about any of this clearly.

"Ashley, I really don't think going after Harrington will make you feel better or—"

She held up a hand, then bent down and continued dusting herself off, straw falling to the loft floor. "Look, Shane," she said, glancing up at him in between wipes of her hands on her gown, "I appreciate that you didn't say 'I told you so' about him, but you're wrong about *me*. I *will* feel better when Harrington hands me a big fat check that will save the McCray Ranch. My parents spent stupid sums of money on this wedding that they didn't have. You very likely know that."

Shane *did* know that. For a few weeks, Anthony had kept his interesting math a secret from his foreman until Shane had found too many deficits. Money was going out faster than it was coming in, not helped by the fact that expected sales of cattle and land hadn't gone through.

"And a long road trip is exactly what I need," she said. "It'll be like the solo honeymoon I didn't expect to take."

She bit her lip, which was slightly trembling. Her face began to crumble. Tears slipped down her cheeks.

He grabbed the box of tissues and held it out for her.

"Whatever," she said, dabbing at her eyes, trying to put some steely resolve in her voice, her expression. It wasn't working. "I'm going and that's that."

"I hope you're planning to change first," he said.

"Of course I am. I *hate* this dress," she added, new tears forming in her hazel eyes. "I'm going to change, pack, let my parents know I'm fine and going on a mission, and then I'm leaving. Jackson Hole, here I come." She turned around and stepped backward onto the ladder and started climbing down.

Jackson Hole. Where he had to be tomorrow to drop off the girls at their grandparents' house. For just a little while, Ashley's situation had wiped that from his mind, but he was going to have to face the Shaws in just a couple of days. And their threat.

Wait a minute.

Huh.

An idea slammed into his head. An idea that could help out both him and Ashley. Maybe save his entire future. Save his *family*.

And hers—if Harris paid her back.

He thought of Ashley McCray in her straw-festooned, snagged, dirty wedding gown—and how she still managed to look elegant. She simply had a regal look about her. Even when she was grooming horses, Ashley looked great. She was what he supposed was called a "girlie-girl." She liked dressing up. Heels. Perfume.

And she was what the Shaws would call a lady. Polite, refined.

Oh, yes. She could help him. And in turn, he could help her. They could help each other.

"I have a bad idea," he called out. "A better bad idea than yours."

She climbed back up until just her head was visible over the floor of the loft. "And what could that possibly be?"

"I have to drop the twins at their grandparents' mansion tomorrow for spring break. Five days. What if *I* drive us to Jackson Hole—I'll drop you at Harrington's summer place, then take the girls to their grandparents."

She tilted her head. Bit her lip.

She looked at him. He looked at her.

Silence.

"I guess we're headed in the same direction so it's not that bad an idea," she said. "The twins would be great, fun company."

Was that a diss? That *he* wouldn't be great, fun company? He supposed she *was* used to him pointing out her problems.

"There's a catch," he said.

Now it was her turn to raise an eyebrow. "Of course, there is. What?"

"In return for me driving you seven hours so you can sit back and process, especially in the dark and in the rain, you'll teach my twins manners. I need them to be little ladies by tomorrow. By the time we arrive at their grandparents' house."

She stared at him in total confusion. "Why on earth would you want them to be little ladies?"

He looked away for a moment, a hard sigh escaping. "Because the Shaws don't think they're being raised right. 'Feral tomboys' is a favorite descriptor. They've dangled a threat to petition for custody."

She gaped at him. "*What?* Willow and Violet are two of the happiest, funniest, most curious, interesting little kids I've ever met. What's wrong with being tomboys?"

"I could hug you right now," he said, then could feel his cheeks slightly burning.

She smiled for the first time since he'd climbed up to the loft. "Huh. I guess we could *both* use a hug."

He tried to imagine hugging Ashley McCray—and couldn't. They just didn't have that kind of friendship. Not that they were friends, really. They just knew each other from the ranch. He just happened to know a lot about her personal life. She'd know about his too—if he had one outside of his role as a father. He'd moved to the ranch to take the job as foreman just a few months before he was widowed. He'd spent the past five years working hard and raising his daughters with absolutely no social life beyond relatives. He was friendly with the McCrays but they'd always kept their relationship strictly professional.

"That's why I think we'd be good travel companions," he said. "We've both got a lot going on right now—so much that we'll probably be in our own heads most of the time instead of getting into dopey arguments about this or that. And I really do need your help, Ashley. Seriously."

She nodded and extended her hand, the earlier worry and unease gone from her hazel eyes. "It's a deal."

After making a plan with Shane to meet at his cabin in two hours—at 4:00 p.m.—so they could hit the road, Ashley slipped out the back door of the stables. She darted into the woods just a couple of feet away. There was a path she could take just on the other side of the tree line that would lead to the back door of the ranch house.

She did not want to be spotted by any guests still hanging around—and the wedding gown and updo would make her stand out big time. She hurried along the path, her *peau de sois* pumps as ruined as her dress by now. Every now and then through a gap in the trees, she'd been able to see a few of her relatives hugging one another goodbye in the parking area, all holding a food container. Her parents must have had the dinners boxed up and handed out so they wouldn't go to waste. She had no doubt the wedding cake was still there, intact. She wished she could smash it.

Sigh.

It was over an hour since the wedding had been called off, and it looked like most of the guests had left.

As she pulled open the back door, she could hear people

talking in the living room. Her parents. Her grandparents—both sets. Her three aunts—her mother's sisters—Daphie, who was recently divorced, Lila, who went nowhere without her two mini Chihuahuas, and Kate, who Ashley could hear threatening to sue Harrington for "breach of expectations."

She sucked in a deep breath and moved to the doorway of the living room.

"There she is!" Daphie exclaimed. "Oh, my Ashley," she added, rushing over and pulling her into a hug.

The hug felt so good. Ashley hadn't realized just how much she needed warm, strong arms around her. In seconds she was surrounded by embraces and hand squeezes and compassionate murmurs.

She'd thought having a purpose—going after Harrington for all the money her parents had wasted on the non-wedding—had perked her up, made her feel stronger. But suddenly, in the comfort of her family, all the hurt, all the humiliation came flooding over her, and her eyes filled with tears.

"I'll kill him!" Daphie shrieked. "When I get my hands on that rat—"

"No, I'll kill him!" Kate said. "What an absolute—"

"Cowardly bastard," Lila added, shaking her head, a Chihuahua in each arm.

Her mother ran over, pulling her into a hug. "Are you okay?" she whispered, stepping back to peer at her daughter, her eyes so full of worry and concern. Catherine Mc-Cray put a hand on either side of Ashley's face. "You'll be okay. You're strong. You're a McCray."

Her father nodded and hugged her next. "I'm so darn sorry, sweetums."

That did it again. The sight of her father's sweet brown eyes so filled with anguish for his daughter broke the dam.

"Someone get more tissues," Kate called. "We actually all went through two boxes already."

Ashley's mom darted off and returned with two boxes. Four hands thrust a tissue at her, and she used them all to dab at her eyes.

"I can't wait to tell that rat fink just what I think of him," Daphie spat, her curly red hair bouncing on her shoulders.

"Well, he ran away like the cowardly baby he is," her mother said. "He's halfway to Jackson Hole by now. Safe from our wrath."

"Not mine," Ashley said, lifting her chin, the tears drying up as her plan came back into sharp focus. "*I'm* going after that rat fink. I'm leaving for Jackson Hole in a couple of hours to demand every cent back that you two spent on the wedding."

"What?" her father said. "Ashley, honey, you don't have to do that."

"If she doesn't, I will!" Ashley's mother snapped. "And not for the money, for the principle! Okay, for the money too. How dare he!"

"I'll go too," Daphie said.

Ashley shook her head. "Actually, Shane is driving me."

"Shane?" her father asked. "Really? He offered?"

"Turns out he has to be in Jackson Hole tomorrow to drop off the twins at their grandparents for spring break," Ashley explained. "So I'm going along."

Her dad was shaking his head. "Ashley, that rat bastard took enough from you. You don't need to waste even more of your time and energy going there to get the money back from him. I'll just sic the sheriff on him. Surely what he did breaks some old Wild West law."

Ashley almost smiled as she envisioned Harrington Harris IV being led away in handcuffs for leaving her at the altar. Until she imagined hearing him whine, *But I don't love her. How could I marry her?* And the sheriff agreeing and uncuffing him.

She sighed. "I want to. The ranch needs it. He's paying us back every cent. Shane's holding on to the engagement ring, which I'll sell when I get back. I need to do this, okay?"

Her parents peered at her, studying her the way they always did when she announced she was doing something a little "out there."

"I do feel more comfortable knowing Shane and his twins will be with you," her mom added. "They're a breath of fresh air—the girls, I mean."

Ashley laughed. "Not Shane?"

Catherine McCray smiled. "I adore Shane Dawson. He's a great foreman. And he's a great dad. I just meant that Willow and Violet are a hoot. Shane is always pleasant, but he's not a comical five-year-old times two. Those girls will cheer you up for sure."

A great dad. She thought about why he needed her help with the twins on the road trip and almost blurted it out. But his issues with his in-laws were Shane's business, and she didn't think he'd want that getting around. Her parents could be trusted, but her aunt Lila was a huge gossip. Ashley glanced at her—she adored Lila, but the woman loved to dish. With the failed wedding, she was already hanging on every word to report back to her friends and acquaintances in the off-leash dog park where she took her Chihuahuas twice a day.

"Well, since Shane's driving you, I feel better about that too," her dad said. "I'd trust that man with my life."

Ashley did like knowing she'd be in good hands. Safe hands. "He *does* like to poke his nose into my business, though," she said, thinking of the times he'd told her Harrington didn't deserve her.

"Mine too," Anthony McCray said. "But in my case, that's his job. Do you know he refused to take a salary this past month because of how bad the books were getting?"

Ashley gaped at her father. "Really?"

"That's nice and all," Aunt Kate said. "But Shane's wealthy, right? His late wife's family is super rich."

"Actually," Lila said, one Chihuahua nuzzling her neck. "His wife had a trust fund, but she never touched it. And Shane left it alone for the twins when they come of age. They lived on their own salaries—Shane's as foreman, and his wife was a teacher, right?"

Interesting. "How do you know that?" Ashley asked. "I mean, about his wife's finances?"

"Oh, it was big news when she married him," Lila said. "That she married a ranch foreman and that they were not living beyond their own means. That the wife went from her parents' mansion with an indoor *and* outdoor pool to a cabin next to a barn. Plus, I know one of her cousins and got all the scoop."

"Huh," Ashley said again.

"I heard that Shane lets the grandparents pay for summer camp and trips with them every summer to amazing places, and he's fine with gifts for the girls," Lila added, "but on a day-to-day basis, they live on his salary."

"Which he hasn't taken the past month," her father reminded them.

Ashley's busted-up heart softened toward the foreman a little more. Not that being proud and making his own way made him a saint, but that he turned down a salary to help out her father, to help their ranch survive, when he probably needed it…that was something.

Anthony McCray nodded to himself. "Now, *there* is a good man."

"It's good to know they exist," Daphie said.

Ashley crossed her arms over her chest. "Well, he may be a great guy, but I can't say I'm looking forward to sitting next to him in his SUV for the next couple of days. Shane and I are night and day. He's been tsking me all year over Harrington and our arguments." Ashley's chin wobbled. "And he was right too. I'm such an idiot." She covered her face with her hands, the tears threatening again.

Her mother put an arm around her shoulder. "No, honey. You were just in love. And Harrington won us all over. But now he's shown us who he really is."

Ashley nodded, dropping her hands. She sucked in a breath. "I'm getting back our money. I'm going to keep my mind focused on that. And I'll be fine."

"Sweetheart," her dad said. "You really don't need to go after the money or have anything to do with that lying coward again. We'll get through this—just as we would have had the wedding gone ahead. Let's just move on."

Ashley shook her head. "I need to do *something*. Something to help me deal with how stupid I feel. How angry I am. Family and friends flew in from all over the country. Cousin Ben wasted his army leave on a wedding that didn't happen. Harrington is going to pay us back."

"I get it," Daphie said. "When my ex walked out on me, I presented him with a bill for my suffering—twice weekly therapy and *retail* therapy."

"I don't think it's the money so much as the last word Ashley is after," her eighty-two-year-old maternal grandmother said.

"Oh, Grammy," Ashley said, gently hugging the dear woman. "You've always known me so well."

But it was both. The money and the last word.

And maybe, if she was very honest, she'd admit that she was holding out a little hope that Harrington would take one look at her and tell her he was sorry. That he made the biggest mistake of his life by not showing up, that he just got scared, that of course he loved her and wanted to marry her.

Her chin wobbled again. How did a man spend a year with someone, share in her life, get close to her family and friends, propose, plan a wedding, whisper in her ear just the week before that he'd never been so happy, that he couldn't wait to spend the rest of his life with her, that she was his everything, and then decide days later that he was wrong about all that?

Maybe he would change his mind when he saw her again. And what if he did? What if he took one look at her on his doorstep, his "Sweet Ashley" as he always called her, and realized he'd made the biggest mistake of his life?

And if he *did* say that, what would she say in return? Did she actually want him back? If she *did* take him back, how could she necessarily believe anything he said at this point? How could she ever trust him again? He didn't show up to their wedding! He'd *texted* her that he didn't love her.

He made a fool of her in front of everyone she cared about. How could she possibly want him to change his mind and love her again?

She happily accepted the fresh round of hugs she got from her family. The aroma of her grandmother's White Shoulders perfume—which had been her great-grandmother's trademark scent—made her feel instantly comforted.

And right now, she needed all the comfort she could get. Her entire life was up in the air. Of course her head was a jumble of crazy thoughts. She'd just have to see what hap-

pened when she arrived in Jackson Hole. How she felt. How
he felt. Maybe she'd take one look at Harrington Harris IV
and vomit. Tell him he was a low-down dirty rat coward
and hold out her hand for the big fat check that would save
her family's ranch.

And maybe she'd take one look at him and realize that
their love story wasn't over. That all he'd have to do to get a
second chance from her was admit he'd made a terrible mistake. That he knew now, with a little time to think, a little
time apart, that she *was* the one for him. He'd beg forgiveness for the awful way he'd gone about getting to that point.
They'd elope to Vegas, and she'd still make him pay for the
wedding that wasn't.

Anything could happen.

Suddenly she was really glad she wouldn't be making
the trip alone.

Chapter Three

Shane was due to pick up the girls from the birthday party at 3:30 p.m., but at 3:00 p.m. he received a phone call from Allison Waterly, the birthday girl's mother. There was an "unfortunate incident," and could he please come pick up the twins *immediately*?

Uh-oh.

He was in the middle of packing and quickly threw swim trunks in the suitcase open on his bed, his mental list of what he needed to bring zipping out of his head.

"Willow threw a cupcake at one of the other children," Allison said. "Hard. And she also refused to apologize."

Oh, Willow, he thought. Why are you throwing cupcakes at anyone?

"I don't know what led up to it," Allison continued, "but as an example for the other children, I'll need you to pick up the girls. Of course it's wrong to punish Violet for Willow's actions, but when I asked Willow why she threw the cupcake at Dylan, Violet shouted it was because he was a 'dumbhead idiot,' and we don't use words like that."

He sighed long and hard internally.

"I'll be right there," he said. "And sorry."

He headed down the hall, grabbed his keys from the hook by the door and went out to his SUV, glancing over at Ashley's cabin about a quarter mile down the path. She was likely in the middle of packing too.

He'd been second-guessing himself for offering to drive her to Jackson Hole. Maybe he should have encouraged her to stay home. He didn't think confronting the ex was a good idea or a good use of her time and energy when an email would do—and document her request just fine. But now, en route to pick up the girls, he was reminded of how badly he needed Ashley's help with them. When she taught them manners, he could ask her to cover: *Why they can't go around throwing cupcakes—hard—at children. Even if they're "dumbhead idiots."*

He sighed again and got in his SUV and drove out. When he arrived at the Waterlys' home and headed up the walkway, the front door opened. He could see the twins sitting on the entry bench, bright red parting gift bags in each of their hands. They popped up when they saw him coming.

Allison gave him the same look of pity that the McCray relatives had when they learned he was a widower. "Willow did finally apologize to the boy she threw the cupcake at," she said, giving both girls a satisfied nod.

"And I also apologize," he said to the woman. "I know managing a party full of kindergartners is hard enough without having to call a parent for early pickup."

"No worries, Shane. Thank you for coming, girls."

He gave each twin a sharp look.

"Thank you for having us," they said practically in unison.

Allison smiled, and with an arm around each girl, he ushered them out, the door closing behind them.

"We'll talk in the car," he said.

They weren't exactly hanging their heads on the way to

the SUV, which meant Willow felt justified for what she'd done, and her twin agreed.

Once they'd pulled away from the house and were on the road, Shane eyed Willow in the back seat. "Okay, tell me what happened."

In another glance in the rearview mirror, he caught Willow's face fall, her lower lip slightly tremble. She looked at her sister. Violet eyed her, then frowned and looked down.

Huh. He gave them a few seconds.

Willow kept her head down now. "That dumbhead stupid idiot Dylan said that it's weird that we don't have a mother like everyone else." Her voice was low, practically a whisper, and he could tell that she was trying not cry.

"And what did you say?" he asked. He realized a second too late that he should probably say something about the stupid and dumbhead and idiot, but what they were talking about seemed more important than shutting them down over word choices.

He wondered if their grandmother would agree, given what the issue was. If Beatrice Shaw were in the car with them right now, would she chastise them for their language? Or would she be more focused on what had upset Willow?

Especially because it involved their mother. Beatrice's daughter.

Willow was still staring at her lap. "I said we *do* have a mother. But that she died."

Violet bit her lip. "And I said that our mom is in heaven. And that means she's always with us."

"You know what that dumbhead stupid idiot said?" Willow asked, scrunching up her face in anger. She met his eyes in the rearview mirror. She was on the verge of crying.

"Hang on a sec," Shane said, pulling over. He set the car

in park and turned around to face his daughters. "What did he say?"

Tears filled Willow's eyes. "He said that our mom is *not* with us because she's *dead*."

Violet's eyes filled too, her face crumpling. "And he said that dead people aren't walking around or making pancakes or doing anything."

"And that's when I threw my cupcake at him," Willow said.

Shane got out of the car and opened the rear door. Both girls hopped out. He kneeled down and they came in for a hug. "Your mom *is* always with you. She is." He pulled back a bit and touched his hand to the region of his heart. "She's in here. For me and for you two. Always."

"I knew Dylan wasn't right," Willow said, her face brightening.

"He's never right," Violet added.

"You know, you wouldn't have gotten in trouble if you'd just told him that. When you get mad, use your words. Your voices. Next time, if you have something in your hand, like a cupcake with frosting, don't throw it at the person you're mad at. First of all, you won't get to eat it that way. Am I right?"

They girls both laughed.

"And no matter how mad you get at someone, throwing things at them is wrong," he added. "It's like hitting. Not allowed, okay? And neither is using bad words. You can tell someone they're wrong without calling them names. Understand?"

"Yes, Daddy," Willow whispered. "I'm sorry." Her sister echoed her words.

"I love you girls so much," he said. "And I have a surprise for you."

"We're not in trouble?" Violet asked, her sweet face brightening.

"You already got in trouble," he said. "You were booted from the birthday party. It's settled as far as I'm concerned."

Both their narrow shoulders sagged with relief.

"Let's get back in the car and I'll tell you the surprise," he said.

They raced in and buckled up. He pulled back into traffic. "How would you like to take a road trip—with Ashley? And me, of course."

He knew the answer before he asked, of course.

"Yay!" Willow said.

"Yay!" Violet seconded, pumping her goody bag in the air.

"Where are we going, Daddy?" Willow asked.

"You know how I'm taking you to your grandparents tomorrow?" Shane asked, eyeing them in the rearview mirror. "It turns out that Ashley has to go to Jackson Hole too. So we're all going to drive together. It's a long trip. We'll leave in about a half hour and stay overnight at a hotel. But there are rules for the road trip."

"What rules?" Violet asked.

"I want you two to be kind and respectful to Ashley," he said. "By respectful, I mean that you shouldn't ask her questions that she might not feel comfortable answering."

"About her wedding?" Willow asked.

"Exactly," Shane said.

"What shouldn't we ask her?" Violet asked. "And what *can* we ask?"

"Well, you can ask her if she's okay. You guys were there at the wedding. You know what happened. That the wedding *didn't* happen after all. So it's fine to ask her how she is. But I don't think you should ask her questions about why he didn't show up. Stuff like that. She might not want to talk about it, okay?"

He got two solemn nods.

"Is Ashley very sad?" Willow asked.

"She's definitely sad," he admitted.

"We can draw her pictures to cheer her up," Willow said.

"And give her candy and a toy from our goody bags," Violet added, holding up the bright red gift bag.

"That's really nice," he said. "So when we get home, we'll pack for the trip. You'll be at your grandparents' house for five days, so double-check your suitcases that you have play clothes *and* dress-up clothes."

He'd do a final check before they left.

"And scrunchies," Willow said. "Nana doesn't like when our hair is in our faces."

"Or when we're loud," Violet added.

"Or chew with our mouths full."

"Or run hard in the house."

"Well, since you know all that, it'll be easier to remember not to do those things, right?"

"I never remember," Willow said.

Violet nodded. "Me either."

"It's *important* to remember," Shane said. "It means to think before you act. I know it's not easy—for adults *or* five-year-olds. But try, okay? Sometimes, even when something isn't important to you, it's still important to someone else, like your nana, so you do the thing for *them*."

"Okay, Daddy," they both said.

"You know what my favorite thing is about going to Nana's and Pops's house?" Violet asked.

"What?" Shane said.

"They have so many pictures of Mommy. All over. They even have pictures of her when she was little."

"I love looking at those pictures," Willow said.

Shane's heart constricted in his chest.

Almost five years after losing Liza, looking at photos of her still wasn't easy. He figured it never would be. He'd loved her very much. They'd had a good marriage. There had been ups and downs, like everyone had. But they'd been solid. And happy.

And just like that, she was gone.

He wasn't about to lose the girls too. Not when he could do everything in his power to keep them. If that meant guiding Willow and Violet to be little ladies on the way to Jackson Hole so that they'd impress—or simply *not horrify*—their grandparents, so be it.

"You take good care of our girl," Ashley heard her father say to Shane as the last of the bags were stacked in the cargo area of Shane's SUV.

Oh, brother. She wasn't one of the horses or cows. She wasn't ranch equipment. Their foreman was simply giving her a ride because he needed her help. But she knew her father was comforted by the idea of his trusty foreman watching out for "our poor baby," which her aunt Kate had actually referred to her as earlier, so she let it be.

She *was* grateful she wasn't making this trip alone. Shane had his downside—butting into her business, getting know-it-all-y—but he *was* trustworthy, and she felt absolutely safe with him. And he came with two absolutely adorable bonuses. She loved that Violet and Willow were already buckled into their booster seats in the back, their faces full of excitement about the trip—because Ashley was unexpectedly coming along. Their sweet heroine worship of her always made her smile, but right now, it was a real balm to her busted-up heart.

And finally, after another round of hugs with her parents, aunts, uncles, cousins and grandparents, the SUV doors closed, the engine started—and they headed down the long drive.

Shane had mentioned he had to make a few quick calls since he hadn't planned on leaving for Jackson Hole today, but the grandparents had been thrilled to hear the girls would be arriving early and he'd been able to change his hotel reservations for the overnight stay.

The seven-hour road trip would be broken into two days of driving, giving Ashley a lot of time and space to think and process. They'd be on the road for a little over two hours today, arriving at the lodge Shane had booked in Bison Creek for a late dinner and maybe a swim in the heated pool before the twins' 8:30 p.m. bedtime. Then they'd hit the road again bright and early, stopping to see a couple of sights along the way, and arrive at the Shaws' home by late afternoon.

Then he'd drop her off at Harrington's.

Shane had planned everything, from the route to the timing to kid-friendly places to stop for breakfast and lunch tomorrow and a petting zoo just a half hour outside Jackson Hole. How she appreciated having him take the reins. To not have to do any of this brain work and research herself—figure out the route and where to stop, not to mention driving for hours by herself without knowing how things would go when she reached her destination. Having him as the driver didn't change that—she still didn't know how things would go when she arrived—but at least she didn't have to concentrate on driving while she worried about it. He'd also let her know he'd put the engagement ring in the safe in the ranch's office.

While she'd been packing, he'd texted the entire itinerary to her along with: I'll wait, of course, while you and Harrington talk. Shouldn't take long to tell him off and get your money back. Then we'll drive home.

She hadn't mentioned that she might not be returning home with Shane. That she and Harrington might want to *really* talk. See how things felt with the pressure of the wedding off the table… Which was why she now found herself thinking that she probably should have brought the ring with her. In case it was slipped back on to her left hand.

She hadn't mentioned that to anyone.

She could barely admit it to herself that she felt a stirring of hope.

"Are we there yet?" Willow asked in a very exaggerated whine.

Violet giggled.

Ashley turned around and grinned. "Um, we've got today and most of tomorrow to go."

"I was kidding!" Willow said, her big green eyes twinkling. "Daddy said we're not allowed to ask that."

"That's right," Shane said, smiling at his daughters in the rearview mirror. "Every parent's favorite rule of the road."

Now the girls were whispering. Something about candy?

"Ashley, since you might be sad," Violet said, "do you want something from our goody bags from the birthday party we went to?"

"Oooh, whatcha got?" Ashley asked. "And it's very nice of you two to be concerned about me and want to cheer me up with treats. Thank you."

The girls beamed at her.

"Three fun-size Snickers," Willow said.

"And four Dum-Dum lollipops," Violet added.

Ashley smiled. "I will definitely take a Snickers. Any cherry lollipops?"

She heard more whispering—loud whispering, which made her smile. "You give her a Snickers," Violet said. "And I'll give her a lollipop 'cause I have cherry."

Once she had her treats, the girls went from quiet to whispering again. She caught Shane glancing at them in the rearview mirror. With a *look*. Ah—she knew what that look was probably about. He'd instructed the girls not to ask her questions. She thought about telling them that they could ask her whatever they wanted. But then again, she'd probably take their earnest questions to heart and get all upset again.

Father knows best, she thought. *Let it go. Eat your Snickers.*

They played a round of I spy. And I'm thinking of a number between one and twenty. At Ashley's turn to think of a number, Willow guessed sixty and Violet ninety, since both girls could now count up to one hundred by tens, and they all laughed. Then the twins started singing the chorus from their favorite song, and Ashley joined in, which earned her serious bonus points since she knew the words. Then they asked Shane to put in their favorite kiddie mystery podcast.

Five minutes later, she turned around to ask them where they both thought the runaway dog in the podcast was hiding, and she was surprised to see Willow and Violet conked out, fast asleep.

"Wow, they're out cold," she whispered to Shane.

He smiled. "No need to whisper. They sleep through the blasted rooster every morning—unlike me—so you won't wake them by talking. It takes a lot of energy to be them. They nap easily and sleep hard at night."

"I wonder if *I'll* ever sleep again," she said, letting out a sigh. "My entire life is up in the air."

"In the air? What do you mean?"

"I *mean*… I can't really know what will happen when I get to Harrington's."

He glanced at her and she caught the confused look on his face. "You *know* what will happen. You'll hand him the bill for the wedding, he'll pay without hesitation because it's probably the equivalent of a weekend getaway to the Harrises, and we'll be on our way."

"Well, yes, I'm definitely going to ask for the money. But there's always the possibility that Harrington and I will decide to work things out."

A quick look at Shane revealed his face kind of scrunching up. He pulled over on the service road and put the SUV in park.

"What are you doing?" she asked. "What's wrong?" She instinctively looked back at the twins, but they were as fast asleep as they'd been two minutes ago.

He dropped his hands off the wheel and slightly turned to face her. "You've got to be kidding me, Ashley. You *are* kidding me, right?"

What was he talking ab—

Oh.

The lightbulb went off. He was talking about Harrington. About her saying that things might work out between them.

Clearly he hated Harrington. That much had been clear from the way he'd always pointed out the guy's every…im-perfection. But she'd never given much weight to his opinion on that point before, and she wasn't about to start now. It was her relationship, so her feelings were what mattered.

"Shane, you don't go from about to marry someone to magically losing all your feelings for that person because they…" *Left you at the altar. Humiliated you—in front of your family and friends and people you never met, since the Harrises had invited a bunch of their own close friends.*

Said in a text that they realized they didn't love you.

She glanced down at her lap, her heart so heavy she might slump over.

"Right," he said. "But you don't hope to get back together with that person either."

She bit her lip, uncertainty *and* a flare of anger shooting up in her gut. Why was she talking to him about this?

"Oh?" she asked with as much sarcasm as she could get into the tiny word. "What do you do, then?"

"You deal with how bad it hurts. And day by day it'll get easier. Until one day, you'll realize you don't feel like you were drop-kicked into a herd of running cattle. You'll feel more like yourself."

Her gaze shot to his face. *Kind of specific there, Dawson.* It occurred to her that he might be talking about himself. How *he'd* dealt with heartbreak.

She certainly wasn't going to argue with him that he didn't understand that kind of pain. He'd lost his wife to a terrible car accident on a rainy night. The mother of his two baby girls. Violet and Willow had only been three months old. For five years he'd been raising them on his own. Yes, he had family close by—she'd met his kindly parents many times when they came to visit him and the twins. But on a day-to-day basis, he was alone with two little girls, all their lives changed in an instant. And he'd been grieving all that time. It couldn't have been easy.

"Let me ask you something," he said suddenly. "What did you—what do you—love about Harrington Harris?"

She felt herself bristle. "I could list fifty of his good traits. But loving someone is about much more than why they're a good person. It's about chemistry and how the person makes you feel, how you *feel* about them. It's about the inexplicable. And yes, the list of traits, of course."

"Let's hear the top ten traits of Harrington Harris IV," Shane said, staring up the engine and pulling back onto the road.

She shot him a glare. Yes, she was defensive. But rightly so. How dare he? She didn't have to justify herself to him.

To herself, maybe. But not to anyone else.

She cleared her throat. "On our first date, we were on our way to dinner when he saw a stray dog limp into the woods and asked if I'd mind if he went after it to bring it to a vet. It took us two hours to find the dog. Harrington carried him out, wrapped him in a blanket in his car, and we took him to the vet. Over a thousand bucks later, Harrington found a foster family for him until he could heal, and that family ended up adopting him and named him Woody."

Shane scowled. "Did you make that up?"

"The name? Of course not. They named him Woody after being rescued from the woods."

"No, I mean the entire story. Your ex-fiancé doesn't strike me as the type to give up the surf and turf and hundred-dollar bottle of wine to save an injured stray."

Ashley gaped at him. "You think I made it up? That I sat here and lied to your face?" Now she was indignant.

"Just doesn't seem like him."

"That's because *you* don't know him. You saw him around the ranch when he came to see me or pick me up or drop me off. You overheard bits and pieces of our private conversations and came to all kinds of unfair conclusions. Harrington is a good guy. Yeah, he can be impatient and a little self-absorbed sometimes. But no one is perfect."

He kept his eyes on the road. "I suppose not."

Ashley straightened up in her seat and looked out the window. She should steer the conversation to small talk.

"Wow, we're only in Weaverton?" she asked, noting the sign for the town limits.

"We've been driving for twenty-five minutes," he said.

"Gonna be a long trip."

"Yeah," he agreed, still scowling. "No argument from me on *that*."

Now *she* was scowling.

Special EDITION

Believe in love. Overcome obstacles. Find happiness.

Available Next Month

Taming A Heartbreaker Brenda Jackson
Her Secret To Keep Makenna Lee

....

A Surprise Second Chance Anna J. Stewart
A Little Bit Of Love Synithia Williams

4 brand new stories each month

Special EDITION

Believe in love. Overcome obstacles. Find happiness.

MILLS & BOON

Keep reading for an excerpt of a new title
from the Special Edition series,
A CAPE COD SUMMER by Jo McNally

Chapter One

The Sassy Mermaid Motor Lodge didn't look too terribly bad at night. Thanks to traffic delays, Mom's insistence that they stop at what felt like every other exit to "see what looked interesting" and Lexi getting lost on the dark, winding side roads of Cape Cod, she and her mother didn't arrive at their motel until two in the morning.

Not just the place where they were staying. It was *literally* their motel. Or at least…*Mom's* motel. Phyllis Bellamy had inherited the Sassy Mermaid Motor Lodge from an uncle no one had spoken to in decades. And their first time seeing it was right now. In the dark.

There were a few cars in the parking lot of the long, low, two-story motel, so the place was at least pulling in *some* money. That would make it easier to sell, which would happen just as soon as Lexi could convince her mother to dump this place. But despite the No Vacancy sign being lit, it was definitely not full. The lawyers said the motel had thirty rooms, and there were only ten cars parked there. The reception office was located near the center of the building, but it was dark, too.

"Thank goodness I have the keys, right?" Mom shook the giant ring of keys the attorneys had sent her. Each was carefully labeled—apartment, office, laundry, pool, storage one, storage two, etc. Lexi parked in front of the office and stared into the darkened room beyond the plate glass.

"It feels creepy to just let ourselves in like this."

"Don't be silly." Mom hopped out of the car. "It's *my* motel, so we're not trespassing. Oh, wow—I can smell the ocean!"

Lexi got out and stretched. It had been a long three days since they'd left Des Moines, and she'd driven most of it. Not because Mom hadn't offered to drive, but because her mother was quite possibly the world's worst driver. Lexi's life might be a flaming hot mess right now, but she still wanted to keep *living* it awhile longer.

She took a deep breath as she stretched, and realized what Mom was talking about. The rich, salty aroma of the ocean was heavy in the breeze. She could hear the surf splashing against rocks coming from somewhere out there in the night. For all her doubts about this journey, Lexi was looking forward to spending a little time near the ocean. But right now, exhaustion was catching up with her—she was hitting the proverbial wall, barely able to stay on her feet.

"Let's get inside and hope that mystery uncle of yours left you some comfortable beds."

"Right. Let me find the key here…" Mom flipped through the keys, her bright pink hair falling over her face. It had been a little like watching a butterfly leaving its cocoon to watch her mother transform over the past year. From a meek housewife to a fearlessly liberated woman, and all because her husband—Lexi's father—had left her for a woman younger than two of his children.

Meanwhile, Lexi had followed the opposite path since her own life imploded. She'd gone from being confident and successful to nursing her emotional wounds and avoiding everyone she used to know or work with. Maybe Mom's year of living dangerously would rub off on *her*, now that they'd escaped Des Moines and Chicago. Never mind that neither of them had ever been to Massachusetts before and knew nothing about running a motel. Details, details. With any luck, she'd convince Mom to sell by the end of the summer. That was all the time that Lexi could give to this project. It was mid-April now, so they should be able to get this place on the market and sold by August.

"Okay, sweetie, I got it open." Mom waved her hand to get Lexi's attention. "I feel like this should be a more momentous entrance, but we don't want to wake up our guests by popping champagne in the middle of the night." She pushed the door open and a tiny bell rang above it. They both froze, but they didn't hear any movement inside. Whoever was watching the office had obviously gone home for the night. The lights from the parking lot cast a soft light through the windows into the office. There was nothing surprising—an ice machine, a reception counter, a coffee counter and a few chairs scattered around. All in shades of brown and gold. There was a door in back with a sign that said Private.

Mom giggled, whispering for some reason. "This is so exciting! My very own motel and a brand-new life on the *ocean*. I've seen the ocean exactly once in my life, and your father bitched the entire weekend we spent in Virginia Beach. It was too hot, it was too sandy, there was nothing to do, blah, blah, blah." She pushed the back door open. "This must be the residence. Where's the light switch? Oh, there it is." She hit the switch and the room lit up.

"Jesus," Lexi muttered, "turn them back off."

The sign out front said the Sassy Mermaid had been open since 1948. From the looks of things, this room hadn't been updated once since then. It was wood, layered on wood, layered on wood—parquet wood floors, paneled walls and a plywood-coffered ceiling. There was a well-worn braided rug of brown, gold and orange in front of a brown plaid sofa to the right. Over the sofa was a giant oil painting of a tri-masted schooner speeding across an angry sea. On the left wall was a kitchenette with a small sink, an apartment-size refrigerator and a hot plate. Along the back wall was a twin-size day bed with a rusted white iron frame. Beyond the kitchenette was a staircase that was partially enclosed, showing only the bottom four steps. If this was the so-called living quarters the lawyers emailed her mom about, there was no way the two of them could stay here.

Lexi walked across the room to check out the two doors in the back. The first was a small bathroom with one of those old metal shower stalls that belonged in a camp or cabin somewhere. Spots of rust looked like brown snowflakes on the sides. The other door led to a weird combination of hallway and storage closet, with painted plywood shelves narrowing the space even more. The shelves were packed to the ceiling with cleaning supplies and boxes of who-knew-what. There was a door marked Exit at the back.

"Do you really think Uncle Tim *lived* in here?" Mom was moving papers around on a small desk in the corner. "The lawyers said—"

"Clearly the lawyers had no clue what they were talking about," Lexi said. "We'll figure it out in the morning, but for now, why don't you take the bed and I'll sleep on the sofa. I'm exhausted—" There was a sound behind her. A footstep on the stairs. *We aren't alone!* She spun toward the narrow, carpeted staircase...

"If you're here looking for drug money, you're going to be very disappointed." A rough male voice spoke coldly, but calmly, with a heavy New England accent. She could see bare feet and legs coming down the stairs—long legs, with one calf sporting a large, ornate tattoo of a ship's anchor. The intruder took another step and Lexi backed up as he spoke again. "If you don't get your dumb *ahsses* out of here, you're going to find yourselves sitting in the back seat of a police *cah*...with fresh bruises." Another step. He was wearing blue boxer briefs, and nothing else.

But Lexi didn't spend much time thinking about the man's physique. Not when he was uttering threats with a dangerous growl. And carrying an iron fireplace poker. She put herself between him and her mother. She was the daughter of one large, angry man and had almost been the wife of another. She didn't intimidate easily. Not anymore.

She didn't see his face until he stepped onto the bottom landing. He was tall, with dark hair and startling blue eyes. Those eyes were cold as steel right now, his square jaw tight. He'd started to raise the fire poker, but he stopped when he got a look at them.

"Who the hell are you?" he asked.

"I think—" Mom was using her full *Mom* voice, low and cold, which had always sent her three children scurrying "—*we* should be asking that question, young man." The guy was at least mid-thirties, maybe even forties. From his tan and the weathered lines on his face, she'd guess he spent a lot of time outdoors. Mom continued. "I *own* this motel, so why don't you tell us who *you* are and what you're doing here. Or maybe we should call the police to sort this out?"

The man's jaw dropped. "*You're* Curly's niece?"

"If by Curly, you mean Timothy Neely, then yes, I am."

He set down the poker in the corner and stepped into the room, apparently forgetting he was in his underwear. "Damn. I didn't think you'd be here until the weekend. Uh...

I'm Sam Knight. The estate lawyers—" he pronounced it
law-yahs "—have been paying my cousin and I to keep the
old place open for, well…you, I guess. Phyllis, right?" He
started to step forward as if to shake her hand, then looked
down. Color rose in his cheeks. "Oh…son of—excuse me."
He stepped into the bathroom just long enough to grab a
brightly colored beach towel, which he wrapped around
his waist.

Now that he wasn't clutching a weapon in his hand,
Lexi tried to shift herself out of fight mode and join the
conversation.

"And you *live* here?" That came out as more of an ac-
cusation than a question, but she was so damn tired, not to
mention being extremely wary of this rough-looking guy
making himself at home on her mother's property. Although
he didn't look quite as tough now that he was wearing a
green beach-towel skirt covered with pink dolphins and
yellow starfish.

"No," he answered, having the grace to look a little guilty.
"But someone has to take the overnight shift. Tonight was
my turn." He glanced up toward the top of the stairs. "I had
no idea you'd be here tonight, or I wouldn't have stayed upstairs."

Mom let out a loud sigh of relief. "You mean this isn't the
living quarters?"

"For the owners? Hell, no." He glanced around the room
with a look that mirrored their first impression. "This is
basically just an extension of the office. The bed's there
for someone to use if they're covering the office overnight.
The upstairs is a full two-bedroom apartment. Do you have
luggage to bring in? I can take it up for you."

"But weren't *you* covering the office overnight?" Lexi
sounded contrary. She knew it from the warning look on

Mom's face. There was just something about this guy that set her on edge. Or maybe it was the fourteen hours of driving she'd done that day.

His gaze settled fully on her for the first time. He did one of those annoying head-to-toe appraisals, and she bristled. Sam raised one eyebrow, and she could swear she saw a glint of amusement in his eye. "And you are…?"

"Oh, this is my daughter, Lexi," Mom answered for her. She was a thirty-six-year-old woman and didn't need her mother speaking for her. But right now, exhaustion was pressing down on her more every minute.

"The only bags we need tonight are there by the door." Lexi nodded at the two small-wheeled suitcases. "I really need to get some sleep before I start dealing with—" she gestured in his general direction "—this."

Her tone made it sound like he was the bellhop. She really didn't care at this point. She wanted a bed and she wanted it now. She just prayed the upstairs was a hell of a lot nicer than this time capsule from the forties. She brushed past him, being sure to keep her eyes away from the towel around his waist, and headed up the stairs. He scrambled to turn on the light switch on the wall behind her.

"I thought I was sneaking up on a robbery, so I left the lights off."

Mom followed Lexi as he grabbed the bags. "Do you have a lot of robberies here?" Her voice made the question sound naively innocent, as if she was asking how often it rained on Cape Cod.

"At the motel? No. But every small town has its share of bored teenagers looking for mischief. Once tourist season starts, that number goes up substantially." He called up to Lexi. "There's a double light switch at the top of the stairs on the right."

She flipped the switches and looked around with relief. The apartment was, most importantly, clean, and second, *not* brown. The floor plan was open, and it had a nice living area with textured laminate floors the color of driftwood. The decor was a blend of midcentury modern and coastal, with a large blue sofa facing a wall of windows with a sliding glass door. There was a small white brick fireplace in the corner. The beadboard ceiling was vaulted, giving a sense of space. Behind her was a bright kitchen—not huge, but efficient. The counters, including the long peninsula, were blue and white tiles in a checkerboard pattern. A little busy for her taste, but it was cute. A hallway led past the kitchen, presumably to where the bedrooms were. The layout reminded her of the shotgun houses she'd seen in New Orleans—long and narrow. But livable for the short time they'd be here.

Her mom and Sam stepped up into the living room, and he swept his arm around, giving a bullet-point tour as he pointed. "The sliding door leads out to a big deck above the motel office. Obviously, that's the kitchen back there. Bathroom over there with a shower. Two bedrooms share a full bath down the hall. They don't have the view this space does, but they're pretty good sized. The apartment gets wider as it goes back. There's an outside entrance back there with stairs down to a private parking area behind the motel."

Now that he mentioned it, she could see the apartment was pie-shaped, narrowest at the window wall. It certainly wasn't as traditional and ornate as the house she'd grown up in, but it was bright and inviting. This would be her home for a few months, until she could convince Mom that neither of them belonged in Winsome Cove.

That was the deal she'd made with Max and Jennifer.

All three Bellamy siblings agreed someone needed to keep an eye on Mom until she came to her senses. Going a *little* wild after the divorce was one thing. But insisting she was going to move to Cape Cod to run a motel she'd just inherited was a lot more dramatic than dying her hair hot pink, or trading her Talbots wardrobe for one from Forever 21.

Phyllis Bellamy had been the quintessential stay-at-home soccer mom and socialite housewife throughout her forty-year marriage to Bob Bellamy. She'd kept the house spotless. She'd joined Dad at the country club every Friday for dinner. She'd hosted bridge club and run fundraisers for all the most socially acceptable charities. She'd attended the United Methodist Church every Sunday, always sitting in the same center pew. But she'd never once run any kind of business. When she'd insisted she wasn't going to sell the motel until she'd "checked it out," they figured they had to protect her.

Lexi had been first up, since she was unemployed and had already been living with Mom for a few months after losing her job, her Chicago apartment *and* her reputation. Max and Jennifer had promised they'd each take a turn here in New England if she couldn't get Mom to sell right away.

"Point me to the smaller bedroom." Right now, she just wanted to sleep. "And please tell me the bed is made." She took the handle of her suitcase and turned toward the hallway.

"Uh, yeah… I gotta get my stuff out of there first." He moved ahead of her. "That's the room I was using tonight. Like I said, we didn't expect you for a few more days…"

She waved her hand. She didn't care. "Are the sheets clean?"

"Well…they were fresh tonight but I'll change them—"

"Don't bother." What a weird welcome to Cape Cod—a

towel-clad hottie threatening her with a fireplace poker before offering to make her bed.

Sam turned on the light in the bedroom and dashed around, grabbing a T-shirt off the dresser and yanking it over his head. He gripped khaki shorts in one hand while he picked up a small duffel bag. "I'll, uh…give you a better tour of the place tomorrow."

"Yup. Whatever. Good night." She crawled into the bed and fell onto the pillow. "And goodbye."